WHISPERING ROOTS

Also by Valerie Georgeson and published by Macdonald

THE TURNING TIDES

SEEDS OF LOVE

WHISPERING ROOTS

The Shadow of the Elephant
VALERIE GEORGESON

GUILD PUBLISHING LONDON

This Edition published 1988 by
Guild Publishing by arrangement with
Macdonald & Co (Publishers) Ltd

Printed and bound in West Germany
by Mohndruck, Gütersloh

For MahaGanesha

ACKNOWLEDGEMENTS

The author would like to thank the following:

South Shields Central Library, particularly Miss D. Johnson
(Local Studies Librarian, Borough of South Tyneside Libraries),
Mrs E. Georgeson for local knowledge,
Mr G.H. Brown, for help with research, and for use of his poem,
Come Forth Dark Night.

The author also wishes to acknowledge the following
publications:

BLAKE COMPLETE WRITINGS: ed. Geoffrey Keynes,
Oxford University Press, 1966

EYE DEEP IN HELL: by John Ellis

GALLIPOLI AS I SAW IT: by Joseph Murray,
William Kimber & Co. Ltd.

Ridley Family

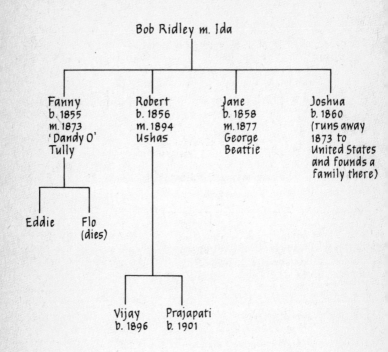

Bob Ridley m. Ida

Fanny
b. 1855
m. 1873
'Dandy O'
Tully

Robert
b. 1856
m. 1894
Ushas

Jane
b. 1858
m. 1877
George
Beattie

Joshua
b. 1860
(runs away
1873 to
United States
and founds a
family there)

Eddie

Flo
(dies)

Vijay
b. 1896

Prajapati
b. 1901

Beattie Family

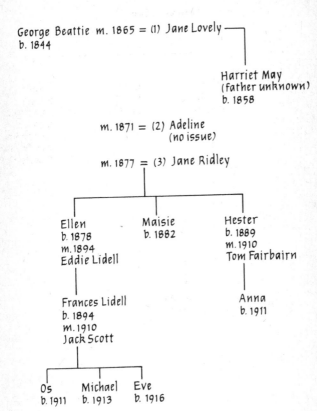

George Beattie m. 1865 = (1) Jane Lovely ———
b. 1844

Harriet May
(father unknown)
b. 1858

m. 1871 = (2) Adeline
(no issue)

m. 1877 = (3) Jane Ridley

Ellen
b. 1878
m. 1894
Eddie Lidell

Maisie
b. 1882

Hester
b. 1889
m. 1910
Tom Fairbairn

Frances Lidell
b. 1894
m. 1910
Jack Scott

Anna
b. 1911

Os
b. 1911

Michael
b. 1913

Eve
b. 1916

PART ONE
June 1902

Who's he that seeks the Dragon's blood?

CHAPTER ONE

Down on the beach, the sands were cooling. Lost in the trail of horseshoes by the water's edge, the two girls wandered on, oblivious to the sinking sun, until a shadow fell across the younger's path. Frances looked up, startled, and saw the girl ahead. Her shape was black, the curves half formed, a bare outline against the shimmering rocks. What had happened to the long, hot afternoon? Dazed by day dreams, Frances stopped, shivered and looked doubtfully after the retreating figure. Hester, born to Frances' grandma in her later years, stood in the awesome authority of aunt over her. She was supposed to look after Frances, but she was lost in her own dreams, kicking at the foam, shading her eyes to follow the long trail farther up the beach.

'Hester!' Frances called at last. 'Hester! It's getting late!' Hester turned suddenly. Frances stepped back in fright, over-balanced, then sat down, in the shallows.

'What did you call me?' Hester's voice pursued her. But Frances picked herself up, wringing out her petticoats, as she scampered to dry land.

'Hester.' She was in for trouble and she knew it. Her aunt bore down on her, black eyes blazing from the shadowy face.

'How dare you call me Hester!?'

'Why shouldn't I? It's your name, isn't it?'

'Auntie Hester to you!' Blinking in the red glare, Frances didn't know whether to stand her ground or run. But she was hungry, and it was late. The urgency of the situation gave her courage.

'You ought to go and wake Grandma.'

'Well, I'm not!'

'But Hester . . . ! I mean, "Auntie" . . . '

'Don't argue with me, child!' Hester Beattie, thirteen years old, stuck out her sprouting breasts and stamped her foot. But Frances shrugged and turned to walk along the beach, alone. 'Come back here!' The shrill cry was lost, as the little girl began to run over the hard sand, the cold waters of the North Sea lapping her feet.

Who was the horseman, who had charged down the beach, hooves kicking at the foam? Hester turned into the sun, pursuing her dream of the stable lad, his big black eyes inviting her, his smile daring her, his body teasing her. Was he out exercising the young stallion, Bonny Lad? He had let her ride him once. Her arms ached at the memory, tearing at the reins, screaming at the horse, controlling him. And she'd done it, though they'd all said she couldn't, even him, the stable lad. He'd admired her for it, and a new thought had passed across his face, as she'd slipped down the greasy side of the horse, back to earth. Hester saw that thought, and answered it with her eyes, and as she helped him groom the stallion afterwards, she had let his hands explore her, groaning with delight, till, maddened with delay she had turned on him, tearing at his clothes, kissing and biting his neck, surprising him. Yes, she had surprised even the stable lad! She smiled at the memory, shading her eyes against the angry sun, searching for the hoofprints in the sand.

Yes, who was the horseman? Frances, back turned against the sun, dreamed her own dream. Who was he? Why, he was a knight, a real live knight, holding his sword in the air, and crying, 'For England and Saint George!' Miss Turnbull had told them all about Saint George at school. He had been sent to save England on the eve of disaster, with the king in the very jaws of death! King Edward the Seventh on the eve of his coronation,

14

struck down with appendicitis! Just to think of it made you want to cry. Surely Saint George would save him? He might even save her, if she asked him. Frances, turning to drag her feet up the soft sand to the dunes, caught sight of the old familiar landmarks. The twin piers of North and South Shields, ships coming and going in the busy harbour, and the town itself, with its dismal roofs, temporarily transformed by the lurid sky. Shields. She wished God would send a bolt of lightning to destroy it! And especially her granda's flower shop! And even more especially, Auntie Hester! She was sick of the lot of them! 'Cry Harry for England and Saint George!' She charged up the dunes and almost fell over her grandma, lying on the ground.

Jane Beattie, cradled in the dunes, stirred in her sleep, but dreamed on. She lay, mouth open, white hair trailing, silver in the sand. Gazing down on her, Frances' heart melted. It seemed a pity to wake her. Poor grandma. She'd had a hard life, you could tell that just by looking at her. She looked sad, somehow; but not sour and forbidding, like Frances' mam. No, disappointment had not made grandma bitter. Asleep, she looked so warm and nice. She made you feel like you could just go and talk to her, and tell her all your troubles and then she'd soothe you like ointment on a bruised skin. Frances touched her lovingly. Jane stirred, then, with a sharp cry sprang out of sleep.

'What's wrong?' Her panic-stricken eyes searched the shadows. 'There's something wrong.' Then she saw her granddaughter. 'Oh! It's you!' Frances nodded, backing off, watching, feeling somehow betrayed. There was a chill in the air. Jane shivered. 'What time is it?' Frances shrugged. 'Late.' Jane sighed, looked up at the paling light of the heavens and scrambled to her feet, shaking the sand from her dress. 'Where's our Hester?' Again Frances shrugged. Annoyed, her grandma rasped at her. 'Well go and find her, then! You were supposed to stay with her! How can she look after you if you don't? Go on! It's getting dark!' For a second, Frances stayed, watching the woman, startled out of sleep, nervously rearrange her dress. Then, she turned suddenly, to scramble across the dunes, onto the beach, running, running towards the distant figure of her Aunt.

★ ★ ★

15

'I told you so! We've got to get back home to the shop!' Frances was waving for all she was worth. But Hester turned away, covered her ears and walked on. Oh their Hester *was* a little madam! Granda was right. He'd belted her one only this morning for being cheeky when he told her off for slouching, and he didn't know the half of it! 'Hester! Stop, will you!' Crying with frustration, Frances ran on, panting, 'Auntie Hester!', till she ran into her shadow.

'What!?'

'We've got to go back! I told you! Grandma's waiting!'

'Let her!'

'Grandad'll be furious if we're late!' Hester snorted.

'Huh! What do I care! I'm going to follow the horse tracks.'

'But they probably lead all the way to Cleadon Hills!' Hester looked down the beach towards the distant cliffs, and the hills beyond. She smiled.

'Fancy!'

'Hester . . . ' Frances looked at her aunt shyly. 'Do you know who the rider is?'

'I might.'

'Who?'

'Shall I let you into a secret?' Hester was swinging on her heel, showing off. Frances shrugged doubtfully. 'I think it's Joe, from the stables.'

'So?'

'He likes me.' Hester's cheek bulged from her exploring tongue. 'I like him an' all!' Her laugh was dirty. 'I let him put his tongue in me mouth last time he kissed me!'

'Hester Beattie! You'll get germs!'

Hester roared with laughter and took off, at a smart pace, trudging through the sand, followed doggedly by Frances.

'You can't go up to the hills! You've got to come back home!'

'I won't! I hate home!'

'So do I!'

'No you don't. Or you wouldn't be so keen to get back there!'

'We've got to.'

'Why?'

'I don't know really. We just have. They'd all be upset if we didn't.'

'Good. I'd like to upset me Dad. He upsets me enough!'

'What about Grandma, then?'

'Me Mam? Huh! Her an all!'

'All right, what about *my* mam. And Auntie Maisie. They're your sisters! Surely you care about your own sisters, left at home working in the shop, while we're out enjoying ourselves?'

'Them? Don't be soft! Our Ellen's a born martyr . . . '

'My mam's not a born martyr!'

' . . . And Maisie's daft! Nowt to choose between them really! Let them work if they want to!'

'All right then! If you don't come, Auntie Hester, I'll tell on you! I'll tell Granda!'

'What about?'

'The stable lad!' Hester's shape grew against the sun, as she swung on the fleeing child.

Maisie hugged herself, rocking to and fro in an ecstasy of grief, as she stared at the pails of flowers.

'I knew it!'

'What?! What did you know, our Maisie?' Annoyed, Ellen turned the notice on the shop door to 'CLOSED'.

'As soon as I saw that new moon through glass, I knew!'

'What?!' Ooh, but their Maisie could be irritating!

'About the king, of course!'

'Oh I see!' Ellen sneered. 'Of course! Why didn't *I* think of it?!' Maisie missed the irony in her sister's voice. 'Of course! That's why he got appendicitis!' Maisie nodded excitedly.

'Eeh, Ellen, do you think I've got . . . "powers"?'

'Eh?'

'No. But do you?'

'What powers?'

'Why, to foretell the future, man!'

'You great soft jelly!' Ellen exploded. 'You don't really think that you seeing the new moon through glass could give the king appendicitis, do you?'

'Why not?'

'Give me strength!'

'You've got to admit it, Ellen. I *did* see the new moon through glass, and the very next day he did go down with it! *And* they had to cancel his coronation!'

'You're crackers.' Maisie sniffed and tossed her head.

17

'It *is* a bad omen, Ellen. Deny *that* if you can!'

'If it's a bad omen, pet, it's you it's bad for! *You* saw it!'
Maisie's jaw dropped in consternation.

'Eeeeehhh!' she wailed. The realisation struck her like a
thunderbolt. 'Am I goin' to get appendicitis an' all?'

'Our Maisie! I give up! You're crackers. You are really.'
Maisie's lower lip trembled, then gathering up her wounded
pride, she turned and walked into the back scullery.

Ellen smiled. You couldn't be angry with her. Not really. She
was simple was their Maisie. It wasn't her fault. The hunched
back banged awkwardly against the door frame, and a tiny sob
escaped from her, as Maisie slipped out of sight. Now there'd be
red eyes at supper time. What a life! As if *he* wasn't enough!
Ellen raised her eyes to the little balustrade above the shop, and
the glass door of her father's office beyond. She could hear him
pacing to and fro, like a caged lion. Why couldn't the bloomin'
king have waited till after his coronation before he got
appendicitis? Really, it was very inconsiderate of him! I mean!
All them flowers wasted! It was a disaster. Ellen looked at the
wilting blooms. The perfume of lilies hung heavy on the air. Ah
well! She'd have to do her best to save them, at least till after the
king's operation. After all, operations were dangerous things. He
might die, and then people'd want flowers for his funeral.
Looking on the bright side, Ellen began gathering up the pails.

'What did you say?' Her father's voice roared in the office
above. Ellen looked up, fearful for her husband.

'What did you say?' George Beattie, patriarch of Beattie's
Florists swelled with rage. The young man before him quailed.

'I only asked if you could've insured against it.' He stammered.

'Gormless! That's what you are, Edward Lidell! Gormless by
looks and gormless by nature! I don't know what our Ellen ever
saw in you!'

'Yes, sir. I mean, no sir.'

'This was an act of God, Eddie!'

'Yes, sir. Like our Frances.' George darted him a look. Was
Eddie playing games with him? Perhaps he wasn't as gormless as
he looked!

'Frances? What about her?'

18

'She was an act of God, wasn't she? I mean, we never meant, Ellen and me . . . '

'Rubbish! It was the act of a conniving cowardly little man, to get my daughter pregnant, and marry your way into my business.' Eddie's heart pounded, but his eyes remained fixed to the floor. 'You've brought us bad luck, Eddie.'

'It's not my fault the king got bad!' Eddie retorted at last.

'It's your fault we ordered so many flowers!' George glared at him. 'Write to the Newcastle merchants! See if they'll have them back!' Eddie gaped. What sort of a fool's errand was the old barsket setting him on now?

The voices upstairs had dropped. Ellen returned to her task. Poor Eddie. Ellen sighed. What a family! And, talking about families, where was their Frances, she'd like to know? It was far too late for a lass of her age to be out, even if she *was* with her grandma! The scent of lilies caught in her throat. She coughed, and took them down to the cold cellar where they would keep till morning.

> 'The silvery moon was shining down,
> And love lit up my heart,
> As we swayed to the tune we knew so well,
> In the days when we were apart.'

At least Maisie'd forgotten about her premonitions! As she peeled the potatoes for supper, she was crooning softly to herself. Maisie sighed longingly. When would her true love come, riding on his white charger, to carry her off into the sunset? When? Oh when?

Jane's pulse was pounding. The air was still. Too still. The gentle breezes of the afternoon had given way to an unnatural calm. The dunes towered around her. She looked up at the walls of sand, their shadows growing ever longer. Where were those children? She would go and see. Feet slipping on the slopes, hands grasping at the sharp grass, Jane clambered up the dunes, panting as she reached the top, to stand, silhouetted against the setting sun. It hung behind her like a molten womb, suspended, its rays setting fire to the horizon. And the crescent of the moon waited, poised over the glassy sea, the only movement on the beach, the figure of the little girl, running through amber rivulets, across the sand, pursued by Hester. She soon caught up with her and grabbed her by the arm. Orange flares broke the waters, blazing from beneath the sea as though some fire breathing monster, wakened from a long sleep, stirred in its depths. Frances looked up, saw her grandma, and screamed for help.

Alarmed, Jane picked up her skirt and slid down the dune onto the beach. Hester was beside herself. Her eyes were wild. Like one possessed, she pulled the younger by her hair, twisting and riving, till the child was on her knees, begging for mercy.

'Oh, Hester, please, please, stop it! I won't tell! I promise! I won't tell!'

'If you do, Frances Lidell, I'll make you so sorry, you'll wish you'd never been born! Do you hear me?'

'I promise I won't. Cross my heart and hope to die!' Then Hester threw the child from her, and she fell sprawling on the sand, smashing the imprints of the horses' hooves.

'Hester! What's going on?' But Hester's eyes slid from her mother's. Helplessly, Jane turned to her grand-daughter. 'Are you all right, Fran, pet? Come on, love. Up you get. Stop crying now!' She helped her to her feet, her anger against Hester rising. But her daughter's dark shape was already pressing on up the beach to the road. So Jane bit back her fury and took the younger's hand, leading her, gently, in the footsteps of the elder. Frances' nose had begun to bleed. Dark red, the drips fell down the front of her dress. The sight of them frightened her and she stopped in her tracks, howling.

'Look what she's done to me!!'

'Tut! Oh now look at you!' Helplessly, Jane called after her daughter. 'Hester, come back!' But the girl kept on, charging up the hill as though the devil was behind her. 'Eeh, I don't know what's got into her.' Jane shook her head. 'It must be her age.' She sighed. 'Where's your hanky, pet?' She applied it to the child's bleeding nose. Putting her head back, to stem the flow, Frances stared at the fermenting heavens. Gold outlined the rearing clouds, and low growls threatened, as though a tiger prowled.

'Hurry! I think there's going to be a storm!' At the roadside they stopped to empty sand from their shoes, and stare back at the transforming sea. The fire had darkened now. Crimson currents ran in the tide and the blood red sun sank beneath the weight of a violet sky. 'Eeh, I hope our Maisie gets the washing in!' Jane panted, as they sped homewards up Bent House Lane. Then, as though reminded by the clattering roll of thunder, she added, 'There's no need to cause ructions by upsetting your granda or your mam, so we'll say nothing about any of this, eh?'

Half the cats of the neighbourhood were careering towards her, as Hester turned the corner into the lane behind Victoria Terrace. Slipping on a fish head, she saved herself by hanging onto a pair of her father's combinations, still hanging on the line. Theirs was the only washing left out to the mercy of the coming storm.

'Maisie!' Hester called, as she came into the yard. Maisie started, and the fish lad fell over the flower boxes, in surprise.

'Where did you spring from?' Maisie gabbled.

'Wait till Dad hears about this!' Hester jeered. 'You, canoodlin' with a lad, in the back yard!'

'I wasn't! And you'd better keep your trap shut, little sister. Or else!' The fish lad was beating a hasty retreat, and Maisie shouted her message after him. 'Tell him it'll be all right!'

'Tell who, our Maisie?'

'Sh!' Maisie peered through the kitchen window. But it was only their Ellen.

'Where's Granda?'

'He's in with Alderman Wilson, talking about the new Town Hall. So you can't go telling tales to him!'

'Let's see your letter.'

'No! It's private!'

'I'll tell Mam, then. She's just coming up the street.'

'If you do, Hester, I'll tell on you.'

'What? What'll you tell?'

'I'll tell about that young stable lad up on Cleadon Hills! I've seen you making eyes at him!' Thwarted, Hester barged off into the house, where she disappeared up the maze of stairs, and locked herself in her attic room.

Maisie was taking in the washing as Jane and Frances came up the lane.

'You're looking very pleased with yourself, Maisie,' Jane remarked as they passed her. 'Have you done the suet?'

'Aha,' Maisie said absently. She was grinning from ear to ear, and hadn't so much as glanced at her niece.

'Has the king died?'

'Not that I know of, Ma.'

'Then what're you grinning about?'

'Nothing.'

'There's something fishy going on. I know that.' Maisie whooped with laughter and shaking her head, Jane left her, giggling uncontrollably in the lane. When they entered the empty kitchen, the child hid behind her grandma's skirts, while she spied out the lie of the land. Jane could hear Ellen down in the cellar with the flowers. She was spraying them. Good. That'd keep *her* out of the way! Now where was George? Advancing quietly up the back stair, she heard his full mayoral voice. He was in the parlour with Alderman Wilson. So, the coast was clear. She hurried Frances up to her room at the top of the house, bathed her wounds, then firmly told her to rest till supper.

'Can I not have a story, Grandma?'

'A rest would do you more good.' Jane backed towards the door.

'I'm lonely.'

'Go to sleep now!' Frances watched the door close, and listened. Her grandma crossed the passage. She stopped outside Hester's room. Was she going to tell her off? But there was silence, a long silence, as Jane stood, paralysed, afraid to try the door of her daughter's room. Perhaps it would be better to leave it, say nothing. Her hand was shaking. There was a sob from the room behind her. Poor Frances. Her anger rose. She tried the door. It was locked.

'Hester!' There was no reply. Jane raised her voice. 'Hester! Open this door!'

In the kitchen, Ellen watched Grace the cat demolish a tail end of salmon.

'What's this?'

'It was a present,' Maisie said haughtily.

'For the cat?' Ellen shrieked.

'I can give it to whoever I like.'

'But that's salmon!'

'It's Grace's favourite!'

'You pander to that animal!'

'Why shouldn't I? She's the only one round here that cares about me.'

'Cupboard love!' Downstairs the sisters shrieked.

Upstairs Jane hammered on Hester's door. In the parlour, unable to think for the din, George was puce with rage. Striding into the passage, he reached for a stick, and hurled it against the dinner gong. Alderman Wilson put his hands to his ears as it resounded through the now silent house.

'I'm afraid it's dinner time, Jim. Thank you for calling.' Mayor and Alderman shook hands, and the visitor departed into the threatening night.

How had he ended up with this household of troublesome women?! At dinner, George's eye fell on his son-in-law, and his lip curled.

'Gormless by looks and gormless by nature!' He muttered into his soup. Ellen bristled.

'Say something to him, Eddie! Defend yourself.' Edward Lidell clanged the spoon in his cup and kept his silence.

'Grocer's son!' George snarled.

'Why shouldn't he have tea with his supper, if he wants to?'

'Ellen . . . !' Jane warned. Another wave of thunder passed in the distance. Silently the assembled family listened as it rolled and rumbled lazily across the town. Ellen sighed.

'I think we might light the lamps. It's so gloomy in here.' Jane darted Ellen a look, and shook her head. Ellen frowned. Now what was wrong? Why shouldn't they light the lamps?

'I knew a dog called Gormless once,' Jane said by way of making conversation. Eddie groaned.

'Gormless by looks and gormless by nature.' George was right on cue.

'You're only jealous, Da!' Ellen told him. George's red mouth parted the mass of grey beard in shock. 'You only wish you'd thought of it yourself. That's all!'

23

'Thought of what, dear?' Jane asked.

'Young fellow me lad . . . ' Gritting his teeth, Eddie almost swallowed the soup spoon. 'Young fellow me lad only thought we should have insured against the coronation being cancelled, if you please!'

'That's a good idea!' Jane looked admiringly at her son-in-law. Frances jumped as her granddad roared in wordless fury, throwing down his napkin like a gauntlet. 'Have I said something wrong?' Jane asked. 'Maisie do pick up your father's napkin.'

'Pardon?' Guiltily, Maisie looked from father to mother.

'I said, pick up your father's napkin, pet.'

'Oh . . . Yes. Sorry.' As Maisie bent, pages rustled in her lap. But another wave of thunder mercifully distracted her father's attention.

'Ellen, light the lamps!' he ordered. Jane sighed and signalled to Frances to pull the hair across her face. Hester shuffled uncomfortably.

'Is there any news of the king?' Ellen asked, as she lit the first lamp. The gas flared green, phosphorescent, in her face. George shook his head.

'Might he die, Granda?' Frances asked, wide-eyed. Jane put her finger to her mouth. But George saw her.

'Why shouldn't she ask? Our Frances has an inquiring mind. She takes after me!'

'Yes, dear.'

'I hope he does die!' All heads turned on Hester.

'That's a dreadful thing to say.' Ellen snorted in disgust as she paused over the mantel to light the second lamp.

'It would be better for us!' Eddie sighed. 'All them flowers in the cellar . . . we could turn them into funeral sprays, and wreaths.'

'Poor man.' Jane sighed.

'Hah! Be a darned sight better for this country if he *did* die!' George shouted. 'I tell you, this illness is no accident!' All eyes were on the patriarch. 'It's a judgement from the Almighty!'

'It's appendicitis, dear!'

'Exactly. God's judgement.' Ominously another roll of thunder passed them by. George enjoyed the moment, then went on, 'When the old queen died, the old morals died with her. Now this . . . this Don Juan . . . '

'What's a Don Juan?' Frances asked.

'Sh!' Jane told her. Frances shrugged and sighed.

'This Don Juan is going to drag the country in the gutter, with his loose morals and loose women! Everybody'll use him as an excuse to go rampant! It's the end of the family as we know it!'

'Sh,' Jane warned him, indicating the two young girls at the table. George flushed and looked at them. His eyes narrowed. He pointed across the table at Frances. She was pulling her draggled hair across a livid eye.

'What's the matter with *her*!' he shouted.

'She fell down, George.' Jane tried to calm her husband. 'She's all right. Children are always falling down.' Hester was staring straight ahead of her. George frowned.

'Is that true, Frances? Did you fall?' Frances' stormy eye stared out from behind her hair. 'Tidy yourself up!' Ellen sped to her daughter's side.

'Tut! You've had a nose bleed as well, haven't you?' She clucked. 'Clumsy girl!'

'I asked you a question, Frances! Did you fall down?' Frances couldn't look at him. She darted a glance at her grandma, who nodded mutely, then said, very quietly,

'Yes, Granda.' George glared at his wife. There was more to this than met the eye.

'Where did you fall?' George demanded. Again Frances looked at her grandma.

'Em . . . '

'On Bent Lane!' Hester put in. Her mouth was tight.

'Let the child answer for herself!' George bellowed. 'Where did you fall?'

'On Bent Lane, Granda.'

'Hah!' George sat back in his chair. Once more the napkin was thrown to the ground. 'Women! I can never get to the bottom of anything in this house!' Maisie's papers rustled as she bent to retrieve the napkin for a second time. 'You're all in cahoots against me!' With that George rose from the table and stormed from the room.

Ellen coughed, as she resumed her place. Eyes darted from one to another, but no one said a word. Finally Jane spoke.

'Maisie, dear, I think we might have the meat roll now.' Stuffing her letter up her sleeve, Maisie rose and went down to the scullery. Frances was crying.

'Go to bed, pet,' her mother told her. 'We'll bring you a milky drink later on.' Sniffing back her tears, the child left the room. Now, only Jane, Hester and Frances' parents were left at the table. It became necessary to make conversation.

'Mind, I think Queen Alexandra's nice,' Jane said. 'She puts up with a lot. Eeh, and she loves her children, you know. They call her "Motherdear". Did you know that? Like one word. "Motherdear". Isn't that nice?'

'Yes, Ma.' Ellen agreed. 'That's very nice.' Again the thunder grumbled down the coast. Ellen looked distractedly through the window.

'It's building up,' Eddie said.

'I wish it would break and get it over with.'

Frances was still hungry. It wasn't fair. She wanted some meat roll. Maisie did a nice bit of suet. Her grandma said so. Maybe they'd bring her bread and dripping with her milk. She shivered between the cold sheets. Hester Beattie! Huh! If her grandad found out what she'd done, she wouldn't half be in for it, and serve her right! 'Auntie Hester' with her pants down and her bum stuck up in the air, getting walloped! But her granda didn't know, and she wasn't getting walloped, was she? Frances sniffed. Caked blood blocked her nose. It was worse than having a cold. Her eye throbbed, and her head hurt where Hester'd pulled her hair.

'Nobody cares about me!' she wailed, as Jane came in, carrying a tray of steaming milk, and buttered bread.

'That's not true!' A smile fluttered on Jane's face, then died.

'I hate it when Granda's in a temper.'

'We have to make allowances, dear.'

'What for?'

'Things are a bit difficult, love, and then . . . ' Jane sighed, and Frances waited, dying to know more about her granda's temper. But Jane saw the gaping mouth and merely said, 'Eat your supper.' Disappointed, the child sucked the butter from the bread. 'Properly now!' Grown ups weren't half boring!

'Where's me Mam?' Suddenly Jane laughed.

26

'You know what she's like when there's a thunderstorm!'

A loud clap volleyed overhead. Ellen screamed, and raced Maisie to the bedroom where the sisters flung themselves under the big brass bed, shaking.

'You nearly had the chamber pot there, our Maisie!' Ellen giggled.

'Get away with you!' Maisie reached for the end of the eiderdown and pulled it underneath the bed to keep them warm. 'It might be a long night!' But as they lay stiffly waiting for the next clap, Maisie began to moan.

'Shurrup, man. You're getting on me nerves!' Ellen hissed. A pair of boots came into the room. The women watched. The boots stopped beside the bed. Suddenly Eddie's face appeared, upside down, staring at them from under the valance.

'I want to go to bed!' he said.

'Well you can't!' Ellen snapped.

'It's *my* bed!'

'It's hers as well!' Maisie squeaked.

'I don't know why you can't shelter under Maisie's bed. Why d'ye always pick on this one, eh?'

'Because, Eddie, there's a load of junk under Maisie's bed, and our cat couldn't get in there!'

'Tell her to clear it!'

'I *am* here you know! And I'm not deaf,' Maisie objected.

'I want to go to bed.' Thunder cracked, shaking the tiles on the roof. The sisters screamed. 'It's a dog's life!' Eddie sighed and, pulling a couple of blankets from the bed, he left them, to shake down on the sofa in the scullery.

'Anyway, you *don't* care, Grandma. If you did, you wouldn't side with our Hester.'

'I didn't side with her.'

'You let Granda think I fell!'

'So?'

'So, why did you let me get into trouble when it was her that was to blame?'

'But you didn't get into trouble, Fran. Did you, eh?' Frances looked at her grandma. Her face was in the shadow of the candle. 'Your Granda wasn't angry with you, was he?'

'I suppose not.'

'No. He never is. But what would have happened if he'd found out what Hester did?'

'He'd have walloped her!' Frances said with relish.

'Exactly. And you wouldn't want that now, would you?' Frances thought better of expressing her real thoughts on the subject. 'And he'd have taken it out on me as well!'

'Why?'

'Well . . . Hester's my daughter, isn't she?' And I'm only your grand-daughter,' Frances thought, longing for her grandma's white hand to reach out and hold her own. 'So, it was better not to tell him.'

'We lied.'

'No we didn't. We just didn't tell him, that's all.' Jane's brow creased with irritation. 'And anyway, Fran, you must have done something to set her off!' Frances said nothing. 'What was it, eh?' Frances shook her head. 'Come on, you can tell me.'

'I promised.'

'I won't tell anybody else. What did you say to her?'

'It's a secret.'

'From your Grandma?' Perhaps telling would make her grandma love her more. But she couldn't. She'd promised.

'It's a secret.'

The storm was moving away again. It came in waves, passing, then coming back again, like the tide.

'I don't like you having secrets from me, Frances.'

'It's not my secret. It's hers. Only I promised not to tell. Just like *we* didn't tell granda.'

'I see.' Jane had stiffened. A wicked gleam came into the child's eye.

'What was Auntie Maisie reading under the table?'

George belched as he placed the meat loaf back in the larder. Women! Huh! Why couldn't he have had sons; someone sensible to talk to? He jumped guiltily as Eddie came in with his blankets.

'Ousted by the women, eh?' He sized up the situation at a glance. The perfume of flowers rose from the cellar. It caught George on the raw.

'If the king *doesn't* die!' he declared, 'I'll sue the bugger!'

As he passed Ellen's room, George heard the sisters whispering under the bed.

'I've got a lovely pair of kingfisher stockings, and an emerald skirt.'

'You'll look like a parrot, woman!' Ellen objected. 'All you need's a red feather!'

'You've got no taste, our Ellen! I wouldn't be seen dead in a red feather.'

Ellen groaned, but decided not to pursue the subject.

'When are you going, anyway?' Paper rustled as a letter was drawn from inside a sleeve. 'Ooh, it stinks of fish!'

'Don't be so snotty.'

'Well, he's hardly a knight in shining armour, Maisie! I mean! A fishmonger! You could do better!'

'Listen who's talking! The pot calling the kettle!'

'All right, Maisie! I only said!'

'Huh!' Maisie unfolded the piece of paper, and showed her sister. 'Here. *If* you're still interested! He wants me to go on Thursday week.'

'*Where* are you going, Maisie? And with whom?'

Maisie jumped and hit her head on the bed springs. Her father's boots stood square in front of her nose.

'Em . . . the chapel . . . em . . . '

'Mr Platt's asked us to a meeting about the Sunday School trip.' Ellen answered for her.

'Why does nobody answer questions for themselves in this house!' George's roar was drowned in an almighty blast from the heavens, which sent the women into hysterics.

As George's door closed, Hester's opened. She was sitting at her attic window, staring at the sky.

'Hester . . . ' Jane's voice invaded her thoughts.

'Yes?' She turned and stared, unblinking, at her mother.

'Hester, we've got to talk.'

'I don't see why.'

'Hester!'

'Well, I don't!'

'Why did you do it?'

'What did Fran tell you?' Jane paused. There was alarm in her daughter's voice, and her own chest caught with fear.

'Nothing. She wouldn't say a word.'

'Good.'

'What is it, Hester? What is this "secret" of yours?'

'If I told you, it wouldn't be a secret any more, would it?' Mother and daughter stared at one another in the half dark.

'You must tell me.' The mother's voice was unnaturally tight. Hester stared at her, wondering.

'What do *you* think it is?' she asked her at last.

'What do you mean?'

'What are you scared of, Ma? Me?' Jane gasped. 'Go on, Ma, tell.'

'There's nothing to tell.' Jane was defensive.

'Have *you* got a secret, Ma?'

'What makes you think I have?'

'Everybody should have at least one, don't you think, Motherdear?'

'How dare you speak to me like that. I should have let your father belt you, like you deserved.'

'Then why didn't you?'

'You little . . . !' Jane's hand lashed across her daughter's face. Hester stared at her mother for a long time. She was shaking.

'I hate you,' she said at last. 'Both of you.' The words hissed out of the darkness.

'You don't mean that.'

'Yes I do. I'm old enough to know my own mind.'

'You're growing up. Yes. But you're not old enough yet. You're a turmoil of emotion at your age.'

'I'm old enough to know.'

'Know what?!'

'Things.' Jane bit her lip. 'I'm a big girl now, and I'm learning!' A crackle scorched the roof of the house opposite. Hester yelped with glee.

'Isn't it magnificent!' she said, her face vivid with excitement.

'Come away from the window. You might get hit.' But Hester ignored her.

'I like it,' she said.

Voices, voices, whispering. Across the corridor, in the attic room opposite, Frances heard Hester and her grandma talking. She heard the voices rise and fall in anger, and she was glad. Then, she heard the door open and close, and her grandmother going down the stairs to her own room, where she and granda would lie in bed, talking, whispering. But she never heard what they said; couldn't piece together the scattered words and phrases, so that they made any sort of sense. What were they saying, her family? What were their secrets? With invisible threads, they reached out, winding round her heart, pulling tight, first this way then that. Were other families like this? Or only hers?

'Frances didn't fall, did she?' Jane sighed and turned onto her back.

'No. It was Hester's doing.' George snorted with fury, silent, counting the seconds between the thunder and the lightning. 'It's quite a storm isn't it?'

'Getting close,' he said. The lightning flashed. Jane drew the blankets over her head, but George pulled them back again. 'We've got to talk,' he said. 'It's no good burying our heads in the sand.' His hand reached out and touched her. She grasped it anxiously.

'Don't, George! Don't! I can't bear it! Raking up the past!' But George had made up his mind.

'The past's alive, Jane. It's taken flesh and blood.'

'Poor Hester.'

' "Poor"!' George roared. 'By God, that young woman would eat us alive as soon as look at us!'

'It's not her fault!' There was a long silence. George sobbed.

'Lord God, forgive me. For I have sinned.' Jane stirred uncomfortably. When she spoke it was in a small, tight voice.

'We're all sinners, George! And it's no good taking it out on Hester!'

'I don't take it out on her!'

'You do! You've always had it in for her. You hate her! You can hardly blame her for hating you back!'

George spoke in a quiet voice.

'*You're* always gentle with her, Jane. Does she love you?' He felt her grief, knew hot tears scorched her cheeks, though she said nothing. 'You spoil her.'

'I'm afraid.'

'Of Hester?'

'Yes . . . no. Of what happened. The sins of the fathers, George.'

In the silence, lightning flashed, scorching the midden roof. Jane jumped, and George took her in his arms. Laying her head against his cheek, she felt the wetness of his tears, and was all compassion for him. 'It's not Hester I hate.' He wept. 'It's myself. When I see her, I see my own bestial nature, rearing up at me.'

'You've got to forgive yourself.'

'I can't, Jane. I forgave *you*, long ago, but . . . '

'Do you remember how it was, when we first met?'

'A young fresh girl, Jane. Like our Frances is now. That's what you were. I was jealous of your beaux.'

'Were you?'

'Yes! Do you remember when Ronnie first came courting?' Jane nodded. 'He was a nice lad was Ronnie.' George laughed harshly. 'He saved you from rape, and got himself killed for his trouble, then, years later, when we were all old enough to know better . . . '

'I was your wife. You can't rape your wife.'

'I did, all the same. Maisie and Ellen asleep upstairs, and I raped you.'

'We're none of us without sin.'

'I was jealous, Jane.'

'I know. But then, so was I. I was jealous of Alice Minto. You had a son by her! You still see her, George!'

George squirmed. 'Hester reminds me, Jane. She reminds me of what I am. That's why I can't stand the sight of her.' The thunder prowled, growling over distant roof tops. 'I wasn't fair to you. I'm not fair to you even now.'

'If only I could see Robert again. He is my brother, George! I'd like to see him once before I die!'

'Hasn't he caused enough trouble?' Jane sobbed, and George comforted her, rocking her to and fro, as the thunder rolled. 'I'm sorry, Jane. I can't. I'm sorry.'

Jane sighed, biting back thoughts of her brother Robert, changing the subject for George's sake.

'I was remembering the trial . . . Jack Purvis's smarmy face. Getting away with murder. I wonder how he feels now?'

'Only good people hate themselves for the wrong they do. The others turn into devils to torment us.'

'Are we good, George?'

'George sighed. 'We'd like to be.'

'Is anyone? Really good, I mean?'

'Our Frances is.' The old man's voice lightened. 'She'll be the saving of this family yet.'

'What about Hester?'

'Hester? Huh! If she's going to stand any chance at all, you're going to have to stop spoiling her, Jane.'

'But I don't!'

'You do! Take those riding lessons, for a start! I can't afford riding lessons! But just because that little madam wants them, she's got to have them!'

'I'm sorry, George. But she needs an outlet.'

'She needs discipline!'

'And love.'

'Love.' George dropped his voice. Hester was a living reminder of a part of himself; a part he hated. How could he love her? But Jane's mind was running on more practical themes.

'Maybe if she took up the piano instead? That's very disciplined. And cheaper!'

'All them scales . . . ' He sighed, 'I'll think about it.'

'Thank you, George. I do love you, dear.'

'And I love you.' His lips were wet on her cheek. He fumbled for her, and she let him make love to her, a friendly embrace, reassuring. Then he turned over and fell asleep, too exhausted to hear the cacophony of the growing storm. Jane lay, eyes wide, staring at the flashing sky, memories whispering. Hester, standing at the window, as the lightning scorched the tiles of the roof outside; laughing, enjoying the danger, lusting for it. Jane knew that feeling, and understood it. Hadn't she felt the same? Robert's last night home. They had gone to the circus. There were elephants, and tigers, and a man at the centre of the ring, lashing his whip. She had sided with the tigers. They resented the man's sway over them, just as she had resented George, and she'd longed for them to spring, to hurt the man. She had shared their blood lust, but hers had broken all the boundaries of love. She had betrayed George. What if he *had* betrayed her first? Hers was the greater betrayal. The fault was hers. And now, Hester was growing up. The past made flesh. Oh yes, she understood George's feelings about Hester. Hadn't she slapped her on the face? And in slapping her, wasn't she punishing herself? Thunder growled into a deep roar, rattling the window panes. Jane closed her eyes against the thought and willed sleep to come, willed the sandman to throw his sand in her eyes; sand; walls of sand; sleep; oblivion. The shadowy dunes. Frances running on the beach, pursued by Hester! Yes, the children were growing up. In the depths of the sea, the fiery monster stirred and Jane muttered uneasily in her sleep.

Voices, whispering; the secret threads reached out, weaving a web around the child in the attic. Sobbing, Frances threw back the bedclothes, and sprang to her feet to watch the purple clouds roll angrily across the window pane. Thunder clattered over the great dome of the Queen's Hall opposite. Like an army on the move, the storm gathered its strength at last and hurled itself against the enemy. Legions rode for her, horses' hooves galloping, drumming onwards. Knights, swords flashing through the darkness, severed the knots tied about her strangled heart. The sobs grew louder. Nobody loved her! Nobody! Nobody, except . . . her grandma. She loved her grandma and her grandma loved her. She was sure she did! After all, if she loved her, her grandma *must* love her in return! The scent of decaying lilies rose up the stair. Frances hurled open her window. In fact, if it wasn't for Grandma Beattie, she didn't think she could stand living in this house at all! The storm was passing. Fury spent, it loitered, grumbling, over the distant sea, and Frances breathed the cool air that came with the rain.

CHAPTER TWO

The king did not die and the family sat, silent, round the break-fast table next morning, while George read the papers. His eye rose from the page to catch his son-in-law trying to read the news on the back page. Ellen coughed. Eddie jumped guiltily and George resettled the paper. Frances' toast crackled painfully in the ensuing silence. She raised her hand to her mouth, hardly daring to eat, and wondered when somebody was going to say something about Hester. For the strained atmosphere surely meant a row was imminent, and what could it be about if not about Hester! At last they would all see how badly Frances had been treated. Her grandma had seen to it, as she knew she would. Then, at last, Eddie could bear the silence no longer.

'Are you going to sue the king, then, Mr Beattie?' There was an ominous pause. Eddie fled into the shop. Ellen had a violent fit of coughing and, trying not to smile, Jane joined Maisie at the stove.

'Do you need any help, pet?' Maisie moaned, and turned a swollen face to her mother. 'Eeh. You're martyr to your teeth and no mistake.'

'She says it was the thunder set it off.' Ellen giggled.

'I see nothing to laugh at in your sister's misfortune!' George reprimanded. Frances frowned, bewildered, then her eye caught the headline, as George turned back the paper. 'The King. Doing Well!' Her heart sank. She had thought herself the centre of the world, and found she was barely on its periphery.

'Well! Honestly!' Ellen objected. Turning her annoyance on her daughter, she bustled Frances from the table. 'You're going to be late for school Fran, if you don't get a move on!'

'But I've not had me bacon, yet, Mam!' Frances wailed.

'Is that my fault?' Ellen snapped, darting an accusing look at her sister, who moaned pitifully in return.

'Home sweet home!' George flung down his paper. The door to the cellar had edged open. The reek of roses and dying lilies mingled with the pungent smell of frying fat. 'Will somebody close that door!' Then he marched up to his lonely office, to brood over the accounts.

The weather had broken. Drizzle fell from the brim of Frances' hood, down her nose, drip, drip, as she and Hester began the long walk to the new schools in Mortimer Road. The injustice of it! To have to suffer Hester's company all that way, after what she'd done to her! 'Look after our Frances, mind, Hester! I'm relying on you!' her grandma had said, as the pair left for school. Huh! Fat chance of Hester looking after anybody! She needed somebody looking after *her*! Not that Hester relished the company any more than Frances.

'So you didn't let on about the stable lad, after all, our Fran?' Hester sneered. Frances shook her head. 'Mind you don't neither. Or I'll have to frighten you some more!' Frances set her mouth.

'It wasn't because I was scared, I didn't tell on you. It was because I promised. So there!'

'Prig!' Hester jeered. Then, silently, they suffered one another, trudging together, but not together, on through the rain to Mortimer Road Schools.

Frances was in Standard II, and doing well. In fact, she quite liked school. She could read and write, was good at her tables and sums. Miss Turnbull said even her needlework wasn't bad. She got on with the other children too, sons and daughters of miners, railway and ballast workers, dockers . . . the school drew children from all over the southern part of the growing town. But it was reading that Frances really liked most. She would pore over her books for hours, escaping into other worlds, whereas sums were Hester's strength. She was in the Seniors and once arrived at school, Hester turned to go in her own gate, without a backward glance, disowning the younger child. 'Good riddance to bad rubbish!' Frances muttered under her breath, as she went on to the humbler, junior entrance. She shivered as she took off her oilskin in the cloakroom. Her feet were sopping wet. She glanced at the line of stockings drying on the pipes. But the bell had gone, and the school was assembling to give thanks for the king's recovery. Frances' heart was no longer in it. It was hard to give thanks for someone else's deliverance.

But nobody was giving thanks in Beattie's flower shop. The white lilies had gone brown at the edges.

'It'll be my fault,' Ellen said fractiously.

'If it's not mine,' her husband reminded her.

The picture of misery, a scarf tied round her chin, Maisie's eyes reproached them all; it's me gets all the blame round here, never mind you lot!

'Eddie!' The three jumped out of their skins, as George bawled over the railing down into the shop. 'Fetch my wife!' Eddie scuttled off at such speed, you'd think somebody'd set fire to his pants.

'The Old Barsket!' Ellen muttered darkly, staring up at the office door.

'Here here!' Maisie sighed. 'D'you think me toothache'll be gone by Thursday?'

'Why Thursday? Oh aye! Your fishmonger!'

Jane couldn't seem to fix her mind on the need to economise. Head aching after a restless night, the subject of Hester pursued her with fierce urgency.

'I'm sorry, George, but I'm really worried! And our Ellen and Maisie aren't much help. Hester has such tantrums! And, I mean, if she can't cope with her temper, how's she going to cope when she starts having "feelings"?' Desperate for an answer, Jane clutched at the only straw which had come to hand. 'What about them piano lessons?'

George raised his eyes to heaven. As if piano lessons could be the answer to anything!

37

'They'd be cheaper than horse riding, anyway!' George was half-way to giving his consent. Anything for a bit of peace. And Jane gabbled on, relieved to have found some course of action.

'Mind, she'll need a piano, to practise on! They make nice pieces of furniture do pianos!' But there was still the need to economise. 'We'll maybe get one second-hand. I'll look in the paper, shall I?'

'If you like.' George took his arm away, itching to get back to the accounts. Jane seemed relieved, but a new idea had crossed George's mind. 'What about our Fran?'

'What about her?'

'I hope she won't feel left out.'

'Fran? Well, surely, our Ellen and Eddie are responsible for her, eh? I mean, you can't afford piano lessons for them both, can you?' George shook his head and bent to his accounts. 'I'm sorry about the flowers, George.' He looked up, surprised. 'I do love you.' She kissed him gently on his balding head. The crusty face crumbled and George laid his cheek on her hand. 'There's a lot of us to keep, I know. And I'm not much good at spinning out the housekeeping.'

'It's not your fault, Jane.'

'If I could have given you a son to help you . . . '

'Not your fault.' He sighed. 'Eddie's not much cop.'

'No.' Jane agreed. 'Sometimes I wonder he had the gumption to get our Ellen in the family way!' The grandparents exploded with laughter, and, opening the door, Maisie was surprised to see the old barsket, one hand round his wife's waist, the other riding up her skirt, and she giggling and laughing like a schoolgirl!

'What do *you* want?' George bellowed.

'It's a letter. It's just come. It's for Ma.'

George snatched it from her, and Maisie fled, grinning, and muttering, 'Eeh! Well I never! Well I never!' Opening the letter, Jane flushed with pleasure.'

'It's from Harriet! She's coming home for our silver wedding!'

George's hand flew to his brow. 'Oh no!'

'George! She *is* your stepdaughter!'

'You've changed your tune. You two used to be always at one another's throats.'

'That was in the old days, George. Poor Harriet. She never got over Robert. That was the trouble. Ending up an elderly

38

spinster, like that. Tut! Well, we're all older and wiser now, aren't we?'

George's face was inscrutable.

Frances' best friend, Muriel, was waiting for her after assembly.

'Hurry up, man. We'll be late!' Muriel flounced on ahead, and Frances smiled to herself as she followed. She was a bit bossy was Muriel, but she was a 'canny lass' all the same, and anyway, Muriel's mam was a dancing teacher. Frances had been to their house more than once to watch the classes, held in Mrs Blunt's front room. It was a big room, and there was no furniture to speak of, only the bare boards on the floor, a tinny piano and a long form for pupils to sit on while waiting their turns. Frances had sat on that form and watched Muriel and the other girls, longingly. They were practising for a display at the Miner's Hall. They were going to wear costumes with spangles on and everything!

'What've you done to your eye?' Muriel whispered, as they paused outside Standard Two.

'I promised not to let on. But it was our Hester. Don't tell anyone!'

'Cross my heart and hope to die,' Muriel said dramatically, as they opened the schoolroom door, to be greeted by a frown from Miss Turnbull. Mind, their teacher was lovely. She had black hair, piled up on her head in a bun, and she wore lovely dangly earrings with amethysts in them. Frances watched as the sun peeped from behind the clouds, and glanced off the purple stones to dance across the white walls of the schoolroom. She was asking questions about Saint George.

'Can anyone tell me which other countries claim him as their patron saint?' No one could. 'Well, there's Ethiopia, Venice, Russia . . . '

'Catholics an' all, Miss!'

'That's true. Catholics turn to him for help sometimes, when they've got a problem. Yes, Frances?'

'Do you have to be a Catholic to ask Saint George to help you?'

'I don't suppose so. Why? Have you got a problem, Fran? You certainly look as though you have! How did you do that to your eye?'

'Her Dad belted her!' Cissy shouted out.

39

'Sh.' Miss Turnbull turned angrily on Cissy.

'I fell down,' Frances declared. 'On Bent Lane.'

'Well. You'll have to be more careful won't you?' Frances bristled as the class laughed.

'Clumsy clart! Clumsy clart!' They chanted.

'Will you be quiet!' Miss Turnbull banged her cane on the desk. 'Now! Do any of you know of any instances when Saint George is supposed to have saved England?'

He saved the king last night,' Frances stated.

'Well, I suppose he might have.' Miss Turnbull smiled. 'But he is certainly supposed to have appeared, at the head of a heavenly army to help the crusaders once.' Now this was something! The girls were all agog. A hero saint appealed to them hugely, and enthusiasm grew to adopt him as their class's patron, never mind England's. It was the talk of the playground, as Frances and Muriel swung from rung to rung across the ladders, hanging in the shed roof.

'I think it's a smashing idea!' Frances panted, turning upside down, hair hanging to the ground. 'He might even help me against our Hester.'

'My Mam says she's got all the makings of a trollop!'

'What's a trollop?'

'I don't know. But it's not nice.' Frances swung herself to the ground, and looked up, watching her friend on the rungs.

'Can I come for tea tonight?'

'My Mam says you've got to ask your folks before you come, next time. She says she can't have you worrying them, not knowing where you are.'

'Oh.' Frances was disappointed. 'It must be nice to have a proper Mam.' Muriel, upside down, stared at her friend quizzically.

'You've *got* a proper Mam! Haven't you?' Muriel's hair hung down invitingly. Suddenly Frances pulled it and ran off, laughing down the shed.

'What tickles me is Harriet remembering at all!' Jane was pacing up and down the kitchen in her excitement.

'Auntie Harriet's a stickler for anniversaries and that, Ma!'

'What'll we do to celebrate?'

'You could hire the Queen's Hall. Have a party.'

'Eeh! I wonder if your Dad's let us? I mean it is our silver wedding!' Jane's eyes twinkled at the prospect. But Ellen was frowning, as she wired the best of the coronation lilies into a wreath.

'Do you think the Frasers'll notice they're not fresh?'

Jane's practised eye assessed the situation. 'No. I shouldn't think so. People's eyes are usually too full of tears to see properly at funerals.'

'Mrs Fraser's a good customer, mind, Ma. We don't want to upset *her*!'

'We've got to salvage what we can!'

'I know, Ma, but I mean, it's not good business, is it? Not in the long run!'

'Your father knows best, Ellen!'

'I'm only trying to . . . '

'I know just what you're trying to do! You're trying to spoil my good mood, that's what!'

'I am not! Face facts, Ma! It's no good sticking our heads in the clouds!'

'Mind who you're speaking to, my girl!' Tears of vexation flooded Jane's eyes. 'My job's to keep your father happy, Ellen. It's not easy. Give me credit!'

'Yes, Ma.' The words stuck in Ellen's throat. Pandering to the old barsket might make him happy in the short term, but he wouldn't be so happy when business slumped. 'I'm only thinking of the future, Ma.'

'You're being selfish, Ellen, as usual. You none of you think of me, do you? I've spent my life trying not to rock the boat.'

'Yes, Ma.' And Ellen locked in her tongue. What she had to say on that subject would really put the cat among the pigeons!

'You all seem to expect *me* to keep everything together in this family. Well, it's time you and Eddie grew up, Ellen; took your share of the responsibilities! You've got a child now, in case you'd forgotten.'

'And what do you mean by that?'

'You neglect her. You do, Ellen. You've never forgiven her for trapping you into marriage. As though she could be blamed just for being born!' Ellen turned her face away, shaking her head in distress. 'You can't run away from the truth, pet.' Jane's voice was softer now, but Ellen came back with shocking ferocity.

'No, you can't, Mam! And the truth is, you've stolen our little girl! It's *you* our Fran dotes on!'

'I don't encourage her, Ellen! I've done my share of child rearing! Now it's your turn! You made your bed!' Jane threw the wreath aside, and stalked up to her room. Ellen stared after her, white-faced with fury. So, her Ma thought it was *her* kept everything going, did she? Huh! It was Ellen! Slaving in that damn shop, cleaning the house, waiting on them all hand and foot, while she . . . she . . . Ellen was crying. She looked down at the half-finished wreath. Why, if she didn't have time for Frances, it was because she had so much work to do!

Hester'd gone to a friend's for her dinner, so Frances came in alone at twenty to one.

'I can't see to you! You'll have to find your grandma. We're doing the Fraser funeral,' her mother told her, bitterly.

'We're going to have Saint George for our class saint.'

'Eh?'

'Mind out the way, pet,' Eddie told her, as he ferried the wreaths and sprays out to the yard. 'I want to get this lot off.'

'Maisie, our class is going to have a patron saint.'

'Ma, I'm in agony, here!'

'You want to see the dentist, our Maisie!'

'Grandma . . . '

'Would you like your egg soft or hard boiled, pet?' Jane asked with a meaningful glare at her daughter.

'Soft, please.' Frances sighed and followed her father out into the yard. He rang his bell as he swung into the lane, his bicycle laden with offerings, looking for all the world like a float at a flower carnival.

'Eeh, I hope they won't notice them lilies!' Frances turned to see her mother, anxiously watching her husband go.

'Mam, why's Grandma in a mood?' Ellen looked down at her daughter, tight lipped.

'Why?'

'She's hardly said a word to me this dinner time. Have I done something?'

'No. It's not you, pet.' Ellen brooded for a moment, then spoke up. 'There's only one person your grandma really cares about,' she said bitterly. Frances frowned.

42

'Who's that, Mam?'

'Her brother, Robert Ridley.'

'Have I heard of him?'

'Your granda can't bear to hear his name. He was a bad lot and no mistake!'

'Why? What did he do?' Ellen looked this way and that and whispered in her daughter's ear.

'Don't let on I told you, mind, but your grandma's precious brother stole all the takings from the shop, and ran off with them.'

'Eeh!'

'Your grandma tried to cover up for him. Why she'd even given him her diamond engagement ring, to help him get away! If you ask me . . . ' Ellen nodded sagely, but Frances' mind was running on ahead.

'Where did he go?'

'India. You'd think she'd've been glad to be rid of him! But no! She still hankers after seeing him, all these years later. It's a disgrace!'

'Will he ever come home again?'

'I should think not! Your granda would never allow it!' To her consternation, Ellen heard her little daughter saying, sympathetically,

'Poor Grandma.'

Twenty minutes later, a soft boiled egg inside her, Frances was back on the road to school. Poor grandma! No wonder she looked unhappy. Why couldn't her granda forgive and forget and let Robert come home again? Maybe that was why he was always in a temper! Oh dear! Everybody was unfair to her grandma. And it wasn't true she didn't care about anybody else. She cared about Frances! Why she'd given her a note for Miss Turnbull, hadn't she? She pulled it out of her pocket, and looked at the envelope. It was sealed. Was it about her black eye? Did it say Hester'd done it? What else could it be about? Stuffing it back in her pocket, Frances ploughed on, dutifully handing her teacher the note once in class. Miss Turnbull read the note thoughtfully, then scribbled a reply and sealed it, before handing it back. Frances waited, looking at her teacher, who merely smiled and told her to sit down. She was disappointed. She had expected some reaction, even sympathy, but none was forthcoming. So she went back to her seat, beside Muriel, and got on with her sums, trying hard not to think about romantic places like India.

At tea time, coming in the back way with her letter, Frances came across her mother and father, whispering in the yard. Eddie kept glancing up at the window, where her granda worked.

'You tell him.'

'No, you tell him.'

'*Me* tell him how to run his own business? It'd sound better coming from you.' And then they saw her.

'Hallo, pet. Had a nice day at school?' Her mother forced a smile.

'We've got to write a composition.'

'What about?'

'Saint George.'

'That's nice.' They waited for her to go in, before resuming their whispering. But Frances didn't care. She was in on one of the secrets! She knew about her grandma and her 'secret grief'. Feeling almost conspiratorial, Frances handed the note to her up in her bedroom. Jane looked pleased with its contents, and went up to the office to tell her husband, but said nothing to Frances. Disappointed, and puzzled, Frances went back downstairs, took out her doll and pram and started pushing it round the kitchen. What had grandma written to the teacher? And what had been the reply? Perhaps it was too serious a matter to talk to Frances about! Perhaps their Hester was going to be expelled! But neither her grandma, nor Miss Turnbull had looked cross, had they? It was all very strange.

'You're in me way!' Maisie objected, as she came through, searching for Ellen to help in the shop.

'How's your toothache, Auntie?' Frances asked.

'It'd be all the better if your mother would do some serving instead of gossiping in the back lane!' Seconds later, voices were raised outside and Ellen came in, banging against the pram, followed by Maisie and Eddie, as the shop bell rang.

'We were *not* carrying on, our Maisie!' Ellen was shouting in answer to her sister's accusations. 'We were discussing business!' Now the yard was free. Frances wheeled her 'baby' outside, and rocked it quietly to sleep. Secrets, secrets! At least now she had her own to nurse.

* * *

44

Maisie was in a state of high dudgeon at supper time. She served the potatoes, tight-lipped, and pale, while Eddie and Ellen sat watchful, staring at the old barsket as if waiting to say something. He just kept sighing, and ate without noticing what was on his plate, while Hester looked like the cat that got the cream. She had come in early, singing, and there was mud on her boots. Where had she been? Nobody but Frances noticed, and she sat, like the wise monkey, 'sayin' nowt'.

'Our Ellen suggested "The Queen's Hall" for our silver wedding do, George!' Ellen jumped, and immediately denied her mother's charge. 'Yes, you did, Ellen!'

'I only said . . . '

'Well you can unsay it, then.' Her father told her. 'It's far too expensive!'

'Ah, George!' Jane's mouth drooped.

'Now don't you start! As if I didn't have enough trouble! We've got to tighten our belts!'

'It's not *my* fault the coronation got cancelled,' Jane objected.

'Does it matter whose fault it is?!' George roared.

'I hear the king's going from strength to strength,' Eddie informed them.

'He would!' George snorted.

'Well, it wouldn't have made much difference if he *had* died!' Eddie's tone was defiant. George's eyes narrowed.

'And why not pray?' George spoke the words slowly. His voice was threatening. Eddie's jaw opened, then closed again. Ellen kicked him under the table.

'The way the business is going . . . '

'What do *you* know? Throwing out perfectly good blooms!'

'They were past it, Dad,' Ellen put in.

'Rubbish! They'll do to pad out the fresh! After supper, you can get yourselves down there, and sort them again! I've had enough profligacy in this house!' George had on his 'don't answer me back voice', and no one did. 'And while we're on the subject, Hester . . . ' Hester jumped. 'You can say goodbye to your riding lessons!' Hester gasped, the sudden target of her father's wrath. She didn't know whether to shout or cry, so she just sat, as if paralysed, mouth open.

'You look as if you're catching flies, dear,' Jane told her gently. Hester closed her mouth. 'We thought you might like to take

45

piano lessons.' Hester looked at her mother in disbelief. 'Frances' teacher, Miss Turnbull has agreed to take you on.' So that was what the letter was all about! Hester! Frances glared at her aunt across the table, but her eyes met with accusation. Hester was not pleased, and she blamed Frances for her displeasure.

'We've not got a piano!' Hester pointed out.

'There's an old one at the chapel. I'll have a word with Mr Symthe. I daresay he'll let us have it at a reasonable cost.'

As she searched in her toy box after dinner, Frances dreamt of the silver wedding. There had been talk of a party! A posh party at 'The Queen's'! They'd never had a party there! Come to that, they'd never had a party at all! They'd arranged the flowers, and done the catering for plenty of other people's do's and dances, and Frances had sat at her window staring out at the dome of the hall across the road, the light pouring out from the doors below onto the dark street. Ladies, dressed in the colours of jewels, alighted from the carriages, dainty feet stepping onto crimson carpet, swishing up the stairs, under the glistening chandeliers. She'd heard the music, and, if she went down, to sit, in the dark, looking out of their dining room window, she could see through the great windows of the ballroom opposite, as the dancers twirled and whirled, round and round, a sea of colours, till, at last, Frances would fall asleep and have to be carried up to bed. If only her granda would let them have a silver wedding do there, just once. It would make up for not letting poor grandma see her brother! And Frances would so like to be one of the dancers . . . Snapping out of her dream, she picked up her top and whip and ran down to the yard to play.

Hester didn't cry. She never did. She had homework to do. French. She would go up to her room and get on with it. See if *she* cared, if they stopped her pleasures! She liked French. She dreamt of Paris sometimes. Perhaps one day she might see it. She might even work at the Folies Bergères. Hester's dreams at thirteen years betrayed a deep-rooted desire to shock. She wanted only the opportunity. There was a timid knocking on her door. She ignored it, and continued writing. Then the door opened, and Jane walked in.

'I thought you'd like some tea.' She put the cup down beside her daughter, who continued as before. Jane stood for a moment, then went quietly to sit on the bed and wait. Hester sighed deeply. Outside, in the yard, Frances was playing tops and whips. She could hear the top singing as it whizzed round and round, and, as it slowed, she heard Frances catch it with her whip, and set it off again, careering across the yard. Then it stopped.

'Go on! You can do better than that!' Ellen and Maisie, resorting flowers, salvaging the living from the dead, egged on the little girl. There was silence, as Frances wound the whip around the top.

'The nights are drawing in,' Jane said. Twilight dimmed the window of Hester's room. 'You'll hurt your eyes. Let me light a lamp for you.'

'Thanks,' Hester said, without looking up. Jane lit the lamp, then sat, fidgeting awkwardly, wondering what to do. Suddenly, she got up and began to tidy Hester's things. Hester's back went rigid. Her mother was picking up her shoes.

'Hester, where have you been to get your boots so muddy?'

'Oh . . . Jean and I had a walk in their garden at lunch time.' The boots were caked with mud. Jane looked closer. A pungent smell caught her breath.

'Do they keep horses?' she asked. There was a silence. Hester's throat went dry. 'Where were you really, Hester?'

'We went for a walk on the hills. That's all.'

'With your friend?'

'Of course.'

'Which friend?'

'Jean. I told you!'

'Look me in the eye and say that.' Hester turned to face her mother.

'I went for a walk with Jean.'

'I don't believe you.' They stared at one another. 'What were you doing, Hester?' Frances' top was spinning. It whirred in the yard below. It whirred like the whip of the ringmaster, while the tigers prowled; Robert's last night, before George had raped her . . .

'What's Fran been saying?'

'Fran?' Jane frowned. 'Why?' Hester said nothing. 'What have you been doing, Hester?'

'Nothing.'

47

'Hah!'

'I've been seeing a lad at the stables, if you really want to know.' Jane gasped, and sat on the bed. The past made flesh. Her voice trembled when she spoke at last.

'What do you mean, "seeing" him?' Hester laughed loudly. 'Hester! How dare you! How dare you! Laughing in my face! What am I going to do with you, Hester?'

'Are you going to tell Dad?'

'What is there to tell Hester? Hester, are you all right?' Hester's laughter increased. 'Who is he? Tell me! Who is he?'

'The stable lad at the riding school. His first name's Joe. I don't know his surname.'

'And have you . . . have you "been the whole way" with this lad?'

'Wouldn't you like to know?'

'Tell me you're just saying things, to frighten me!'

'Perhaps I am, Ma. Perhaps it's just your own dirty mind!' Perhaps it was. Or perhaps it wasn't. Either way . . .

The fault was hers. Unable to face any more, Jane ran, shaking, from her daughter's room. Her head swam. Blood pounded in her ears. The sound of the whip in the yard echoed in her brain. Memories bombarded her from every side. She had sided with the tigers. She had shared their lust, resenting the sway of the man at the centre of the ring, controlling them, searing them with his lash. She fled down the stairs to the kitchen. But the sound of the whip held her. She went to the window and looked out. Frances stood, feet firmly planted in the middle of the yard, whip raised, and the top spun. The child felt the eyes on her back. She turned and saw the white face of her grandmother, through the glass, and she smiled. Then she pointed to the spinning top, giggling with excitement, looking back at the white face, innocent of the horror in the eyes. For Jane felt herself to be the top. The child raised the whip, and again it lashed, wheeling through the air, it whirred and whizzed, it whistled and spat. And it caught at the top, stinging, searing. And the sisters, watching, shouted on the little girl, poised to strike the top again. Drowned by applause, muzzled by the glass, the scream was without sound. But the sisters saw, and Frances, catching their expression, let the whip drop, turning to see. Behind her own reflection, caught in the green swirls of the glass, she saw her grandma's agony; hands on her ears, the face a face no more. Jane was an open mouth, screaming silently.

The women moved, babbling with distress. Figures came, writhing behind the window, pulling at her grandma, tearing her away from the glass. And Frances stood, whip fallen to her side, feeling somehow that it was all her fault. Deaf to sound, the drama at the window came and went, like a dream. Now the child's reflection stayed alone. And as she moved slowly towards the glass, her image spread, swirling through the green, dispersing her in colours, orange, brown, red, blue. Red? Her mother saw, coming back into the yard.

'Put your head back! That's it. Good girl.' Cold and wet, the rag stopped the flow of blood, and Frances' eyes met the dark shape of Hester, standing at the lamplit window of the room above.

CHAPTER THREE

Frances stared out of the darkness, at the dome of the Queen's Hall, face wet with tears. They were all in bed, her family, all in their separate rooms, while she sat at the dining room window, looking out. She was not alone. She had her doll, Mary Ann, for company.

'I wish there'd been a ball tonight, Mary Ann,' Frances said, sighing. 'That'd've cheered us up, eh?' She gazed on the doll's face, impassive in the moonlight. 'What happened to Grandma? Do *you* know?' Mary Ann seemed to shake her head. 'Neither do I. Nobody tells me anything.' But they had told her something, hadn't they? Her Mam had told her about Grandma's brother, Robert. Frances'd always known Grandma had brothers and sisters. She'd had a sister called Fanny once, and a brother called Joshua. Uncle Josh lived in America, and he was younger than Grandma, and great aunt Fanny was dead. But this other brother, Robert, had been news to her. Was he still alive? He must be, if Grandma wanted to see him. Poor Grandma. Was it because of him she'd got upset? Maybe she'd had news of him. Maybe he'd been stealing things again. He must be a horrible man for Granda to hate him so much. All the same, he *was* family and Grandma loved him. Her Granda was rotten, keeping him away. The clock on the mantel struck two. Frances shivered, and pulled her blanket round her. 'I wish there was a ball tonight, all the same.' She sighed longingly, staring at the blank windows of the hall across the road.

Ellen and Eddie were staring up at the dark ceiling of their room.

'What's the time, Ellen?'

'The clock just struck two.'

'Oh.' Eddie sighed. 'Light the lamp, pet. I want a cup of tea.'

'You and your tea!' Murmuring, Ellen lit the lamp, slipped on her dressing gown and went down to the kitchen. The clatter of the kettle drew Maisie. Silently, she descended the stair, and stood in the doorway.

'Is that tea you're making?' she asked plaintively. Ellen dropped the kettle in the sink.

'Eeh! Our Maisie! You'll give me heart failure! Creeping up on's like that!'

'I couldn't sleep.'

'Neither could we. Eeh, I don't know. I can't stop thinkin' about it. What got into Ma, eh?'

Eddie shuffled in in his slippers, yawning.

'I reckon it's . . . you know . . . her . . . you know . . . ' He flushed.

'What's he mean?' Maisie asked.

'I don't know.'

'You know . . . her age . . . '

'The change? Rubbish!' Eddie sat down, deflated. 'Honestly, Eddie, why couldn't you say? He's not so shy when he's in bed, you know!'

'Shurrup, man.' Eddie was shocked, but his wife laughed. 'Maisie's not married!'

'So?'

'She doesn't know about . . . "things".'

'She will soon if she carries on the way she's going!'

Eddie said nothing. He was looking at his sister-in-law's hunched back, heaving up and down with laughter. Ellen shook her head. '*We*'re in no position to put her right, are we now?' Eddie frowned. Really Ellen ought not to encourage her. Maisie was simple. A man might take advantage.

'Maisie,' he began, 'I tend to think of myself as a sort of

51

brother to you.' Ellen and Maisie stared at him, amused at the unaccustomed authority of his tone. 'Men, Maisie, are not to be trusted!'

'You can say that again!' Ellen whooped.

'Shurrup, will you, woman!' Eddie shouted, nettled. 'I'm talkin'!'

'Huh!' Now Ellen was sulking. 'You're good at talking when you're with us, but you're not so good when it comes to "him".'

'And what's that supposed to mean?' Eddie asked.

'You never said *owt* to the old barsket about the Fraser business, I notice!'

'How could I, man? In the circumstances? The poor sod had enough on his plate, what with her yelling fit to bring the house down, and our Fran bleeding all over the place!'

'I hope she's all right.'

'If you ask me,' said her father, 'our Fran's the only one in the family that is!'

'What's that about the Fraser's?' Maisie asked.

'They've put in a complaint. They say the flowers for the funeral weren't up to scratch and they're not going to pay. And I don't blame them!'

'Oh my hat! Dad'll go mad!'

'I couldn't say owt tonight now, could I?' He appealed to his sister-in-law.

'You know what *I* think?' Two pairs of eyes looked expectantly at Ellen. 'I think you'd *like* this shop to go under, Eddie!'

'Eh?'

'You would! Then your father could take us over, couldn't he?'

'Rubbish!' But Eddie shuffled uncomfortably in his seat, as Ellen banged down his cup of tea in front of him.

'You can put your own sugar in!'

'But I thought Dad wanted to take over Lidell's shop?' Maisie said innocently. Ellen looked daggers at her, while Eddie laughed.

'He did, Ellen. Admit it. The old barsket's been angling to take over my Dad's grocery business right from the start. It'd serve him right if the boot ended up on the other foot!'

Upstairs, Frances listened to the voices of her Mam, her Dad and her auntie, murmuring in the kitchen, and felt comforted. Her eyelids drooped, her head sank to the cushioned window seat, and she fell asleep. Later, their tea drunk, they all trooped back upstairs. But Maisie stopped on the landing.

'Sh!'

'What's wrong with *her*?'

'I thought I heard something.' She pushed open the door to the dining room, and saw Frances asleep in the moonlight.

'Eeh!' Ellen squeaked. 'What's *she* doing down here? The little minx!'

'Don't wake her,' Maisie said. And Eddie lifted his daughter, gently, taking her up to her attic room, and folding her once more in her blankets. He looked down on Frances' face for some minutes. Sometimes, when he thought about it, he was surprised to find he had a daughter. She didn't seem to take after him. Not much anyway. Had Ellen played him wrong? He shook his head. Impossible. He touched the little face soothing the frown away. It was a Beattie face all right. She belonged to their camp, not his. But still, it was all for the best. After all, what could Eddie give her? He was trapped in this house, bound hand and foot, just as he had been at home, with his Mam. They wouldn't let him be a man, none of them. He was a weed, like his father before him. Eddie sniffed, tucked in his daughter, and went back downstairs.

Next morning, Frances stayed off school. She was pale and nervy. Ellen, Maisie, and Eddie were specially kind to her, but it was her grandma that Frances really missed. The doctor'd given her a dose to calm her down, and now she lay sleeping. But, as usual, no one would tell Frances what was wrong.

'Granda, why did Grandma start screaming?' George looked sadly at the child, standing at the open door of his office. He patted his leg.

'Come and sit on my knee.' Frances came slowly, nestling up to the huge grey beard. 'Do you love your old granda?' he asked softly.

'Yes.' She answered doubtfully.

'I love you too.' His voice was gruff with emotion. Frances pulled away from him in panic.

'Is Grandma going to be all right?'

'Of course she is, pet.' George reassured her. 'She just got upset. That's all.'

'Because of our Hester?' He looked at her strangely.

'What do *you* know about it, Frances?' She wriggled uncomfortably.

'I promised not to tell.'

'I see.'

'But, if you said first . . . '

'You'd not be breaking any promises, eh?'

'No.'

'All right. She's been a bit naughty, Fran. She's done something she shouldn't.'

'What though, Granda?'

'She's been naughty with a lad.'

'I thought it must be that.' George was shocked. 'I saw her with the lad from the stables once. They were holding hands and everything.'

'Everything?'

'He kissed her, Granda!' Her eyes were wide with shock. But George was relieved.

'Promise me you won't go on like that, Frances.'

'I promise.'

'Good girl. We'll be keeping a tight rein on Hester from now on, so don't you worry about her any more. Now, how about telling me what you've been learning at school, eh?'

'We've been learning all about Saint George, Granda! How he kills dragons, and rescues maidens and that.'

'Oh.'

'Did he really, Granda?'

'It's what's called a myth, pet.'

'What's a myth?'

'Well, like the parables in the bible, it's a way of telling you about something that makes it easier to understand. But it doesn't mean to say that it actually happened.' Frances was disappointed. 'Now in the case of Saint George . . . well he's like the goodie, fighting off evil. The dragon's the devil, really. And the maiden, well, she's the innocent victim. So, Saint George's saving the innocent girl from getting into the clutches of the devil. That's what it means.'

'Will he save me, Granda?'

'I'm sure he will, pet.'

'What's he look like?'

'Who? The devil or Saint George?'

'Saint George, man!'

'How about you telling me?'

'Well . . . he's huge. And he's very fierce. And he rides on a white horse, and he's got black armour on.'

'Black?'

'Yes. Shiny black. He's handsome, but he's scary. I'd like to marry somebody like that.'

'Eeh, well, there's not many men answering to that description in Shields!' Her granda laughed.

'*You're* called George. And *you're* fierce, Granda.'

George was taken aback. 'Aye but I'm no saint, pet,' he told her gently.

It was growing dark, when Jane rose at last. She had slept for eighteen hours, drugged by laudanum. Frances was already in bed. She went upstairs to see her. The child was reading.

'Caught you!' her grandma said.

'Are you all right now?'

'Yes, pet. Did I give you a fright?' Frances nodded, looking warily at Jane, as she sat on the bed beside her. 'They tell me you had a nose bleed?' So, her grandma cared. She'd come up to see her, to comfort her. Suddenly the child sobbed, her arms reaching out for love. Jane rocked her to and fro nervously. 'Will you do something for me, Frances?'

'Aha. What?'

'I want you to keep an eye on Hester.'

Frances looked at her grandma in astonishment.

'Spy on her, you mean?'

'No. Not spy on her exactly . . . just . . . well, you do go to the same school.'

'The seniors is separate from the juniors, Grandma.'

'I don't want to have to ask the teachers. It's better kept in the family.' Jane was speaking almost to herself.

'What, Grandma? What's best kept in the family?' Jane sighed.

'It's not so much what Hester's done I'm worried about, Fran. It's what she might do in the future. She needs protecting from herself.'

'But, what might she do?'

'It's in her blood, you see. It's not her fault. We should all be extra kind to her.'

'What's in her blood?' Jane was near to tears.

'She takes after . . . after . . . ' Robert, Frances thought. She takes after Robert, the brother who stole and ran away. But Jane reached out and found another thread. ' . . . My sister, Fanny,' she said at last. Frances' eyes opened wide with astonishment.

'Fanny's dead now.' Jane's words began to flow more freely, as the story tumbled out. 'But she used to run after the lads, when we were young. She got herself into all sorts of trouble. And she drank. Yes, she drank herself to death in the end. But not before she'd sent her husband and her child to the workhouse.' Frances gasped.

'I never knew that!'

'Your granda cut them off. I can't say I blame him.'

'Fanny. Is that not short fo·Frances?' Jane started as if out of a dream. 'Was I called after her?'

'Yes, but . . . Fran, you're nothing like *her*! Nothing! You mustn't think that!' But what *was* the child to think? If Hester had Fanny's blood, then so had she!

'Has she got anything to do with Granda's bad temper, then?'

'What?' Jane looked puzzled.

'You said we had to make allowances for Granda, because of something. Was it because of her, or . . . ?' Dare Frances mention Robert? The words stuck in her throat, and she found she could not.

'Your granda's not bad tempered, pet! Well, not all the time!'

'No, not all the time.' Frances stared at her grandma, commanding her to say more. It was as though the child had a power over her. It was the power of innocence. For Frances only sought to know the truth. It was her family. It was her right. But Jane was not innocent and her eyes slid from hers.

'Yes. It's because of her,' she said. But Frances did not look satisfied with her answer. Distraught, Jane left her, feeling she had done more harm than good.

Frances looked after her grandma, eyes black with shock. Her mind spun with confusion. Robert, Fanny, blood. Frances shared their blood, just the same as Hester. Would she then grow up like Hester? Her grandma had been worried about 'the future'. And her granda'd made her promise not to be like Hester and chase after lads! What terrible thing was going to happen to her, then? Maybe Saint George could help her! Frances slid out of bed, onto her knees and gripped her hands tightly together.

'Please, Saint George, save me from bad blood. Save me from me Auntie Hester, and other dragons. Thanks very much.' Then Frances climbed back into bed, pulled the sheet up tight, and, brain anxiously working, trying to piece the tangled threads together, Frances finally escaped into sleep.

In all the fuss about Hester, Maisie's activities had gone unnoticed by all. By all, that is, except Eddie. Now, decked out in her finery, she stood before the mirror and tried out her smile. Her mouth warped and spread. There was a fault in the glass. How could she see herself properly in this blooming thing?! Her cheeks were a bit pale, mind. Turning to her bureau, Maisie opened it, pulled out the drawer at the back, then, twisting a knob, a tiny piece of wood sprang out, to reveal the hidden niche behind. Maisie smiled with pleasure. She enjoyed working the secret drawer. Then she reached in, and pulled out a tiny box. 'Rouge Brunette' it said on the lid. Quickly she applied the red to her cheeks, slipped the box back, then the drawer, locked the bureau behind her and no one was any the wiser. That was better. She looked like she had a bit of life in her now. She was all set. She was going out on the town with the fishmonger! Turning to check her hat from the side, Maisie caught sight of her hump. It wasn't so bad really. And if she moved just slightly to the left, the flaw in the mirror smoothed it away, as if it had never been. Perhaps this mirror wasn't so bad, after all! 'Look like a parrot', indeed! A queen more like! Maisie was singing, as she passed through the shop.

> The silvery moon was shining down,
> And love lit up my heart,
> As we swayed to the tune we knew so well,
> In the days when we were apart.

'Stop her, Ellen!' Eddie hissed at his wife.

'Have a nice time!' Ellen called after her. 'Don't do anything I wouldn't, mind!'

'Give Mr Platt our best regards, pet,' Jane reminded her.

'Eh?' Maisie stopped, puzzled.

'Yes, Maisie, remember and tell Mr Platt I send my apologies to the Sunday School Committee!' Ellen said between clenched teeth.

'Oh aye!' Maisie grinned. 'I will. Ta ta!'

'Ta ta, love.' Eddie gave Ellen a look.

'I wash my hands!' he whispered.

'Yes, pet. You always do!' his wife spat at him.

George was out. He often was; on council business mostly. It had been a heavy day, close, cloudy, with a strange, orangey sky. But now it was twilight, the clouds had cleared. Jane stared out through the shop window. The crescent of the moon had grown. It was at its quarter. Not silvery, but yellow, golden, it hung in the heavens. And the stars? She would like to go and look at the stars . . .

'I think I'll just pop out for a bit of fresh air.' She pulled her shawl around her, and opened the shop door.

'You do, Mam. It's nearly closing time anyway.' Ellen encouraged her. 'It'll do you good.' Scarcely noticing the horse drawn tram, Jane crossed the street, and entered George's nurseries by the little gate, alongside 'The Queen's'. She liked it there. The balmy summer air comforted her nerves. The honeysuckle in the hedge went to her head like wine. Yes, dusk was her favourite time. Walking slowly up the lane, she stared up at the stars. So far away they were; the heavens so vast. What did she matter in the end? What did anything matter? She sighed. The greenhouse loomed dark with foliage, splashes of red, and yellow glaring from the glass. George's chrysanthemums. He grew them at all seasons now. Once, when she was young, before she'd married George, she had cut her wrists on the glass of this very greenhouse. Then, she had been close to death. It had been an accident of course. George had saved her, carried her back into the house, and tied the bandage tight to stop the flow. Memories. They had been married now for twenty-five years. Their marriage had stood, was it in spite of everything, or because of everything? There were no secrets between them. They had hurt one another to the full. They had forgiven and they had gone on loving. What did any of it matter now?

Jane sank onto the old seat George had put beside the hedge. He often sat there, smoking his cigars. The only place he could get any peace, he often said. He was right. It *was* peaceful. Night smells. She breathed deeply. Night scented stock . . . He must have planted it especially, right beside the chair. Dear George. He was a sensual man, sensitive. His gruff exterior his only armour. Poor George. What with this business of the coronation, the Fraser's, Hester . . . Oh, Hester! The trees whispered. Jane shivered. An owl hooted close by. Wings whisked in the half light, and a dark shape loomed out of the tree, up into the sky, dropping, claws outstretched, then away with its burden back into the trees. The owl lived a secret life. It knew the darkness and was unafraid. She might almost envy it.

Walking back across the street, Jane saw that the lights in the shop were out. Upstairs, in Ellen and Eddie's room, a lamp had been lit. Shadows crossed the curtains. But she did not see the little girl, in the darkness, sitting at the dining room window, watching her. The sky was like black velvet. Stars twinkled, red, blue, yellow, and white. It was late. Turning in by the lane, Jane entered the house the back way.

'Ooh! What a fright!' Ellen was sitting by the kitchen fire, drinking cocoa.

'Sorry, I'm sure,' Jane said. 'George back yet?' Ellen shook her head. 'Maisie?'

'Oh yes.' Ellen lied. 'She'll be in bed by now.'

'You go on up. I'll wait for George.'

'No, Ma. You need your rest. I'll give him his cocoa. Don't worry now.'

'We're a lot of night owls these days, Ellen!' Jane said, as she went upstairs.

Ten minutes later, Maisie's head peered cautiously around the door.

'Coast clear?' she whispered.

'Why aye. Come on in. Tell's all about it! I'm dyin' to know!'

'There's nothin' to tell.'

'What d'ye mean? There must be, man! When're you seeing your fishmonger again, eh?'

'I'm not. I'm finished with him!'

'Why?'

'He's got a kiss like a sink plunger! He's set me toothache off!'

★ ★ ★

59

Frances waited till the noises stopped, and even Maisie was fast asleep, then padded silently upstairs to her own room. Poor Grandma. Why didn't anyone keep her company when she went out? Was she nursing her secret grief about her brother over there in the nurseries in the dark? Didn't anyone care? She reached for Mary Ann and cuddled her, giving her the comfort she would have liked to give Jane. Time and again, Muriel had asked her to stay for tea, and time and again, though Frances had longed to go home with her friend and share the easy atmosphere of her family, she had refused, hoping that her grandma would want her, would let her in on her secret, the secret Frances already shared, had she but known it. Poor Grandma. Crying for her, Frances went to sleep.

The air was thick. Noises; creaks, and bumps, cracks and rattles jerked Jane from sleep, as the house lived and settled round her. George shifted, then snored again. But Jane was stifling. The room, behind its thick curtained window, smothered her. She could die like this. Entombed. Seized with panic, she got up, went to the window, and threw back the curtain. Suddenly she was bathed in light. The sash slid noiselessly, the sweet night air swam towards her, and the world stilled. Moonshine on roofs, on walls, on the yard below. A sudden crack, the lash of a whip. George grunted, and woke up.

'What's wrong?'

'Nothing. I couldn't sleep. I wanted some air.' Again the whip cracked. Like gunshot, it echoed on the night air.

'Somebody's in a hurry!' George, dredged from sleep, yawned, as a horse galloped up the hill towardls the Village.

Upstairs, in the attic room at the front of the house, Frances stirred. Hooves pounded through her dreams. A lonely horse galloped, galloped for dear life. And then it was gone; horse shoes on the shore; Hester tracing the tracks. Fire on the horizon. Who was the horseman? Was it she? Why was she so afraid? What was she running from? In her sleep, Frances sobbed, murmured her prayer to Saint George, and, in the silence of the night, slept again.

He was at Jane's side.

'Sh! George'll see everything's all right. Don't you worry.'
Outside, dark wings fluttered, and came to rest.

'What's that?'

'Bird of some sort. Come back to bed.' Jane let him lead her,
let him tuck her in, and said goodnight before he slept again. But
she did not sleep. At last, she reached for the bottle of laudanum,
and counted the drops into her glass. Then she drank. Then she
slept; and dreamed. And the whip commanded her. She cowered
from it into her corner. And she hated the figure at the centre of
the ring, the figure in black and gold who wielded the whip.
Fierce with anger, she poised to pounce, but the figure turned,
and it was a little girl. Her chestnut curls tumbled from beneath
the black top hat. Her little legs stuck out beneath the spangled
coat. Yes, Frances was the one with the whip . . .

Jane shut out the day behind drawn curtains, and opened them at
night. She felt free then. George was often out of an evening, and
as the day waned, Jane would retreat to the nurseries, where she
sat on alone into the darkness, leaving the work to her daughters,
Maisie and Ellen. Hurt, Frances watched her grandma, as she
crossed the busy street, leaving them. One day, the little girl
raced down from her room, flying out of the shop, and across the
road, dodging the traffic.

'Grandma! Grandma!' Jane turned, and the breathless child
caught up with her, smiling and panting. 'Can I come with you?'
Jane pulled back. There was a look of fear, even hatred in her
face.

'No, you can't! Get on with your homework!' But the words
were drowned by the sound of horses, a team of them, pulling
the tram up the hill. Then Jane walked away, into the dusky
gardens beyond, leaving the child, alone.

Ellen was scrubbing the counters, while Maisie took the pails of
flowers down to the cellar. Eddie was in George's office, sorting
the day's takings, and George was out. Only Hester remained in
the upstairs part of the house. At the bottom of the stair, Frances
heard her thumping five finger exercises on the piano. Opening
the door a crack, Frances stood and watched. Suddenly, so
suddenly that Frances jumped. Hester crashed her hands down
full on the instrument.

'What do *you* want?' she shouted.

'Nothing.' Hester glared at her. 'I was lonely, that's all.'

'You must be, or you wouldn't come looking for me!' Hester laughed.

'Can I have a go on the piano?'

'With pleasure! I hate the thing!' She shifted over, and Frances sat beside her on the long stool. 'Start with the left hand. There. Lift your wrists!' She slapped the child, who looked at her with accusing eyes. 'Don't look at me like that! You've got to suffer for your art!'

'Why?'

'It's the sacrifice artists have to make to get inspiration.'

'Oh.' Frances was put out. 'In that case, I don't think I want to be an artist.'

'Don't worry. I don't think you're in any danger!' Frances sobbed suddenly. 'Now what's wrong?'

'I miss me grandma!' Frances wailed. A strange expression came to Hester's face.

'I tell you what,' she said. 'If you're lonely, why don't we go up to the hills tomorrow, instead of school, eh?' The wicked grin challenged her and she gasped with pleasure. 'Don't tell anybody, mind! Not even Muriel!' Frances shook her head, a defiant look on her face.

'I won't tell anybody! And especially not grandma!'

The next day, the two girls came down to breakfast, in a state of high excitement. But, Ellen and Maisie were run off their feet, keeping the house and shop going, Eddie's Mam was ailing, so he had to help his Dad, Jane was still sleeping, after a poor night, bedevilled by nightmares, and George, worried to death about her, went up to the office 'to write a letter', with nothing inside him but a cup of tea. So, no one noticed that Hester and Frances, unusually friendly and giggling, were only too ready to set off 'for school'.

It was a fine day, breezy but dry. Clear of Westoe, they struck out towards Harton, and got lucky, when a passing cart gave them a lift to the village. This was the life, jogging along a country road, breathing the fresh air! Hester, who had raided the larder in the night, brought some lamb and tomatoes out of her schoolbag, and shared them with Fran.

'I wish we had some pickled onions,' Fran complained.

'Huh! Hark at her!'

'All right. I only said! This is smashing. Thanks, Hester.'

'Don't mention it.'

'I wonder what Miss Turnbull'll say, tomorrow?'

'Tell her you've had another nose bleed!'

At Harton, the pair waved their driver goodbye, and set off for the hills. The sun was already high in the sky when, thirsty, they stopped at the farm. It was an adventure. No doubt of it! Frances enjoyed the warm sweet milk the woman had given them, and it was even nicer to be out in the fresh air, looking down on the distant view of Shields. But once they'd had their drink, Frances was itching to be home.

'You know, I'm beginning to wish I'd never brought you!'

'We'll never get home again for dinner time, if we don't go now!' Frances panicked.

'Go then!' Hester told her, and started walking off. She wasn't going to leave Frances to make her way back on her own, was she?

'Hester! Don't leave's!' she yelled after her.

'Come on, then! Ma told you to spy on's didn't she? Well, now's your chance!' With sinking heart, Frances realised where Hester was planning to take her. What a fool she'd been. Powerless to prevent her, the child followed Hester, down the miry tracks, into the stable yard. And there he was. The stable lad.

'Where've you been?' he asked, grinning.

'Ma kept's in.' Hester grimaced. She was sort of dancing round him, ogling, and he seemed to like it.

'Who's she?'

'Her? Oh just me niece.'

'Niece?' He guffawed. 'Are you sure she's not your sister?'

Hester shook her head. 'Me Mam got carried away in her old age!'

'Like mother like daughter, eh? Do *you* want carrying away, like?'

'Depends where to!'

'Well . . . ' He looked towards the hayloft. Hester glared at Frances, who was shifting awkwardly from foot to foot. 'Get lost, eh?'

'But, Hester, I'm hungry, and I can't go home on me own.'

'Oh here!' She threw her an apple. 'Go for a walk. A long one.'

63

Giggling, Hester let the lad take her hand, pulling her across the yard, into the barn. His hand reached out and tweaked her bottom. Echoing laughter followed Frances out of the yard, down the track and back onto the hills. She trudged on and on, sobbing. She knew Cleadon a little bit. Her Mam and Grandma had taken her there a few times. But she'd never been alone. There were funny people on the hills. As every twig snapped, Frances jumped, looking fearfully behind her. Maybe a man was following her, or a gypsy, or . . . or . . . a ghost! Feet thrashed through the grass closer and closer. Voices. There were two of them! Then a man and woman, arm in arm, walked up to her, smiling.

'Hallo, hinny? Lost your way have you?' Frances was speechless with fright. 'Never mind.' The woman took her hand. 'We'll lead you to the path again. You come out by the white horse!'

'White horse?'

'Aha. Do you not know it?' Frances shook her head. 'Well, it's not much, pet. Just something scratched out of the limestone, that's all. We'll show you.' She let them take her on towards the main path. At least she was safe with them. 'There now. Look up there!' Frances looked, and sure enough a white horse stood etched from the hillside, amongst the grass.

'Why's it there?' she asked, wide eyed.

'Well, pet.' The woman was pleased to get a word in. 'A lady that used to ride a lot on the hills fell off her horse one day and got herself killed. And her husband did that in memory of her. Isn't it romantic?' Frances nodded.

'There. Can you find your own way now, eh?' The man was eager to get on with his courting. He pulled at the woman's hand.

'All right, Jack. I'm comin'!' she said, waving goodbye. 'Take care, pet! Go home now!' Frances watched them go. They were nice. She'd felt safe with them. But now they'd gone. She looked up at the horse. A shiver went up her spine. Suddenly she started running, up the path, through the gorse bushes, catching the thorns, scratched, bleeding, one thought in her mind. She had to get back. Her grandma had given her a sacred trust, to watch over Hester. She loved her grandma. Stumbling onto the track, she ran, mud up to her ankles, down the lane, and into the yard.

There was no one in sight. A few horses neighed. Hooves, restive, shuffled in their stalls. Where were they? Oh yes. The hayloft. Frances glanced at the open door of the barn. Slowly she walked towards it. There were noises, moans and grunts, animal sounds, coming from inside. A piece of straw floated down. She looked up. Hester's dress was over her head, and the stable lad, bare bottom high in the air, was bumping up and down on top of her. Hester was in trouble! He was hurting her. The moans grew louder. Frances yelled,

'Stop it! Get off her!' Reaching for a hayfork, she brandished it in the air, making jabs at the exposed buttocks.

The lad screamed, 'Get her out of here!'

Then Hester's livid face glared down, as she threw back the skirt, 'I thought I told you to go for a walk!' she yelled.

'You would, wouldn't you!' Hester dragged her along the track, past the farmhouse, home.

'I thought you were in trouble!' Frances sobbed.

'Poking your nose in!'

'What was he doing to you?' Hester laughed. 'Were you being naughty?'

'Yes!' she spat. 'If you like!'

'I *don't* like it! I mean, what'm I going to tell Grandma?'

'Tell her the truth! Tell her I've been naughty!' Hester threw her head in the air and marched ahead, leaving the child, tired and sore to trail behind.

For once, Eddie took a hand in things. He walloped Frances, till her behind was black and blue. She wailed and she howled so much, they might have heard her down at Tyne Dock! She was sent to bed early, where she lay shivering with shock, wondering what her granda was going to do to Hester.

'At least your Fran told the truth,' Maisie said. 'I do think you were a bit hard on her, Eddie. I mean it wasn't her fault. She's only a bairn.'

'She knew she was doing wrong!' Eddie said firmly.

'She didn't know what *they* were doin', though!' Ellen snorted.

'I wonder what's going on in there?' All looked up at the closed door of George's office. It was strangely quiet.

'Go on, Maisie. Put your ear to the door.'

'Eeh no! *I* don't want a thrashin'!' Maisie said reasonably.

'Sh! Here comes Ma!' Now three pairs of eyes focused on the white face of Jane Beattie, as she came out of the kitchen, a cup of hot milk in her hands.

'I thought I'd just take this to the bairn,' she said apologetically. 'If it's all right.'

'Well, of course it is! You go on up, Ma.' Surprised, Ellen encouraged her. Jane turned back, and started up the stair to Frances' room.

'What's got into Ma? You'd think *she* was to blame, the way she's carrying on!'

No one had ever knocked at Frances' door before. She turned over and looked at it doubtfully. Then the knock came again.

'Come in,' she said at last. Jane, a tired smile on her face, came into the room and sat on the bed beside her grand-daughter.

'I thought you'd like this.' She handed her the cup and Frances cradled the warm drink in her hands. 'You're cold, pet. He shouldn't've thrashed you like that. Tut! You were in enough of a state when you got in, God knows.' Frances began to cry. 'Eeh now. That's enough tears, pet. Don't cry. You'll set me off.'

'I let you down, Grandma. I'm sorry.'

'You? You let *me* down? Eeh, Frances!' She took her in her arms, comforting her.

'I thought you didn't like me any more, Grandma!'

'What do you mean?'

'I thought you didn't love me.' Jane's tears wet the child's hair, matting it against her face.

'Is that why you went with Hester?' Frances nodded dumbly. 'In that case it's me that should be sorry! And I am. I am sorry . . . sorry . . . sorry.' She sang the words, rocking the child in her arms. 'She's got the devil in her has our Hester!' And Frances knew she couldn't ask what Hester had been doing, or why it was so bad. 'You know, your granda said once, you would be the saving of this family.'

'Me? How?'

'I don't know. Just by being you, I suppose.' Frances pondered.

'Maybe we should ask Saint George to help us, as well, Grandma.'

'Saint George? Why?'

'Well, he kills dragons and monsters and that. And Granda says they're devils really. So maybe he'd kill our Hester's, eh?'

'Dragons!' Jane went pale. 'Do you think he might?'

'I don't see why not, Grandma. She mostly gets her own way. She even gets piano lessons, and she's naughty.'

'I know it must look like she does, but not really.'

'*I* want to go to *dancing* lessons, Grandma.'

'Do you?'

'Muriel's Mam gives them in her house.'

'Eeh, I don't know what your granda'd have to say about dancing lessons!'

'But I want to . . . and if our Hester . . . ' Downstairs, a whip lashed. Jane held Frances closer. Hester screamed. It lashed again, whining through the air. Again, Hester shrieked with pain.

'It's not her fault. We should all be extra kind to her . . . '

'It's all right. Sh. There now.'

Frances was comforting Jane.

Then Frances slept, satisfied at last. The late evening sunlight mellowed into gold, and fell on her smooth brow. All was well with her world. If she had been punished, then so had Hester. And whatever were the dragons of the past, she would not be afraid, with her grandma at her side. Robert, Fanny, Hester. They were all dragons. But she would stand and fight them, for her grandma's sake. She was riding along the beach, on a white horse . . .

The sun had set, and darkness filled the house as Jane too sank into a deep slumber. The owl flew across the roof tops, a dark shape against the starry sky, and, in the yard, Grace began to howl. Jane stirred. The howl of the cat amplified in dream into the roar of a monster. And it was chasing her. Where was she? In a maze. She couldn't seem to find the way out. And the monster was getting closer. She stumbled. Thorns hurt her feet. Blood. She had to find a way out. Had to get away.

'Sh! Sh!' George rocked his sleeping wife, and she clutched at his arms, deep in her dream. Suddenly, the bushes cleared. She started to run, sand under her feet, soft sand. If she could only reach the sea . . . she ran on, but the sea got no nearer. And all the time, she could hear the monster closing in on her. And the sand grew into walls, great walls, and she had to climb the walls of sand, but the sand crumbled under her feet. And all the time, the beast was getting nearer, nearer . . .

CHAPTER FOUR

It was the end of term, holiday time, but what was there to look forward to apart from Aunt Harriet's visit? Harriet was her granda's stepdaughter from a previous marriage, and had gone as a companion to a titled lady, years ago, in London where, according to granda, she had picked up some very funny ideas. Added to that, Aunt Harriet was very bossy. So Frances wasn't looking forward very much to her imminent arrival, and the weeks spread out before her; five long weeks stuck in the house, everybody at loggerheads! Frances didn't blame her grandma for getting up late. She would as well, given the chance. What was there to get up for? She was fed up. Muriel's Mam had taken her off to Hexham to her auntie's. There was nobody to talk to, nobody to play with, except them at Sunday School. And Frances didn't like Sunday School on principle. After all, she'd jammed her little finger in the Sunday School door, hadn't she? It was enough to put anybody off! But, her granda'd go mad, if she didn't go. Since the events on the hills, he'd put his foot down 'with a heavy hand', as Maisie'd put it, dragging Hester and Frances off to the chapel on every possible occasion. So go Frances did. She sat, dreaming of ballet shoes, and spangled frocks, while the teacher's words fell dully on her ears.

'Now who can tell me the parable about the man that built his house on shifting sands?' he asked. Davey Lawson put his hand up. 'Good lad, Davey. Stand up, and tell it to the rest of them.' Davey stood, coughed awkwardly, blushed, and began.

'Well this bloke, he built a house on sand. And this other bloke built a house on rock. And one day there was a storm and the bloke that built his house on sand, well, it fell down, like.' Davey stopped, his mouth clamped shut.

'And . . . '

'And the other bloke that built his house on rock, well it was all right, like.'

'Exactly. Thank you Davey, you can sit down now.' Thankfully, the lad sat. 'Now, who can tell me why the house built on the sand fell down?'

A variety of responses were shouted out. 'He used the wrong cement!' 'He had rotten bricks.' 'He couldn't build a house for toffee!'

Exasperated, the teacher prompted them. 'Think of our own beach here in Shields. What happens to sand, when the wind blows, or you walk on it?'

'It moves, sir.'

'That's right. It moves. You can't depend on it. So it's no use building your house on sand, is it?'

'No, sir!'

'You've got to have strong foundations, rock hard, to weather the storm. Now, life's like that . . . ' Frances recognised the philosophical tone creeping in. She'd heard it often enough from her granda. Sometimes he preached at the chapel as a lay preacher. 'Life is hard,' the teacher was telling his class of eight year olds. 'Unless our lives are built on the solid rock of morality, we too will be unable to weather the storm.'

'What's morality, sir?' A small voice chipped in. The teacher looked very sad, and shook his head as the clock struck three. There was immediate bedlam. 'Next week . . . ' The teacher's voice rose in threat, 'we'll answer the question set by our young friend here, "what is morality?" '

'You were very good, Davey.' Frances whispered admiringly.

'Oh it's nothing,' he replied airily. 'Me Mam expects me to make me mark in life. She says you've got to start young.'

'And you've started.' Frances felt a growing respect for the lad. 'Do *you* know what morality is, Davey?'

70

Davey nodded. 'It means being good.'

'Oh.' Frances thought for a minute. 'How do you know what's good?'

'Your Mam tells you.'

'Oh. Davey . . .'

'Aha?'

'What if your Mam doesn't tell you?'

Davey was foxed. He shook his head, frowning. 'I hadn't thought of that.'

'I think I'd better ask me grandma.' With that Frances got up and left the lad to his mystified thoughts.

'Well, pet,' Jane explained. 'If we don't behave, if we're naughty, eventually it'll catch up with us. Our lives'll fall about our ears, just like the house built on shifting sand.' Frances was weeding her little plot of garden, in the nurseries.

'Our Hester was naughty.'

'Yes.'

'So, when she gets married will her house fall down?' Jane smiled and shook her head. 'No, pet. Not exactly. It's a parable, you see.'

'Like Saint George?'

'Yes. Like Saint George.'

'I see. Because he stands for good and the dragons stands for evil, like Granda said!'

'Yes. The dragon is Evil. All the evil things we've ever done.'

'Eh? Grandma?'

'It's true . . . Our sins never die, they take a form to haunt us.' Jane stared through the child. 'And by their shadows, we know them. They grow into monsters, pursuing us in dreams . . . and one day, one day, they catch up with us . . . !' Frances shivered and looked away.

'I hope the dragon never catches up with us!' she said tearfully. Jane started.

'You'll be all right. You've got Saint George to look after *you*.'

'And you, Grandma!' Frances dug her fork into a clump of daisies with relish. 'Eeh, these are funny, Grandma!' Jane looked at the flowers. They were tipped with red. Frances dug in deeper. She heaved out the clump, holding it high in the air.

Then a tail, hanging from the mass of root flickered and she dropped the plant in fright.

'It's just a worm. That's all.' Jane bent down to show her. 'Look!' Frances covered her eyes. 'Look, Fran! You can't be squeamish in this life! You've got to face things!' Reluctantly Frances opened her fingers and looked between. 'You see? It's not as bad as you imagined. It's just a common worm, not a dragon at all!' Frances laughed.

'No! Not like Uncle Robert, and Fanny and Hester!' Jane went white. Had Frances said something wrong?

'They're not dragons!'

'But I thought . . . '

'What did you think?'

'Well, they've all done naughty things.'

'I see.' Jane drew in her breath, sharply. 'And what do you know about my brother, Robert?'

'Well, that he stole the takings from the shop and ran away with your engagement ring.'

'He did no such thing!' Jane's tone was sharp. Frances dared not argue. But her face puckered in confusion. Her Mam had said he had. And that meant, either her mam or her grandma was telling lies! Which of them was it? She began to cry.

'I don't understand. Did Fanny and Hester do naughty things, then?'

'Yes.' Jane sighed with vexation. 'Now come on, love! That's enough talk about dragons! All you have to do is not let your Auntie Hester get you into any more trouble! You've got to be good enough for the pair of you!'

'That's not fair!'

'What's "fair" got to do with anything?' Frances stared blankly at her grandma. Was this what Granda meant when he'd said that about being the saving of the family?

'But, Hester hates me. She's always having a go at me.'

'Turn the other cheek. When she's nasty, you be nice. Like I said, you've got to be good for the pair of you.'

'Why should I?' Riding down the beach on a white horse was one thing, but being good enough for two was quite another!

'She's family, Frances. That's why. You can't get away from your family ties.' Her grandma's voice frightened the little girl.

72

'For my sake! You must look after poor Hester. Promise me!'
Frances nodded.

'I promise.' The grip on her arms relaxed. Her grandma smiled. 'That's it. Now come on. Put your weeds on the compost heap and we'll go home. It's tea time, and your Auntie Harriet's expected.' Suddenly Jane bubbled with delight and the woman and the little girl ran helter skelter across the street back into the shop. Honestly, her grandma's moods weren't half funny!

Harriet stood in the kitchen amidst a pile of trunks and boxes.

'How long're you planning on staying, Auntie?' Ellen asked anxiously. Ignoring her, Harriet spread her arms wide in an extravagant gesture,

'Eeh, Jane! I've got some wonderful news!'

'Oh? What's that, Harriet May?'

'My employer's dead!'

'Well now that *is* good news!' Jane obliged.

'And . . . and . . . you'll never guess what!' Harriet May paraded round the scullery, displaying herself in all her glory.

'Eeh, Auntie, you look smashin'!' Maisie said. Jane sniffed, Frances hid behind her, and Hester stood in the shadows watching with interest. For Aunt Harriet was a most extraordinary sight. Always blessed with a taste for the exotic, like a summer rose, overindulged by the sun, it had become overblown. The dull hair was now a deep, burnished orange, and she wore it loosely tied at the back. The emerald bow matched the velvet hat and the suit, which fell from her ample form in luxurious folds. Her shoes and blouse were the colour of port wine, and she wore a shawl about her shoulders, printed with peacock feathers. A bangled arm reached down to hitch up the skirt and the family gasped to see the red silk stockings.

'You've gone to town, Harriet! I'll say that!' Jane commented, while Ellen giggled, spluttered, and escaped into the shop.

'Yes, but you haven't guessed!' she said.

'You've married one of them Bohemian artists you're always on about.'

'Don't be so daft! No . . . much better than that!'

'I give up,' Jane said. 'You tell us.'

'She's left me all her money!'

'Eeh!'

'Eeh!'

'Eeh!'

'For goodness' sake will somebody say something other than "eeh!" '

'What are you going to do?' Jane asked.

'I've bought myself a nice little flat in London, and I'm all set to enjoy myself!'

'Good for you, Harriet.' Jane was generous. 'I'm sure you've earned it. It can't have been easy being a companion to her ladyship all those years.'

'How do you get your hair that colour, Auntie?' Maisie asked.

'Egyptian henna, dear.' Bracelets rattling, Harriet removed her hat, and shook out the orange mane. 'We're very keen on the oriental in our set.'

'It seems to me, Harriet May, you've taken her ladyship's place, as well as her money.'

'Well, Jane dear, I've got the brains, you see. She never had, poor thing. She could never hold her own amongst the intelligentsia. She relied on me to do that for her. Position and title, are not everything, as you will all learn.' She addressed the younger members as though she was at a public meeting. ' "The rich man in his castle, the poor man at his gate" and all that cant, are definitely out. In fact, to tell you the truth, my own misfortune of birth has put me beyond all the normal restrictions of society. I am not bound by convention. And this, I may say, the real people, with the real minds, with actual, feeling souls, do genuinely respect.' She paused for effect. 'Yes! Being a bastard is a positive advantage in life!' There was a stunned silence. Maisie gasped, and Frances' small voice piped up from behind Jane's shirt, 'What's a bastard, Grandma?'

Bundled out into the yard, 'to play', Frances turned to see accusing eyes, watching her, from the kitchen window. Why wouldn't they tell her what a bastard was? And if it was something naughty, why did they act like it was her fault? They always wanted to keep things secret! Grown ups, huh! Even if they'd answered her, would they have told her the truth? Did they ever tell her the truth? Her Mam, her very own Mam, had told lies about her grandma and her brother, Robert. He wasn't a thief at all! But in that case, why wouldn't her granda let him come back home? Frances' mind spun with confusion. Seeking distraction, she rummaged in the shed, and pulled out an ancient umbrella. Its catch was rusty, but she got it up, and held it over her head, turning her back to the house, as though shielding herself from it. She wished there was somewhere she could go. If only Muriel hadn't gone off to Hexham for the holidays! If only they lived by the sea! But there was only the yard and the back lane. She pushed open the yard gate, and edged out into the dirty lane. Dead flowers, rotten food, potato peelings, lined the walls, and nestled between the cobbles. She wandered out, walking up and down the lane, umbrella high in the late afternoon sun, dreaming of dancing lessons, and barely noticed Grace, returned from a foray into the great outside world, until the cat howled. Startled, Frances saw her, at her feet, staring up at her.

'Hallo, Grace! been visitin' some of your friends, have you? Huh! You're lucky. I wish I had a friend to visit.' Grace started washing herself, as though embarrassed, and Frances bent to whisper in her ear. 'How do you manage, living with them grown ups? I mean you seem to keep out of trouble, and do what you want. Why can't I?' The cat looked at the little girl wisely, then wandered off, nose in the air. 'I see.' Frances sighed, standing. 'You're like the three wise monkeys, our Grace. Hear no evil, speak no evil, and see no evil.' Yes, she thought, as she followed the cat indoors, I'll just keep quiet and pretend I'm not there. I'll not ask any questions any more, except for things like 'Will you pass the salt?'

'Will you pass the salt, please, somebody?' Maisie passed it to Frances automatically, and Frances sprinkled it on her dinner without a word, watching the grown ups, taking in the ripples and the undercurrents of their conversation, like the audience at a play; never tempted to join in, but anxiously trying to work out what each of the characters was up to. Her Dad, Eddie, had never liked Harriet May. And he liked her even less now she had money.

'I don't hold with women having money,' he said. 'They only squander it. Don't you agree, Mr Beattie?' George frowned as he toyed with the peas.

'Live and let live, Eddie. I mean,' Harriet put in, 'I don't hold with people having teapots on the table at dinner time. Tea is surely for tea time after all, but I've not said anything, have I?'

'Why shouldn't Eddie have tea with his dinner if he likes?' Jane was surprising them tonight. She was bright and cheerful, just like her old self. 'After all, it's only a convention to have tea at four o'clock. And you believe in flouting conventions, don't you?' George half-smiled, but kept his eyes on his peas.

'I believe you should either flout convention, or abide by it,' Harriet asserted. 'There's no half measures!'

'You see? That's what happens!' Eddie said bitterly. 'Give a woman her own money and her head fills up with all sorts of rubbish.'

'What rubbish?'

'Flouting convention!'

'Sh! Please!' Jane looked warily at her husband.

'Fat chance *I've* got of doing any squandering,' Ellen muttered. 'I never *see* any money.'

'That reminds me . . . ' Maisie said, 'I've not had me pocket money for a fortnight!' George was unusually silent. Intrigued, Harriet began to dig for clues.

'The age of the woman, Eddie, is upon us. Of course a downtrodden little weakling like you is too afraid to admit that women have the brains, the ability, nay the right to live their own lives!'

'Women's Rights! I might have known!' Ellen sighed.

'Ssh!' Jane hissed, but George, the old patriarch, said nothing at all.

'Once we have the franchise the world will change, and for the better!'

'You've forgotten your banner, Harriet!' Eddie sneered. Still George kept his silence, though his temples twitched.

'Eddie, you're a working man.' Eddie frowned. Now what was she getting at? 'You are one of the downtrodden, just as I am. Women and workmen should band together.' George opened his mouth, eyes blazing, then closed it again. 'The Independent Labour Party will, one day, unite us in the cause!'

'The cause of what?' asked Maisie.

'The women's cause! Too long have we been the power behind the throne. Now we shall sit on it!' Maisie guffawed, and Harriet's fist thumped hard on the table. It was some time before the bracelets came to rest. 'We women will show you men the way!'

'I wish *you'd* get on *your* way!' Eddie jeered.

'Watch your manners, Eddie!' George spoke at last. 'Miss Beattie is a guest in this house.' Eddie's stud popped, under the strain of suppressed rage, and his collar sprang awry. But, encouraged by George's unusual show of tolerance, Jane spoke up.

'Well, I wouldn't mind having the vote!' George glared at her.

'And what would you do with it?'

'Vote for you of course, dear.' Harriet raged at the marital display. She hated it. She knew that when his wife smiled at him like that, George would give her anything, even the vote. To Harriet, who had had to fight for everything in life, it was an insult. But there was an ally in the camp. Hester squirmed as her father smiled down on his clever, playful wife.

'I wish *I* was a bastard!' she said. George's hand flashed across Hester's cheek, and she fell, howling, to the floor. Hear no evil, see no evil, speak no evil. Frances shut her eyes, shut her mind against the anger, and the hurts, and the fears. She ran out into the yard, found the old black umbrella and paraded up and down, up and down the lane, under its fragile protection.

'I'm off out to see how me Mam's gettin' on.' Eddie was struggling with his collar, in the kitchen, where Ellen and Maisie were washing up after dinner.

'You make it sound like they live in Timbuctoo! They're only next door, man! Honestly, all you need do's shout loud enough and they'll hear you!'

'I believe in showing respect,' Eddie said punctiliously, as he struggled with his collar stud. 'So, I shall do my parents the honour of paying them a proper visit. Which is more than you ever do.' Ellen's colour was rising.

'You're just usin' them as an excuse to skive off out of *her* way!'

'Well! If Lady La-ti-Tiddle says one more thing about women being better than men . . . !'

'She's right an' all!' Quickly, Eddie slipped his jacket back on, and made for the door. Then, with the hopeful words, 'I'll give them your love, shall I, pet?' he scarpered.

'Don't bother!' 'pet' yelled, throwing the dishcloth after him. 'And you needn't let them go thinking Lidell's can take over Beattie's, either! Because *my* Dad'd rather go bust, and so would I!'

Eddie turned out of the yard of number 18, Victoria Terrace, and went in by the back gate of number 16, of the same. Frances saw him from the top end of the lane, and hid behind a dustbin, watching. That meant her Mam and Auntie Maisie would be alone in the kitchen, washing up. What if her Mam had told her the truth and it was her grandma who had lied? She would ask about the 'bastard' business once again. Then, if her mother told her the truth about that, she would believe her about Uncle Robert as well. If not, she would ask her grandma what a bastard was, and if *she* told her, then it was her who was telling the truth. So, with her childish logic Frances hoped to solve her mental dilemma. She waited till Eddie had gone into number 16, then made her way back down the lane.

Eddie's collar sprang awry even as he entered the kitchen.

'Well hallo, Eddie, son! Long time no see, eh?' complained his mam, huddled in a rug by the fire.

'Are you not sweltered, Mam? It is July, you know!'

'Huh!' she replied. 'Your collar's cock-eyed!'

'Yes, Mam.'

'And how are *they*?' Ma Lidell's head jerked at the dividing wall.

'Ellen sends her love.'

'Stuck-up tart.'

'She is me wife, Mam!'

'I never see you now. And what about my grand-daughter, eh? What about *her*? That lot next door's no better than they ought to be! Huh! I don't think I like the idea of my grand-daughter living in a house of sin!'

'Mr Beattie's a lay preacher, Mam!'

'Hypocritical . . . '

'Mam . . . ' Eddie warned. 'He is me father-in-law, you know.'

'The goings-on in that house are enough to make your hair curl!'

'I wish I'd never told you.'

78

'No wonder Shields is going to the dogs with him at its helm!' Eddie sighed.

'Aye, I have to agree with you there, Mam. He can't run a florist's shop let alone a town!' A crafty look came into the old lady's face.

'How *is* business, son?'

'Ailing.' Eddie smiled in spite of himself.

'They'll not look so superior when we buy them out, eh?'

'Mebbe not, Mam.' He tried to stop himself, but he couldn't help dreaming of the day when he saw, over the shop door of number 18, the name, 'Lidell's'. Aye, 'Lidell's Grocers and Florists'. It'd look good that. Eddie's own little empire.

'I wonder, should I keep the old barsket on, in a consulting capacity, Mam?'

'He *is* your father-in-law, son.' His mam grinned wickedly and threw back her rug. 'Eeh,' she said. 'I'm feeling a lot better now!'

Ellen had surprised herself with her own fierce loyalty; in spite of her resentments. Would she really rather go down with the ship than let the Lidells in? Yes! She would! She was a Beattie! And a Beattie was somebody! That lot next door, huh! Eddie's Mam was a crafty old bitch. She'd worn her husband down with her nagging tongue. He worked all the hours God sent in their shop, while she cossetted herself, putting on the aches and pains. 'Eeh I don't feel well!' She had the men running round her like she was the centre of the world. Of course Eddie and his Dad were a pair of weaklings, but even so, there was no need for her to be such an old shrew! After all, look at Ellen!

'If them Lidells take charge of Beattie's shop, it'll be over my dead body,' she hissed at her sister, as she helped with wiping the plates. 'We've got to tighten our belts, Maisie!'

'I don't see why I should have to do without me pocket money!'

'You'd just buy penny dreadfuls, if you had it!'

'It's the only bit of romance I'm likely to get!'

'Mam, what's a bastard?' The sisters turned, in surprise. Frances had crept in, unnoticed.

'Nothin', pet. Run along and play, eh?' But Frances hung about, kicking at the table legs. 'Now what?' her mother asked. Frances dared not ask the real question in her mind: Mam,

79

should I believe you or me grandma? Instead, she sought the consolation prize.

'Grandma says if it's all right with you, me dad and me granda, I can start dancing classes.'

'Does she now? Well why doesn't your grandma ask your dad and your granda, herself, eh?' Frances fidgeted plaintively. 'Because she knows there's not the money for dancing classes, that's why?'

'Ah, Mam!'

' "Ah" yourself! I think everybody in this house has taken leave of their senses apart from me!' Frances sighed and turned to go. But where should she go to? It was getting dark outside. Up the maze of stairs to her room? Out into the darkened shop? Standing on the threshold, she heard her mother say,

'Kids!'

'Did Hester say, "I wish I'd *had* a bastard, or I wish I *was* a bastard"?' Maisie whispered.

'I wish I *was*,' Ellen whispered back.

'Never!'

'Mind if she carries on like this, she *will* have one! She was lucky this time.' Ellen sighed with envy. 'I only did it the once, then our Frances was on the way and I was stuck!'

'You're luckier than me! I've never done it at all.'

'Maisie Beattie! I should just hope you haven't!'

'I'm going to get left on the shelf, I know I am. I'm twenty, Ellen!'

'What's all this whispering about?' The sisters jumped and turned guiltily to see Harriet May, at the scullery door.

'Oh, just our Maisie. She's scared she's going to get left on the shelf.' Ellen blushed, remembering, too late, that Aunt Harriet was also a spinster.

'Nothing so terrible about that, Ellen. Of course I chose to avoid the married state. Men aren't all they're cracked up to be, you know.'

'I do know,' said Ellen with feeling.

'Anyway, I just wanted to give you your presents . . . ' In the shop, Frances' ears pricked. Presents? Did someone say something about presents? Harriet placed her parcels on the table, and the sisters crowded round, shrieking with delight, as the rest of the family swarmed into the room. 'This one's for

Jane. One for Frances! There, Pet.' The child's eyes bulged at the huge parcel. 'One for Eddie. Where is he?'

'Gone round to his mother's. She's poorly, you know.'

'George. This is for you.'

'Oh. Thank you, Harriet.' He opened the wrapper and found his favourite cigars inside. 'It's very generous of you, I'm sure.' Jane was stroking a Paisley shawl in pure silk.

'Look at this, Ellen!' Maisie shrieked with delight. 'It's the spitting image of our cat! What is it Auntie?'

'A pyjama case. See? It opens here.'

'Ooh!' Ellen was dabbing herself with perfume, as Frances tore away the last shred of paper from her parcel.

'It's a box, Grandma.' Frances sounded disappointed. Taking it from her, Harriet opened it up. There was a doll inside. Frances gasped with pleasure, holding out her arms for it, but Harriet held it back.

'Now this is no ordinary doll!' She set it on the table, on its stand, and began to turn a key at the back. Slowly, the doll raised one leg and, to the tune of a tinkling music box, it twirled round on the point of its toe. Frances was thrilled. She flung her arms round her auntie's neck.

'Oh, Auntie! How did you know I wanted to be a dancer?'

'What's this?' George was sharp.

'Nothing, dear.' Jane soothed him. 'Just a childish whim. She wants to start dancing classes, that's all.'

'What's this family coming to?' he roared. 'You're all going down the road to perdition!' With that, he banged out of the kitchen.

'I notice he didn't include himself,' Ellen pointed out. Everyone laughed. Everyone but Frances.

'What *is* a bastard, Grandma?' Frances asked, as Jane tucked her in.

'Never mind about that, pet. I'll wind up your doll, shall I?' Frances watched in silence as the key turned. 'I told you not to build your hopes up about them dancing classes, didn't I?' The little girl said nothing. 'Don't you like your doll?'

'Aha.' Frances stared, as the doll twirled, and the music whirred. Jane hesitated, then, with a gentle goodnight, she turned to go. From her bed, Frances watched the doll circling, whirring, ever more slowly to the dying tune. Then there was silence. So many questions and no answers. She heard voices in the next room. Grandma must be giving Hester her present from Aunt Harriet. What were they saying to one another? Voices. Whispering. They reached out, winding about her heart, whispering threads. Frances got out of bed and turned the key, twisting it round and round, until it would move no more. Then she let it go, and the doll danced and the music played, and the whispering stopped.

Maisie and Ellen were putting the dishes away, when Jane came down again.

'Where's Harriet May?' she asked.

'She went up to the office,' Ellen told her. 'I told her Dad was best avoided when he was in one of his moods, but *she* said, she knew how to handle him, thank you very much. Honestly, Ma, I don't know how you stand it. She treats us like servants! Eddie couldn't take it. He went to see his Ma, just to get out of her way!'

'Mind,' Maisie reminded her, 'she's been very generous.'

'Lady Bountiful! Huh!'

'You're only jealous!'

'I am not! She's no better than me! "I chose to avoid the married state", I don't think! She'd've got married like a shot if Uncle Robert would've had her! Isn't that right, Mam?'

'Stop bickering you two!' They stared at Jane in surprise.

'Well, Ma,' Ellen whined, 'she waltzes in here as though she owned the place! I mean, she's not even family!'

'Harriet May is your stepsister, and don't you forget it!'

'Yes, but Ma, she isn't really. I mean she said it herself. She's a bastard. Not even a blood relation.'

'Sweet Jesus, what have I spawned?' Tears sprang to Jane's eyes. 'I only hope and pray our Frances turns out better!' With that, Jane pulled her new shawl close and went out into the darkness. Ellen looked at her sister in amazement.

'What did I say?'

Upstairs, in the office, George inhaled deeply on a cigar.

'Well, Harriet,' George sighed, as though it hurt him to admit it, 'you've done well. I'll say that for you.'

'Yes, Dad.'

'Never thought you would. But there you are. Life's full of surprises.' Was there a sneaking regard in George's expression?

'Of course, you've got three fine daughters of your own . . . '

'Hah!' His tone rang with disillusionment.

'Hester's growing up. I see she's learning the piano.' George breathed out a ring of smoke. 'Thirteen. Quite the young woman.' Harriet considered Hester's possibilities. 'You'll have to watch her, George.'

'I didn't ask you here to talk about Hester!' Harriet inclined her head and waited. George coughed. 'Harriet May, you're a . . . a . . . woman of the world . . . '

'How's business?' She'd hit the mark. Clearly taken aback, George responded too quickly.

'Business is fine! Never been better!' Harriet didn't believe him, but smiled all the same.

'Good. So, what *is* wrong? In your letter, you said I was needed urgently. Why me, all of a sudden?'

'I didn't know who else to turn to,' George sighed. 'Over the years, I've come to see that you, Harriet, are more like me. You have brains. Sense. You're like a man.' Harriet bit back a smile. 'Yes, I've grown to respect you, Harriet May.' She put on the required expression of amazed gratitude and, encouraged, George continued. 'So, in my anxiety over Jane, I naturally turned to you.'

'Jane?' Harriet was genuinely surprised.

'She's been acting strangely, Harriet. Hysterical at the drop of a hat. Not sleeping. Nightmares. Been on the laudanum.'

'Oh dear.' For years, after her mother's death, Harriet had lived on sufferance in this house, through her stepfather's second marriage, then his third, to Jane, only to be thrown out, to fend for herself, at last, and all at Jane's bidding. And now they expected help from her?!

'What do you want *me* to do?' she asked sweetly.

'I thought if you talked to her, woman to woman . . . ' He looked hopefully at the sweet smile, and felt a genuine regret. 'I've not always been fair to you, Harriet.' Harriet snorted in spite of herself, and George eyed his stepdaughter warily, before going on. 'I loved your mother. She was my first love. Even though she had strayed. And I took you in. I did my best. But you weren't my own, and I . . . I'm sorry. I admit it. I never really loved you.' Harriet's eyes narrowed. 'I'd like to make it up to you.'

How?'

George's cigar had gone out. He fumbled for a match. 'I'd like to help you. Give you some advice.'

'What sort of advice?'

'Financial.' The wily old devil, Harriet thought. She put on an innocent expression. 'You've come into money, Harriet. You're going to need expert guidance . . . '

'What had you in mind, George?'

'A short term investment, I thought.' He looked at her, swallowing hard. Swallowing his pride. She smiled.

'What in?'

'The shop, of course!' George barked at her. Was she pretending not to understand?

'Oh. Why didn't you say, George? You want a loan, do you?'

'I'm not asking for a loan! This is an investment opportunity, Harriet! It would pay dividends!'

'Oh! Like shares, you mean?'

'Yes! Exactly. Like shares!' George was relieved. He struck the match and lit his cigar.

'I see. Yes. I'd be interested in that.' She settled back comfortably in her chair, watching him.

'You're a wise woman, Harriet May! I always said it.' Harriet smiled.

'Have you a good solicitor, George?' He started in surprise.

'What do we want a solicitor for? We're family, aren't we?'

'Well, George, of course it's kind of you to say so, but actually, I'm not, am I?' He stared at her. 'In fact, I'm not related to any of you, by blood, at all! I think we ought to do it properly don't you? After all you're a man of the world.' There was a long silence.

'Of course,' he said at last. 'We'll do it properly. And I'll give you a good price, when you want to sell again.'

'*If* I want to sell, George.' Her eyes were steady, cold. It was like looking into the eyes of a snake. Heat rose up George's spine. He looked away, into the empty grate.

'No need to tell the family about any of this,' he said gruffly.

'None at all.' Harriet rose to leave. 'Oh, and about that other

business . . . Jane . . . I'll see if I can find out what's wrong, shall
I?'

It was late. Ellen had gone to bed, and Eddie, back from his
mother's had crept in beside her at last. She put out a hand to
him.

'I missed you,' she said forlornly. Eddie's eyes, ready for sleep
a few seconds before, sprang open, in surprise.

'Oh yes?' he said hopefully.

'Give me a cuddle.' Immediately Eddie obliged. 'I hope she
doesn't stay long,' she whispered.

'Who?'

'Who do you think? Lady La-ti-Tiddle!'

'Oh. Her! Aye.'

'She'd no right to talk to you like that, Eddie.'

'No!'

'I mean, I might say things sometimes, but I'm your wife!
She's not even family!'

'True!'

'And the family's got to stick together, haven't we, Eddie?'

'Yes . . . Ellen . . . ?' Eddie sniffed suspiciously.

'D'ye like me perfume? It was me present from Auntie.'

'You smell like a . . . a . . . '

'Eddie!'

'Attar of Roses, pet.'

Through the kitchen window Maisie saw them, in the yard, Jane
and Harriet, whispering. What were they talking about? The
whistle went on the kettle, and the two heads turned. They
looked at her, through the glass, as though she was a stranger. It
made her flesh creep.

'Would you like a cup of tea?' she shouted. They nodded and
turned their backs again to continue their conversation. Maisie
spooned the tea into the scalded pot. She felt nervy tonight.
Jumpy. It was dark out there in the yard. No moon, that was it.
Downstairs in the cellar, a rat scratched. Grace's ears twitched.
She raised her head and went to the cellar door. 'Go on, then.'
Maisie let her through, and watched the white speck on the end
of her tail disappear into the darkness below. The tea would be
brewed by now. She could do with a cup herself. Her tooth was

nagging. That was probably why her nerves were so raw. The pain shot through her, red hot. A sudden screech from below made her jump and the tea spilt, scalding her hand. 'Sugar!' she hissed. She wanted to cry. It wasn't the pain. It was something else; a feeling. In her simple way, Maisie's heart overflowed with love for her family. She ached to look after them. She wanted to fold them in her arms, like she did Grace, and hug them close, so no harm would come to them. But she couldn't. She was nothing. Just a fool. Just Maisie with the hump back, simple Maisie Beattie whose every instinct warned her of something lurking in the darkness of the night. Something that frightened her. Grace padded back upstairs, and laid the head of her victim on the hearth.

'Good girl!' Maisie gave her a titbit from the roast and watched, as the cat, job done, enjoyed its reward. Then she picked up the cups and took them to the kitchen door. Her mother was crying.

'They're none of them any use to me! George doesn't want to know.'

'Typical of men!' Harriet grunted.

'Yes. If they don't like something, they just ignore it, stick their heads in the sand. Ellen and Maisie are no good. I mean look at them! Ellen's far too wrapped up in herself to be bothered about anybody else, and our Maisie's . . . well . . . ' Maisie cringed. She didn't want to hear, but felt compelled to stay. 'Maisie's feeble-minded. Simple. She can't help it, I know, but, it's no use to me. Our Hester's nothing but trouble, and Frances's too young.' Harriet murmured her sympathy, but Jane came back on her sharply. 'And you're no better, Harriet! You went off and left me, up to me neck in it! Oh yes! You like to think you're hard done by, but think on! You got away!'

'I was thrown out!'

'I needed you, Harriet. The house and shop to run, the bairns . . . . You belted our Maisie till she was black and blue . . . don't try to deny it! What else could we do but send you away? And to think, I once saved your life!' Harriet sobbed. 'I'll never forget that night as long as I live. You a pillar of fire in your bride's veil . . . '

'You stole Robert from me.'

'Don't kid yourself, Harriet! He never wanted you. You just

86

imagined he did!' There was a long silence. Maisie scarcely dared to breath. Then, at last, she heard her mother weeping. 'You always let me down, Harriet. Always, right from school days. Trying to get me into trouble, blaming me for all your own misfortunes. Why couldn't you have been nice? Then we could have all got on and helped each other, instead of . . . You left me alone, and with so much to face. George and that Alice Minto . . . ' Jane was crying steadily. 'I needed comfort, Harriet. I needed love. That was why . . . If I could only undo what was done!'

'I know all about needs, Jane. You don't have to tell me.' Harriet's voice was bitter.

'Poor Harriet.' In the darkness, Maisie felt Harriet May bristle. 'Perhaps we can help each other?.'

'Oh?'

'Our Hester . . . She needs to be kept out of trouble. Out of the way of men. You need companionship.'

'I see.'

'In your circle, Hester might find her place.'

'Perhaps when she's older . . . '

'You owe me that much, Harriet! Don't let me down again!'

Suddenly Harriet turned, as if to go, and saw Maisie standing in the doorway.

'I thought you might like your tea out here,' Maisie said coldly.

'That would be nice. Thank you dear.' Changing her mind, Harriet took both cups, and graciously handed one to Jane. Maisie watched as Harriet raised her cup, and Jane responded, clinking hers against it.

'It seems you've got your way, Jane.' Maisie turned her back on the darkness and left them to it. Aunt Harriet was clever. Maisie was simple. Her Mam had said so. but she was not a fool, and fools rush in . . .

CHAPTER FIVE

Frances came down next morning to a complete change of atmosphere. What had happened in the night, while she slept? The first thing was her Mam and Maisie whispering in the kitchen. Their voices were resentful, bitter. And then, an event which *never* happened, her grandma actually came down for breakfast! She had a guilty look about her, but was bubbling underneath with a new hope and spirit. Ellen and Maisie clammed up, as soon as they saw her. Grandma seemed put out, at first, but soon shrugged off her hurt, when Aunt Harriet came down, and she started chatting nineteen to the dozen with her, as though they were the greatest of pals. Then came Hester, sullen as usual. And Jane and Harriet kept on looking at her, funny like, especially Harriet, till Hester began to feel uncomfortable. What was going on? And where was her granda? He never missed his breakfast. Finally, he came, ate a bite of toast, without a word, smiled politely at Harriet, then went back upstairs, leaving his tea. He looked as though he'd shrunk, somehow and he was uncomfortable with them all, while Auntie Harriet was easy. She was a woman, come into a fortune, luxuriously trying out the extent of her new-found powers.

Pulling on her jacket, Frances looked at Grace, sleeping on the window sill. At least *she* hadn't changed. She just slept through everything, taking nourishment, when she needed it, and wandering off when she felt like a change of scene. Hear no evil, see no evil . . .

Waiting for Hester in the yard, Frances considered the shed. Her big black umbrella was inside. She opened the door and wrenched it out, toying with the handle, even as Hester emerged, snapping back at Aunt Harriet, 'I can manage on me own, thank you very much!', tearing the coat from her hands to shrug it on, as she stalked out of the yard. 'Wait for me!' Frances flew after her, shoving up the umbrella, struggling to get it through the gate, and out into the lane. Hester had been sent on an errand by Aunt Harriet, and Frances had hoped to go with her. It was something to do in the school holidays.

'What've you got *that* for?' Hester stared askance at the umbrella. Frances didn't answer. 'Well, don't think I'm going to walk with you, carrying that old thing. You look a proper fool!' Frances sighed, hiding under the black canopy, following on behind, and wondering why Hester was even more spiky than usual. Did she know what had happened? Or was she, too, puzzled and upset by the change? Letting Hester go where she would, Frances wandered off alone, through the maze of back lanes, pondering. In the night, some great event had taken place. Her world had changed its axis, and now, instead of Granda, Harriet was the pivot of the family.

'Look who it isn't!' A sneering voice challenged her. It was a girl called Sally from their school. 'What've you got that great black umbrella up for? It's not even rainin'!' Suddenly Sally laughed. 'You look as if you've been to a funeral!'

'I have,' Frances said at once.

'Oh.' Frances hadn't noticed how far she'd walked, and she now found herself at the back of Ocean Road, where Davey lived. 'What're you doing here?'

'I've . . . I've come on a visit!' Frances blustered. Sally was taken aback, and Frances felt obliged to knock on the back door of Davey's Mam's, to prove her lie. Mrs Lawson opened the door, somewhat surprised, and found herself supplying her young caller with cake and tea.

'I've been to a funeral,' Frances said airily, 'and now I'm

89

making me calls.' She put down her crumby plate, with a haughty nod, and got up, reaching for her umbrella. 'I'm sorry I can't stay any longer, Mrs Lawson, but I do have other calls on me time.' With that, Frances departed, leaving the stupefied lady to whisper to her son, 'My, she's a precocious little madam, isn't she?'

Frances went home in triumph, and a new cocky manner emerged. What did she care what people thought? She didn't need anybody and nobody needed her. She was a big lady now, who went calling, as independent as you like! Even her grandma, too wrapped up in her new companion to notice her any more, could be discarded. Others too had changed their manner, to accommodate the new pattern of allegiances in the house. Ellen and Maisie put up a front of mockery, against Jane and Harriet, which, as time went on, became more and more brittle . . .

'How long's she been in there?' Ellen and Maisie were gazing out of the kitchen window at the locked midden door.
   'Three quarters of an hour.'
   'Eeh!'
   'She took a book in with her.' Maisie thought for a moment, then asked,
   'How long was it?' Ellen looked at her in astonishment.
   'Our Maisie! You nearly cracked a joke!'
   'What do you mean, "nearly"?!'
   'Mind, we shouldn't laugh. It's a terrible thing, constipation.'
   'Yes, Ellen.' Maisie straightened her face, looked at her sister, then laughed again; 'What was that she said about us women being the power behind the throne?'
   'She said we had to sit on it.'
   'Aye well. She's doing that all right!' The midden door creaked open. Walking through the yard, Harriet May paused to wonder why her nieces were having hysterics over yesterday's boiled cabbage.
   'I don't see anything funny in bubble and squeak!' she complained, as she entered the kitchen.
   'What's your book, Auntie?' Ellen dared not look at Maisie.
   'The Decline and Fall of the Roman Empire.' The sisters shrieked with laughter. Flushing, Harriet asked where Jane was.

'Still in bed I expect!' Ellen said, wiping away her tears. 'Sometimes she doesn't get up till tea time!' And she screamed and roared all over again.

'Disgraceful!' With that Harriet May stalked upstairs and knocked loudly on Jane's door. Maisie's mood switched suddenly.

'What's she want with Ma?' she asked, frowning.

'They're going out.'

'Where?'

'Newcastle.'

'What for?'

'How would *I* know? Ma never tells me anything!'

'Huh! Them two's thick as thieves these days!' Maisie looked askance as Harriet May and Jane flounced out, eyes alight and ready for adventure. Ellen sighed enviously.

'I've not been to Newcastle for ages!' The laughter had gone, and left them with a day like a pricked balloon.

Jane was enjoying herself. Like a girl, out on the town, she window-shopped. Glad to miss the bubble and squeak, which Maisie always burnt anyway, she sat with Harriet, at the window of a tea shop, eating cream cakes and watching the world go by, deep in thought.

'I think I liked the cigar box best,' Jane said at last.

'Well, I wouldn't fork out that much for him!' Harriet sniffed. 'Is he still seeing you-know-who?' Jane nodded.

'Alice's got rheumatics now, you know.'

'Serve her right!'

'So, he doesn't get much joy there any more!' There was a twinkle in Jane's eye. Harriet's mouth gaped, then she exploded with sudden laughter. Heads turned to look. 'Sh! You'll get us thrown out, woman!' Harriet stifled her giggles with a handkerchief, as Jane whispered on. 'The lad's in his teens now. You can't wipe out the past, Harriet; just make the best of it. Anyway, as you know very well, *I'm* in no position to complain!'

'Nobody's perfect, pet. And you're no worse than most. Now don't start crying again! You always did like creating dramas! Your moods are like the weather these days. Unpredictable. You were laughing a minute ago. Who'd be a woman, eh?'

'True,' Jane sighed. 'Do you think it's the change?'

'Men, religion, they drive you into the ground between them.'

'Harriet May!'

'Well they do! It's well to be seen God's a man! Look what a mess He's made of things!'

'Eeh!'

'I think nowt of either of them!'

'Eeh well, each to their own, Harriet.' Jane fiddled with her teaspoon and flushed before she spoke again. 'Em, I've been meaning to ask you, Harriet. Have you said anything to our Hester yet?'

'No. Not yet.'

'But you *are* going to?' Harriet's lips pursed.

'I said I would.'

'Only I'll have to talk George into it.'

'You'll have no trouble on that score.' Jane's heart jumped. Now what exactly did Harriet mean by that? Shaking off the sudden sensation of uncertainty, Jane pushed away her empty cup and sat up in a business-like manner. 'Now! Back to important matters. This cigar box, I'm going to buy . . . ' Harriet groaned. 'I've been thinking. I could get his name engraved on it . . . or, better still, our two initials intertwined. "On the occasion of our Silver Wedding." '

'Very romantic!' Harriet sneered. And so it was settled. Back to the silversmiths they went. Arriving home like truant school-girls, they fled upstairs, giggling, to hide the present.

'Now what?' Ellen asked Maisie in disgust.

'Oh!' Maisie suddenly remembered. 'I bet you what you like, they've been shopping for the silver wedding!'

'I'd forgotten about that,' Ellen said, dismayed. 'I suppose they'll be expecting a cake for it, won't they?' Maisie and Ellen looked at each other and sighed. As if there wasn't enough work to do in the shop!

Frances watched, as Ellen and Maisie began making the cake, decorating it with white roses, silver bells, and horseshoes.

'Will I have to give Grandma and Granda a present, Mam?' she asked.

'You?' Ellen looked at her sharply. 'You're only a child! They'll not be expecting owt from you!'

'She could make something, Ellen,' Maisie suggested. 'If she wants.' Did she want? Frances couldn't decide. Upstairs, Hester was learning a special piece on the piano for the party, and was resenting every moment of it. You could tell that by the way she was banging down the keys. It was purgatory just to be in the house with her. It would be nice to go down to the beach. Frances could call on Davey Lawson and go down with him, if she had an excuse for it.

'I could make something out of shells, if you'd let's go down the beach to get some, Mam.'

'Do what you like, pet,' came the careless reply.

Davey Lawson was a good audience. He lapped up the precociousness despised by his mother, and was in a fair way to becoming slave to 'that forward little lass' from Fowler Street. Willingly, he scanned the shoreline, seeking out the tiny, pastel shells for her. His pockets were jam-packed with them. And, as he worked, Frances played. She twirled over the hard sand, hair flying, stopping to stand on one leg, swaying, as she raised the other into the air, arms struck out, desperately trying to keep her balance.

'Are you pretending to walk the tightrope?' Davey asked.

'No, you clot! I was dancing. Couldn't you tell?'

'Oh yes. So you were,' he said humbly. Frances smiled again, accepting his pile of shells, as a ballerina might accept a bouquet, curtseying deeply. Davey didn't know where to put himself.

'My grandma wanted to go on the stage, you know.'

'Honest?'

'Honest. She wanted to be an actress like Lily Langtry.' Davey's eyes widened.

'Your grandma?'

'Aha. But she married me granda instead.'

'Heck!' Davey let a wave slide over his boots without even noticing. 'Actresses are naughty.'

'I know.' Frances sighed, shaking her head like a schoolmistress with a class of wayward children. 'There's a lot of that in my family.' Davey's eyes were nearly popping out of his head. 'I've heard them talkin' about it. Me Auntie Harriet's a bastard. Auntie Maisie's been out with a man, I know for a fact, *and* she wears rouge. She keeps it hidden in her bureau. I found it one day when they were out. And, oh yes, Grandma Lidell says my

Dad *had* to marry me Mam. I'm not sure why, but that was something to do with *her* being naughty an all . . . and . . . I saw Auntie Hester once, doing things with a lad!!'

'What . . . things!' Davey could hardly get out the words, he was so winded by the onslaught of 'naughtiness'.

'Well!' Frances spoke with relish. She looked to the left and to the right and then bent forward to whisper in Davey's ear. Davey went pink, then purple, then ran into the sea to be sick. He was quite pale when he returned to her side. 'Don't tell anybody, though,' Frances hissed. Davey shook his head. As they walked back up Bent Lane, Davey was thoughtful.

'I don't like leaving you to go home on your own,' he said, as they approached Fowler Street. 'Will you be all right?'

'Oh yes, Davey,' Frances said lightly. 'I don't mind any of them at home! And anyway, I've got Saint George to look after me.'

'Oh. That's all right then.' He smiled politely. 'Thanks for a very interesting afternoon.' And he shook hands with her before he went. Left to herself, Frances suddenly felt frightened and alone. She wandered home, dragged dismally upstairs to the attics, and laid her shells on her bed. What was she going to make out of them now she had them? She picked one up and fingered it. Its brittle structure broke and crumbled in her hands.

George was late home again. Harriet, hair in papers, had finally gone to bed at midnight, and the others had retired long ago. Only Jane's lamp burned on. A pair of horses trotted up the hill toward the village and Jane sighed, breathing in the sweet night air at her window. It had been a busy day. She hugged her secret present close. She had enjoyed herself. She hadn't felt this happy for a long time. The feeling took her by surprise. It made her light-headed, feverish. 'No worse than most.' No she wasn't. Everything was surely going to be all right at last, with Harriet's help. Wings fluttered over the back lane. Every night the bird came a little closer, now lighting on the midden roof. Jane smiled. The midden. Harriet's 'throne room'. In spite of herself, Jane laughed. And the owl settled. Jane watched him; silent; watching her.

The next day, Ellen felt poorly with her cough, so Jane surprised

94

them all, by helping in the shop. She was gay, careless of the resentment that greeted her behind the counter.

'What's the matter with you lot?' she teased her daughters. 'I've never seen such long faces! You want to cheer yourselves up. Have a holiday!'

'Chance would be a fine thing.' Ellen sniffed. Then Jane's eyes twinkled.

'What do you think, Harriet? Shall we take them all out for the day, eh?'

'Just the women,' Harriet smiled. 'The men are banned.' Ellen and Maisie watched them plan the outing together. Jane was giggling and laughing. Her face was flushed.

'She's living in a fool's paradise if you ask me,' Ellen said. 'I'm sure we'll none of us enjoy ourselves if Auntie Harriet's got anything to do with it!'

'Why can't I have a holiday?' Eddie complained.

'How can you have a holiday,' his wife sneered, 'when you never work!'

Eddie was more cowed than ever. George had taken over the accounts again, and Eddie had felt himself slowly eased from his position of ascendancy. He shuffled awkwardly under his Mother's scrutiny.

'What's keeping the old barsket going? That's what *I'd* like to know!' She rasped.

'I don't know, Mam.'

'Well, you ought to know! You should make it your business to find out!'

'I can hardly just ask him, can I?' Ma Lidell ruminated.

'They're going out for the day, you said?'

'On Thursday, aye. Only the women, like.'

'Not him?'

'I suppose if there's council business, he'll have to! But it won't be to the seaside!' The old woman pursed her lips in a cunning smile.

'As long as he's out . . . I've got an idea, son!' Eddie looked at his mother with dread.

In spite of themselves, even Ellen and Maisie enjoyed the sensation of delightful wickedness. They prepared themselves for the festival, pressing their best clothes, pinning on lace, crimping their hair. The night before the great event, Ellen came down late, for something to soothe her cough. Maisie was still in the kitchen, drying her hair by the fire.

'What's that funny smell?' Ellen asked.

'I've been doing me hair.'

'What with?'

'Senna.'

'Eh?'

'You know, that stuff Auntie Harriet uses. It's supposed to turn your hair red. It's not done much for mine, mind.'

'Did you say, "senna"?'

'Aha. I got some at the chemist.' Ellen looked at the remains of a large packet on the kitchen table.

'These are senna pods, man. For the relief of constipation.'

'Eh?'

'They're for CONSTIPATION!' Ellen was howling with laughter. 'What you wanted was henna! Henna with an "h"!' Then Maisie started up, screaming blue murder about how her hair was going to fall out, or turn purple, or God knew what! Coming down to see what all the fuss was about, Harriet looked at the packet on the table. 'I'm sorry, Auntie. You've had it now! Our Maisie's bought out the whole of Shields!'

The disaster of Maisie's hair began the holiday with a swing. Giggling and laughing at her expense, the women paraded down the coast road, in search of further amusement. This was more like it! This was what holidays were supposed to be like, Frances thought, as she ran on ahead to the fair. No need for Davey Lawson now! No need to play the know-all grown up. She could hear the barrel organs playing half a mile away. People were screaming, and laughing, and eating candy floss. She wanted some of that, like any other little girl. It was like pink cotton wool, and stuck to your chin, and your nose, and it was sweet. Or should she have a toffee apple? But at the very entrance to the fairground, they were stopped short by Maisie who, lured by the attractions of the weighing machines, was dying to know whether she was thin or not. She insisted on 'having a go'. Sitting too suddenly in the chair, the mechanism broke, the bell clanged, and the man shouted out for all the world to hear, the terrifying words, 'Twenty stone!'

Maisie was furious. The man made her pay and threatened to sue her for breaking his chair. But then, the whole Beattie tribe descended on him, declaring him to be a charlatan, because their Maisie was seven stone at most, and anyway, her Dad was the mayor. Muttering, the man retired to repair his contraption, while the family processed victoriously into the fairground, Frances glad, for once, to be one of their number.

But once on the threshold, they paused. Noise and colour assaulted their senses. Signs and hailers demanded their attention from every corner, threatening to split their fragile unity.

'Come and see the fat lady!'

'Eeh, our Maisie. You could earn your fortune here!' Ellen dug her sister in the ribs and set them all off laughing again. But Maisie stood long-faced, sniffing back the tears.

'I'm not a freak!' She stamped her foot. Jane sighed.

'There now, Ellen. Look what you've done!'

'I want a go on the helter skelter!' Frances pulled at her mother's arm. Ellen shook her head.

'Maybe later on. Come away now. Oh no! Where's Hester?' All turned to look. They saw her, drifting off into the crowd.

'Hester!' They called out. 'Hester!' Hester looked round angrily. 'Come back!' Pushing her way through the crowd, Harriet reached her niece. They watched as she put an arm round her and talked to her; saw how Hester sulked, shrugged, sighed, then came back to them. 'Hester and I are going off on our own for a bit,' Harriet announced. Jane opened her mouth to object. It was supposed to be a family outing, after all! They should stick together! But, on second thoughts . . .

'Maybe it'd be best,' she said. 'Hester's getting a bit old for merry-go-rounds. We'll go with Frances.'

'Look!' Maisie's voice breathed enthusiasm. 'There's a palmist! Hey, who wants their palm read?'

'Not me!' Jane laughed. 'Are you ready, Fran?' The child nodded enthusiastically. 'Right, let's find something nice and quiet to start off with. Oh! Look over there! Would you like one of those pretty paper parasols?'

'I wouldn't mind going with you, Maisie,' Ellen said, linking arms with her sister. So Jane and Frances found themselves alone in the fairground, stuck with one another.

* * *

Blinded by the light, Harriet and Hester stumbled into the nearest tent. The air was heavy. Harriet fanned herself with her gloves.

'It's a Hall of Mirrors!' Hester turned to go. But Harriet laid her hand, gently on her arm.

'It's cool in here. And there aren't many people.' She smiled invitingly, paying their entrance fees herself. So, Hester followed on, stopping short behind her aunt at the first mirror. 'You and I are alike,' Harriet May informed her. 'We have strong wills, good brains. But, all the world can see is that we're different.' Her neck distended like a giraffe's, the large head swinging dangerously above. She tried the next mirror along. 'That's why they don't like us. They would have us apologise for living, if you please!'

'*I* didn't ask to be born!'

'Indeed not! Most women allow themselves to be used; to be forever at the mercy of their emotions, at the mercy of men! But, we know better! Romance? What's that? Sheer nonsense!'

'Yes!' Hester laughed at the image of her aunt, her left side shrunken and twisted, while the right had grown tall and fat.

'Hester, you can trust me!' The image waved and swam. Hester averted her eyes. 'I'm going to help you.'

'How?'

'How would you like to do as I did? Take up a situation with an intelligent woman . . . ?' Hester frowned.

'Be a servant, you mean! I'd be no better off than if I was married!'

'It's not so bad. Look where it got me!' Harriet's smile, fractured by the glass, flashed out at her. 'You'd have to be finished, of course! I was, you know. Languages, the piano . . . And in return, you'd see the world! Mix with the intelligentsia! Be accepted for what you really are in a more liberal society. Think about it, Hester. My requirements, though exact, are few. You would benefit greatly in my employ.'

'*Your* requirements? *Your* employ?' Her aunt was glad to see the girl was smiling. She certainly had possibilities. She turned from the mirror to look at the reality.

'You've got me wrong, Aunt Harriet! You see, I like men! It's just I don't want to marry any of them!' Stepping back, Harriet shrivelled to the size of a midget.

* * *

98

Maisie and Ellen came reeling out of the palmists.

'She's crackers, Maisie! How could she say your head rules your heart? You haven't *got* a head!'

'You cheeky thing!'

'We've wasted our money! She couldn't read nursery rhymes let alone palms!'

'She was sniffing away at that ectoplasm!'

'She was sniffing away at your hair! She could smell your senna pods!'

'She said I was psychic.'

'Physic, man! She thought you were dosin' yourself!'

'And when she said, "You long deeply for your soul mate . . . well, dear, you are going to find him", I nearly died! Ooh Ellen! I wonder what he'll be like?'

'*Your* soul mate? Hah!'

Eddie was run off his feet. George had gone over the road to the nurseries to fetch some tomatoes for the shop, and Ma Lidell had stolen in, to rummage in his office. For, once George got inside them glasshouses of his, he lost all track of time. He could be in there for hours. He always found plenty to do. The sun was glaring down. The plants would fry in that heat. He raised the windows at the top, and started rolling down the blinds, one by one, to shade them. Beads of sweat grew on his brow. He took off his coat, pulling up his sleeves. Anyway, if the women could skive off, so could he! He wiped his forehead with his handkerchief. He was getting old. Sixty years old. Jane was young yet, forty-four. Fear gripped him. Getting old. Past it. Out of step with the times. The women getting the better of him, taking over. A household of women. And he didn't understand any of them! Even Jane! She'd changed; drifted away from him. Had he evaded his responsibilities, passing Jane on to Harriet? She seemed happier. But was she just cocking a snook at the past, trying to get away with murder like Jack Purvis? He remembered the inquest. She had accused Purvis of trying to rape her, and then of killing Ronnie. Jane had stood up in court, told the truth and shamed the devil. No one had believed her. No one but George. George sighed. He was burning, overcome by heat. He looked up. There wasn't a cloud in the sky.

* * *

99

Frances looked up at the parasol. It was flimsy, not at all like her big black umbrella. Was she not pleased? Jane considered her a moment, then took her by the hand.

'How's Saint George these days, pet?' Her eyes twinkled.

'I don't know, Grandma. I expect he's off fighting dragons and that.' Frances' eyes evaded Jane's. She hadn't forgiven her for neglecting her. Jane bent down, speaking gently.

'There aren't any, pet. They're just bogies in the night. Like when you think your dressing gown on the door of your room is a ghost, waiting for you in the dark.' Frances looked at her, warily.

'You mean, there's no such thing as ghosts?' Jane smiled and shook her head.

'No, pet. Not ghosts. Not bad blood or anything! Everything's all right. The past's over and done with! We should be thinking about the future!' She laughed. 'What'll we go on first!' Frances looked round the fairground and her eye lighted on the carousel.

'Can I go on that?'

'Whatever you like, pet! All you've got to do is enjoy yourself!'

Eddie glanced nervously through the shop window. His Ma was a long time up there. His customer chose some white carnations, which he mixed for her with irises. Their scent was heavy and he felt sick in the sultry air of the room. A loud bang made him jump. He glanced up at the office door. At last, Mrs Lidell appeared, pale and furious. Eddie put his finger to his lips, and taking payment from his customer, showed her out.

'It's her!' Ma hissed, as the bell clanged on the shop door.

'Who?'

'Your Lady La-ti-Tiddle! She's put money in the business!' She left, fuming, 'I'm not serving in here for them! I wash me hands! And you, son, you should do the same!' Eddie stood, numb with shock. So the old barsket would rather let *her* in on the business than his own son-in-law! What was the point of working all the hours God sent? He was needed next door, wasn't he? His kith and kin needed him. Right then! George Beattie could stew!

George's shirt was wringing wet. He'd have to change. Mopping his brow, he picked up the tomatoes. Red, ripe fruits. He held one to his nose and smelt it. It had the musty greenhouse smell he loved . . . Would Jane be as courageous now? Or, under Harriet's influence, was she fooling herself she could run away from the past, shelving her burden? Did anyone ever really get away with anything? He bit into the fruit. It cut sharp and sweet through his thirst.

The horses began to move. Slowly, at first, the carousel revolved, and the horse she sat on rose and fell. Frances grinned. It was wonderful! All the colours, bright in the sunshine, and the music, banging in her ears, stirred her. She sat high in the saddle, smiling at her grandma as she passed her for the first time.

'I'm Saint George, Grandma! Look! I'm holding out my sword!' She yelled, pointing her parasol high into the air. Jane smiled, and waved.

'Hold on tight!' Yes, everything was fine. She was relieved to feel at ease with the child again. Her and her 'Saint George'! Jane smiled, remembering an old flame. Dear old Ronnie. He'd been born on Saint George's Day. Had given her a red rose once. A long time ago. Saint George and the dragon. Memories. The shadow lengthened before her. Deepened. Darkened. She was engulfed by the shadow of a man. Turning, Jane came face to face with Jack Purvis.

'Grandma! Look!' But Jane's back was turned. The horse rose and fell. The music blared. Her grandma was talking with a man. No. She was pushing him away! People were looking, crowding round. Frances craned her neck to see behind, but the carousel whisked her off again, faster, faster. Coming round for the third time, she saw the man, walking away, her grandma swaying as she looked after him. The horse rose and fell, and when she swung back into view, her grandma was lying on the ground.

'Grandma!' The little girl on the carousel screamed, as she went on circling round and round. 'Grandma!'

Round and round the dancer twirled, slower and slower, the music flagging, faltering, ceasing. And when it stopped, the child's sobbing could be heard again, forlorn and intermittent. And then she wound the toy up, and again the doll careered into a spin, her leg rising and falling manically, in time to the music. It gave Frances comfort for the cords were tight around her

101

heart, and no one listened to her. Her grandma had said every-thing was all right! But how could it be? They all said it was the heat, or something called 'the change', and what her grandma really needed was rest. But they were wrong. It was the man, the stranger, who had frightened her. Who was he? What had he got to do with them? With the Beatties? Heavy feet, unaccustomed to the attic stairs, dragged up to her. It was her granda. Frances' heart leapt. Someone cared. She looked at the door, as it opened, and his grey face peered in at her.

'Are you all right, pet?' She nodded dumbly, but her cheeks were streaked with tears. George melted. Smiling gently, he sat on the bed, his book beside him, his great arms circling the child, warm and comforting as a bear.

'Granda, you believe me, don't you? There *was* a man. Honest.' George turned to pick up the book.

'I brought something to show you,' he said softly, opening it.

'They're photos, Granda!' George nodded.

'Very old photos.'

'Who's that?'

'Your Grandma. And that's me, and Auntie Harriet there.'

'Eeh! You don't half look funny!'

'People always do in old photos. Look at this one.'

'Who is it?'

'Did the man you saw this afternoon at the fair look anything like that?' Frances stared at the picture, frowning, then shook her head.

'No. He was taller, Granda. I'm sure.'

'All right, pet. Not to worry.'

'Who is that with Grandma?'

'Your uncle.'

'Uncle Joshua in America?'

'No. You've got another uncle. Or you did have, once. His name was Robert. He went to live in India.' Frances looked back at the photo.

'He looks dead,' she said.

'Do you think so?'

'Yes. But then, so do you. It's funny, everybody looks like ghosts in old photos!'

'But they're not, pet. Not always. Don't mention this to your Grandma, eh? It's just between you and me.'

102

'Yes, Granda.' He tweaked Frances under the chin. 'When can I see her?'

'Maybe tomorrow, eh?' He smiled and was gone, leaving Frances with a new weight on her heart.

Next day, she was allowed in to see her grandma. She was sitting up in bed, reading, and she looked up, smiling when Frances entered the room.

'Hallo.'

'Hallo, pet. Come and sit by me. Here, I've got some chocolate. Would you like some?' Frances nodded and ate the sweet solemnly.

'Are you better?'

'Yes! Of course I am! It was only the heat!' Her grandma's smile was bright. Too bright. There were red spots on her cheeks. Child and woman looked at one another for long moments, and the bright smile faltered.

'Who was the man, Grandma?'

'What man?'

'You know.' Jane shook her head, the smile fixed hard. 'You were pushing him away, just before you fainted.' Again, Jane shook her head.

'No, pet. You've been seeing things!'

'I wasn't!'

'Well then, he must've just been somebody in the crowd, that's all!' Frances looked away. Her grandma was lying. She knew she was.

'It's funny, isn't it?'

'What?'

'I mean, it's funny that you were alive, and knew people and did things, even before I was born.' Jane's smile softened.

'Yes. I suppose it is to you.' There were tears in Frances' fearful eyes. She sighed. Who had told the truth? Her mam or her grandma . . . or neither?

'Now what's wrong?'

'I wish I could go to dancing classes.'

Auntie Harriet spent long hours up in Jane's room. Frances heard them talking, behind closed doors. Was she telling Harriet about the man at the fair? Why her? Why not Frances? Or the rest of them? But the Beattie women were busy. There was a 'do' to cater for at 'The Queen's' over the road and they were making raised pies, trifles, and meringues, till the larder was filled to bursting. Even Jane came down to help at the last minute, sculpting the swan out of ice to grace the centre table. Chin cupped in hands, Frances watched, entranced, as her grandma quickly cut the long neck, curving it gracefully, then carved the body, wings folded, feathers smooth, knife slithering on the surface, where it had begun to melt. Then, at the last minute, Granda and Eddie went across with the swan, and set it on the centre table of the banqueting hall, where it would be admired and then melt. It didn't bear thinking of! Pleading tiredness, Jane went to bed early. And Frances took her chance of asking Maisie.

'Auntie, do you know who the man was?' Maisie looked up from her magazine. 'The man I saw Grandma with at the fair?' Maisie sighed. They were alone in the kitchen. She looked out at the dark window, remembering. Maisie shook her head. 'Why won't she tell us?'

'Because she thinks we're none of us good enough,' Maisie said bitterly. There was a long silence.

'How are you getting on with your silver wedding present?'

'I've not started yet.'

'Eeh! Fetch your shells down now. Go on! I'll help you.' Passing Jane's room, on the way to the attic, Frances heard her grandma, rummaging about. She was heaving something heavy across the floor. She stopped and panted. Then, Frances heard the sound of a key turning in a lock, and a lid, creaking open. Papers rustled and were torn. Then a match was struck, and Frances smelt fire.

'Grandma!' She tried the knob, but the door was locked. 'What are you doing?'

'Just clearing out some old letters. Go to bed now! Good night!'

'Goodnight.' The child answered doubtfully, and went slowly up to her room. Even from the high dormer of her bedroom, craning her neck, Frances could see across the street. For some time, she watched the ladies and the gentlemen dancing, through the windows of the ballroom. Bright colours glowed; lights shone. Then a shadow passed along the side of the hall. Frances

104

glimpsed it, as it turned up the lane to the nurseries. It was her grandma. She had gone out. Heavy-hearted, the child left the window and turned to wind up her dancing doll.

'Fran? I thought you were bringing down your shells?' Maisie stood at the door.

'I couldn't be bothered, Auntie.'

The moon was a golden orb, high in the sky, when George came home. Stealthily clicking the sneck on the back gate, he looked up and saw the shadow of ragged wings, moving across it. The great owl soared over the chimney tops and glided down toward the house, coming to rest on the scullery roof, where it settled to its vigil at Jane's window. Jane. Dreading his bed, George took refuge in his office, reading the well-thumbed pages of a book.

> The rainbow comes and goes;
> And lovely is the rose, The Moon doth with delight
> Look round her when the heavens are bare,
> Waters on a starry night
> Are beautiful and fair;
> The sunshine is a glorious birth;
> But yet, I know, where'er I go,
> That there hath past away a glory from the earth.

He could hear Jane's childish voice, even now, echoing down the years, from the platform of a school. His heart caught in his throat. He closed the book, and lay back, staring helplessly into space. There was no refuge, no escape.

It was the silver wedding at last. But a shell had fallen off Frances' box. She should glue it on again. It looked a mess. The dinner gong! She had to hurry. All thumbs, Frances dipped the shell in the glue and tried to set it back in place. Fiddly thing!

'Stick, will you!' she yelled at it. Then, holding her breath, she carried her offering, gingerly, down the stairs to the dining room, where all the presents waited, on the sideboard.

'I've not wrapped it, Auntie Harriet. The glue's still wet.'

'Never mind. Put it here.' Harriet tried to take it from her but Frances insisted on setting it in place herself, 'in case more shells dropped off'. Then Ellen and Maisie scuttled in with the soup tureen, and Eddie dragged in his resisting mother.

'You'd have complained if you *hadn't* been invited!' Eddie hissed in his mother's ear. She managed a smile of greeting and, at last, the stage was set. It looked somehow forced and haphazard.

'Come on, Hester!' Harriet commanded. 'Strike up now!' Hester launched into a rendering of 'Hearts and Flowers' on the pianoforte, and the happy couple came into the room, arm in arm.

'Thank you, dear!' Harriet called to her niece. 'We have enjoyed your playing long enough!' The piece unfinished, Hester struck a discordant note and darted a poisonous look at her aunt, while Ellen and Maisie giggled, ladle poised over the soup tureen. But, George was clearing his throat, and the soup had to wait, as he stood, ready to make a speech.

'Twenty-five years ago today, Jane and I were married. On that day, I considered myself to be the luckiest man alive. I still do.' He turned to his wife, eyes brimming with tears.

'Sentimental old fool!' Harriet May muttered.

All eyes were now on Jane. She sat, slumped in her chair, staring at her empty plate.

'I had a big speech prepared . . . ' George faltered, caught up in genuine emotion. 'But I've . . . forgotten it.' He sniffed back a tear. In spite of herself, even Harriet felt a pang in her heart. 'I just wanted to say, "thank you", Jane. And to let you know I love you . . . more than ever . . . ' There was a long silence. Eddie began to clap, and one by one the rest of the family joined in the applause. But when the applause died, Jane had still not moved. Silence descended. A feeling of unease gripped the company. A feeling of guilt. Why had they not made more of this celebration? Ma Lidell wriggled, wondering if the soup was getting cold. Then the tear dropped. It rolled slowly from under Jane's lashes, down her cheek, and fell into the empty plate. George touched his wife gently. 'Are you all right, dear?' She could not look up. She bit her lip and shook her head. 'What's wrong?'

'Where's me old dinner set?' she gasped. George smiled with relief and laughter rippled round the table.

'Oh, is that all? I thought I'd done something terrible! This is my present Jane; to you. A brand new dinner service, in best china.' She was staring at her plate. A dry sob scraped her throat;

106

long and low it ground on and on, till, at last, it failed. A chill had fallen on the company. Powerless to prevent her, they sat frozen in their chairs as Jane stumbled from the table, reaching for the door, running down the stairs, and out of the house. Eyes met. No one spoke. George looked blankly round the table. What had he done? What was wrong? Then Frances saw. She saw the green dragon curl its tail round the rim of the tureen; She watched it stride across the dinner plates, stacked on the sideboard; it crawled into the soup bowls and hid in the coffee cups, beside each guest. Flaring its fire, red and gold, it reproduced itself in every nook and cranny.

Suddenly, crying out, Frances scraped back her chair and dashed out. George tried to stop her. Panting, he followed his grand-daughter down the stairs and through the shop. The door was wide open. Through its arch Frances saw her, stumbling across the street. People were shouting. Hooves pounded in the road. The tram was coming, careering full speed down the hill. Standing at the kerb, Frances shouted helplessly,

'Come back! Grandma! The tram!' But Jane was deaf, blind. George was too late to stop Frances, as she dashed out, to pull back her grandma, by her skirts. People screamed. Terror in the horses' eyes, rearing, trampling, crunching under foot. The tram swerved, crashing to the ground. Then there was silence. Thick and red, the blood oozed from Jane's head, trickling through the straying strands of white. Frances touched it, gently putting back the fallen pins.

'Grandma, your hair's come undone.' Blood stuck to her hands. Puzzled, she looked at it, then, up at the old man, standing, crying beside her. Passengers were moaning, scrambling from the wreck. A horse whinnied, and tried to rise. The family came out and stood stunned, watching, as Frances wiped her hands on her dress and looked at them again, shaking her head at the thick dark blood. 'I can't get it off,' she said.

PART TWO

1905

Here come I, Saint George; from Britain I have sprung.
I'll fight the Dragon bold, for my wonders have begun.

CHAPTER SIX

She heard the opening bars and, with thumping heart, giddy and light as air, Frances walked out alone, to centre stage. She was a snowflake, whirled and tossed by the wind, spinning, dancing through the haze of smoke which curled up onto the stage from the auditorium. She stood out starkly against the backdrop, of lurid swirling blues. No matter that her feet pounded on the boards; no matter that the lacy skirt was made of old curtains; no matter she had no technique; Frances' heart was in it, and for a few short minutes, she made them all believe. The dance ended in silence. Frances faltered, suddenly exposed, then Maisie began to clap. The miners stamped their feet and cheered. George wiped a tear from his eye. And Ellen and Hester had to admit,

'Mind she's good!' Flushed with joy, Frances picked up the box of tinsel snowballs from the wings, and ran back on stage, throwing them joyfully into the audience. Hands rose to catch them. Eddie missed his, and laughed as it fell into the lap of young Davey. Then, as the dancer curtsied for the last time, Davey Lawson silently laid his adoring heart at her feet. The debut of Frances Lidell was an astounding success.

Going home in the hansom together, the family glowed with pride. But Frances hardly listened to their praise, and, as the frost glistened outside, on the road, she imagined she was the snowflake, flying, floating over the moonlit roofs of the town, away from the shop, Shields, everything she knew and hated.

'There's some cold stotty cake, pet, if you're hungry!' Auntie Maisie brought her down to earth with a bang. Frances sighed.

'No thank you, Auntie.' Politely, she loosened Maisie's grip on her arm. Maisie fell silent. So, 'the bairn' still spurned her auntie, did she? Not good enough for her, was that it? Yet Maisie worshipped the lass. Night after night, she'd cuddled her in her own bed, after her grandma'd died. Time after time, she'd mopped her up after a nose bleed, or nursed her after a fainting fit. Why, she'd done more for her than her own mother! But nobody loved Maisie Beattie, did they? As the cab turned into Fowler Street, Maisie sighed, resigning herself to a loveless fate.

Alone in his room above his mother's sweetshop in Ocean Road, Davey Lawson opened his snowball. And as he drew out the little bag of candy inside, he prayed that Frances would be a good girl and come back to Chapel so he could see her regularly again. He'd told his Mam about Frances' family, and what they'd done. She'd shaken her head, and wished the Salvation Army onto them. But the tinsel glittered temptingly in Davey's grey life. Frances Lidell beckoned him on like a fairy. He stowed his snowball away in a drawer for later. Whatever his Mam said, he could still dream, couldn't he?

And so could Frances, high up in her solitary room. Her nightlight glimmered by her bed, lighting up the corners of the room, casting shadows on the walls. The little dancer stood alone on her plinth. Should she get up and turn the key? It was cold. Ice frosted the window panes and stood in the brimming jug on the washstand. Frances nestled deeper under the blankets, shivering. Why had she not said 'yes' to her auntie's offer of a hot bottle? Because, by her little acts of kindness Maisie was trying to possess her, to make her love her! But what was the point? People only *said* they loved you. They never meant it! Frances needed no one and no one needed her. The nightlight burned brighter, as she slumbered. The shadow of the little dancer grew longer. Then the flame flickered, and another shadow, deeper, darker, reared behind the dancer, engulfing her . . .

. . . and Frances was dancing, dancing, round and round, swaying, swooning. A ballroom. Yes . . . like The Queen's; huge. So huge, she couldn't see where the floor ended and the walls began. Round and round . . . fading into darkness; swirling; spotlights picking out the couples; swaying. Who was she dancing with? Nobody. Alone. Music coming to an end. People clapping. Then they all made way, crowding back to the sides; a floor show; like an arena! Spotlights picking out the horse-drawn carriage, clattering into the ring, driving round and round; then out of the ring and away out of sight. And now a horse came on, a beautiful horse, prancing and dancing all on its own. Lovely! So fine, so elegant, its neck arching, legs high in the air, picking its feet up high, leaping and twisting . . . Trying to get away! Darkness all round! Only the horse spotlit in the circle of light . . . trying to get away! Something behind it, chasing it; horrible, ugly, bellowing; a monster, attached to the horse by a thread . . . a thread so fine you can't even see it. No! Oh no! The monster is eating the horse and the horse can't get away!

'Wake up, pet! Wake up?'

'Get off me! All of you! Help?'

'You're havin' your nightmare again, pet. Everything's all right!' Frances stared up at the livid face of her auntie Maisie in the light of the oil lamp. 'It's that great monster . . . ' Maisie looked at the huge wooden carving, on the floor beside the washstand. 'It's enough to give anybody nightmares is that!'

'It's not a monster! It's an elephant!'

'With human legs and four arms? And what's it doing standing on a mouse? Did you ever hear the like?'

'It belonged to Grandma!'

'Aye and look what happened to her!' Maisie could have bitten out her tongue. 'I'm sorry, pet. I didn't mean . . . ' She sighed again. 'Do you want to come in with me for the rest of the night? Eh?' Frances shook her head, retreating further under the bedclothes. Maisie sighed. 'Eeh, I wish I understood you.' She tucked her in. 'Better now?' Frances nodded and reluctantly, Maisie left.

* * *

Bathed in sweat, Frances watched the shadow of the elephant, on the wall behind the little dancer. Did the elephant threaten, or protect her? And why had grandma kept it hidden under her bed? Frances got up, pulling the eiderdown around her. If it hadn't been for her, the elephant statue and the other things would have been destroyed after the funeral. But she had wanted them and her granda could deny her nothing at that time, even dancing classes. He had asked her if she knew what had made her grandma run out into the street. And she had told him,

'It was the dragons, Granda. They chased her out.' He had looked shaken and upset. Then he had touched her cheek gently, and said Yes, she could learn to dance, if it would help her forget, and she, of course, had assured him it would. Only it hadn't. She pulled open the drawer of the washstand and took out a box. Inside was a dried up rose and a faded, blood-stained drawing. That was of an elephant too. Who had drawn it? What did it mean? Pondering, Frances dropped it back into the drawer, but she held onto the rose. Hesitantly, as if to propitiate the statue, she placed it, an offering at its feet.

'Please, I don't want any more bad dreams,' she said, then crept back to bed and went to sleep.

It was a harsh winter. The dazzling snow lay three feet deep in the back yard, and a silence descended on the world. Maisie's twenty-third birthday came and went, and still no suitor carried her off into the sunset. Late at night, she sat up, secretly reading the lurid novels of Elinor Glyn. Erotic passions coloured her dreams; ladies sprawled on the tiger rugs of her imaginings, and she went to bed, drenched in Attar of Roses, swooning as though under the influence of ether. Ellen looked askance on Maisie's secret 'life' and pointed out that 'marriage is not all it's cracked up to be!' But Maisie's gentle heart was aching for affection and, in desperation, she wrote to the Sunday Papers.

Frances didn't know what anybody saw in papers and, for her, Sunday was the most boring day of the week. There was no school, no dancing class, no shop; only The Glebe Chapel in the morning, and homework, or improving reading in the afternoon. And the Sunday following Maisie's letter, seemed no different from all the rest. She was doing her French homework on the scullery table. Ellen had gone next door with Eddie to visit the Lidells. George sat in his office, snoring, while Maisie was reading the paper. Upstairs, Hester was practising on the piano. Frances sighed, as the strains of the Moonlight Sonata drifted down the stair.

'La plume de ma tante est sur la table,' she muttered as she wrote in her exercise book. Maisie was searching through the newspaper furiously. Suddenly she flung open the pages, adjusted her spectacles and read avidly. Then, she gasped and went pink. 'What is it, Auntie?' Frances asked curiously.

'Nothin'! Nothin' to do with you, anyway.' More curious than ever, Frances left the table and went to peer over Maisie's shoulder.

'Go on, Maisie! You can trust me!' Maisie hesitated.

'Promise you won't laugh?'

'Cross my heart and hope to die.' Dying to share her secret, Maisie pointed out the lines in the paper. They read, 'Spinster, 23 seeks honourable gentleman with view to marriage. Non-conformist preferred.' Frances giggled.

'Did you put that in?'

'Why not? I've no intention of ending up an old maid, and I've got as much chance of meeting anybody, stuck in this shop as I'd have if I was in prison!' Frances nodded in agreement, as she continued reading down the column.

'There's a lot like that, Maisie. Look, here's a man looking for a wife . . . ' Maisie slowly read, 'Christian man, affectionate, steady, wants hard-working wife to help run business. Good looks not vital.'

'Eeh, that sounds interesting.' As Maisie considered the advertisement, her heart skipped a beat. Had fate stepped in?

'You'll have to write to him, Maisie. I tell you what, we could write it together!' Her aunt's look made Frances' heart melt with pity.

'Yes,' she whispered. 'You tell me what to say, and I'll write it.' If she penned the note herself, it would take all day. So, as the opening bars of The Moonlight Sonata began all over again, the aunt and the niece crept upstairs, to begin their task.

But Maisie's letter brought a disappointing reply. The man was sixty, with dropsy, and a bookshop in Newcastle. He wanted an unpaid skivvy, and although Maisie might well have ended up a rich widow eventually, the prospect meantime did not fill her with joy. So the gentleman was dismissed. Still, her own advertisement brought in five letters. Three they discarded at once, as not fitting for a lady. But the other two needed further investigation. Maisie agreed to an assignation with each of them in Newcastle. The excitement kept Frances going through the spring. Evading the suspicions of the old barsket was problem enough, but safeguarding her naïve aunt was even worse. So, Frances insisted she go along each time as chaperone, thereby also hoodwinking George, who thought Maisie was merely taking her on improving excusions. They visited museums together, went round the keep at Newcastle, and even went to the theatre. Frances was enjoying herself enormously. But the best of it was, that on the fourth attempt, Maisie found herself a young man.

He was called Will Stoppard. He was twenty-eight, a stutterer and he ran a village pub in Northumberland, with his Dad. He liked music hall and Frances found herself enjoying a whole new world of grown up delight, as she sat beside the happy couple in the stalls. Will and Maisie teetered on the edge of marriage all through the spring, and Frances had begun to dream of bridesmaid's dresses, but Maisie hesitated. If she married a publican her father would never speak to her again! So she had better be very sure of herself before she burnt all her boats. But how could she be sure? Toothache and indecision kept her awake many a long night as April approached, and spring increased her agitation still further. 'Eeh, me sap's rising!' she explained. Frances urged her to throw all decency to the wind, risk everything, leave the shop and fly to the waiting arms of her beloved, to try the life out for herself. But Maisie was afraid.

'I'd miss Grace!' she wailed plaintively.

'You could take the cat with you, man!' Frances insisted. 'She'd like the country! Think of all them rats, and moles and things she could chase!' But still Maisie dithered, until, at last, she came up with an idea.

Her toothache had been 'agony' for three weeks. Even George was sick of the sight of her tied up in a scarf like a suet dumpling, ready for the pot. Everyone urged her to 'do something!' So, at last, Maisie went to the dentist. She came back pale but resolved.

'He says I've got to have them all out!' she announced.

'All of them?' Ellen asked in horror.

'Well, I might as well while I'm at it. It'll save trouble later on. The only thing is, he says I'll need a holiday after it, to recuperate, like.'

'Eeh, you will, Maisie,' Ellen agreed. George was horrified. A holiday? Away from home? And what were they supposed to do in the shop, he'd like to know?'

'Well, Dad,' Ellen told him, 'if she's got to have one, far better have it now before Auntie Harriet comes and whisks our Hester off!' Hester scowled.

'I don't know that I want whisking off!' she muttered. 'Not by Aunt Harriet anyway!' George frowned, but kept his silence.

'All right, Maisie,' he said at last. 'Have them out. You can take a week off after Easter.'

She came back in a cab, white and shaking. She'd had gas, but it had made her sick.

'I told you not to have any dinner!' Ellen scolded her, as she tucked her up in bed. But in two days, Maisie was up again and raring to go. Ellen clucked as she helped her pack her bags. 'Are you sure you're fit to travel now?' Maisie nodded furiously. She was going to have her holiday, come hell or high water!

'How are you going to eat, Auntie?' Frances queried.

'I don't care, pet, just so long as I can kiss!' came the stoic reply. George took her to Newcastle Central Station on the Monday morning, when he went in to buy flowers for the shop. Pangs of guilt tore at her, as Maisie waved to the disappearing figure of her father on the platform. To think he was paying for the holiday! If he only knew! Well, she'd done it now! She was a fallen woman!

'There's a card from our Maisie!' Ellen announced, coming in from the shop a week later. 'Having a lovely time, wish you were here. The farm is very nice and the weather is good.'

'Is that it?' George sneered.

'It says a lot for *her*!' Ellen said. Frances picked up the card and smiled.

'Can I take a red rose from the shop?' she asked.

'What for?' Granda roared.

117

'For school. We all have to give each other one. It's Saint George's day!'

'Oh.' George was assuaged. 'Nobody can say I'm not a good patriot. Aye, you can have a rose if you like, pet.'

Frances enjoyed her long and lonely trek. It couldn't last long enough for her. She could day dream to her heart's content. One minute, she was the great actress, playing in Shakespeare, the next, a ballerina, dancing on her points, but always, she was alone. She would enjoy the adulation of the great British Public, as she travelled about the world, wrapped in furs and diamonds. It was what her grandma had wanted, and what had she ended up with? A life of drudgery tied to a shop, smothered by the scent of flowers. She remembered her grandma's white face, and the blood . . . Frances swayed.

'Are you all right, pet?' An old workman took hold of her arm and sat her on the wall of a house. The world was swimming. She hadn't fainted since January and usually she did it during school assembly, not on the way to school. 'Nerves' the doctor had said. He'd recommended raw liver every morning for her blood, and egg flips at night. Everything was nerves according to him. Once she'd stayed out for three hours. He'd said she hadn't wanted to wake up. But she wasn't going to faint now! She was in the school play today! They were doing the ancient mummers' play 'Saint George and the Dragon'. And she was playing Father Christmas, even if it was Easter! So she couldn't be ill, could she? Cold and clammy, Frances, nevertheless, insisted she was better. She thanked the workman, then, holding her rose tight, she went on to Mortimer Road Seniors.

The whole school was going to watch, including the boys. Muriel's Mam had come in to help, and Cissy, who was playing the dragon, was having trouble with her tail.

'I know I should've practised with it,' she wailed, as she fell over it for the umpteenth time.

'If in doubt, roar!' the teacher told her. The school hall bubbled with excitement, and heads turned, as the cast paraded in. There were a few giggles, the teachers shushed, then everyone settled down. Frances was in her element. She felt quite safe behind her Father Christmas whiskers. Nobody would know who she was! The children clapped and cheered, and hissed at the dragon who died marvellously, and then came back to life! So Muriel, who was playing Saint George, had to gird her loins and start again, jabbing away with her little wooden sword, as Frances stood at the side, watching. The school went mad. There was an uproar of excitement, as they geeed on first the dragon, then Saint George. Muriel and Cissy were getting carried away with themselves. Cissy fell over her tail, right on top of Frances, and Muriel helped her up. Everyone laughed as the dragon handed the knight his sword back and the fight began again. But the tail had become caught up in Frances' long robe. And the dragon was pulling Father Christmas along behind him. Everyone laughed. Then, suddenly, Father Christmas was on the floor. He'd fallen over too. And there was red stuff on his beard. The teacher rushed onto the stage, pulled off the whiskers, and Davey Lawson, sitting with the boys of his own class, saw his beloved lying pale and bleeding on the ground. 'She's dead!' The whisper went round the school, as Frances was carried out. Davey helplessly cursed the dragon for dragging her down.

'That Cissy Green's a proper twerp!' he told his neighbour, pity stirring the male heart.

It was the same with Will. At first, he had been shocked by Maisie's appearance. She arrived, pale and exhausted, a scarf about her face. When she spoke, her mouth puckered like an old man's, and she lisped. But, he did his best to look after her, not allowing her to lift a finger in the kitchen. He cooked blanc-mange and creamed potatoes for her, which she spooned into her toothless mouth while he read the newspapers out loud.

'The Ppppprince and pppprincess of Wer . . . wer . . . '

'Waleth,' Maisie unused to toothlessness, lisped where Will stuttered.

' . . . arrived in Bombay to a tumultuous welcome by the Indian ppppperpeople.' Will's Dad shook his head and hid a smile. They were a daft pair and no mistake. 'The perprincess was greeted with an address from the women, Parararparsee, HerHindu and Mahommmmedan. A coconut and a bowl of werwerwater werewere perpassed seven times round her h . . . h . . . '

'Handth?' Maisie guessed.

'Head. And then rice was thrown at her . . . '

'Eeh, thath terrible!' Maisie objected. But Will continued,

'. . . . as a sign of good ferferfortune. The Herhindus circled her with little lamps . . .'

'For God's sake you two!' Will's Dad laughed. 'Will you get out of here and leave me in peace!'

'Ber ber but Dad . . .'

'I can manage this pub on me own! I've done it before. Go on! Before you drive me mad!'

'I don't know that Mer Mer Miss Beattie is up to it, Dad!' Will complained.

'Do her good! Borrow Bill Davidson's pony and trap, why don't you? Give her some fresh air!'

He'd taken to Maisie had Will's Dad. At first, he hadn't liked the idea of a woman coming to stay. He had his reputation to think of, not to mention his licence. But anybody could see Maisie Beattie wasn't a trollop. Will was safe enough in *her* hands! Chortling to himself, he watched the unlikely pair go at a trot down the lane. Maisie bunched up in a rug, Will, holding the reins. His Dad'd suggested he take her to Cragside for a treat. The rhododendrons were out in the gardens. All colours they were, purple, white, pink, red, gold . . .

'Ooh itsth tho lovely, Will,' Maisie gasped. Taking her arm, he led her up to the house, where the housekeeper showed them round. Maisie's eyes bulged. It was amazing! They had electric in the house! You could switch lights on and off! They had contraptions! Things that cleaned the carpets, washed clothes, did the ironing! Wherever you turned some astonishing novelty drew the eye. It was an Aladdin's cave. Will smiled. His Dad'd judged her right. She was loving every minute. In fact, she had to be dragged forcibly away from the ironing, with the new fangled electric iron, and would have finished the lot if the hot tea, supplied by the housekeeper, hadn't made her gums ache again. Tired and happy, Maisie settled back between her cold white sheets that night. She yawned. It must be the fresh air, making her so tired. She took a couple of aspirins for the pain and dropped off almost at once.

Next morning, she awoke as the cock crowed. She sat up suddenly, wondering where she was, but remembered, as she heard the knock on her door. For a second, Maisie didn't know what to do, then she reached for a shawl and wrapped it round her, before going to the door and opening it. Will stood outside, blushing, a cup of tea in his hands.

'You should've stayed in berberberbed . . . I mean, I would've brought it to you in berberberbed . . . I mean . . . oh heck. Here.' He thrust the steaming cup at her. This was the life. Maisie had never had tea in berbed before. She was usually the one that took it to the rest of them! Cautiously she sipped, fearful of setting off the ache in her jaw. Then she dressed and came downstairs. Will was packing a picnic. They were going to spend the day down by the river. Maisie's heart fluttered. She was definitely feeling better.

'You've got some cercercercolour in your cheeks today!' Will congratulated her. Maisie smiled. He might as well have told her she was beautiful, because that's how he made her feel.

They walked, the hamper between them, along the riverside, seeking a spot in the shade. A rocky pool, hidden by bushes, swept by the leaves of low lying trees, came in sight. There was a rope hanging from a branch. Will had swung from it, as a boy.

'I've had some ferferferfun here,' he told Maisie. She gave him her toothless smile. He was getting used to it now. Then they settled on a rug, and lay back, listening to the whispering leaves, till they felt hungry enough to eat. Afterwards, they sat, sipping lemonade in contented silence.

'Fancy a walk?' Will asked. Maisie nodded. 'Are you up to climbing? It's a bit rocky!' 'Up to climbing' indeed! She'd show him! Laughing, she strode on ahead of him. The rays of the sun filtered through the leaves, dappling the swirling waters. Their laughter echoed along the river bank, like the memory of childhood, drifting in and out of the trees. Then, her foot slipping, Maisie stopped, steadying herself, and looked about her. She could see Will, getting nearer, his moustached face peering through the bushes.

'You can't catch me!' she called. Picking up her skirts, she scrambled on into the greenwood, her young man in hot pursuit. His steps were dull on the peaty earth, but the snapping twigs told her he was nearer. She looked back, startled; he stopped, staring. Maisie's smile faltered. What was wrong? She touched her hair, straggling about her cheeks, and Will saw a wild creature, half woman, half faun, standing in the trees. Her eyes, dark and wide, looked fearfully at the man as he approached. The humped back quivered. She was the deer, he the hunter, and he would master her. Maisie's foot gave on the soft earth, but his arm caught her, and pulled her to him. She began to fight, and he spoke soothingly, calming the wildness, feeling the small heart beating madly against him. Her cheeks were pale, the naked mouth vulnerable. Gently he placed his lips on hers. His tongue met no resistance, and Maisie's knees began to give. The peat, soft like cushions, welcomed them, and his hardness melted her all to softness. Gentle, giving, Maisie saw Will's face transform, as he took his pleasure. His eyes burned bright, energy coursing through him, flushing his face, tightening the sinews in his arms and legs, making him into a man. It was what he was, after all. And, when all was said and done, Maisie was a woman. It was what they were meant to do. It was simple, natural. It was nice. She enjoyed his joy, which swept her on a wave of ecstasy, echoing through the woods, a cry like a will o' the wisp, like happiness set free.

Their happiness roamed all afternoon. Splashing in the pool, naked, Will teased her by hiding her clothes behind a stone. Blushing, she crept into his arms and let him dry her skin. Luminous, soft and white, it reflected light, like the moon reflects the sun. He marvelled at it, wishing he could paint. And she marvelled at the dark hairs on his arms and legs, and on his back. She loved his back, and hung there, hard against him, rocking, swooning with delight, as he dried himself. And then they dressed, and lay down under the trees, drifting off to sleep. Warm for late April, a cuckoo sang, flies hummed, and Will snored. Maisie turned onto her side, and looked with admiration at the exposed torso of her lover. His chest, like a barrel, moved her. She put her arm across it, and held him. He looked so vulnerable now. He had given his all, and now he needed her protection. Playfully, she touched the dark moustache. His lip twitched. One eye opened, and he smiled.

'Want something?' he asked. Maisie giggled.

'I was just thinking . . . '

'Best not to.'

'I never knew such happiness existed.'

'Maybe it doesn't.'

'Is this me?' He pinched her and she yelled.

'Yes.' He laughed.

'It's as though the world outside, Shields, everything, didn't exist . . .'

'I know what you mean. And it doesn't, not at the moment, not for us.'

'I wish this day could go on forever.'

'It will.' He looked at her, his eyes soft and clear. 'In here.' He pointed to her heart, and she took his hand, holding onto it.

'Why us? There's so much misery, and temper and lies in the world, Will . . . and, when you're involved in it, like when I'm at home, it *seems* real enough, though it doesn't here, just now.'

'Happiness and unhappiness live side by side, Maisie. All you have to do is turn over the coin. But you need to trust one another to do that. And once trust's been broken . . .'

'I trust you, Will. I don't know why.'

'Question why, and you're not trusting any more.'

'Is that all happiness is?' Will sighed, and turned to face her, his hand gently stroking her sunken cheek.

'Happiness, unhappiness, what difference will any of it make in a million years' time?' Maisie stared into his eyes, wondering.

'Will?'

'Mmmm?'

'You're not stuttering.'

CHAPTER SEVEN

'There hath passed away a glory from the earth.' George arranged his offering of white lilies in the little vase, and stood back to admire the effect.

'It's a nice inscription,' Ellen said brightly. 'The gold stands out well against the black marble.' The family grunted their approval, and George blew hard on his handkerchief. The anniversary of Jane's death was always hard for him.

'I'm glad you could all be here. It would have pleased her.'

'We are family, Mr Beattie.' Frances could have killed her father for his hypocrisy. Her Mam was right. He was a weakling, not a man. She nestled closer to her granda's side, and he grasped her hand gratefully. Frances hadn't wanted to come. But family ties won her over, and she came, with the rest of them, decked out in sombre shades. It was cold for July. Now they had paid their respects, surely they could go? A large splash touched the black stone. They looked up at the ashen cloud, hanging over them, like smoke. There was a loud click. Aunt Harriet had put up her umbrella. She held out her arm to Hester, offering shelter. But Hester glared darkly at her aunt. Another splash wet her shoulder, then, resignedly Hester accepted the offer, as first George's, then Ellen's, then Maisie's umbrellas went up, a circle round the grave. The sight of them made Frances shiver.

124

'Come on, Dad,' Ellen said gently. The rain pattered overhead and spat at their feet. George nodded dumbly, and the line of black umbrellas turned to go home, through the rain.

An atmosphere of oppression hung over the dining room, as the family sat, listening to the pouring rain outside. Frances stared at the streaking window panes. Ellen sighed, and Hester, dark rings under her eyes, bit her nails.

'Don't do that, dear,' Harriet told her. Hester's jaw stiffened. One last snap of the teeth, and she dropped her hands into her lap. Eddie was itching to roll a cigarette. Should he go out to the back yard midden, and suffer the cold and damp to satisfy his urge? Why not? He stood, coughing an apology.

'Where do you think you're going?' Eddie pulled himself up to his full height.

'The throne room, Harriet! The throne room!' No one laughed. The joke had worn thin. It was just what they called the midden now. That was all. Eddie went, Hester began picking her nails and Maisie's teeth clicked.

'For heaven's sake, Hester. Play the piano!' Hester stared at her fingers, inspecting the damage, as though she hadn't heard. Harriet sighed. What was the matter with the girl?

'I feel a presence,' Maisie said slowly. Alarmed, even Frances turned to stare at her aunt. There was a long silence. Maisie's teeth clicked again. 'She's here.'

'Who? Ma?' Ellen gasped.

'Don't be so soft!' Harriet spat.

'I know.' Maisie sniffed at the air, head on one side, listening. 'I can feel her shade . . . ' A sound like a pin dropping, made them all jump.

'It's your teeth, Maisie!' Harriet spoke with exasperation. 'You were done with them dentures! You know you were! You should've complained at the time!'

'Shush!' Maisie's finger was on her lips. A shadow seemed to pass across the room. Suddenly Hester got up and sat at the piano. Harriet smiled. Now, at last, they would have some suitable entertainment. Hester raised her hands high into the air, and plunged into a long series of complicated scales.

Eddie wet the paper, and sealed it. It was a good shape. He liked

125

it. A job well done. Rocking on the throne, he reached for his matches, and set light to the shaggy end of the tobacco. He inhaled deeply, then slowly breathed out the long wreath of smoke. The midden was the only place he could get any peace. He didn't belong anywhere. He lived in a kind of no man's land. Not that he minded. It had its compensations. He'd got the length and breadth of this family and his own, and he liked neither of them. He didn't much like serving in shops, either. But what else could he do? He had to eat. For the minute, he was stuck. The strains of Hester on the piano filtered through the pattering rain. He grimaced and inhaled deeply. Anyway, George didn't give him any stick, not since Eddie'd got to know about Harriet and the money. They had a gentleman's agreement of a sort. And, when all was said and done, he'd inherit half of Beattie's shop in the end. It wasn't so bad. He'd make Harriet buy him out, sell up his share and bugger off. He'd have a packet what with that and the money his mam'd leave him. Who cared about business anyway? Let them both go hang, the Lidells, and the Beatties! He'd just keep quiet, let them all think what they liked, and then when the day came . . . freedom! Even Ellen didn't know what he was planning. Even Ellen. The smoke curled as Eddie smiled. Yes, he was a wise monkey and no mistake. There were no flies on him. Or were there? Maybe one. One fly in his ointment, Frances. His daughter. She didn't like him. Why should she? All he'd ever done for her was tan her hide. Yes, the old barsket had her affections, if anyone did. That was the fly. His own daughter . . .

More like Jane every day, George thought as he listened to her. She put her heart and soul into the poetry. Frances had a natural sense of drama, a born actress, and the old familiar lines from Wordsworth's 'Intimations', breathed life into George's memory. Was Frances also thinking of her grandma? Her voice had a searching quality, as though her heart ached for something lost. It struck an answering chord in the listeners. George mourned Jane and lost youth. Harriet mourned an enemy who had been her only true companion. Ellen ached for a husband, though, to all intents and purposes she had one. Maisie mourned past happiness. Would she ever see Will again? Why didn't he get in touch with her? Or was he waiting for her to make the first move again? Frances ached for freedom. But what did Hester want? Her gold cross glittered in the gaslight. It stood out sharp against the dull grey dress. She was biting her nails again. Consumed by guilt, she whipped herself, for driving her mother to despair with her wickedness. She hated her body and the sensations she had been unable to resist, and now was bent on its utter subjugation. She changed overnight; worked till her fingers bled, making wreaths for the shop, or practising on the piano. She went with George to chapel, but it didn't satisfy her, and instead began to visit the new Anglican church of Saint Michael and All Angels, up the road. George watched, bemused, but Harriet only shrugged and said,

'It could've been worse. She could've gone into the Sally Army.' She believed Hester would 'grow out' of her religious phase. Mr Freud had written about such things. Young women of a morbid turn of mind either had crushes on their women teachers, or turned to religion. A spell with Harriet in London, seeing the sights, mixing with the intelligentsia would soon bring the girl out of herself. George had grave misgivings about Harriet's set, but, she was an educated woman, and she'd got on in the world. He was forced to admire her for that. And she *was* a woman. Hester needed a woman, and her sisters weren't up to much. Jane had put Hester into Harriet's charge. Why not let her take her then? Harriet hated men, God knew. Well then! Hester'd be safe with her, wouldn't she? Frances' voice drifted beneath his thoughts . . .

> Heaven lies about us in our infancy!
> Shades of the prison house begin to close
> Upon the growing boy . . .

Maisie sniffed back the bitter tears. She'd had a taste of freedom. She knew what happiness was. Her teeth clicked in her agitation.

'Oh, Maisie! Do something about them dentures, for heaven's sake!' Harriet objected.

'Oh shut up!' Maisie shot out of the room, crying. Everyone looked at one another in amazement.'

'What's got into *her* lately?' Ellen asked.

'It's grandma, I expect,' Frances lied. 'She's missing her.'

★ ★ ★

Harriet put pressure on George and George, in turn, put pressure on Hester to go to London. It was a great opportunity. But Hester resisted, kneeling in the dark pews of St Michael's, praying for guidance.

'Oh God the Father of Heaven: have mercy on us miserable sinners,' the vicar intoned.

'Oh God the Son, Redeemer of the world: have mercy on us miserable sinners,' Hester replied with the congregation. Her guilt felt more at home in the Anglican Church than it did at the Glebe.

'Remember not, Lord, our offences, nor the offences of our forefathers; neither take thou vengeance of our sins: spare us, good Lord, spare thy people, whom thou hast redeemed with thy most precious blood, and be not angry with us forever.' Hester was weeping, as she wailed,

'Spare us, good Lord.' Yes, perhaps God would spare her, if she punished herself enough; if she suppressed the sickening urges within. The knuckles of Hester's hands were white, as she gripped them in prayer. But still her guilt was unassuaged. Was even this enough? One Sunday morning, on her way to Matins, Hester had, on an impulse, gone into St Bede's Roman Catholic Church. She had passed it on her way to Saint Michael's, many times, and felt unaccountably drawn to the place. The Latin mystery, the incense, the statues to the Virgin, all the trappings of Roman Catholicism attracted her and the service itself satisfied her emotions. Afterwards, she had lit a candle to the Madonna, and stared up at the serene face of the Virgin for a long time, praying for forgiveness. She had felt at peace then and the notion of becoming a nun, from that time, had held a serious attraction for her.

'Oh Lamb of God; that takest away the sins of the world, grant us thy peace.' Peace. Yes. That was what Hester wanted, above all things. Peace. Why could they not leave her to go her own way, instead of pushing her onto Harriet? When else had she known peace? Those few precious moments in the arms of some man, afterwards. Yes. That was the only other time. So! It seemed she must either indulge or deny herself to satisfy her nature. But her father wouldn't hear of her entering a convent! She dared not so much as mention it to him. And as for men . . . they'd sooner lock her up! That left Aunt Harriet. Hester shifted uncomfortably on her hassock. Why not try it? What had she to lose? She might even like it! The vicar, about to pronounce the blessing, was alarmed to see the anxious woman in grey recklessly flying from the church.

Frances watched jealously from the door, as Harriet supervised Hester's packing. It seemed, once she'd decided to go, she couldn't get away fast enough! George had shut himself in the office, and the others were all working in the shop. Frances should be down there too. But she couldn't tear herself away from the feverish activity upstairs.

'Never mind, Frances! No doubt your turn will come!' Harriet stroked Frances' cheek, as she slipped out to fetch Eddie. The trunk and boxes were packed and he was needed to carry them downstairs. Hester stood behind them, as behind a wall, daring anyone to approach or try to change her mind. She smiled broadly at the girl by the door, and looked round expansively.

'Well! Good riddance!' she said. Frances laughed, in spite of herself, and Hester, whooping, leapt over the boxes to snatch up her niece and swing her round joyously. 'Don't you wish it was you?'

'Yes! Oh yes!' There were tears in Frances' eyes. Hester set her down, thoughtfully.

'I've not been very nice to you. I'd like to give you something to make up.' Frances, head on one side, stared at her aunt, as she took the gold cross and chain from round her neck. 'Here. Do you want it? It's all right. You can. I don't need it any more.'

Eddie complained non stop, as he took the bags and the boxes down.

'Why couldn't you have packed the trunk downstairs? Women! I'll do myself an injury, heaving a great thing like that down three flights!' But George came to the rescue, rolling up his sleeves;

'I'm not in my dotage yet!' he roared, taking hold of the handle at one end.

'Be careful, Dad!' Ellen warned. But George enjoyed panting and sweating, swinging the box onto the cart by himself, under the admiring eyes of the lady customers.

'We're not going on that!' Harriet objected, as Eddie got up front, and took the reins.

'There's a cab coming for you, Harriet.' George gasped, purple faced. Hester was coming up behind, eyes bright, pink with excitement, itching to be gone. George looked at her for a moment, then suddenly held out his arms. 'Come on, pet. Say goodbye properly, eh?' Hester looked suddenly afraid. She hesitated. Was she going to run away? Harriet frowned.

'Go on, Hester. Say goodbye to your father.' Bracing herself, Hester walked into the outstretched arms, which enfolded her, and held her close. Then she began to cry.

'There now, love,' George comforted her. 'It won't be too long before you're back. We'll miss *you*, you know.'

'I was feeling so happy!' Hester sobbed. 'And now . . . now, you've spoiled it all!' George was astonished.

'What have *I* done?' He looked from one to the other. Harriet raised her eyebrows.

'Come along, dear. The cab's coming . . . ' Hester blew her nose, the pink flush faded into pale and she joined Harriet in the cab. As they jolted off down the street, Frances stood in front, waving, with the rest of the family. But neither Hester nor Harriet looked back.

'We're going to be short handed in the shop!' Ellen observed. Maisie wiped a tear from her eye.

'I'll miss our Hester,' she said.

'You great soft 'app'orth!' her sister sniped. 'Come on Fran. You can help me clean out the cellar!'

Sweeping up the fallen petals, in the dank, dark room below stairs, she felt for all the world like Cinderella.

'What'll happen to *me*, Mam?' she asked at last.

'What do you mean?'

'When I'm grown up?'

'How should *I* know? Tut! I expect you'll leave school, and work in the shop for a bit, then you'll probably get married.'

'Oh. Who to?'

'Some nice young man.'

'There aren't any, Mam!'

'How do you know?' Frances stared at her mother. Ellen sighed, the pail hanging empty in her hands. 'You're wiser than's good for you, me lass,' she said sadly. Then she looked at her daughter, through the glow of the lamp. 'I don't know if I should encourage you really.' Frances watched and waited, as her mother struggled within, exploring the unfamiliar relationship of mother and daughter. 'But you're growing up now, and . . . and . . . I'd not want you to end up like me. I mean, look at's.' Frances looked. 'I'm a drudge. I work from morning till night and I keep my husband's bed warm. And what for? I get no fun, no thanks for what I do. I'm no better off than I was before I got married, in fact worse. At least then I had my dreams, like you.' Frances'd never thought of her mam having dreams.

'Why did you get married then?'

'I was expecting you, pet.' Ellen was frank. Frances' legs turned to jelly. It was one thing knowing about it, in her head, but quite another when her mother confessed it to her. For suddenly, and for the first time, Ellen had touched her daughter's heart, and her advice carried more weight, because of that. 'So, Fran, if you dream, dream about becoming something, pet. A teacher maybe. Something where you can earn a bit of money and keep your self respect, aye but keep yourself to yourself. Don't dream about men. Don't make my mistake. There now. I've said it. I daresay I shouldn't've. But I have. Come on. Fill the pail for me again, there's a love, or we'll not be finished before bedtime!'

So, Frances bore the guilt for her mother's unhappiness! If it hadn't been for her, she would never have married her father, never have stayed in the shop. The thought had never occurred to Frances. Yet, how could she be to blame? She hadn't asked to be born, had she? Family ties, pulling her this way and that, dragging her down. Well, when the day came, she would take her mother's advice. She would become something! Yes. After all, Hester had escaped. Why not her?

And why not Maisie? Almost three months had passed since her holiday at Rothbury. Memories of dappled sunlight and warm skin troubled her heart. Will had been right. The day *had* gone on forever. But now she was back at home, she wished it had not. The coin of her happiness had been turned. Better never to have known love than lose it. Why had he not spoken before she left? He only had to say the word. But words were not Will's strong point; nor Maisie's, come to that. And how were they to get together again? She did have some pride, and you can only have your teeth out once in your life! She had thought they had been of one mind, she and Will. Her thoughts had run on marriage. But what about him? Had she mistaken him? And if not, why didn't he, at least, get in touch with her again? At night, she dropped her dentures into the glass beside her bed, turned on her pillow and wept.

'Oh, Ma. Please, Ma. Tell me what to do.' But Jane's ghost was silent; it fluttered in Maisie's heart, cast shadows on the walls, and left with the dawn. A new day began, another day in Beattie's shop, working, morning till night, she, Ellen and Frances. There was no escape. And every now and then, letters, and postcards dropped through the letterbox, to tell them how green Hester was finding life on the other side.

Hester slept late on a feather bed, and woke to the ringing of Harriet's telephone. Yes, Harriet actually had a telephone. She slipped into her silk kimono, and padded across the softly carpeted hall to pick up the receiver.

'Bloomsbury 214,' she spoke in her poshest tones. 'Miss Beattie's residence.' Another suffragette wanting Harriet to speak at a meeting. She made a note and went into the tiny kitchen to make the tea. China tea, of course, not common or garden Indian. Harriet had nine different kinds of tea in her kitchen. Hester drank some, then took Harriet's in to her, sitting on her bed beside her, as her aunt yawned.

'What sort of a day is it?'

'Overcast.' Hester rose and went to the window.

'Don't bother to pull back the curtains, then. Let's stay cosy for a while.' Harriet watched her niece, from her pillows. 'Come back, dear.' She patted the bed beside her.

'The place is filthy. There's dust everywhere!' Hester shook out a fringed shawl, that was draped across the dressing table mirror, and the dust rose.

'So what? Come and talk to me.' Hester replaced the shawl, and came obediently to sit on the bed.

'There was a call from Mrs Nagler,' she said, in the tones of a good secretary. 'She wants you to speak in Birmingham on the 23rd.'

132

'Franchise?'

'Trade Unions.'

'Mabel Redfield would do better at that!' Harriet saw how Hester's brow cleared. She hated the meetings and the speeches. She hated the late nights, sipping wine or coffee, as women sprawled on sofas, discussing the vote, and had little to offer of a constructive nature, when it came to the subject of improving a woman's lot.

'You don't like the movement, do you?' Harriet challenged her. Hester shrugged.

'Not much.'

'Why?'

'It won't get anywhere, that's why!'

'Oh?'

'All them women sitting about gossiping!' Harriet sat up in bed, and put down her cup.

'You don't think women are up to it, is that it?' Hester shrugged again. Harriet smiled impatiently. 'You're going to have to learn to trust your fellow woman, dear.' Harriet put out her hand, and gently touched Hester's. 'You mustn't become a misanthrope. We shall have to teach you to trust.' Hester withdrew her hand. Harriet said nothing, but lay back, considering the situation. 'You've had a difficult life, dear. It's going to take time for you to achieve your personal liberation. But, I'll help you, all I can. You can be sure of that.' Hester had not expected gentleness. She had disciplined herself, she had worked, she had sweated blood to bring herself up to the required standard. And now she had reached it, instead of a whip, she was offered cake and candy. Her harsh and domineering aunt was as soft as jelly. This was not what Hester wanted. It did not satisfy her need for punishment. The hand reached out again. Hester looked down at it, soft and white. She let Harriet's fingers spread across her palm, but the nerves did not tingle in the skin, as they had when Joe had touched her. 'You have the hands of an artist, Hester,' Harriet told her. 'You shouldn't be washing dishes and dusting. I'll get a maid in to do that.'

'Yes, Aunt Harriet,' Hester agreed graciously. Then she withdrew her hand and flexed the fingers, covering her distaste with a smile. 'They're getting rather stiff. I think I'd better go and do a few scales.' Disappointed, Harriet let her go.

'Whatever you think best, dear.'

Meetings and late night discussion groups gave way to visits to the theatre and concert halls. Harriet and Hester went to Paris and Berlin. They saw light opera, 'Tom Jones'. They saw Mrs Campbell act, Annette Kellerman swim, and Marie Lloyd sing. They watched 'Mrs Warren's Profession' by Mr Shaw. They read the latest books, and saw the exhibitions. Gloating letters arrived back home in Shields, throughout the summer and the autumn, where the women thirsted for news of the good life. Frances began to keep a scrap book of all the postcards, mostly photographs of actresses Hester had seen. It wasn't fair, Hester seeing all the ballets, when Frances'd not been to *one*! How could she tell whether she was any good herself, if she never saw professional dancers on the stage! And Maisie wasn't much help any more. She never took her to shows now. What was wrong with her and Will? Frances had liked him. Sitting at the dining room window in early November, Frances watched the ladies and gentlemen arriving at 'The Queen's'. She never tired of watching. She was quite sure that, one day, she would be one of their number. She would be a famous dancer, feted throughout the world. She would travel to Paris, Rome, Berlin, Moscow, New York; she would dress in beautiful gowns and go to balls far far better than the ones over the road!

'There he is again!' Ellen was peering over Frances' shoulder, at the street below. A lone figure stood in the shadows at the side of the hall, staring mournfully up at the Beattie windows. It was Davey Lawson. Maisie came up behind and giggled.

'Fancy, our Fran! A beau at your age!' Embarrassed, Frances turned away from the window and stood, warming her hands at the fire. 'You should be so lucky!'

'Do you think we should ask him in, Maisie?' Ellen asked.

'Eeh, I don't know. He might be shy.'

'It might be just what he's waiting for an' all!' Ellen said. 'I mean, all this fairy tale about men making the running, is crackers! When it comes down to it, men're bone idle, and born cowards. They'd never do anything if we women didn't get them moving.' Maisie frowned.

'What do you mean, Ellen? They don't like it if we tell them what to do, do they? I mean, if I was to chase after some man, he'd think I was . . . you know.' She nudged Ellen, indicating Frances was all ears, and she dare not elaborate.

'The trick is to make them think *they* did it . . . that it was all their idea. It never is of course, but you've got to let them *think* it is. They're just overgrown kids really.'

'Oh. I see.' Deep in thought, Maisie went to stand beside Frances at the fire.

'Well, are we going to ask your admirer in, Frances, or not?' her mother demanded.

'No!' The tone was truculent.

'All right! All right! I only asked!'

'I don't want any admirers!'

'You'll change your tune!'

'No, I won't!'

'All this about you going on the stage! Look what happened when you were in that school play! I ask you! How could *you* ever go on the stage? Stage fright, that's what it was!'

'It was not! I fell over Cissy's tail!'

'Huh! She'll change her tune! Won't she, Maisie.'

'I expect so,' Maisie said, absently stirring the fire with the poker.

'Honestly! You're like a wet weekend! The pair of you! Especially you Maisie. One minute you're over the moon, the next down in the dumps! Anybody would think you were in love!' The poker clattered on the hearth. Maisie changed colour. 'Our Maisie!' Ellen grinned. 'I do believe I've hit the nail on the head!'

'Don't be so soft! Mind you . . . ' she went on, 'on the subject of needing cheering up I was thinking it might be a good idea if you and me went out again, Frances, like we used to.'

'Oh, Maisie!' Frances' eyes were shining. 'Do you think we could?'

'Why not?' Ellen watched jealously. She had opened her heart to her little girl, and here she was, rejecting her, in favour of Maisie. They were like a pair of conspirators and they were leaving her out.

It was just like it was before! Frances helped Maisie with the letter.

18, Victoria Terrace,
Fowler Street,
South Shields

Dear Will,

It is a long time since we were last in touch. You must think me awful! But things have been very busy at this end and what with one thing and another I have not had the time to put pen to paper. I am very well, and so is the rest of the family. Hope you can say the same. But Frances has been a little low of late. And I wondered if you could suggest something to help her out of the doldrums. I know you got very fond of her at one time. She is a good girl and deserves a bit of cheering up. It's her birthday soon too. We both miss our little trips out to the theatre and that. Well, that's all for now. Give my regards to your father.

Yours sincerely,
Maisie Beattie

They waited three days before the reply came.

'You're perky this mornin', Maisie!' Eddie remarked gloomily, as he reached out a hand from the depths of the bed and took his cup.

'There's a frost!' Maisie told him. 'Nice and sparkly outside!'

'What's *she* got to be so happy about?' Ellen asked after she'd gone. Eddie shook his head and yawned dismally.

'They've maybe invented a tooth powder that actually sticks and sent her a sample!'

Frances' birthday treat was a trip to Newcastle to see Henry Irving in Tennyson's play 'Beckett'; or at least, that's what it was in theory. In fact, they went to Balmbra's Music Hall with Will. Frances had heard of Henry Irving and longed to see him, but Will was for the music hall, and after all, the whole thing was *his* idea, wasn't it? He fairly bristled with pride at his own ingenuity.

'I was wondering how to get things back to normal, Maisie,' he said. 'I'm glad I thought of this.'

'Eeh, Will,' Maisie said admiringly. 'You've got gumption, I'll say that for you.' Will's chest bulged. He had a present for

Frances, a real silver charm bracelet. Thrilled, Frances let him put it on her wrist.

'Thank you, Uncle Will.' She smiled at him, gratefully. 'It's the nicest present I ever had.' Will flushed with pleasure, and the three of them had the night of their lives, laughing and singing. Maisie winked at Frances, and Frances winked at Maisie. Their little letter had worked a treat!

Christmas came, and Frances danced in another display at the miner's hall. She was singing this time, as well as dancing, quite the star of the show! But George was less than pleased, as she launched into 'Burlington Bertie', dressed in men's clothes! Rakishly, she tipped her hat to one side, and flourished her cane, as she stepped out in her dance routine. The pointed toes stuck out incongruously from beneath the sharp, creased trousers. But it was precisely this incongruity that pleased the audience. The feminine mocked the masculine, gently, so that even the rakes, watching her, could see themselves, and laugh. Davey Lawson thought her the most winsome, gorgeous girl, he had ever seen. He sidled up to George, after the show.

'Congratulations!' he said. George glared at him. Was the lad being funny with him? Squashed by a look, Davey retreated to his mother's side.

'Music Hall trash!' George raged on the way home. 'I shall have to have a word with Muriel's mother!' Frances and Maisie dared not look at one another, but Ellen sensed their mutual guilt, brooding jealously on their companionship.

'How's the boyfriend?' she asked at last. Maisie jumped, and went red.

'I don't know what you mean!' she blurted out. George looked at his daughter through narrowed eyes. Had Ellen hit the nail on the head?

'Davey Lawson is not my boyfriend, Mam!' Frances said quickly, to stop Maisie giving herself away. The clever little minx! Ellen thought.

'He's sweet on you, though!' Distracted, George laughed.

'So that's it! He was trying to butter me up! The sly little . . .' But George seemed pleased that his little grand-daughter could arouse such passion. 'So! You're going to be a little heart breaker, are you?'

'Huh!' Frances said.

'Doesn't his Mam run the sweet shop on Ocean Road?' Maisie asked, recovering herself. George nodded.

'They've been after our recipe for black toffee for many a long year.' He leaned forward in the cab, and whispered, 'Maybe, deep down, that's what Davey's really after!'

'Don't be silly, Granda!' Frances snorted. And George laughed till the tears ran down his face. Ellen sat back, watching, waiting. Their Maisie and Frances were up to something, and she was going to get to the bottom of it!

Christmas dragged. The shop stayed open till lunch time on Christmas Day, and they were all exhausted by the time the 'CLOSED' sign was turned on the door. Harriet had taken Hester to Biarritz for Christmas. It was *the* place to go; the King's favourite, and so everyone's favourite. They missed them over the Christmas dinner. Cold pork, cabbage and pickle graced the festive table. There had been no time to cook for themselves. Business came first. But it was Jane they all missed most. She had been the centre, the pivot of the household. She had made the place seem warm and cosy. Without her, there seemed no point to Christmas. George went out on Christmas night. Alice Minto, for all her rheumatics, kept a welcoming hearth, and George felt lonely in his widowhood. He had bought Alice a garnet necklace for her Christmas box, small token gifts for her children, but for his son, his own son, he had chosen a set of instruments for his draughtsman's trade. The instruments were silver plated, and presented in a leather case, with a plate, engraved, 'For James, from your everloving father, George Beattie.' Alice looked in silence on the gift, for some time. It was as near as George could get to publicly recognising his son, and she knew it had cost him. The evening wore on, as George put off his departure for home, and reached for the Christmas port.

Sitting by the fire in Fowler Street, the older members of his remaining family cracked nuts in the silence. Ellen was fidgeting.

'I don't like it,' she said at last. Maisie frowned.

'What?'

'Dad, going to *her*!'

'Try and stop him!'

138

'Let the old barsket have his fling if he likes, woman!' Eddie said loudly. Frances, playing with her revolving doll over by the window, looked up.

'Sh!' Ellen warned. Frances sighed and closed her ears. More secrets. Well, what did she care? She and Maisie had a secret of their own, hadn't they?

'What bothers me . . . ' Ellen whispered, as Frances turned back to her play, 'what bothers me is that son of his . . . ' Eddie frowned and looked at his wife, alarmed. Ellen nodded. 'Makes you think, doesn't it?'

'What makes you think?' Maisie asked.

'Nowt makes *you* think!' Ellen snapped; then she whispered again, 'I don't know about you lot but I'm not goin' to let Alice Minto's bastard get his hands on this place, if *I* can help it!' Eddie looked worried. 'After the work I've put in here, I want it all, when Dad's gone!'

'You'll not get it all, in any road!' Eddie snorted.

'Eh?'

'Nowt.' Ellen stared at her husband. Was he hiding something from her? Everybody else was, why not him? 'Look, Ellen, if it worries you, *I'll* have a word with the old barsket, eh?' Ellen said nothing, considering the possibility. 'I think he'll listen to me.'

'You're very sure of yourself all of a sudden!' his wife sneered.

'Eddie's been gettin' on well with Dad, Ellen. Haven't you noticed.' Yes, Ellen had. And that was another thing . . . The door opened suddenly, and George came in, slightly tipsy. Maisie and Ellen exchanged horrified looks. Their father never drank; wouldn't tolerate a drop in the house! Frances looked up from her play and smiled at him. His expression softened.

'Are you all right, my pet?' he asked. She nodded, and as she started winding up her toy again, her bracelet jangled on her wrist. 'We'll have to get your new charms fixed for you, eh!' he said jovially. 'Hand them over, Ellen. I'll have a go!'

'It needs a jeweller, man!' Ellen objected but fetched them all the same. Ellen had given Frances a lucky silver horseshoe. Maisie had found a silver cat.

'Take it off then!' George told his grand-daughter, and Frances removed the bracelet and gave it to him.

'It's a nice piece of work, mind.' He frowned, trying to remember through the haze of port. 'Who gave it to you, eh?'

'Uncle Will,' Frances said absently, as she finished winding up the doll. Maisie froze. Slowly the penny dropped in her father's fuddled brain. The musical toy began to play. Ellen threw back her head victoriously.

'I knew it!' she spat. 'Uncle Will indeed!'

'Shut up, Ellen!' Eddie said, and gripped his wife's wrist hard.

'Get your filthy hands off me!' she screamed at him.

'Don't you dare speak to me like that, wife!' Ellen blanched, and Frances thought she was going to die, as her granda turned on Auntie Maisie.

'Can anyone enlighten me as to the identity of "Uncle Will"?'

'Yes!' Ellen whipped her hand away and Eddie flung out of the room, banging the door behind him. 'Ask Maisie! Ask her where she takes Frances for their educational trips! Ask her, if he isn't her fancy man! My God, I've had my suspicions for a long time, but now I know!'

'Be quiet!' Ellen clenched her fists and watched, as her father approached Maisie.

'Go on. I'm waiting.' Maisie, pale and trembling told the truth, the whole truth and nothing but the truth. Flushed, and giddy from the unaccustomed alcohol, George reeled.

'A publican!' he roared. 'By God, I'll teach my girls not to be harlots, if it's the last thing I do.' His hand lashed Maisie's face. She fell back against the sofa. The musical doll faltered and stopped. There was a wet stain under Frances' chair, where she sat, watching and listening, paralysed by guilt and terror.

CHAPTER EIGHT

The moon was waning. Pale rays of light carpeted the marble floors and the scent of burning pine hung heavy on the air, as Harriet looked up at the stars. She was on the edge of the world. Would she fly into paradise, or fall into hell? The low, insinuating notes of Beethoven's Moonlight Sonata drifted from the room behind her. Hester's playing controlled her emotions, hesitating teasingly on the notes of the crescendo, dropping softly to the gentle conclusion, leaving Harriet desiring more. The gentle breeze stirred the leaves in the garden, and rippled the still waters of the lake beyond. Then, at last, the silk of Hester's skirts whispered behind her, and silently, she came to stand at Harriet's side. Why did she sigh? Was she bored with Italy? Or worse still, bored with Harriet?

'It's chilly for May, isn't it?' The girl was smiling up at her, eyes large and playful. Harriet smiled, relieved.

'There's still snow in the mountains.'

'Yes.' Hester stared across the dark lake. 'Shall we go and see it?'

'If you like, dear.'

Hester threaded her arm through hers, watching the flush of pleasure that crept over Harriet's face.

'You're so nice to me, Auntie.'

'As long as you're happy.' Harriet patted the hand, resting on her arm, and wondered at the amusement in her niece's face. Was she laughing at her? Her heart lurched for an instant. Jane had blackmailed Harriet into taking charge of her daughter, and Harriet had agreed, intending to indulge her resentment with a vindictive twist. Yes, she had meant to get her own back on Jane, seducing the wayward Hester, not protecting her. But the plan had backfired on herself. She had not seduced her. She had fallen in love. No one had ever loved Harriet May. Not George, not Jane, nor her brother Robert. They said she had dreamed up Robert's feeling for her. She had looked a fool, and her bitterness had turned her against all men. But the need for love remained. And when she went to London, her mistress, whose leanings were tolerated with amusement in her liberal set, made use of it, corrupting her for her own pleasure. Harriet had meant to do the same to Hester. But Hester was not Harriet. She was not soft and vulnerable. And, to her dismay, Harriet had found the position of power had been reversed. 'Are you playing with me, Hester?' Her voice was trembling, as she looked into the mocking eyes.

'If I am, at least I don't bore you, Aunt Harriet.' Hester laughed.

'Do *I* bore *you*?' Hester frowned, irritated.

'Only when you go on about it. You give me everything I want! Why shouldn't I be just as happy as a sandboy?'

'But you're not content.' Hester shrugged. 'Never at peace with yourself.' A dark shadow fell across Hester's face. 'I'm sorry. I didn't mean to upset you . . . If I don't make you happy, it's my fault.' In spite of herself, Hester was touched by her aunt's naked pathos, and found she could not strike her down. Suddenly, she was crying. Harriet took her in her arms and comforted her, rocking her, to and fro.

'I'm not nice, Harriet. I'm not. Really, I'm not. You should get rid of me, before I hurt you.'

'You only think you're not nice, because it's what everybody's been telling you all your life! Stop doubting yourself.' Hester looked back into Harriet's eyes. 'I don't doubt you. Why should you?'

'You trust me?'

'Yes.'

'Thank you.' Her aunt was a fool.

'No need to thank me, Hester. I love you.' Harriet felt her words falling like raindrops on the lake. Whirling pools of emotion rippled from the centre, spilling out into the silence that followed. Her heart stopped. She had jumped. But where was she? In heaven or hell? Her eyes reached out to Hester's, pleading, 'Say you love me. Save me from falling into hell'. And the girl stared back, feeling the power she had over the woman, excited by it. Her lips parted in a slow, sweet smile. She took Harriet's kiss; she accepted it like another treat, giving in to the sensation, allowing it to lead her where it would. And afterwards, lying together before the crackling fire, she savoured her conquest.

Maisie's glasses were all steamed up. They should warn you about that when they sold you the books, she thought, as she wiped the lenses with her apron. There was a knock at her bedroom door. She jumped, hiding the novel behind her back, as Frances came in.

'There's a postcard from Aunt Harriet and Hester. Look!' Maisie gazed on the rosy-topped mountain and the mirror lake.

'Eeh!' she said dreamily. 'Isn't it romantic? Just like me book!'

'What're you reading, Auntie?' Frances was trying to get at the book behind Maisie's back.

'Elinor Glyn,' she whispered. 'But don't tell your granda. I'm in enough trouble.' Frances grinned, grabbing the novel and opening it at the marked page. 'You're too young!' Maisie told her, hastily taking it from her.

'But I want to know about "love" and that, Auntie,' Frances explained innocently.

'Well, you won't find out about it in there!' Maisie retorted.

'What's love like?' Frances giggled.

'Get on with you!' Maisie slapped her hand. 'What does the card say?'

' "Idyllic surroundings, wonderful weather, charming companionship. Don't you envy us? Love, Harriet and Hester." Can I keep it?'

'No! It's addressed to me! Go on up now! It's bedtime!'

* * *

143

'I want to know about love and that.' Maisie shook her head, listening to the musical doll up in Frances' room. She didn't want to shatter the child's illusions. Not yet. Let her believe in her knights in shining armour for a while longer. Maisie yawned and lay back against the pillows, pulling her hair net tight behind her ears. Will. Dear Will. She missed him. She looked over to her teeth, soaking in the glass. He wasn't like the heroes in the novels. Thank God. If he had been he'd have expected her to be like the heroines. No! Will was too shy to be a hero! He needed looking after as much as she did. Was she daft to hanker after him in the face of her father? Harriet's postcard stood, propped up against the glass. Was this feeling for Will really love? She looked absently at the postcard. It wasn't what she'd expected. Yet, God had been kind to her. He had given her a taste of real passion. Real. Yes. That was it. Maisie wasn't wearing rose-tinted glasses. And if she wanted to see Will again, she was going to have to do something about it, because he wasn't going to come galloping out of the mist and sweep her off her feet! Her father stood between them like a mountain, just as real and twice as ugly! How was she going to tackle him when, at the moment, he wasn't even speaking to her!

Next morning, Maisie was reading the paper, over breakfast, out loud, as usual. ' "The wedding bells rang out all over Spain, and flowers showered down upon the royal pair. Then, suddenly, a dream turned into nightmare. The procession was making its way back from the church, when a bouquet, thrown at the bridal coach, exploded, shattering fragments into the air. The Prince and Princess of Wales were in the carriage immediately behind and watched with horror as the groom, King Alfonso, handed his bride, Princess Ena, out of the coach, her white dress spattered with the blood of a dying soldier." Eeh!' Maisie wiped her eyes with her apron and sniffed loudly. Then she raised her voice so that her father would hear. 'The path of true love never did run smooth.'

'Tell your aunt not to be such a sentimental fool!' Frances sighed and began repeating the speech.

'Tell the old barsket I heard!' Maisie snapped. George clenched his teeth.

'Tell your aunt, that if she doesn't show more respect, her

father will throw her out on the street, where she deserves to be!' Maisie went pale, and bit her lip, saying nothing, as George stormed out of the room. Then the flood gates burst.

'You asked for it, Maisie!' Ellen told her. But Frances, deeply sorry for her aunt, and feeling guilty for having given her away, threw her arms around her and comforted her.

'It'd serve him right if I walked out right now!' Maisie said bitterly. Frances stared at her aunt. There was a look of determination on her face. It filled her with a strange excitement. She leant in close, and whispered in her ear.

'Take me with you!'

It was five o'clock in the morning. Lurid swirls of light curled through the river, like spilled paint. Frances shivered. She was grey with lack of sleep.

'I hope we're doing the right thing!' Clutching her carpet bag, Maisie followed on, as Frances led her past the brigs, water sucking at their sides, slapping against the staithes, and on to the steamer.

'The tide's on the turn. They'll be going out with it!' Frances urged her aunt on, looking to left and right, looking behind; like shadows, they crept on board, hiding as a sailor came up on deck, ducking out of the way as the captain started giving his orders. It was a small ship, carrying coal. Maisie groaned as they opened the door to the hold and saw the blackness.

'Are you *sure* it's a good idea!' she said more loudly. But Frances shoved her from behind, and in they went, falling onto the hard lumps, sprawling as the ship rocked, lurching out of its berth. In the darkness, Frances grinned. They had done it! They'd got away unobserved, stowed on board a real ship! She wondered where it was going. New York! She might see Great Uncle Josh at last! Or perhaps they were bound for somewhere exotic like India, or the Cape.

'What possessed me to wear me best dress?' Maisie wailed.

'Sh! We'll have to lie low till we're well out of harbour, Auntie!' Maisie groaned, shifting uncomfortably on the coals.

'I can't breathe! The air's full of dust.' And then she started coughing. Frances reached for a hanky and stuffed it in Maisie's mouth. 'Mind me dentures!' Frances stifled a giggle, as feet ran over their heads, and voices called urgently. Smells; coal and dust, tar and sea, filled her nostrils. This was adventure; romance. This was escape. The engines chugged, and water churned. A new life awaited. She might change her name. Who should she be? The toast of New York, Miss Frances . . . Thingummy! Her grandma's brother had stowed away and made good in America. Why not them? A pilot had come on board to take them over the bar.

'Where're you bound?'

'Yarmouth first, then on to Fishguard with whatever we can pick up.'

'Yarmouth!' Maisie was delighted. 'That'll be nice!' But Frances' heart sank. Yarmouth wasn't very exotic. God was surely playing some sort of joke on her! Suddenly the little door opened, and sailor's head appeared.

'Blimey! Look what we've got here! A pair of flounder!' Black and dishevelled, the women emerged from the hold amidst the laughter of the crew.

'Never mind, hinnies, I'll take you back with me in the coble!' the pilot promised jovially.

At least he couldn't leather them in public. Cold with fear, they sat alongside George Beattie, as he drove them back to Fowler Street. Two scruffy lasses from the quay, they were ushered in the back way, through the kitchen, observed only by the children and the cats. Ellen and Eddie stared in disbelief, as they stood, heads hung low, before the master of the house.

'You have blackened the name of Beattie!' George roared. There was a snort from Frances, and the two culprits burst into uncontrollable fits of laughter, as George looked on, ready to burst with impotent rage. Tears of mirth washed the sooty cheeks. The wind taken from his sails, George could only sit in the rocking chair and wait.

'Yes, Dad,' Maisie said at last. 'We have blackened the name of Beattie.' Frances turned her face to the wall, howling with laughter, 'and I for one will do it again, unless you agree to allow me me bit of freedom.'

'Freedom?' George was aghast.

'Aha. Freedom. You made me promise not to marry Will. And I agreed. But I don't see why I should be stuck here till I rot, and never get out or anything. So, I am now going to lay down my terms!' Ellen and Eddie quailed, retiring to a safe distance, as Maisie continued under Frances' admiring glance. 'I will continue to work in this shop, all hours of the day and night as I do now, and I will not disgrace your name again, if you agree to let me go with Will to the music hall at least once a month, and let our Frances come as well,' she said as an afterthought.

'I draw the line at Frances!' the old barsket said darkly. Frances looked desperately at her aunt. But Maisie had pushed her father as far as he would go.

'I don't blame you, Frances,' he said to her. 'You were led on by your aunt.'

'I was not! It was my idea in the first place! I wanted to run away!' Choking on her tears, Frances fled to her room, followed by her helpless mother.

'If you're tired of Como, we could take a trip to the Alps.'

'Oh yes!'

'It'll be hard going!'

'Good.' Harriet sighed. She might have known it wouldn't last; that the restlessness would return to drive her loved one on, away from the lapping waters of the calm lakes. She would be sad to leave Como and the little villa they had called home. But Hester had gone on and on about the mountains and the snow so that, in the end, Harriet had given in. She watched Hester packing. Her feverish haste to be shot of the beloved place hurt Harriet. Banging the cupboard doors, wrenching open the drawers, Hester was stamping on Harriet's most cherished memories, and she could not bear it. Quietly, she left the bedroom, and went sadly to stand on the verandah looking up the shimmering lake. They had had such lovely times here, boating, picnics by the lakeside and ambling into the lower hills to pick spring flowers. They had been happy. But Hester didn't want happiness. She was young. She had not suffered as Harriet had . . . not yet. She could afford to trample on her happiness, counting it as nothing. And what did Hester want? Harriet shook her head. Whatever it was, she couldn't give it to her. She could only go along with her as far as she was able, hanging on as long as she could. Yes. Whatever it cost, she would go with Hester to the mountains. So, raising her eyes from the still lake, Harriet looked up cautiously at the icy peaks.

But hills look much easier from the safe distance of a hotel lounge, and Hester grew impatient. They had come all this way, and all Harriet would do was sit, sniffling, surrounded by handkerchiefs, and stinking of eucalyptus! When it came down to it, she was just like any other middle-aged woman, mutton dressed as lamb!

'It's all right when you're sitting pretty in a nice warm room! Oh yes! Then you'll go on and on about the new woman, pushing ever onwards to new heights of achievement! But when it comes to getting off your backside and climbing a tiny little hill . . . !'

'I was speaking metaphorically, Hester! And that hill is anything but little!'

'Well, I am not going to sit in Gmunden drinking chocolate and eating cream cakes till *I'm* the size of a house!' Harriet pulled her shawl closely round her spreading form, as though to hide it. 'I shall go alone.' Hester threw back her head. 'And when I come back, I shall leave you here and go my own way!'

'And where do you propose *to* go? You've got no money! You're completely dependent on me!' Hester's eyes burned with fury. Harriet bit her lip. She shouldn't have said that. She was making matters worse. She sighed. 'I'm sorry,' she said. 'That wasn't fair. I'll come with you. We'll go climbing together. I promise.' Hester kissed her aunt enthusiastically.

'Oh thank you! I do love you, Harriet May!' Harriet smiled bleakly.

From Gmunden they drove to Bad Ischl, where they picked up their guides, and started off on the long trek up the Schön. It stood more than two thousand feet above sea level, and the soft grassy slopes soon gave way to harsher, steeper climbs. Down below Harriet could hear the tinkling bells of the cows. Above her was mist and water, ice and snow. Hester set a hard pace. At first, the guides laughed at her, muttering something in German about 'mad Englishwomen'. But Harriet's feet blistered in the new walking shoes, and she had to stop to catch her breath time and again while Hester stood, staring down at her, impatiently, before driving them on again. And then, the guides stopped smiling. They didn't like this slip of a girl with a will like iron who dominated them and the woman. They took Harriet's arm and helped her, shouting ahead that Hester should slow the pace.

They would tire, and have an accident, they said. But Hester only laughed, and burned on up the mountain.

'*Achtung! Dies ist nicht der Weg*!' The guides warned her not to leave the recognised path, but Hester wouldn't heed them. So, they waited in the mist, refusing to go on, as Harriet struggled after her, alone. And she began to hate the mountains. Hard and cold, they were without mercy, making no allowances for human weakness. Why did Hester have to climb, and subdue them? Harriet stopped, heart pounding, under an overhang, knowing her defeat. She turned her face into the rock, and cried. Hester would surely give her up now. Then a voice came from above. Harriet looked up. Through the swirling mist she saw Hester, a dark shape, arms outstretched, head thrown back defiantly.

'Hester! Come back! You'll kill yourself!' Distantly, the voice answered her.

'There is no God!' But the mountain caught the blasphemy up in swirling snow clouds, to send it falling softly back to earth, dispersed, in tiny flakes. So that's what it had all been about! To climb the highest peaks, and challenge the very existence of God! The poor, pathetic child! Sheltering under the rock, Harriet was overcome by compassion. Had she brought her niece to this, by selfishly forcing her own needs on her, without thought of hers? Hurling her cries at the invisible sky, Hester stumbled down through the mists, to fall, defeated and sobbing, into Harriet's welcoming arms.

George stared balefully through the window at the young man mooning about, outside.

' "Lawson's" Huh! They're no gentlemen! They'll rue the day they started up in competition with us! Why, they know nowt about catering! Sweet sellers! That's all they are!'

'Aye,' Maisie said, nodding slowly. 'But they *have* got the telephone, and that makes all the difference if you want to get an order in quick! We can't stand on our laurels.'

'Maisie's right, Dad. It'd be nice if we got the telephone in!'

'Voices going down wires! It's the work of the devil, mark my words!' And with that, George stomped up to his office. Ellen shook her head.

'As if telephones could be the work of anybody but good Shields lads. He must be going ga-ga!'

'It's not the devil's puttin' him off telephones. It's Will! He blames the whole idea on him!'

'Tut! He's going ga-ga,' Ellen repeated, staring through the window. Davey Lawson's vigil had been rewarded. Frances was coming home from her dancing class, and he galloped across the road to her, barring her way to the shop.

'Oh hallo, Davey,' she said nonchalantly.

'Hallo, Frances. I was wondering if you'd let me walk you home from your classes in the dark winter evenings.'

'Why?'

'Em . . . em . . .' Davey flushed, 'Em . . .'

Frances threw her bag over her shoulder and rocked on her heels, laughing up at him.

'You're sweet on me, Davey Lawson, aren't you?' The flush deepened. Davey nodded, agony leaving him bereft of speech. 'Well, you can if you like.'

'Oh thanks!' Davey jumped with joy. 'And can I see you on Saturday as well?'

'Na! I'm goin' out on Saturday . . . to the music hall!' She turned contemptuously and left him standing, in the street.

South Shields Empire Palace of Varieties had everything. And this week, the world famous escapologist Houdini was going to free himself from his water torture cell before their very eyes! He was top of the bill, and would come on last, so they sat back and enjoyed the performing dogs, the trapeze artist, and joined in singing, 'I do like to be beside the seaside', with Mark Sheridan. And then, the slapstick comic came on. He was called Jack Scott. He did an act with a girl. They were supposed to be decorating a room. The stuff got everywhere. He was very young, but he was clever and had them all in stitches in the pit.

'He'll go far!' Will foretold as they applauded. He looked nice. Frances liked the way he'd grinned cheekily at the audience. He had gall! She admired him for that. And then, Houdini came on and, at last, the show was over. Reluctant to part with her Will, Maisie suggested they all went round the corner for a cup of tea, before he started out on the long journey home.

It was a hot, steamy café, and it took them ages to get served, but they didn't mind, because all the stars popped in between the shows, and they watched eagerly, as they grabbed a sandwich and a cup of tea.

'Mind if I sit beside you?' It was him! Jack what's-his-name!

'Be our guest!' Will said expansively. 'We've just seen your act. Mind, it's smashing, man!' Jack Scott snorted with derision.

'It's nothing! Nothing like it should be! It's her! Maria. My assistant. Working with her's like working with a cart horse! A pregnant cart horse!' Frances blushed. 'Oh. Sorry. I forgot there were ladies present.' The cheeky grin followed the apology and Maisie and Frances laughed. He could have got away with murder.

'Our Frances here's a dancer, you know!' Maisie told him.

'Oh yes?' Jack showed a polite interest. 'What sort? Ballet?'

'Yes, and song and dance, and acrobatics too. I'm not as good at that as my friend Muriel, mind. She's double-jointed.'

'How old are you?'

'Not old enough!' Will put in, touching him on the arm. Jack sat back, smiling casually.

'Oh well. Next time I'm on the bill, pop in and see me. We'll see what we can do!'

And Frances dreamed herself out of Fowler Street. The smell of grease paint, the steamy café, the free and easy air of Jack Scott and his like, filled her being. She let Davey escort her to and from her class, like a faithful spaniel. But her mother misinterpreted her dreamy expression.

'She could do worse,' Ellen whispered to Maisie, watching the growing girl as she went upstairs to do her homework. 'Lawson's is doing well!'

'Aye well,' Maisie said bitterly. 'They're not living in the dark ages, are they? Why don't you get your Eddie to have a word with the old barsket about getting a telephone and a proper delivery van, eh?'

'Him? He doesn't care about this place! Not any more.' Ellen sighed. 'I don't know what to make of him. He doesn't seem to care about anything really. Do you know, he voted labour in the last election?'

'Eeh! Ellen!'

'I know. It's the beginnin' of the end, Maisie.'

'Tut tut! Where is he now?'

'In the throne room, reading the paper as usual.' Maisie shook her head. As far as she was concerned, newspapers in the throne room were for one thing, and that wasn't reading.

'Aye,' Ellen watched young Davey through the window, as he walked reluctantly away. 'She could do worse.' Suddenly, on impulse, Ellen ran to the shop door, and opened it, shouting down the street,

'Davey! Davey Lawson!' He turned, surprised. 'Why don't you come for your tea, pet?' She was smiling. Davey hesitated. He didn't want to push his luck. 'Sunday. You could come for your tea after Sunday School. You still go to the chapel, don't you?' Davey nodded, confidence growing.

'Thanks very much, Mrs Lidell,' he said. 'I'd consider it an honour!' Ellen came back inside.

'What are *you* playing at, Ellen?' Maisie was grinning.

'His voice is breaking, Maisie.'

'I noticed! Aye, our Ellen. She could do a lot worse!'

But Frances' mind was not running on marriage. As Eddie sat in state, perusing the labour news, Frances was upstairs reading a novel, between brown covers. It was by H.G. Wells, it was called 'Ann Veronica' and it had been left behind by her Aunt Harriet on her last visit. The old barsket had thrown it in the bin, and called it filth, hurling abuse at 'the new woman', whomsoever she might be! But Frances had rescued the book and read it avidly. She was only too aware of her family's determination to get her married, and settled with a husband, and the inevitable progeny in the shop. She was fifteen now. She would be leaving school this summer. Time was short. She didn't want to be a teacher or a typist, like Ann Veronica. But she did want her independence. Frances' heart fluttered. There was no one she could confide in. Even Muriel's Mam drew the line at going on the stage. Suddenly she had an idea. Her eyes lit up. Perhaps Davey would help her!

There was bedlam in the house. Eddie rushed in from the throne room yelling,

'The land tax bill's been rejected by the Lords! Parliament's been dissolved! There's going to be another election!'

'Eeh!' Maisie and Ellen looked up at the office door. It opened slowly. George's head peered out.

'It's the beginning of the end,' he said. 'It'll be strikes next, and then . . . revolution!' Shaking his head, he turned to see Frances standing at the bottom of the stair. 'Harriet May and her "new women" are to blame!' he told her, before disappearing into his office again. Frances smiled to herself, and looked over the railing into the shop. Her mother, head on one side, spoke archly.

'Oh hallo, pet,' she said. 'I thought you'd like to know I've invited your young man to tea on Sunday.'

'What do you mean, *my* young man!' Frances was puce with rage.

'Davey Lawson, of course. I *thought* you'd be pleased.' Then Ellen beat a hasty retreat into the kitchen, leaving Maisie, starry-eyed, looking up at her. Even Maisie put her under pressure. Oh, why didn't she and Will just elope and be done with it! Frances stormed back up to her room. Her family were the giddy limit!

Muriel obligingly came for tea on Sunday too, at Frances' invitation. Ellen was put out, and the ritual was passed in stilted conversation, well salted by requests to pass the sugar. When, at last, the agony was over, Davey rose, relieved, and said, 'Well thank you very much for a wonderful afternoon, Mrs Lidell.'

'Oh it's not over yet, pet!' Ellen told him.

'Isn't it?' Davey's face betrayed his disappointment.

'I thought you might take these two young ladies out for a stroll. Get away from us old folks!'

'But it's thick snow outside, Mam!' Frances objected.

'Good idea, Ellen!' Maisie backed her sister. 'They could play snowballs.' Muriel and Frances exchanged disgusted glances. Honestly, you'd think they were still kids!

Embarrassed at having his courting done for him by the mother, and knowing he wasn't wanted by the daughter, Davey made his excuses as soon as they were outside. But Frances hung onto his arm.

'I want to talk to you.' Muriel raised her eyebrows, and muttered something about being a gooseberry. 'Don't be daft, Muriel!' Frances told her. 'It's not love talk, or anything like that. It's just something private I want to discuss with Davey.'

153

'Huh!' Muriel stood, hands on hips, a hurt expression on her face. 'I see! "Private!" I thought we were supposed to be friends!' Then she stalked off home, leaving Frances dejected and angry.

'She's got a point, Frances.'

'Muriel's not my only friend,' Frances explained gently. 'You're my friend too, aren't you?'

'I give up,' he said. 'I'll never understand women!'

'You give up rather easily, don't you?'

'You're just teasing me, Frances Lidell and I wish you'd stop it.'

'I'm sorry.' Suddenly, Frances felt rather ashamed of herself. Now she'd upset both of them. She took Davey by the arm and gently pulled him away from the shop. 'Come on. Let's go to the park,' she said. His eyes lit up. Willingly, he allowed himself to be led on.

Some children had made a huge snowball by rolling it down the hill. It stood in their path, frozen solid to the spot. Davey guided her round, and into the bushes.

'My feet are getting wet!' Frances complained, stopping to empty some snow from the top of her boot. Davey held her arm, steadying her, and as she stood, recovering her balance, he drew her in to him, folding her inside his overcoat. Frances froze. His body was warm. She could feel his heart beating, the blood pumping, faster and faster with desire for her. Awkwardly he lowered his face and nuzzled her cheek, nudging her chin up so that he could reach her lips with his mouth. She couldn't think. His hand reached round the back of her head and held her firmly. She liked it. She frowned, puzzled. Her lips opened to question what was happening, and she found her mouth covered by his. She wriggled, but he held on tighter still. He was strong. She had thought of him as a boy, as though she had grown up and he had somehow stayed still. But he hadn't. And she liked what he was doing to her. It was something she had not reckoned with. At last, he finished kissing her, and pulled away, looking down on her, smiling.

'Davey Lawson!' she scolded him.

'Now,' he said. 'What was it you wanted to discuss with me?' Frances' mouth opened and closed. She looked puzzled. She must pull herself together. Ann Veronica wouldn't get herself into a flap all because a boy had kissed her!

154

'Well, Davey,' she began. Davey waited patiently, his hand stroking the back of her neck. It sent shivers through her, making it impossible to think. 'Well . . . ' She concentrated hard, 'You know I leave school this summer.' He nodded. 'They'll all expect me to work in the shop.'

'Yes. I suppose they will.'

'And I don't want to!'

'Oh?'

'I'd like to get away, Davey. I'd like to leave home.'

'You will, one day.'

'Yes, but I mean now! I'm stifled in Fowler Street. I want to be free! I want to be myself! Do you know, I even want to change my name!' Delighted, Davey hardly knew where to put himself.

'Your folk would never let you get wed yet! You're too young!'

'I don't mean that!' Davey's expression changed. 'I mean, I want a stage name! I want to go on the stage!' He was the colour of putty. 'I could do it! I've come on a lot with my dancing, haven't I?' Davey nodded. It was true. He'd seen her. She'd be the hit of any show. He cleared his throat. It wasn't so bad really. Just something she needed to get out of her system. He could wait.

'What does your granda say?'

'He doesn't know! You wouldn't dare tell him, would you?' Davey frowned. This was difficult. What was she asking of him? 'I've been writing to a man in the theatre. His name's Jack Scott. He's a comedian. He says he'll get me an audition for Fred Karno's troupe! But I'd have to go to London for that, and I've not got any money.' She looked at him hopefully.

'Neither have I. And even if I had, I wouldn't lend it to you to do something behind your folks' back!'

'You old stick in the mud!' Frances snapped.

'I'll have you know, Frances Lidell, that I have been brought up a gentleman.'

'Huh!'

'Now I know that coming from your family, you might not be able to appreciate the qualities of a gentleman . . . '

'What do you mean?' Now it was Frances' turn to be insulted.

'But, my intentions towards you are honourable. I am going to marry you, Frances, just as soon as you're old enough. And I'd as soon do it with your grandfather's blessing as without! Now, if

155

you want to get this dancing business out of your system, well and good. Get on with it. But don't expect me to assist you.' Frances gaped at him in astonishment. 'I shall be waiting for you.' He turned his back and walked straight into a bush.

'You pompous twerp!' Frances shoved him away. He fell to the ground, slithering in the snow. 'Some knight in shining armour you are, I must say!'

Well, she would go it alone! She'd show the lot of them! Pacing to and fro in her room, Frances worked off her anger. She was fifteen; almost a woman! Like a butterfly emerging from the chrysalis, she was ready to spread her colourful wings and fly! Yet, there they were, all of them, her family, Muriel, Muriel's Mam and Davey Lawson, all waiting, nets in their hands, ready to trap her, impale her, and put her on display! You'd think they owned her! Had she no rights at all when it came to her own future? If only Aunt Harriet was here. At least she'd support her! She believed in the independent woman!

Or did she? Hester was beginning to wonder.

'I look after you, don't I? I give you everything you want!' Hester was marching up and down the room in a temper.

'You go on and on about how women should be independent, and yet you keep me on a leash! I have to ask you for everything!'

'You get ample pocket money!'

'Pocket money! Hah!'

'All right, then!' Harriet's patience finally broke. 'Get yourself a job!' Hester paled visibly. Within a matter of seconds, she had shrunk. 'What sort of a job could I get?' she asked quietly. 'I can't do anything.' Her eyes pleaded with Harriet. Harriet turned away. How could she give Hester what she wanted? How could she bestow an income on her? She would lose the only real hold over her she had left!

CHAPTER NINE

'Read the following passage from "Theseus and the Minotaur" then answer the questions at the end.' Homework, at her age! Muriel had left school already and was helping her Mam at the dancing class, while Frances stayed on, paid for by her granda. He was so old-fashioned! I mean, who cared about ancient myths, when their feet itched to dance? Outside, in the street, a bell clanged. The electric tram was wheezing and rattling its way up the hill. Progress! No wonder Shields had a new mayor! If her granda'd had his way the town would be in the dark ages and they'd still be rubbing sticks together to make fire! What did Frances want with education? She was going on the stage! And she should get on with it now, while she was still young! Folded neatly, between the pages of her book, was a letter. She opened it out and read it for the umpteenth time;

Empire Theatre,
Sauchiehall Street,
Glasgow
March 31st 1910

Dear Miss Lidell,
    Thanks for writing to me. I shall be glad to see your

dragon fly dance when I'm next in the north-east. Perhaps early May, when I shall be at the Tivoli. Do contact me, nearer the time. Good luck with your budding career.

Yours truly,
Jack Scott Esquire

But what if he didn't like her dancing when he finally saw it? This house sapped her confidence, drained her spirits. She looked round her dingy attic room. She was sick of shadows. She wanted the bright lights! She wanted life! The door banged downstairs. The old barsket was home. What did *he* know about 'life'?!

George had just returned from Alice Minto's, and was cock-a-hoop. He had popped the question and been refused, on account of Alice's rheumatics. His son James was well settled now as a draughtsman, with George's help and he'd seen Alice was provided for, so he had nothing to reproach himself with any more. Honour had been satisfied. He stroked the cat, and didn't swear when she bit him, but laughed, and went up to his office like a man reprieved from the death sentence. He had never felt so free. Even his defeat at the last election had been a godsend. He had given over reading minutes of the sanitary committee, and returned to his beloved poetry. He fondly handled the old, yellowing pages, rare copies of Blake, which had come into his hands through the literary circle to which he belonged in his youth. He took in a deep breath, his chest expanding fit to burst his braces, then let forth, singing loudly,

And did those feet in ancient time
Walk upon England's mountains green?
And was the holy Lamb of God
On England's pleasant pastures seen?
And did the Countenance Divine
Shine forth upon our clouded hills?
And was Jerusalem builded here
Among these dark Satanic Mills?

Frances looked up from her book. What on earth had got into the old barsket? She covered her ears and read on; 'Under the palace was a huge dark labyrinth, and, in it, dwelt a terrible monster . . . ' She'd had a dream about a monster once. It was attached to a horse by a thread, a thread so fine you couldn't see it . . . Like family ties! Suddenly, clear as George's voice, singing below, Frances saw that she was the horse in her dream . . . the white horse that was being eaten . . .

> Bring me my bow of burning gold:
> Bring me my arrows of desire:
> Bring me my spear: O clouds unfold!
> Bring me my Chariot of fire.

But who, or what, was the monster? And what did it mean?

Her grandma's statue of the boy with the elephant's head cast an angry shadow on the walls. His anger was the shadow. But why was he angry? What was the dark secret haunting them all? What kind of family tie would create a monster great enough to anger God? Had her mother told her the truth about Robert, and why he was sent away? Her grandma had said not, but hadn't told her version. Perhaps what her Mam said, was right, after all. Perhaps Robert was sent away for stealing and Grandma only denied it to protect his memory . . . Or perhaps . . .

> I will not cease from Mental Fight,
> Nor shall my Sword sleep in my hand
> Till we have built Jerusalem
> In England's green and pleasant Land.

She looked at the wooden statue. Only the innocent could propitiate an angry God. Frances was innocent. You'll be the saving of this family, her granda had said that. So, what sacrifice did she have to make? Or was *she* the sacrifice? Frances was the white horse! Saint George rode on a white horse, to do battle against the dragon. But where was her Saint George? Just a fairy tale. That's all. 'Not a man in Shields'd answer that description.' Her granda'd said so. Then what was the point of staying in Shields, just to be eaten? No! She would cut off her family ties! She would run away. She would change her name. She would be free! She refused to accept the burden of her inheritance. Did not

159

even want to be reminded of it! Resentment gave her courage. Rubbing her hands, she went towards the statue and tried to lift it. It was too heavy for her. She would have to ask her Dad to take it down to the cellar.

'I can't find my way out!' Hester called through the hedge. 'Please can you tell me the way?'

'I'm sorry. I'm lost too!' the man replied. 'But don't go down there. It's a dead end. I've tried it.'

'Oh dear!' Hester sighed. 'I promised to meet my Aunt Harriet at the tea rooms at four. What am I going to do?'

'There's supposed to be a guide!' The man pointed over the hedges to a raised platform with a chair on top. 'You can see the whole maze from there. I wonder where he's gone!'

'For his tea, probably!' They laughed.

'What on earth possessed us to try Hampton Court Maze?' he asked. Hester shook her head. 'Look, why don't we find our way to each other, at least. We could join forces, then. Two heads are better than one!'

'All right.' They walked for ten minutes, coming and going, now near now far, guided by one another's voices. Finally they found each other, at the very centre of the maze. Two trees grew there, a seat between them. The young man grinned.

'Let's have a rest, what do you say?' Hester smiled, and walked towards the seat. He was a good-looking young man, of open aspect, fair, square built, and affable. She liked him at once. It was worth putting on an act for him. 'Let me introduce myself,' he said, holding out his hand. 'My name's Fairbairn. Tom Fairbairn. I'm a teacher, just now, but planning to go on to better things!' Hester smiled approvingly. His grip was firm. She liked it. 'Now! It's your turn. Tell away!' Soon, she was chatting away, all about her unhappy childhood, her grandma who, it was thought, had committed suicide, her enslavement by her Aunt Harriet. Tom's face became very serious. He shook his head, pity pouring from his eyes, brown, like deep pools. He was warm and loving. She stammered, convincingly.

'I'm sorry. It's selfish of me going on about myself.' Then she looked earnestly back at him. 'You know, you're a crafty young man. Actually, you've hardly told me anything at all about *you*!' Then she laughed, and his eyes lit up, pleased at her humour.

She was changeable as the weather. Like several different people rolled into one, her face transformed according to her varying moods. He would never tire of looking at her. 'You said you were planning to go on "to better things"! What better things? I'm dying to know.' His face fell. He thought she would be disappointed. He would have liked to keep up the pretence of the gay young man about town.

'All right,' he sighed. 'If you must know, I'm planning to become a missionary.' Hester froze, amazed. A different act was required of her, an act which suited her to perfection.

'That's beautiful!' she said. 'Have you been accepted?' she asked. Tom, suddenly shy, looked at his boots.

'They haven't turned me down.'

'Then there's hope?' He nodded bashfully. 'Where do you want to go?'

'China.' Hester gasped.

'But you'd have to learn the language!'

'I'm teaching myself. Of course, if they do accept me, eventually, I'll be able to go to the proper classes.'

'Why won't they accept you *now*?' Tom made patterns in the gravel with the side of his boots.

'I'm not married.' There was a silence. He looked up shyly. She was staring at him, with dark serious eyes.

Harriet was getting annoyed. It was too bad. First of all she'd waited for Hester, in the tea rooms, for more than an hour. Then she'd gone searching for her through the gardens, those awful formal gardens. They reminded her of 'Alice in Wonderland' so much, she'd had to stop herself asking the gardeners to paint the roses red! It was unreal, like a stage set, filled with the ghosts of the unhappy wives of Henry VIII. It gave her the shivers! The horrible place was nothing but bad luck! And then she'd seen them, arm in arm, like lovers, coming out of the maze. Her heart sank like a stone. Her legs shook. Who was he? There was no mistaking the sudden bloom on Hester's cheek. Her friend had found a new interest.

Harriet was filled with foreboding. Hester hadn't been the same since the day on the mountain. She had shaken off all Harriet's attempts to help her, laughed when Harriet said she understood.

Perhaps she was right. Perhaps Harriet didn't understand. This new, light, playful Hester was beyond her. But was she real? She was like an actress playing a part, and playing it very well. The return to England had felt like the beginning of the end. There was nowhere else to go. And now Hester played with her aunt, like a cat with a mouse. She flaunted Tom Fairbairn before her. He came to call again and again. Was she encouraging him on purpose, just to tease? Or did she mean business? Harriet's fear grew to fever pitch.

'You can't trust men! Englishmen have always treated their wives badly! Look at Henry VIII! Look at King Edward! He had countless women! Don't be a fool, Hester! Better drop him before he hurts you.'

'You're jealous!'

'I'm not!'

'I need a husband! How can *I* be independent? I've got no income!'

'Not that old nut!' Harriet groaned, holding her hand to her head.

'I'm not married to *you*, Harriet May. And if you want me to stay with you, as your equal, then you're going to have to give me my independence.' Harriet sighed. She felt tired, very tired.

'Promise me, if I give you what you ask, you won't leave me for Tom Fairbairn?' Hester laughed.

'That's a risk you'll have to take.' Harriet had been driven into a corner. She had no choice but to give way. Her lips were dry. The words stuck to her mouth and Hester enjoyed her discomfort.

'Most of the money's tied up. I can't get at it. All I see is the interest. There's only one investment I *can* give you.' She hesitated. Hester looked at her with curiosity. It was something Harriet was loath to part with, that was obvious. Harriet cleared her throat before she spoke again. 'It may surprise you to know, Hester, that some time ago, I bought fifty per cent of your father's business, the shop in Fowler Street.' Hester gaped. This was something she had not expected. 'It's all I have to offer you.'

'Fifty per cent of the shop? That's rich!' Hester roared with laughter. 'It'll do, Harriet! It'll do!' Harriet's heart missed a beat.

'I didn't mean I'd give you the whole of it . . . ' Hester's eyes hardened.

'Nothing less will do. After all, I don't suppose it'll provide me with much of an income.'

'Not as such. No. It's just a nest egg, that's all. Something laid up for the future.'

'Then you won't really miss it, Harriet, will you?'

'You'll stay with me?'

'For the time being.' Hester smiled playfully, but her eyes were sharp as tempered steel.

George was congratulating himself on having safeguarded his business.

'Come up to the office, Eddie!' He winked, and his son-in-law followed him upstairs, watched by Ellen and Maisie in the shop below. George clapped Eddie on the back, and brought him further into the room. He lowered his voice. 'She turned me down!' he hissed jubilantly. Eddie frowned. What on earth was the old barsket talking about? Then the penny dropped. His face expressed first horror, and then relief.

'You mean you asked Alice Minto to marry you?'

'I had to! I'm a man of honour!' Eddie raised his eyebrows and sighed. 'Don't you see, it really lets us off the hook! She's got no come back on the business! No claim! I asked her. She refused. Frances' inheritance is safe!'

'You had me worried there for a minute,' Eddie said, laughing. George grinned like a schoolboy, his voice rising.

'Harriet May's money's tided us over the worst. We're all set for fair weather now.'

'Do you not think we might be well advised to modernise, though?' George's expression was stony.

'By modernise, you mean drop our standards! Beattie's has a reputation in this town, Eddie, and I will not stand by and see that reputation sullied!'

'Whatever you want, George. Anyway, congratulations! If that's the right thing to say, like!'

'Oh it is! It is! Women! I don't know! I've had three wives, and a mistress, and, if you ask me, Eddie, if it wasn't for the children, we'd be better off without them!' Eddie nodded.

'Aye. You're right there, George! I wish I could get rid of

mine, as easy as you got rid of yours!' The men laughed up-roariously at their joke. Downstairs, two women stood, staring up at the open door of the office. Lazy, careless Eddie! Ellen's face was white. Maisie shook her head. Who'd be a wife?!

George's grand-daughter was performing tonight, for the last time, in public. He could indulge Frances, just once more. Yes, he was proud of her. He had no regrets about his natural son, when he looked at her, for she had grown into a beautiful, engaging young woman. One of the 'Daughters of Albion', as Blake called them. Daughters of England. Yes. Her kind, they held the key to the future, not these suffragettes! But good women; women like Frances! He'd like to see her married and settled in the shop with children of her own. His legitimate line. It was what he'd been working for all this time.

'Eeh! Tut! What does she look like?' Davey thought Frances looked rather nice, as a matter of fact, but dared not say so to his Mam! The back of his neck was getting hot and prickly, as Frances leapt and twisted joyously about the stage. 'I mean, it's not as if she was a child any more! Tut! It's a disgrace! Showing everything she's got!' Davey looked round the hall. There were no leering miners, only respectful workmen, watching a young lass showing her skill. Relieved, he turned back to enjoy the performance, and missed the young man, cigarette in mouth, who crept in at the back. Frances was good, and she knew it. At the end, she smiled victoriously and curtsied graciously to tumultuous applause. The latecomer, standing at the back, clapped lazily with the rest. 'Mind! She doesn't half fancy herself,' Davey's Mam said. Was she jealous? Was she afraid of losing him? 'Your son's your son till he gets him a wife.' Never mind! Let his Mam look askance, as she sat, hands clasped primly in her lap. He wasn't going to be a 'mother's boy'! Frances' words still rang in his ears. 'Pompous twerp'. But he wasn't really; not inside. It was the way his Mam had brought him up, with all that 'stiff upper lip' stuff! She had him in starched collars, and his trousers had creases you could cut bread with. It made him feel like a wooden soldier! He was growing up, nearly a man! He had feelings! Blood in his veins! He was going to marry Frances Lidell whatever his Mam thought. But he wasn't daft; wasn't born yesterday! He would play his cards right, play his mother's game as long as he need, and then . . .

Rattling along in the tram, Jack Scott had a glint in his eye, as he inhaled the smoke of his cigarette. She was a shapely lass, pretty too. The footwork was all right. But it was something else attracted him. It was the daring in her. Yes, she was a lass who would rise to the occasion. Obstinate, no doubt. But he liked that too. She'd gone on and on at him, writing letters, coming to see him with that aunt and uncle of hers, whenever he appeared in a Tyneside theatre, going on about auditions. He was working on a new act. He'd gone through six girls in the last eighteen months! They were all useless. What was there to lose? His mind was made up. He was going to offer Frances Lidell the job!

Hester smiled on her lovers, playing them off one against the other. But it was Harriet May who suffered most. For Tom didn't really take Hester's affair with her seriously, and often came to the flat, treating Harriet in loco parentis. She was someone to whom he had to be polite, and persuade of his good prospects. It galled Harriet to be treated in this way, and Hester gloated, relishing her discomfort. At last she was paying Harriet back for the torture she had inflicted. For Harriet had, unwittingly, teased Hester cruelly. She had not allowed her to suppress her sexuality, as she had wanted, but had roused it, and then, failed to satisfy. For, as Hester had made clear, in the beginning, she liked men. And when Tom Fairbairn came on the scene, she saw him at once as her escape and her tool of revenge.

At night, while Hester slept, Harriet lay awake, weeping bitter tears. If only she hadn't given Hester the money! She had given up everything for her. Her friends had deserted her, dismayed at her foolishness over 'that little bitch'. And the 'cause' had left her behind. She had broken no windows, never been arrested, not been force fed. A nucleus of women had formed themselves at the top; Lady Constance Lytton, Annie Kenney, Mrs Lawrence, and the Pankhursts. Harriet May was not of their number. She was an outsider. She belonged nowhere. It was the story of her life. And now if Hester deserted her . . . ! Fear made her nag. She was suspicious if Hester used the telephone, or went out without saying where she was going. It made Hester furious. But Harriet couldn't help herself. She was driven to torment her, just as Hester was driven to respond. She found a book, 'Learning Chinese' under a cushion and tackled Hester with it.

'*Now* tell me there's nothing serious between you and Fairbairn!' she challenged. Hester smiled slowly. The more Harriet struggled against her tormentor, the deeper the knife went in. By her own nagging, Harriet was bringing about what she dreaded most. Hester was going to marry Tom.

'And what are you going to do with this new accomplishment?' Tom teased her. 'There aren't many Chinese in London!'

'I don't know. Perhaps *I* should go to China!'

'They'd never agree to send two of us!'

'Unless . . . '

'Unless . . . Hester . . . will you marry me?'

'I thought you'd never ask!' She laughed. And Tom adored this clever little woman, loved the way she wound him round her little finger. She was so playful and amusing. And yet, she had so deep a faith. What an asset she was going to be as a missionary's wife! He took her home, to Streatham to meet his parents. As Tom's brothers and sisters lunged for the plate of cakes, Hester joined her hands in prayer. There was an embarrassed silence. She smiled sweetly.

'I'm sorry, I assumed, naturally . . . ' She looked at Tom, who joked to his family.

'She's even more religious than *I* am!' They all laughed. Hester dimpled her confusion.

'I suppose, in the orphanage, you said grace before *every* meal?' Mrs Fairbairn asked.

'Oh, I wasn't brought up in an institution, Mrs Fairbairn. I was brought up by an old aunt of mine. Actually, she isn't related by blood at all!' Mr Fairbairn coughed.

'Then who will give you away my dear?' he asked.

'I would be honoured, sir, if you would take the place of my poor dead father.' Mr Fairbairn bristled with pride.

'The honour is mine.' And so, it was all arranged.

★ ★ ★

Harriet was told nothing, until, one day, coming home from her usual walk in the park, Hester sat down to play on the pianoforte. Harriet's eyes caught a flash of gold, as the hands flew over the keys.

'What's that on your finger?' she demanded. Hester stopped playing immediately and showed the ring. Harriet May went white.

'How could you? How could you, Hester?'

'I need a man, Harriet.' Harriet flinched. 'And Tom is strong. He's the only person who could command me.' Harriet was sickened. Such talk was offensive to a suffragette. 'We intend to go out to China together, to convert the natives.'

'God help them!'

'Indeed, Harriet, God will. Through Tom and me.'

'Can you hear yourself? Do you know what you're saying? You're Hester Beattie! Have you forgotten in all this playacting?' Hester shook her head.

'Hester Beattie no more, Harriet. I'm Hester Fairbairn now.'

'Names! Names don't change a thing, you bloody fool! You weren't made for marriage, Hester. I know you weren't!'

'That's what you think!' The words pierced sharply through the unnatural sweetness of her tone.

'Please! Please, listen to me! Do what you like. Leave me, if you want. But please don't marry!' Hester was furious. How dare she ask such a thing of her. 'I promised your mother *I* would look after you.'

'You're too late, Harriet. Tom and I were married this morning.' Harriet's face crumpled slowly and she began to cry, assailed by a confusion of thoughts and feelings.

'Oh God what have you done? What's the family going to say? I take it you haven't told them!'

'Damn the family!'

'If Tom could hear you now! His little saint!'

'As far as I'm concerned, Harriet, I have no family. I've finished with them, for good.' Hester stormed into her room and began to pack. But Harriet followed her. 'It's not too late! You could get the marriage annulled!'

'Why should I?' Hester laughed, and turned a pitying look on her aunt. 'Do you really think you could possibly say anything, that would change my mind?' Harriet's heart pounded. There

167

was one card left for her to play. She could do what Jane had wanted all along. She could tell Hester the truth.

'Listen to me, Hester. Please, listen to me. There is something. Before she died, your mother told me . . . '

'I don't want to know! I told you! I'm finished with my family! Finished! I am Hester Fairbairn!' She snapped her bag shut. 'Tom will send round for the rest of my things tomorrow.'

'Where are you going?'

'My husband has booked a room in a hotel in Paddington,' she smiled. 'Aren't you going to wish me luck for my wedding night?'

That night, Frances left her room, passing silently by the door of George's office. The gas flickered in his lamp and a shadow crossed the page. He shifted uneasily, and read on; 'There appeared another wonder in heaven; and behold a great red dragon, having seven heads and ten horns and seven crowns upon his heads. And his tail drew the third part of the stars of heaven, and did cast them to the earth: and the dragon stood before the woman which was ready to be delivered, for to devour her child as soon as it was born.' The sins of the fathers . . . The dragon with seven heads. And seven mouths. Seven children to consume. George mopped his brow. No wonder Jane had fled, when she saw them, plates and bowls, crawling with them, reproducing themselves before each member of her family! How could he not have seen? Frances had seen! She knew! Frances, his legitimate heir! She would carry on the line, and she alone. For, Hester was safe in Harriet's charge, and Frances was safe in his. Was that someone whispering down in the kitchen? George strained his ears. Only Grace the cat, sleeping on the hearth, dreaming. All the family were in bed. He was tired. Nerves strained. Yes. It was late, later than he'd thought. Silence hung over the house. It hung, like threads in the air, tangible, waiting. It drew him in, beyond time, beyond the threads that bound his understanding, and held him. Then, as the pale shadow fled the house, George felt the darkness coming. A cloud of smoke, glowing like a black furnace was rolling towards him. Was this Satan? The night was filled with him. He prowled the world, a dragon, breathing fire, in search of his prey. Retching, George fell from the silence. His head swam. He cried out, then darkness overwhelmed him.

They were whispering, the voices, the shadows, lurking round his bed. Blurred, as though seen through water, the forms of women stared down at him, touched him, moved him, and he felt life flowing in him again. George, returned from the gates of hell, swam back to the surface of his life.

'He's awake!' Maisie screeched.

'Sh, man!' Ellen reprimanded her sister. He tried to speak, but his lips were dry. He breathed the word, 'Water.'

Ellen put the invalid cup to his lips, and he drank. The water was sweet. He had never tasted water like it. He sighed with the bliss of drinking it. Maisie had gone to fetch the doctor, and now she came in with him, fussing anxiously.

'Well, hallo Mr Beattie!' George scowled. He didn't like new young doctors. He didn't trust them. 'How are we?'

'*I'm* all right. How are you?' George croaked. Unabashed, the doctor took out his little hammer and started testing reflexes. George almost kicked him as he bent, too low, to the knee.

'Well, you're a lucky man, Mr Beattie!' the doctor announced at last. 'You seem to have escaped any obvious damage.'

'What's wrong with me?'

'You've had a little stroke.'

'Rubbish! I want a second opinion!' The voice cracked into a bellow.

'He's all right,' Maisie whispered in Ellen's ear.

'Of course I'm all right! How long have I been out for the count?'

'About thirty hours, Mr Beattie.'

'What day is it?'

'Saturday.'

'What are you about?' he shouted at his daughters. 'Eddie and Frances can't manage the shop on their own! Not on a Saturday!'

'Em . . . Dad . . . ' Ellen was already apologising for herself. 'We closed the shop.' George spluttered with rage.

'Calm down, sir! You'll bring on another seizure if you're not careful.'

'Open it at once! Where's Eddie and Frances?'

'Eddie's out, delivering orders, Dad.'

'Frances could have done that!' The sisters exchanged an anxious look. 'What's going on?' he asked sharply. The women looked at the doctor, shifting the responsibility onto him. He hesitated. 'I don't care who tells me, but somebody'd better!' George gasped, as he finished speaking. His daughters ran to his side, and he struggled against them as they tried to help him.

'Probably better to tell him,' the doctor said. 'He'll only get himself into more of a state if you don't.'

'Why is it that folk think you're deaf and daft, just because you're poorly? Have I no say in the matter?' George was panting. His brow had broken out in a sweat and he was very pale.

'Give him a brandy,' the doctor said quietly.

'There's none in the house.' Maisie looked fearfully at her father.

'We never touch the stuff!' he gasped proudly.

'You will today!' The doctor took a small flask from his pocket and poured out a capful. 'Drink it,' he ordered. George drank, pulling faces like a child. 'Now you can tell him.' The doctor sat, holding George's pulse, as Ellen, crying, told her tale.

'Frances' gone. It was the night you took ill, Dad. She must have crept out while we were all asleep. She left a note . . . '

Ellen took the note from her pocket, and passed it to her father.

'Give me my glasses,' he said. Silently, Maisie passed them and he put them on, reading aloud, ' "Dear Mam, I have been offered a job in the theatre. I'll get paid and everything. It's my only chance. Don't be angry with me and don't worry. I'll be all right. Your loving daughter, Frances." '

The note dropped from his hand. His mouth gaped. A tear crept into the corner of his eye. ' "Get paid and *everything*"! She'll get "everything" all right!' Now George was crying openly. The doctor closed his bag and went quietly. 'Eddie's gone after her, then, has he?'

'No, Dad. I told you. He's out delivering!'

'He's what?'

'Well, what with you being ill, and the shop to run and one thing and another . . . We did tell the police, but they didn't seem very bothered, like.' Maisie was at the door of the room.

'Maisie, what do *you* know about this?' She turned, caught with her hand on the door knob. She shook her head, holding back the tears. 'It's that damned music hall of yours, isn't it?'

George hurled his voice at her, like a spear. 'I hold you responsible for what's happened to my grand-daughter!'

'Why's it always my fault!' Maisie howled, flying from the room.

'Poor Frances . . . ' George shook the tears from his face. 'My poor, innocent Frances!'

CHAPTER TEN

In a pool of light, the dancer moved, fragile, arms arching, reaching out, hands fluttering, in heart rending simplicity. And then the long neck drooped, and the long, graceful legs, strained, as though strength was draining from them, into the most exquisite dying fall, as the arms, folding, like wings about her, came, at last, to rest. The music ceased. The red curtain slowly swished across the scene, and the London audience rose to its feet in tumultuous applause. Jack's eyes shone, as the curtain drew apart to reveal her, alone at the centre of the stage, a surprised expression in her huge, dark eyes. She was the toast of London.

'Have you ever seen anything like it?' He turned to his neighbour, who sat, pale-faced, tears streaking her face.

'Frances! What's wrong?'

She bit her lip, as though afraid to speak. 'Do you want to go now?'

She nodded. The curtain calls were rung again and again. They shuffled past the adoring audience, and out into the damp street. They had just seen Pavlova dance.

Frances took Jack's handkerchief and blew her nose belligerently.

'Come on, dear! It can't be that bad.'

'Oh it is! It is!' she wailed.

'For God's sake, what's wrong?'

'I'm not Anna Pavlova!' For a second, Jack couldn't believe his ears, then he burst out laughing.

'You little goose!'

'Yes! And that's just what I'd look like, next to her!'

'Come on, Fran! You didn't really think you were that good, did you?' He laughed again, more gently than before. There was a pub over the way. Its lights glowed cheerfully in the dark street. 'Fancy a quick drink?' he asked. Frances' eyes grew wide with horror. 'I'm offering you a small port, dear. For the good of your health, you understand.'

'I don't drink.'

'You're in the theatre now!' Jack told her. 'And you must do in Rome as the Romans do!' He took her arm and propelled her toward the open doors.

The atmosphere was fuggy. Smoke came in clouds over the carved partition, between the saloon and the snug. She could hear women laughing over on the other side; they were having a high old time, singing, even dancing! Whereas in the snug, people just sat in tiny groups, whispering. Jack placed her drink on the table.

'Port. Builds you up. Puts roses in your cheeks.'

'Oh. I am supposed to be anaemic.'

'I thought as much. The theatre's a tough life. You've got to be in peak condition if you want to survive.'

'They give me raw liver at home. I used to get a lot of nose bleeds.'

'I expect you bleed too much with your monthlies too, eh?' Frances started and went scarlet. She didn't know where to put herself. Jack was highly amused. She tried to change the subject. 'Why can't we go in there? They seem to be having a lot of fun!'

'For the same reason as you don't like a man talking about your monthlies. You're a lady.' He smiled affectionately. 'I'll try to remember that.' She laughed at the 'try'. She'd forgiven him already. He nodded at her drink. Obediently, she raised it to her lips. Her nose wrinkled. He smiled encouragement, and she sipped the dark red liquid gingerly.

'It's quite nice,' she said, putting the glass down.

'I should think so. It's the best.' She was pleased he'd bothered. 'Oh yes, m'lady. I'm going to do my utmost to look after you!' She was taking another sip. The port warmed her stomach, glowing pleasantly inside her.

'Well! I think I'm going to like it!' She grinned cheekily, and he was delighted, daring to tweak her under the chin.

'Now, about this business of you not being Anna Pavlova . . . ' he began. Frances giggled. 'Well, I'm glad you're beginning to see it like that!' he said. 'You've done very well, Miss Lidell, for a young lady who has been to a local dancing class a couple of nights a week! You're very good, considering. Maybe, if you'd been born in Russia, and spent all your life training hard to be a ballerina, you could've been like her. But . . . ' He paused, and she stared at him with deep interest, 'Personally, I'm glad you're not. Because if you were, you wouldn't be Jack Scott's assistant. There now!' She was disappointed.

'Yes, but, I'm a dancer, not a comic!'

'You can still be a dancer, dear. I don't want competition. You're the feed. Know what that means?' She shook her head. 'It means, you do the work, and I get the laughs!' She giggled, and spluttered on her drink. Jack took it from her and put it down. 'I think you've had enough of that, for a start!'

'Oh no! I've just begun. This is living, Jack! Something I've wanted to do all my life!' Jack raised his eyebrows. 'If only *they* could see me!'

'Who?'

'Them at home!'

'I haven't got a family,' he said. 'I'm an orphan.' Her eyes grew wide. 'There now! Are you sorry for me?' She laughed and shook her head. 'You should be. Nobody cares whether I live or die!'

'You're free!'

'Oh well! The grass is always greener.' He went to the bar, to get himself another drink. Finishing off her own, Frances watched him with more interest than before. But when he came back, there was only one glass in his hand.

'Where's mine?' He shook his head and wagged his finger at her. Annoyed, Frances rose, pulling her purse out of her bag. But Jack pushed her back into her chair. He was angry.

'Never do that again!' he snapped. For a moment, she was

afraid, and then she saw his anger quickly sapping from him. 'Miss Lidell. While you are with me, kindly behave like the lady I know you are! It may be hard to remain a queen among swine. But that is exactly what you are going to do!' Her mouth opened in surprise. He rose, gave her his arm, and she reeled visibly.

'Ooh! I'm beginning to feel rather funny,' she said.

Her face was the colour of Green Park. Jack splashed out on a cab, and told the driver to take it slowly, sitting bolt upright beside Frances, as she drooped over him. Then she moaned and her head fell onto his shoulder. She was out for the count. He put his arm stiffly round her, to steady her. A man might take advantage of a situation like this, he thought. After all, a man had done so before. But, no. Jack would not be tempted, not this time. This one was definitely different. He left the landlady to pay the cabbie, and carried Frances up to her room. She half woke, as he pulled off her boots, and coat.

'I feel sick,' she said. Suddenly, she began retching. Jack fetched the washbowl, and held it in front of her, as she brought up her tea. The landlady came up the three flights, wheezing her way into the room.

'Miss Lidell is not feeling well,' Jack told her. Mrs Rosa raised her eyebrows and sniffed.

'I shall add the fare for the cab to last month's rent. I hope and pray it won't be too long in coming!' And then she went, closing the door behind her. Jack smiled at Frances, who was beginning to look a little better.

'Can you manage to get your clothes off?' he asked. She nodded, and he turned his back as she undressed and slipped into her nightie.

'You can turn round now.' She was standing in a simple shift, like a lost child. Jack nodded coldly.

'Into bed with you! And to sleep. We'll go through the butterfly number again in the morning!' And then he went. Mrs Rosa was surprised to find him in the sitting room, waiting for his bedtime cuppa.

'Must be losing your touch, dear,' she said.

Jack Scott was a hard taskmaster. Frances had never worked so hard in her life! He was a perfectionist and often lost his temper when her timing wasn't right. 'Timing' seemed to be the key to everything. Mrs Rosa sat, knitting away in the armchair, as they worked, and if they got a laugh out of her, then they knew their act would go down well even in Glasgow! After all, they owed her money, and she 'didn't exactly feel in the mood for laughing!'

'Agnes tells me you were offered a job, Jack,' Mrs Rosa said. 'But you turned it down.' Jack gave her a look which silenced her. 'I see,' she said. 'So that's the lie of the land! Well, whatever they say, two people *can't* live as cheaply as one, and they very soon turn into three . . . !' Frances went cold, then warm, her cheeks flushing pink.

'Time we had a break, Miss Lidell,' Jack said in his usual formal manner. 'I suggest we repair upstairs to fry up a bit of bubble and squeak!' Frances sighed.

'Not again?'

'If you can't stand the heat, get out of the kitchen!' Mrs Rosa said sternly, without looking up from her knitting. 'Take my word for it, girl. You're not the theatre type. You'd do far better to go back home!' Jack propelled Frances out of the room before she had time to retort. As she stomped up to light the gas ring, he put his head back round the door, and whispered, 'There was no need for that, you old cow!'

'She's turning you soft, Jack. Be warned!'

'That's my business!'

'And the rent's mine! You should have taken that job!'

'They wanted a solo act. I am not a solo act. I've not got a solo act!'

'You could have. You're full of ideas, you! I tell you! You're going soft! Good God! Your Frances thought Fred Karno ran a *dancing* troupe! She'll be the ruination of you!'

Frances was peeling onions, and crying into the pan, when Jack came upstairs.

'Let me do that,' he said. She shrugged him off and continued chopping.

'I'll show you! I'll show her an' all! I'm not as soft as I look, Jack Scott! And I know Fred Karno trains comics. So there!'

'You heard?'

'Some of it!'

'I know you're not soft. But you're not really the theatre type. She's right about that.'

'I'll change!'

'That's what I'm afraid of.' Frances stared at him through stinging eyes. Her cheeks were stained by tears. 'By God, you look a sight,' he said.

'*You're* no painting!' Jack twanged his braces dolefully, and waggled his toes, peeping out from the holes in his socks. She had to laugh. 'Look, I'll darn your socks for you, if you like.' His face softened. For once, he wasn't acting.

'You don't have to.'

'I don't mind. It's the least I can do. You are keeping me.'

'*I* don't mind that.' They stood staring at one another through the smoke of frying fat. 'Sounds like a good arrangement, don't you think, Miss Lidell?' The fat burst into flames. Frances screamed. Mrs Rosa started up the stairs, shouting at them, and Jack put out the fire with a kettle full of water. Steam greeted the landlady as she reached the third floor.

'What the hell's going on up here?'

'Love, Mrs Rosa,' Jack said cheerily. 'I do believe Miss Lidell and I have agreed to see whether or not two people *can* live as cheaply as one.'

'Not under my roof!' Mrs Rosa expostulated.

'I mean, madam, we are going to marry!' There was a long silence. Mrs Rosa drew herself up to a great height.

'Going soft!' she spat and set off, laboriously, down the six flights of stairs.

Frances was jittery. It worried Jack. There was he, chirpy as a sparrow, and she just went on humming and hahing about how she thought they ought to wait, and was he sure, and it was a bit of a whirlwind romance, wasn't it? It was as though love was something to be ashamed of!

'What's up? Afraid your folks won't like me?' Frances stared miserably through the dirty window. 'Have you changed your mind?' She shook her head. 'Well then, what is it?' But still, she refused to speak. 'You're very young. You're still . . . well, you've never known a man, have you?' She shook her head. He touched her cheek gently and drew her chin round, so that she was facing him. 'Look at me.' The lashes quivered, and then she

177

raised her eyes to meet his. 'I love you. I'm never going to hurt you. Believe me.' She thought she would die, if he didn't kiss her soon. And then his lips touched hers, gently, sweetly. 'See? You're going to like being married to me.' He smiled down on her. 'I bet you've never been kissed before!'

'Oh yes I have!' Suddenly Frances slapped him hard on the cheek.

'What's that for?'

'For thinking you're the only man in the world likely to take a fancy to me!'

'You little . . . !' He was rubbing his cheek. 'I see! So it wasn't fear of me that was putting you off!' Frances said nothing. 'Come on. You'd better tell me. What's wrong? Why don't you want me to meet your folks?'

'All right!' she snapped back. 'If you must know, I ran away.' Jack went pale.

'What?'

'I ran away!' She glared at him, daring him to be angry with her now. 'They'd never've let me go on the stage, if they'd known.'

'I see.' Jack sat, stunned, on the edge of the bed.

'I'm not going back there! Not ever again! I hate Shields. I hate the flower shop. I even hate flowers!'

'Remind me, if I'm ever tempted to buy you any!' he said sourly.

'I'm sorry, Jack.' She wriggled uncomfortably. 'I suppose you'll not want me in the act any more now.' He gave her a sharp look.

'I've no choice! I've built it round you, haven't I?' Frances was relieved and showed it. Jack lost his temper. 'You selfish . . . !' Not for the first time, she felt a little afraid. Then Jack sighed, running his hands through his hair. 'I was rather looking forward to having a family,' he said.

'I see. So it wasn't me you wanted, after all! It was my rotten family!'

'Don't be so stupid!' He wanted to shake her till her teeth fell out. But suddenly he laughed. 'Oh well,' he said. 'Teach me to go cradle snatching, I suppose!'

'I'm not a child!' Frances was outraged.

'You're too young to wed without the consent of your parents.'

'I'll be eighteen in a couple of years!'

'How long do you suppose it'll be before your folk catch up with you?' Frances shook her head. 'And however hard it's going to be, for the next two years, Frances Lidell, I am not going to give in to your charms . . . so don't even try to tempt me!'

At the end of June, at last, they were offered work. Mrs Rosa lent them the train fare 'Much against my better judgement' as she said, with some asperity. Jack's eyes twinkled. She was like a hedgehog, all prickles outside, but soft inside. From under cover of a newspaper, Jack watched Frances, as the train chugged north west toward Cardiff. She was bubbling with excitement. Her cheeks were pink, and the curls escaped wildly from under her hat. There was no doubt about it, Miss Frances Sheridan, as she'd called herself, looked gorgeous! He shook his head, and steeled himself to read the news. But Frances wanted to chat. The newspaper was a barrier between them. She stared at it resentfully, then her cheeks dimpled and a sparkle came into her eye.

'I see another Zeppelin's crashed in Germany!' she remarked brightly, peering at the print on the back page. Jack frowned, and turned the paper to look at the report. He grunted, and nodded, then turned back to column three. 'I thought you were inter-ested in Zeppelins!' she said. 'Wouldn't it be nice to go up in one?'

'No. It wouldn't. That's the third disaster this year!'

'Oh.'

'They're not cut out for civilian purposes! They'll end up being used in a war. You wait and see.' He put down the paper. Frances grinned with delight. She had scored, but she wanted to draw him in still further.

'Why, Jack?' she asked seriously. 'What do you mean?'

'Germany's taking far too much interest in Zeppelins and the like. And now King Edward's dead . . . '

'But he was an awful womaniser!'

'Maybe! But he was also a skilful diplomat. He held Europe together. Even the Kaiser respected him. Now he's gone . . . ' Jack's hands flew apart explosively. Frances frowned. He was serious. 'How else are they going to keep down the workers? Think of the profits to be made by making guns!' Frances shivered. 'The Kaiser wants war; always has. And we are going to let him have it, simply because we can't really be bothered to stop it. It's as if England had a death wish. Well if you wish for something for long enough, you end up getting it!'

'I don't want to die!' Frances was pale and frightened.

'Neither do I.' Jack sighed. 'But there's many who do! And they'll persuade themselves that it's a far far better thing . . . ' Suddenly he grinned, and patted Frances on the knee. 'Anyway, how else are we going to keep the women down! They're getting out of hand and a war'll put them back in their place!'

'Jack Scott!' She walloped him with his own paper and they rolled about laughing till the tears were running down their cheeks. Finally, lying back in his seat, to recover, Jack stared at Frances. He nodded slowly, a smile curling his lips.

'Yes . . . you'd better watch it, Miss Frances Sheridan! Like I said, you've only got to wish for something hard enough, and . . . ' he winked, '. . . I just might not be able to stop myself!'

Frances felt as though she was about to be thrown to the gladiators! She could hear the murmuring of the audience, even before curtain up. At the Cardiff Empire, there was seating for just under two thousand people, and every seat was filled. The gauzy wings fluttered nervously, and her teeth chattered, as Frances waited, beside Jack, for their turn.

Break a leg!' Jack whispered, as he leapt onto the stage. He was in hob nail boots, a butterfly net in his hand. There was an immediate wave of laughter. Frances heard it, rolling towards her, like the tide coming in. Her heart skipped a beat. The band were playing her tune. She did a *pas-de-chat* onto the stage, and stood there, fluttering, turning on points, before her pursuer. The butterfly outwitted the hunter again and again, as he mimicked the pretty steps and bounding leaps of his teasing prey. His clumsy steps and clownish falls had the audience in stitches, and yet, they were on the side of the butterfly, clapping at her narrow escapes, and roaring their approval, when the hunter finally got himself all tied up in his own net. They laughed and cheered, as the curtain fell, and Frances was thrust back onto the stage. 'Well done!' Jack hissed, as they walked forward to take their bow. It was the moment of Frances' life. She glowed with pleasure, skipping off the stage ahead of Jack, into the wings, and up the stairs to the dressing room, whooping with delight.

'Sh!' the stage manager ordered from the bottom of the stair. Frances put a hand to her mouth, to stifle a giggle, and went with Jack into his room.

'I didn't want to tell you this, before we went on, Frances, but Mr Stoll himself was out there tonight. And, judging by our reception, I'd say we're in for a nice long run! Leeds, Liverpool, and, with a bit of luck, on to the Moss Empire.' Frances' eyes were shining.

'Do you really thing so?' Jack nodded.

'I think this deserves a celebration! Come on. Get your coat on. We're going out!'

George's letter had been forwarded by his friend, Dick Thornton, a Shields man, who ran most of the north east's music halls. It reached Jack's agent, in London, and was sent on from there to Mrs Rosa, who sent it to the Cardiff Empire, where it arrived four weeks too late. By this time, Jack and Frances were enjoying a great success. George was losing patience. It occurred to him, that he hadn't heard from Harriet May for some time. He determined to go down to London and see her, in the hopes she might be able to throw some light on Frances' disappearance.

On the rebound from Hester, Harriet had flung herself into suffragette activities with fierce intensity. The failure of the Conciliation Bill had resulted in scenes of unequalled horror on Black Friday, as police and women fought in Parliament Square. Harriet May had not been of their number, but she burned to be part of the backlash against 'brutish male authority'. All her bitterness, all her hatred at Hester's betrayal, was turned against the male sex. Men had always cheated her. Her father had deserted her mother, her stepfather had rejected her, Robert had preferred his sister to herself, and now, Tom Fairbairn had stolen Hester! Or so Harriet persuaded herself. She thirsted for revenge and the women's movement provided her with a suitable disguise for her predilection. 'Swan and Edgar' felt the impact of her hammer on their windows, as did 'Liberty's' and 'Burberry's'. The sound of shattering glass at dead of night, was balm to her soul. She dropped lit matches into pillar boxes, painted out the numbers on houses, slashed the cushions in railways carriages, broke street lights, then ran, like a child, bent on wanton destruction. She was finally caught on Hampstead Heath, painting slogans on seats. She took her cell in Holloway with pride. Blooded, the movement welcomed her into their ranks, and she gloried, in the hardships of her life in gaol.

George heard the news from Harriet's caretaker at Hayward Mansions. Immediately, he took a cab to Holloway, where the warden granted him an interview with Harriet. The gates creaked and clanged, as she was escorted down the corridor, to the bare room where George awaited her. Her clothes hung about her. There were deep shadows under her eyes, and her face was grey and drawn. She walked in slowly, coughing painfully. And when she spoke, her voice grated in her damaged throat.

'Dear God . . . ' George shook his head. 'Force feeding! In this day and age?'

'Be sorry for yourself, not me!' she croaked. Her eyes were bright and vicious as a hawk's.

'What have I done to deserve such women?' George groaned. 'You've set a bad example Harriet May. You and your "independent women"! It's because of you she's run off!'

'You can't blame me!' Harriet whispered roughly. 'I tried to stop her. But she wouldn't listen. It was all Tom this and Tom that . . . '

'Tom?'

'Tom Fairbairn. Her husband.'

'Fairbairn!' George was mystified. The only name he'd heard mention of was Jack Scott. 'Frances is married then? But she's under age!'

'Frances?' Harriet stared at her stepfather. 'I was talking about Hester!' George thought he was going to pass out.

'Hester?' he repeated weakly. 'Hester's married?' Harriet's mouth grew hard.

'Yes!'

'When?'

'A few months back.'

'Why in God's name didn't you tell me?'

'I didn't know myself, till it was all over!' She glared at him.

'Well! Are you going to stand bail for me or not?' What else could he do?

'I'll see about it. Just write down the address where Hester's living . . . ' Harriet did as she was told, observed closely by a prison warder.

'If they've not gone off to China by now! His family's in Streatham.' George was sweating. He could hardly breathe. He stumbled out of the interview room into the Matron's office. Bail could be arranged. It was a first offence, and, in any case, Miss Lovely's health was endangered after her long spell of hunger strikes. The wheels were set in motion. George left the gaol and went straight to Streatham.

His brain was seething. Had all womanhood gone mad? He stared blankly at the slashed seats in his compartment, as the train drew out of Victoria Station. The Pankhursts were obsessed, and led the women of England behind them. They were unreasonable, masochistic, wantonly destructive. Why, he'd even read somewhere, they had the idiocy to believe women would actually cease to menstruate once they got the vote! Envy of men had turned in upon itself, and what, George wondered, would follow? At Streatham, George was in for another shock. His existence was a complete surprise to them all. George swayed, holding his hand to his head, and Mrs Fairbairn, taking pity on him, asked him in for a cup of tea. It seemed Hester had quickly fallen out with her in-laws, and the newly-weds had repaired to a room in Clapham, to continue their blissful married life alone. What had happened?

'Well, I don't like to say, Mr Beattie, with her being your daughter and all, but, as I see it, you can carry your religious zeal too far!' George was reminded of the phase in Hester's life, when she had taken to frequenting St Michael's.

'What did she do?'

'We thought her a sweet, obliging sort of girl, at first. But she soon changed after coming to live with us. Of course Tom wouldn't see it. She went round dressed in black, dark rings under her eyes, and I'm not surprised because she never went to bed! Well, not once the originality had worn off, if you take my meaning. And that's another thing . . . ' Mrs Fairbairn nodded wisely. 'A newly married man expects more than that!' George coughed his agreement. 'She was a stickler for the church services, morning prayers, everything. We went along with it for a while, but,' and here Mrs Fairbairn clicked her tongue in disapproval, 'don't get me wrong, I'm as religious as the next person, but when she started banging the dinner gong at five in the morning for prayers, well!!! You couldn't rest after that! My husband was like a sleepwalker all day at work. His boss was noticing. I mean, you can carry religion too far, can't you?' There was no time to lose. George took the new address, and set off for Clapham. The same slashed seats, the same feeling of unreality dogged him. The afternoon light was fading into twilight, as George rang the bell of number eight. A man in threadbare slippers and sagging braces, answered the door. A smell of cabbage drifted towards him from the back of the house. It made him feel sick. Up two flights, third on the right. George paused, then knocked. A man came to the door, yawning and blinking in the light.

'Tom Fairbairn?'

'Who wants me?'

'George Beattie. Hester's father.' There was a long silence. 'Let me get dressed,' the young man said. George sat on the stair, waiting. Then Tom came out and escorted George to a café round the corner.

Hester had gone to a special service at the church, and Tom had been working hard at his Chinese, when George had called. It seemed the missionary body were now prepared to accept him for training the following year. Hester was pregnant, but after the first idyllic weeks of honeymoon, when her demands had fairly exhausted him, she had begun to shut him out, telling her husband that their intimate relations must now cease, as they were meant only to serve the divine purpose of producing children. Tom couldn't understand it. She drove him with her religious fanaticism, to the extent that he began avoiding church, just to get out of her way. Could George throw any light on her behaviour? After a long and confidential talk, the two men, exhausted and perplexed, parted company in the road. They shook hands, and wished each other luck. They were never to see one another again.

* * *

'Scott and Sheridan' continued on the theatre circuit, without a break. They were now two from top of the bill, and the warm-up for the star performer, at The Birmingham Empire. Its beautiful decor of blue, white and gold, had an aura of luxury about it and Frances was performing with the 'crème de la crème'. She might not be Anna Pavlova but, as she broke in another pair of blocked shoes, she felt she was the nearest thing. She loved everything about theatre life; even the nerves before the show. And then, on stage, dancing in the lights, before that huge mass of people, timing her every movement to their response, she felt completely in her element. She had to be stopped from doing encores, which would prolong the show, but there were always the curtain calls, after which, bathed in the approbation of her public, Frances would retire with Jack to the local pub, for a shandy, before turning in at the digs, for a well-deserved, and extremely long sleep.

Bob, on the door, thought he had an older version of the stage door Johnny on his hands, when George turned up, at last. He gave his card, which was sent up with a call boy to Jack's dressing room. Jack looked at it and went cold. So, the moment had finally arrived. He took a deep breath, and creamed the make-up from his face.

'Tell my visitor I'll be down in a few minutes,' he told the boy. Carefully, he washed the grease away, combed his hair, and put on his jacket. Taking one last look in the mirror, he left his room, and knocked gently on Frances' door. 'Get your skates on, sweetheart!' he said brightly, 'I'm dying of thirst!' Frances surprised him by immediately opening the door, and kissing him, a smacker, on the cheek.

'Was I good tonight?'

'Brilliant! I'll have to watch you!' He laughed. 'If I'm not careful, you'll be getting billing above me!'

'Who's not the theatre type now!' she challenged, hands on hips. He smiled, and said nothing, taking her arm, as they descended the stone stair to the stage door. Her heart lurched. His back was to her, but she'd've known it anywhere. A mixture of guilt, fear and defiance fought within her, as her grandfather turned and looked straight into her eyes. But then, her courage faltered. George looked drawn; not half the man he used to be.

'Granda! What's happened to you?'

'You ask that?' he said ironically. Frances shook her head.

'It can't just be because of me!'

'No. Not just because of you.' George sighed. 'I have only one thing to ask you, Frances. And that is, do you love this man?' Frances' mouth dropped open. She turned to Jack, but he was staring straight ahead, poker-faced. 'Does he make you happy?' Her granda's voice boomed along the corridor. The green baize door opened, and the stage manager gesticulated wildly at him.

'Sh, Granda. They'll hear you on the stage!'

'Answer my question!' Frances nodded, shame-faced.

'Yes,' she whispered. 'I'm very happy, Granda. Please, please let me stay with Jack.' George's face was grim.

'In that case, Mr Scott, I suggest we have a serious discussion, man to man. I'm staying at the Market Hotel. Perhaps you would care to join me for dinner.' Her granda almost bowed, his politeness meant to subdue the adventurer. Jack had to admire him for it. It was a good act, when all was said and done.

'Go on, little'n! Scat!' he ordered. George raised his eyebrows and Frances was appalled. Was she then to be dismissed? Not to mention miss a good dinner?

'I said, scat!' Jack insisted.

After a pause, Frances left them, and walked back to the digs, alone and wondering . . .

Jack did not make the mistake of ordering wine, but contented himself with table water. They talked about the show, the weather, the suffragettes, the new king, and George was surprised to find the young man both knowledgeable and mature in judgement. While Jack, in turn, found George more reasonable than he had been led to expect, and, perhaps most surprising of all, rather sad. He respected him for seeking out his grand-daughter, whom he obviously loved. It was a good dinner. George was not stingy. But he seemed puzzled, bemused by the turn of events both in the world and in his own life.

'I feel that we, as a nation, are heading for some terrible disaster.' George's brow was creased with worry. 'I don't know what it is. Nothing seems real any more. I feel . . . I feel very old,' he admitted, shaking his head helplessly. 'I feel the whole world order's changing, and it's leaving me behind, Mr Scott.' Jack

186

frowned, and cleared his throat. Was the 'old barsket' sincere? or just a play actor like himself? If he was, he was very, very good. There was a tear in the corner of his eye, as he finally looked straight at Jack. 'I'm not going to beat about the bush. I've sounded you out, and, well, as you might expect, I'm disappointed in Frances' choice, but you could be worse. Now, she says she loves you. Tell me honestly. Do you love her?' Jack's eyes did not waver.

'Yes,' he said at once. 'Very much.' George nodded and sighed. 'I'll offer you half my business, to be yours when I die. Meanwhile, you are to make Frances an honest woman, and train under me at the shop in Shields, so you'll be able to take over when I'm gone.' Jack was dumbfounded. He shook his head. Others diners turned, alarmed, as George's voice boomed out. 'You decline?'

'No. No . . . I . . . To be honest, I was just so amazed by your generosity . . . ' He shrugged.

'I love my grand-daughter. She's the pick of the bunch. The rest of them aren't up to much . . . ' Jack sensed the old man's deep disappointment.

'You're asking me to give up the theatre,' Jack said slowly. 'Not only me, but Frances too. She loves the life, you know.'

'No doubt, just now, while she's young. What happens when she's old, and past it? She's flighty, Mr Scott. No sense of gravity! The slightest breath of wind and she takes off. She needs tethering to her roots. She needs security. Can you understand that?' Jack nodded.

'As an orphan, brought up by the church, yes,' he said. George sat back and looked at him afresh. He nodded slowly.

'I daresay you wouldn't say no to a bit of security yourself, then. You'll have nothing behind you.' Jack said nothing, but looked straight back at the old man. 'You've got weight. I'll say that. You're what she needs in that direction.'

'You said, I had to make "an honest woman" of her?'

'If you're a gentleman, Mr Scott, and I'm beginning to think you are, even after what you did to that little girl, you'll put things right now.'

'I've spoiled your grand-daughter, that it?' George nodded, looking away from the despoiler. Unobserved, Jack indulged in a wry smile. 'All right. I give in. I'll marry her,' he said.

George came back smartly.

'And you'll bring her back to Shields, to the shop?'

'We'll have to finish our present contract first, of course.'
George considered the matter, then asked,

'How much longer is there left to run?'

'A couple of months.'

'You'll marry her *now*.'

'If you insist.' Jack was reaching for his packet of Woodbines.

'Try one of these,' George was offering his precious cigars.

CHAPTER ELEVEN

Jack and Frances finally tied the knot in London when they were working at the Hippodrome. It was the week before Christmas, 'a time when disasters always happen', as Mrs Rosa politely informed them over breakfast. But she came along all the same, with George, and the cast of the show, to the little church, close by the theatre.

'Where're the polar bears?' Mrs Rosa asked churlishly.

'The Hippodrome doesn't do circuses any more!' Jack informed her.

'Doesn't it?' she said, looking round the congregation. 'You could have fooled me.' Jack raised his eyes to heaven, and walked on past her to the altar. But, making his way back down the aisle, his bride on his arm, he saw the old bitch had been crying. He might've known! He nudged Frances, and she smiled, as she saw the sodden handkerchief in her hand.

'I don't know why you had to book a room in a hotel for your honeymoon!' Mrs Rosa hissed, back at the digs. 'You've blessed my sheets many a time, I've no doubt! And if we were good enough for you then, we are now.'

'Ah,' Jack winked. 'But were you, Mrs Rosa? And did we?' He laughed in her face. She was astonished.

'Are you trying to tell me that that lass is still a . . . '

'Sh!' Jack was alarmed. 'Lower your voice. I don't want her grandfather to know!' Jack touched his nose with his finger, and Mrs Rosa shook her head. There was no knowing with them theatricals! They were a law unto themselves!

And Mrs Rosa'd given them a lovely reception! The Vincent Sisters had helped, cutting sandwiches, and Nellie Wallace, about to appear at the new Palladium, had brought a cake. The atmosphere was more like a party than a wedding breakfast. But George was in his element. Standing, watching him, in her new white frock, Frances shook her head and smiled. Who would have thought it!

'Well, Jack,' she said. 'All's well that end's well!'

'Yes, dear,' he replied in husbandly fashion. Frances giggled, and clipped him one on the hand.

'Granda's really enjoying himself, isn't he? Look how well he's getting on with Nellie!'

'He's a dark horse, your granda!'

'You can say that again. Do you know, I think, deep down, he's quite proud of me.' Jack nodded. 'He really enjoyed our act, when he finally deigned to watch it!' Jack took her hand, kissed it, and laid it on his arm. 'I'm so happy, Jack. I'd hate to go on with the stage and that, feeling Granda was against it. But now . . . ' There were tears in her eyes. 'Now I feel he's given me his blessing. I don't know how you did it!' Jack pulled a face.

'Nearly time for the show,' he said, checking his watch. Then he cupped his hands, put them to his mouth and called, 'Beginners please!' There was laughter, and the performers slowly left for the theatre.

The show passed in a dream. There was a bottle of champagne, waiting for them in Jack's dressing room, and everyone, from stage hands, to ticket girls, wished them luck.

'Neatest little husband and wife team in the business!' The door keeper called after them into the street. 'Don't do anything I wouldn't now!' Confetti came at them from all directions, thrown by fans, performers, and stage hands, alike, as they got into their cab. A theatre wedding was bliss.

'I feel more like *they're* my family, really,' Frances said, as she waved her fellow artists goodbye.

The cab stopped outside Claridges. Alighting, Frances stared at the portico with awe. She had never stayed at a proper hotel before. It was really plush! She tried hard not to look impressed, as Jack walked her through the foyer. But her air of nonchalance did not deceive the porters. They winked at one another. 'Newly-weds!' they whispered, and jostled one another to carry the two small bags up to the room. Newly-weds always gave big tips.

'Good luck!' the successful porter said, as he shut the door on them. 'And congratulations!'

'How did he know?' Frances hissed. Jack laughed.

'Maybe it was that frothy white dress you've got on under there!' Frances giggled, as she pulled off her coat.

'It is lovely, isn't it? Eeh!' She sighed. 'I still can't believe Granda was so nice about everything. Fancy him buying me a posh frock!'

'Why not? He's your family. Blood's thicker than water!'

'Fat lot you know about it!' Frances teased. Jack smiled, then, suddenly he looked serious.

'Pity your Mam and Dad couldn't come!'

'They had to stay to mind the shop.' Frances watched him, curiously. 'You're very thoughtful, for a man on his wedding night!'

He had waited for Frances a long time, and he tried hard not to be impatient, but she was nervous and, he told himself, he was a blundering idiot. Afterwards, she wondered what all the fuss had been about and her smile was strained. Jack cursed himself. He was beginning to wish he'd jumped the gun, like everyone thought. Disappointed, he put his arms round her and cuddled her, till she fell asleep. Then he slept too, and woke refreshed at six o'clock the next morning. It was still dark. He stroked her breast and she stirred, lazily.

'I do love you, Mrs Scott!' he whispered.

'And I love you, Mr Scott.' Still half asleep, she warmed to his embrace. Moaning, she turned to him, reaching out. Her touch praised his manhood and he responded joyfully, wooing the woman in her, till she softly welcomed him, and he could love

191

her at last, as he had dreamt he would, and she cried out with the pleasure of it.

As the light came up over London, Frances and Jack sat up in bed, sipping champagne. 'You look proud of yourself, Jack Scott!' She laughed.

'I've every right to be!' he said. She savoured the wine.

'Is it going to be like this for ever?' she asked dreamily.

'Well, I daresay I'll be a little bit less energetic when I'm eighty! But, perhaps, by then, you won't mind so much.' She laughed, then coughed, choking on the champagne. He hit her hard on the back and she almost spilt it.

'Careful! You're wasting it!' He took her glass from her, and recovering, she threw her arms round him, exuberantly kissing him wherever she could reach. When she'd finished, she lay back again, purring.

'Know what I feel like now?'

'Already?' He pretended shock. She hit him, giggling.

'No! Not that! Well, not yet anyway . . .'

'What then?' he asked, grinning indulgently.

'A bath in that gorgeous pink marble bathroom!'

'Good idea. Come on!'

'What do you mean "come on"?'

'Last one there's a cissy!' They whooped as they raced to the bath. The water gurgled, spluttered, then splashed, steaming, into the tub.

'It's wonderful!' Frances moaned with delight, as she eased herself into the deep foaming water. ' "Attar of roses." It's what my mother likes. I think Aunt Harriet gave her some once. Or was it Auntie Maisie?' She looked round. Jack had disappeared. 'Where are you, husband?' Immediately Jack reappeared, two sparkling glasses in his hands. 'Oh! Good idea!' She took hers, as Jack got in beside her. He wriggled his toes. 'Jack Scott! Mind what you're doing with them toes! If you weren't married to me already, you'd have to marry me now!' He waggled his eyebrows at her and, clinking glasses, they sipped the champagne. He lolled his head back, savouring the taste.

'For someone who hates her family so much, you do talk about them rather a lot.'

'No I don't!'

'Yes you do! You were at it just now. I think you care a lot more about them than you let on!' Frances shook her head.

'No. Not really. I mean I *do* care about them of course, but . . .'

'Aha! I knew it!'

' . . . but, only at a safe distance. If I had to go back and live amongst them, it'd be different. I'd just end up hating them again.'

'Women! You do talk rubbish!'

'No we don't! And stop poking me under the arm with your big toe!'

'Sorry. He's right, you know.'

'Who?'

'The "old barsket". And he's not such an old barsket, either!'

'Huh! Anyway, what about?'

'You. You *are* flighty.'

'Flighty? Me? Did he say that?'

'Yes.' Frances frowned and sank deeper under the water. Jack watched her thoughts passing across her face.

'Jack . . .'

'Mmmm?'

'You never did tell me what you said to him.'

'When?'

'That night in Birmingham. How did you get him to agree to everything?'

'What do you mean, "everything"?'

'You know! Us getting married. Me being on the stage.'

'Oh. That.'

'Yes. That. You never told me.'

'No. I never did, did I?' He laughed and threw the sponge at her, and when they'd finished wrestling in the bath, they were back in bed, and most of the water was swimming all over the pink marble floor.

But what, Frances wondered, were they going to do next?

'We could work abroad!' she suggested. 'I've got an uncle on the north west coast of America. Uncle Josh. We could go there! Or New York? Or we could try Paris!'

'Let's just wait and see what turns up,' Jack said. But nothing did. And when their contract ended they were back where they started, and Mrs Rosa's, in January, on no money, was cold and miserable.

'Poor Frances.' Jack put down his newspaper. 'You're run down, aren't you? Why don't you go and see a doctor?'

'I'm all right, Jack. Just fed up. That's all. When are we going to get another job?'

'Not till you're in the pink,' he insisted. 'Come on. Let's see if Mrs Rosa knows of a decent doctor.' Unwillingly, Frances went along with Jack's plan. She was pale and she felt sick all the time. Jack had a fair idea what was up, and, though he was wise enough to keep his suspicions to himself, he was as pleased as punch. But, when she came out of the doctor's, Frances fell into Jack's arms, weeping.

'He thinks I might be pregnant!' She wailed bitterly.

'What's wrong with that?'

'Have you ever seen a pregnant butterfly?' He laughed, and suddenly seeing the funny side, she laughed too.

'Shall I tell you a secret?' Jack whispered in her ear. She looked at him, waiting. 'I hope he's right.' Frances frowned. 'Don't do that.' He eased the frown away with his hand. 'You'll be a beautiful mother. And anyway, it's all your own fault. You drank far too much champagne!' She smiled ruefully.

'It's not fair. Men don't have babies.'

'If we did, you women'd be competing with us to see which of us did it better!' She pulled a face.

'Anyway. I might not be! It's early days yet, Jack Scott!'

He shrugged, and they walked on in silence for a while. Then Jack sighed deeply.

'Well, if you are,' he said, 'it'll be the end of the theatre for me!' She swung round, shocked.

'What?'

'Well, I can hardly leave you behind, while I go off doing my solo act, can I? You'd hate it. And the theatre's no place to bring up children. They need a comfortable, secure home, and a warm, loving family around them.' He sighed. 'So you see, dear, you wouldn't be the only one who'd have to make sacrifices.' Frances stared at him for a long time, before she spoke.

'What did you say to Granda, that night in Birmingham, Jack?' The moment had come. He could avoid it no longer.

194

'I agreed to take you home.' Frances went pale.

'For a visit, you mean?' She was clutching at straws.

'No.'

'Tell me I'm dreaming this.'

'No you're not. It's real. Come on. Let's get home.' He hustled her back along the street and into Mrs Rosa's.

'Are you all right, dear? What did he say? Pregnant are you?' she called up the stairs after them. Frances screamed with rage, and slammed her door behind her.

'Lover's tiff,' Mrs Rosa said to the Singing Vincent Sisters. But she jumped when they heard the water jug crash against the wall. 'I'll charge you for that!' she yelled up the stairs.

'You don't understand, Jack! What I've always loved about you is the fact you have no family! You're free. And so am I now! We have a world all our own, in the theatre. I even have a different name!' It was now February. And Frances' pregnancy was certain. But the rows continued.

'A made-up name. "Frances Sheridan." Hah! It's no more real than the theatre. It's a dream world. Pretend. An illusion.'

'It's the world I want!'

'You need your family!'

'Oh? What if there's something wrong with them, Jack?' He frowned, puzzled.

'What do you mean?'

'There is something. I've heard stories. But I don't know what to believe. Something happened once, a long time ago. My mother told me that my grandma's brother ran off with the takings from the shop and that was why Granda cut him off. But Grandma said, he never stole anything at all! She always seemed weighed down by guilt, as though she knew something much much worse. She committed suicide in the end. I tell you, Jack, my family's cursed!'

'Stop dramatising! Whatever they may be, you can't cut off from your roots.'

'I must! Jack, try to understand. They were dragging me down! I've got to be free of them. Please, don't make me go back!'

'It'll be different this time, Frances. I'll be there!' She shook her head. 'Stop it now! You're fighting nobody but yourself.

Your own shadow. There's nothing else. Who cares if somebody stole something years ago.' She was crying bitterly. 'You're just trying to blame others for your own inability to accept what you are.'

'Huh?'

'Frances, you're part of your family whether you like it or not. You have a responsibility to them. You can't escape that, any more than you can escape having this child.'

'Then I'll get rid of it!' Frances screamed. Jack's hand lashed across her face, and she fell back against the bed, sobbing, 'Why didn't God make me a man?'

Jack looked down on her sadly.

'And there was I, thinking I'd made you glad you were a woman!'

Frances stared bleakly at the icy Tyne from the train window, as Jack rose to retrieve their bags from the rack.

'Chin up, Fran!' he ordered. George was there to meet them at Central station. He nodded at the wedding ring.

'None too soon, was it?'

'Too soon for me!' she snapped. George glanced at his son-in-law, who shrugged, and mouthed the word 'women!' It explained everything. George said nothing, but gently helped his grand-daughter onto the Shields train.

'I brought you some flowers,' he said, handing her a bunch of white lilies. Frances smelt them and was immediately sick.

At first, it seemed that George and Jack were the only members of the family on speaking terms. Forgetting her earlier advice to her daughter, that 'she should do something' with her life and forget all about men, Ellen now informed her, 'You're just an inconsiderate, irresponsible, little bitch! You might at least have got married before disgracing our name and running off to go on the stage!'

Her father said she was 'wanton'. 'I don't understand where you get it from!' he declared, which, considering the circumstances of Frances' birth, was rich!

Even Maisie gave her the cold shoulder.

'I feel used, Frances,' she said. 'And . . . well, I've got to say it, I'm surprised at you!'

They were a bunch of hypocrites! And if they didn't want to speak to her, then she was glad! Honestly, you'd think she and Jack'd been living over the brush, the way they were all carrying on! Then, slowly, she began to wonder. What had Jack told her granda that night in Birmingham? Had he let him think she'd already 'been to bed' with him? If so, then he'd really pulled the wool over their eyes! The conniving little . . . ! Her sense of betrayal increased, and she cold-shouldered Jack, both in the shop and in bed. She had never felt so lonely. Morning sickness overwhelmed her in the heavy, scented, atmosphere of the house, and even Muriel's company palled. All she seemed to want were stories about the stars. She never tired of them; but Frances did, and she cried herself to sleep, night after night, remembering the good old times.

'You've got to forgive me, Frances,' Jack whispered to his wife's back. 'Please. Please, talk to me.' But she lay, frozen, silent, saying nothing. 'Whatever I did was for your own good as I saw it.' And then, suddenly, she turned, and spat fiercely at him,

'For *your* good, you mean! Oh yes, Jack Scott! You've got what you wanted all right. You've got your precious family, and a nice secure foot in the business as well! You've used me. Well, you've had all you're going to get out of me! We're finished. Understand?'

Jack said nothing. Perhaps he had deserved her contempt. What she had said was true, so far as it went. But he had really believed what he was doing was right for Frances, hadn't he? Surely what he did hadn't been entirely from selfish motives?

'I love you,' he whispered. But by now, Frances was asleep.

Jack had immediately seen that the Beattie business needed bringing into the twentieth century. As the new king's coronation approached, he tackled George on the subjects of delivery vans and telephones, both of which were obviously essential. But it was a slow job, like water dripping on a stone. And as they smoked their cigars in the office, after shop closing, Jack worked on the 'old barsket'. He had many ideas. Theatre fans often came into the shop, just to look at the ex-comic, and Jack thought they might capitalise on the phenomenon, and advertise. But George would hear none of it.

'For your information, lad, Beattie's has a reputation in this town. And that reputation is not going to be soiled by common advertising!' Eddie smirked with pleasure. And Jack caught him, miming to his wife, that the new son-in-law was nothing but a big head. But it was now the beginning of June, and the coronation of King George was fast approaching. Jack's patience was running out. He must at least get George to agree to the van.

'We've been trying to talk sense into the old barsket for years, son,' Eddie said. 'He'll never give in. All we can do is hang on till he's dead, and then, well . . . we'll see.' He nodded slowly. Jack said nothing. He didn't see how they could hang on. Unlike Eddie, he'd seen the books. Harriet's money was long since spent, and if they didn't cash in on Coronation Year, then God help them! But then, the Great Transport Strike exploded on the nation, and threatened to hit deliveries. Jack outlined the future that was in store.

'Those who don't have their own transport will go to the wall,' he informed George. 'But, if, for the sake of argument, we, for instance, were to get a van, nothing special, just an ordinary van, we'd stand a better chance of getting to the flowers that *are* available. If we don't, the competition's going to beat us into the ground.' George pouted, and sat heavily, thinking.

'Huh! Lawson's'd like to see that! They used to be a sweet shop, you know. An ordinary little sweet shop. Then they started doing catering, and now? Now it's flowers! There's no real gentlemen left.'

'No. Very true.' Jack agreed.

'This strike's a symptom of the change. It'll be revolution next.'

'I expect you're right,' Jack commented. 'And in any kind of war, one has to employ the tactics of the day . . . "all's fair", don't they say?'

'Huh!' George sighed. 'All right. You win! Get your delivery van!'

'And who's going to drive it, I wonder?' Eddie demanded nastily.

'I am!' Maisie piped up to their general consternation. And she did. She learnt quickly, and enjoyed gadding about in the neat little van, the words, 'Beattie's Florists, and Caterers' emblazoned on the side. It was an advert in itself. Jack also tried to get a telephone. But they were too late. They were now in short supply, so, Lawson's got the lion's share of the coronation orders after all.

'We're keeping our end up!' George said cheerfully, patting Jack on the back.

Jack was not satisfied. He knew they could've done better, but he knew too that Frances resented him trying to influence the family business, so he kept his thoughts to himself. Cocooned in silence, Frances' bitterness and resentment towards her husband, grew alongside the infant inside her. The baby was due in September, and it was the hottest summer anyone could remember. Frances thought she would melt away, lying in the afternoons on the bed upstairs, like a stranded whale. Where was the butterfly now? She had been taken over by a baby, and that baby would rule her for the rest of her life. Her hatred was like a fever. It obsessed her. But the fever was not in her alone. Fever gripped the nation. Warfare was in the burning air of summer. Women fought men. Workers fought employers. Class fought class. Then the arrival of a German gunboat at Agadir brought on the growing fear of war with Germany. And many welcomed the idea, including George.

'England is like a boil,' he complained caustically. 'Perhaps Germany will do us the favour of lancing it!'

Amidst such burning hatred, Frances went to bed for her afternoon rest, towards the end of August. Her head was aching. The weight inside her pressed on her bladder. She sighed, and put her hand on the bed, to push herself up. The bed was wet. Her waters had broken. The child was coming. She called out. No one heard. They were all in the shop, or out. She lay back on the bed, panting. It felt so unreal. There was no pain. The child did all the pushing. She cried out, in surprise, as suddenly its head appeared. She looked down on it, in wonder. And then it started again, pushing out of her. Coming in with a cup of tea for his wife, Jack was surprised to see his son, slithering into the world, all on his own.

The silence was broken. Nights of crying exhausted her, as the autumn faded into winter, and 1912 began. Hester had sent them a portrait of her little girl, Anna Fairbairn. She was a pretty child, fair like her father, but fragile, and always crying. She had been born a few months before Frances' son. According to Hester, Tom had gone off alone, China not being a fit place for a woman with a new baby. Hester had stayed behind in London, with Tom's parents, or so she said. Maisie wanted to go down and see her, but Hester put her off. 'The in-laws don't like visitors,' she wrote. George said nothing. Maisie was disappointed, but she had Oswald to dote on. Named after the great Oswald Stoll, the little boy ruled the house. Jack adored him. And to her surprise, Frances was jealous of her husband's affection for him. She became irritable, and George, noticing it, took her to one side. She stood sulkily, as George sat, looking seriously, up at her.

'Are you performing your conjugal duties?' he asked. Had her ears deceived her? That her grandfather should ask such a thing! She stuttered, went red, then looked at the floor. 'I thought as much! Well, I'm warning you, you're going the right way to lose your husband!' Frances was shocked. The idea had simply never occurred to her. She was about to shout that it would be good riddance to bad rubbish, when her grandfather forestalled her. He had obviously thought out the interview beforehand. 'Men need their wives to *show* them they're loved. Jack's patient, but he's a man. Don't try him too much. If you love him, you'd better start warming up a bit!' Winded, Frances shuffled, then sat, abruptly.

'How did you know?'

'I know the signs! I've been watching you and Jack, and I can't just stand by and see you making a mess of things!'

She felt like a child, caught cheating, very small and rather silly. 'I'm no saint, Fran. I seem to remember telling you that once. I've been married three times. My first wife, Harriet's mother, she was grand. But she died. Then I married a woman called Adeline.'

'What's that got to do with . . . ?'

'She wasn't lucky like you. She kept losing her babies. She wanted them all right. She was a *real* woman.' Frances felt the oblique insult and smarted. 'She was warm, loving . . . But she bled. The doctor told us she wasn't to risk pregnancy again, or she might die.' George paused and looked hard at his grand-daughter. 'It's not easy for me to tell you all this, Frances.' She swallowed hard. The old man's natural dignity brought down her pride. She lowered her eyes, as he continued. 'For a long time, we held out. I loved her, you see. I didn't want to hurt her. But, I was a man, and . . . ' Her granda was crying. Frances looked at him, in amazement, deeply moved by his confession. 'I thought I was doing the right thing by Adeline, when I started going with another woman.' He sobbed. 'Her name was Alice Minto.' He paused. Frances was cold with shock.

'Did Adeline know?'

'She never said anything, but she knew. And it hurt her, Frances. I hated myself for it, but I couldn't seem to help myself. And then, we thought Adeline was past danger, and we started . . . loving one another again. But she conceived, and after carrying for a few months, she died, the little boy with her. So much blood . . . I'll never forget it.' He paused, and wiped away his tears with his handkerchief.

'And then you married Grandma?' she prompted softly.

'Yes. And we were fine, till she was expecting our third child.'

'Hester?' George looked at her sharply.

'No. Not Hester. Jane lost the third one. That would have been a boy too. All my sons, my legitimate sons, were lost. But I do have a son, Frances. You've never met him, probably never will. Alice Minto's youngest. You see, after Jane lost the baby, I kept away from her, as I had done Adeline, afraid another pregnancy would kill her, and I took up with Alice again.'

'And that's when she had your son?'

'Yes.' He looked at her meekly. She could not censure him.

'Would you like to see his photograph?'

Frances nodded, and took the dog-eared picture the old man reached out of his wallet. It felt so unreal, and yet the young man was real enough. He stood stiffly, one arm round a spaniel. His soft eyes stared at her, over a spiky beard, afraid to smile. He looked shy, dependable.

'What's his name?'

'James.'

'Does he like poetry?'

'Why?'

'He looks as though he would, that's all.'

'No. More interested in science, really. Science and animals.'

'Nice.' She gave him back the picture.

'I was so glad when you and Jack had yours!' George sniffed back the tears and smiled again. 'A real grandson! Mine! Oh Frances, you don't know what that means to me!'

'But what about Grandma?' George's smile faded. He sighed.

'She found out about Alice one day . . . ' The pain of the memory caught at his mouth, and he stopped, struggling to form the words. 'We were are at Marsden, on the beach. She saw the lad and knew he was mine. Something happened then. It changed everything. I hurt her, Frances. And, I blame myself for . . . ' He could not go on. Frances could hardly bear it.

'What, Granda?'

'For what happened . . . '

'*What* happened Granda?' George shook his head. 'You must have made it up with Grandma. Hester was born!'

George's eyes were vacant. He had receded from her into his memories. Then, at last, his voice came, whispering, out of the distant past.

'I raped her, you know.'

Frances gasped, 'Who? Hester?'

'My wife!' His eyes scorched her. She sprang out of the chair and fled the room, shaking. Her mind raced. Memories, thoughts, feelings, crowded in on her. She was afraid. She needed help, love. She needed Jack. She ran down the stairs into the shop. Jack was not there.

'He's in the cellar, pet!' Maisie told her. Frances hurried through the kitchen, and stood at the gaping door, leading down under the house. The candle glowed in the darkness. Jack was in the far corner, his back to her. He had been bunching up red roses, but now he was tearing away at something. Softly, she went down the stairs, and stood watching, as he pulled at the sackcloth. Then he gasped, and reached for the light, to inspect what he had found: a huge carved statue.

'It used to be grandma's.' Jack turned, almost dropping the candle. For a moment they stood looking at one another. Then Jack spoke.

'What are you doing down here?'

'I was looking for you. I felt lonely.'

'Where's Os?'

'With Aunt Maisie. Do you love me, Jack?' He was stunned.

202

He frowned, as though considering. 'Do you?' Her voice was desperate.

'Yes,' he said. 'Do you love me?'

'Yes.'

'That's all right, then.' Hiding a secret smile, Jack turned back to his discovery, as though nothing had happened. 'What's this? It looks Indian. A god, isn't it?' Frances waited, interested. 'Hindu. Bound to be. I think I'll look him up in the library.' He stood back, excited and pleased. 'What's it doing down here? It's a beautiful piece; made of sandalwood too. I think we should bring it back upstairs, don't you?' Frances frowned.

'It's unlucky.'

Jack was staring at the god.

'Unlucky for whom?'

CHAPTER TWELVE

Michael was conceived during the Royal Variety Performance of 1912. Like Marie Lloyd, 'Scott and Sheridan' (retired), had been omitted from the bill, and they had consoled themselves with a night out in Newcastle accompanied by Will and Maisie. Will and his father had taken over a pub in Gosforth, so Maisie was able to meet up with him more often than before, and Jack, naturally, had accompanied them to the theatre. The two men had always liked each other, and now struck up a real and lasting friendship. But Maisie had complained; 'They natter on about war, trade unions and God knows what! I mean, I go for a night out! A bit of fun! I tell you, Frances, if you don't brace yourself and come with us, next time, I'll ask your mother!' Frances had laughed.

'All right, Auntie! I give in!'

The iceberg had begun to melt. The music hall was a welcome relief from the shop, and became a regular feature of their lives. But tonight was special. And, partly to cock a snook at the 'Royal Variety', and partly to help Will and Maisie out, they all arranged to put up at a hotel, after the show, as a treat. They had booked two double rooms, and, of course, the ladies were to share one while the men shared another. Or, at least, that was what they'd told the folks at home!

'I don't know why you can't just come back in the van, and save yourselves some money!' Ellen had said.

'Bitch!' Maisie hissed in her ear. Ellen went red, and pursed her lips righteously.

'On your head be it!' she said, flouncing off upstairs, to fling herself on her own bed, and cry. Nobody thought of her, did they? Oh no! They were all far too preoccupied with enjoying themselves for that. It wasn't fair! Why should they be allowed to have fun when she didn't? Even bed was for sleeping in these days. Eddie had long since lost interest in sex; or if he hadn't lost interest, he'd certainly lost the ability. God knew what he sat and read in the throne room for hours on end! It couldn't be good for him, all that reading. And, she was damn sure, it wasn't good for her! She ignored the giggling and bustling as Maisie and Fran got ready for the theatre. And, when they knocked on her door, ready to leave, she put her pillow over her head.

'All present and correct, ma'am,' Maisie called out gaily.

'Mam, we're going!'

'Ellen?' Maisie knocked again. 'Are you not going to give us an inspection?' The two women shrugged and left her to it, their spirits unaffected by the snub.

Maisie was driving the van, as usual. They were to meet Will in town. From under the pillow, Ellen heard Jack crank up the engine. She heard it splutter and start, then they were off. Ellen sat, listening to the silence of the house. Eddie had gone next door. His mother was ill. She had cancer of the liver. Her skin was yellow, and she'd whittled down to skin and bone. After all the years of hypochondria, it was hard to take her illness seriously. Ellen snorted. She wouldn't put it past the old faggot to be putting it on! She could be painting her face that funny colour just to attract sympathy. Well, she wasn't going to get any from her! Ma Lidell had never let Eddie go. She'd hung on and hung on, by fair means or foul. And Ellen had had to stand by and watch, as her husband dwindled from a man into an over-grown, ineffectual little boy. Bitterness ate away inside her, until Ellen was as incapable of restoring her marriage as her husband. The devil-may-care expression of her youth had sallowed, till now, her mouth twisted at the ends, and her voice had always the tone of sarcasm in it. Upstairs, a child was crying. She sighed. As

205

usual, she'd been left, holding the baby! Ellen reached under the bed for her bottle of sherry. She poured a tumbler full and drank it down, before going up to little Os.

'It's the upper crust wants war, Will! Not ordinary folk, like us!'

'I don't know, Jack. Being a publican, you hear what people are thinking. Beer loosens tongues, you know. And there's a lot think we should put Germany in her place!'

'I don't believe it. No, Will. Simple people, working people, just aren't used to thinking for themselves, that's all. They ape the opinions of the upper classes. They're like sheep. But if somebody started them thinking . . . '

'There'd be revolution! No, Jack. Let them rule who were born to. They know how to do it. We don't. If they say we have to fight, we will.'

' "Into the valley of death rode the six hundred!" '

'Eh?'

'It's a poem. Never mind.' Maisie yawned.

'H'away, Maisie, let's you and me go to bed, eh? Leave the men to their discussion.' Frances winked. Her grin was infectious.

'Oh aye. Good idea.' Maisie rose from the hotel dining table, and picked up her handbag. 'Goodnight, Will,' she said airily as she turned to go.

'Here, Jack, stop them, will you?'

'Don't panic! They're only joking! . . . I hope!' They laughed. 'All right, girls. You win! How about a little night cap, eh?'

'Not for me, Jack. Thanks.' Frances held out her hand for the key. Jack gave it to her, and Will struggled with his trouser pocket, to extricate his and Maisie's.

'Don't be long, love,' she said, shyly, as she and Frances left the men, and went up to their rooms.

'Have another, Jack?' Will nervously fiddled with his beer glass. 'How about a scotch?'

'Dutch courage, eh?' Jack teased him. 'No thanks, Will. It doesn't help you know, and well . . . I'm not used to drink any more. When in Rome and all that.'

'Oh aye. I forgot. The "old barsket" doesn't allow it, does he? Do you know, I feel as though I know him through and through. And I've never met him. Not once.'

'His bark's worse than his bite.'

'Maisie's scared stiff of him!'

'I don't know. She used to be. But now . . . You've changed her, Will. She's got reckless! Look at her driving!'

'Not if I can help it!' Will laughed.

'And, I mean, she's taking a risk here tonight . . . eh?' Embarrassed, Will looked into his empty beer pot. 'You two beat me. You do really! Why don't you just run away and get married!' Will looked uncomfortable.

'Tell you the truth, Jack. I'm scared.' Jack frowned, non-plussed.

'What of?' he asked at last.

'I'm not sure she'd say "yes" if I *did* ask her.'

'Are you trying to tell me you *haven't* asked her to marry you?'

'No.'

'Good God!' Jack sat back in his chair and looked at Will with new eyes. He shook his head. 'You take the biscuit, you do! I don't know! You'd go and fight for King and country but you've not got the courage to propose to a lass that's given you everything *but* her hand!'

'I suppose it does sound daft, put like that. It's . . . it's just . . . well, I've never got round to it, that's all!'

'Well *get* round to it! And do it now, before people say you only got married because you *had* to!' Will grinned.

'I'd like a nipper.'

'As an interest, they beat football!' Jack was beaming. Will laughed at him.

'Proud father, eh?'

'You're telling me! Go to it, lad! And good luck!' With that, the two men shook hands and departed to their respective rooms.

Number 20 had the 'Do Not Disturb' sign on the door. Number 22 forgot. The porter, carrying the bottle of champagne, stopped and listened outside 20, where there was a lot of giggling and bantering going on.

'Come on! We'll have our own show!' Jack cried, as Frances dressed up in his clothes. 'Watch out, Vesta Tilley!' He laughed and dug out his comb to play the accompaniment to Frances' 'Burlington Bertie'. They were good too! Should go on the halls! He watched through the key hole and was still laughing as he knocked on the door of number 22. There was a scuffle, a male cough, and then the door opened.

'Compliments of Mr and Mrs Scott,' said the porter, handing Will the bottle of champagne and the glasses. 'Shall I cork it for you?'

'Oh! Aye. Thanks very much!' Will said. The porter pretended not to see the lady disappearing under the bed. The cork popped loudly. Startled, Maisie jumped and hit her head on the springs above.

'Ouch!' she yelled. Will covered the 'boing' of the springs with a fit of coughing. Grinning, the porter took his tip, winked and left.

'Cheeky beggar!' Will said. 'H'away, Maisie! You can come out now! It's safe!' Maisie emerged, red-faced and dishevelled. 'Oh by the way,' he said, as she rearranged herself. 'Before I pour out any of this stuff, I don't suppose you'd like to marry me, would you?'

'Eh?'

'Oh, never mind.' Will poured the champagne, with shaking hands.

'What's the matter with you, man? You're pouring the stuff everywhere! Here, let me!' The champagne sparkled in the glasses.

'To us, pet,' Will said, raising his glass.

'To us.' Maisie drank, then sneezed.

'It's gone up me nose,' she said, reaching for her hanky. Will gave her his, and she blew loudly.

'Nice of them, isn't it?' Will was inspecting the bottle of champagne.

'Aye. They're a canny pair!' Maisie agreed.

'It must be nice to be married . . .'

'Yes. It must, mustn't it?' They stood, champagne in hand, looking at one another. At last, Maisie said, 'Shall I take me teeth out, then?' Will smiled, tears in his eyes.

'Eeh, I do love you, pet.'

Maisie adored children. Jack watched her, nursing Michael, soon after he was born, and shook his head. If only Maisie had taken fire that night, as Frances had, she and Will would have had to get married then! He just couldn't understand it. Why hadn't the silly sod proposed? Ellen was reading a letter from Harriet, post-marked Holloway.

'Back inside again, I see!' Jack said by way of making conversation.

'Huh! If she wants to go to prison, I don't know why she doesn't just come here and be done with it!' Ellen complained.

'Come on! It's not so bad!'

'Oh, I know, if you had your way, we'd have the telephone in, and there'd be even more work! Good job they're in short supply, if you ask me! And a good job Davey Lawson's doing so well an' all.'

'Stop moaning, Mam. I'm sick to hear of Davey Lawson!' Frances snapped. 'And stop taunting her, Jack! Honestly, I feel like a referee!' Jack sighed and picked up the paper again. The baby gurgled. Jack looked up, and watched Frances' face soften, as she took him from Maisie. The little hands reached up and touched her forehead. 'Tut! You'd think he knew!'

'Knew what?' Jack asked, smiling.

'I've got a headache!' Frances cooed at the baby. 'Eeh, he's canny, isn't he?' And Os, playing with a toy car at her feet, pulled angrily at her skirt.

'All right, lad.' Jack soothed him. 'Come on. Let's play a game, eh?' Michael turned to watch. The big blue eyes wondered at the bad humour of his brother. He joggled up and down, as if he wanted to join in the game. His hand reached out to the toy.

'Gerroff!' The two year old screamed.

'Oswald Scott! Behave yourself!' Jack told him sternly. But Os was scowling. The baby didn't like it and began to cry.

'There now! Look what you've done!' Frances told her eldest. 'And Michael hardly ever cries!' It was true. While Os had kept them awake, nights on end, Michael slept peacefully and, unlike his brother, suckled at his mother's breast. Frances was proud of this last achievement and Jack loved watching her, as the little mouth closed on her nipple and sucked the milk from her. It was natural, how things ought to be, a real family, living in harmony together. And Frances was enjoying her role at last, accepting, instead of fighting. She even loved Jack more. Her body welcomed his at night. She opened to him as a garden to its gardener, responding to his love and care. And the shadows of the past fled. There were no more nightmares in the old house.

The monster in the roots slept. She was immune to the poisonous whispering, her contentment the antidote. Let her Mam and Dad quarrel. Let Hester do what she willed. Frances was not responsible for them. Only sometimes, when she remembered her year on the halls, she began to fret again. She was still so young. If only she could have had a little longer to be herself, if only Jack had been honest with her, 'if only, if only . . . ' No. She mustn't listen. For the voices of the past were inside her. She must shut them out. The past was past. Let it go. And Michael helped. Responding to her mood, he nudged her out of the past, making her smile again. Instinctively the whole family revolved around him. And when jealousy made Oswald angry at his mother, as now, Jack came into his fatherly role, lovingly disciplining the child and playing with him.

'What's Harriet May want?' George asked, as Ellen passed the letter on to him. 'More bail, I suppose!'

'No. Apparently she wants to die in gaol, for the cause!'

'Silly bitch!' George snapped. 'It just shows women aren't up to having the vote! I never heard of anything so stupid, eh Jack?'

'Well, if you ask me, George, it's all a storm in a tea cup. What difference is it going to make if they do get it? I mean what harm's it going to do to give it to them, if it's what they want? They're not all going to suddenly take over men's jobs, refuse to have children, and start wearing trousers, are they? Look at China! The Chinese government happily passes a bill saying yes, all right we'll give the women a vote. Thank you very much, say the women and off they go back to their pots and pans, just as before. Give it them, I say! Why not?'

'The Chinese women must be a damn sight more sensible than our lot, that's all I can say! Look at that silly bitch, Emily what's-her-name, throwing herself in front of the king's horse!'

'All part of the English death wish.' Jack had got onto his favourite topic. Eddie groaned, and went out to the throne room.

'You've forgotten your newspaper, Eddie!' Ellen called, waving it at him.

'I don't want it! The news is always bad!' He closed the door behind him.

Through the knot hole in the midden door, Eddie watched

Grace, the cat. Spread-eagled on the window ledge, she opened one eye, to observe the fly, buzzing by her ear. The eye closed. Slowly, a bead of sweat dropped down Eddie's nose. He watched it fall onto his trousers. Then he looked back at the cat. Eyes shut, she raised a paw to dab feebly at the fly, which had departed some minutes before. Eddie wished he was a cat. After all, why should he get all worked up about Germany? Huh! It was just a fly buzzing in England's ear. He'd close his eyes and it would go away. Discretion is the better part of valour, he told himself. If only his Ma was still alive. She'd say that. She wouldn't want him to fight. He missed her. New people were in next door now; strangers in his home. It was funny, he didn't miss his Dad. He'd popped off straight after her. He'd had a week to himself, after the funeral. He'd gone hysterical with joy, and then he'd dropped dead, just fallen down in the street, crumpled, like a pair of trousers when you've taken them off. Ma Lidell was the legs to her husband's trousers. He hadn't been able to stand up without her. So he'd died. Eddie'd never thought his Ma would die. She seemed indestructible. It had overturned his world that. Suddenly, he realised how frail was flesh, and he was afraid; afraid of death, afraid of disease, raging unseen within, afraid of living. He hid away in the throne room, hugging himself, as now, watching the cat, as the fly came back and it slept on.

Ellen had gone to bed early. Eddie could hear her snores from down the passage. She always slept heavily after sherry. He opened the door noisily and went in. Ellen snorted, swallowed her tonsils then sank back into the shallow snoring of a lighter sleep. Eddie sighed and sat at the dressing table, staring at his face. In the twilight, he looked pale, ghostly. He pulled down his eyes and stared at the red flesh underneath. Then slowly he began to take off his shirt. He'd been looking forward to this moment all day, ever since he'd first suspected it, when he was sitting on the throne. He raised his arm and looked. It was red and puffy.

'Ellen! Wake up!' he shouted. Ellen spluttered, groaned, and came to.

'I think I've got a lump.' He was feeling under his arm.

'Eh?'

'I think I've got a lump.' He came and sat by her on the edge of the bed.

'Let's see!' Ellen said, and automatically inspected the proferred arm pit.

'Yes. You have.' She was smiling wryly at Eddie's horrified expression. 'It's a boil. You should wash more often, man!'

'That's not funny, Ellen!' Eddie sniffed haughtily, and put his shirt back on.

'Why don't you go down to the cellar and spray the flowers, eh? Do something useful for a change!'

'Do it yourself!' came the loving rejoinder.

But Jack was already down there. By the light of a candle he pumped the water and sprayed the flowers; roses, lilies, the perfume of the blooms of high summer rose up in the drenching water, like a garden in the rain. He didn't mind doing this job. In fact, he quite liked it. And he had company. Ganesha was watching him, the boy, with the elephant's head. He'd gone to the library to look him up. He had been right. Ganesha was a Hindu deity. He had four arms, each with a weapon in its hand, and he was depicted riding on a mouse. Once, long ago, the forces of evil were becoming much too powerful, and were threatening to overthrow the forces of good. In distress, the deities went to Parvati, the Mother of the Universe, pleading with her, to give them a child, a boy, who would vanquish evil and restore the balance. She agreed and, during her husband's absence, produced Ganesha. When the Almighty Father, Lord Shiva, came home, he found this boy barring entrance to his wife. He, a mere child, was the powerful defender of his Mother's honour. None of the gods could get past him, for he vanquished them all, and when his Father, not knowing who he was, cut off the head of the innocent boy, Parvati, beside herself with grief and rage, threatened to bring about the dissolution of the entire world. To appease her, Shiva restored the child to life, by giving him the head of the first creature he saw, an elephant with one tusk. So, Parvati was pleased and the world was saved . . . The candle flickered, and the huge shadow engulfed the cellar walls. Jack shivered. 'To save the world'. They were on the brink of war, even now; the war to end all wars; perhaps it would be the end of the world . . . a rat, emboldened by Jack's stillness,

212

scurried in the corner. Jack let it be. It could be the vehicle of the god . . .

Frances listened to the arguments on both sides, as she made up the orders for the shop, wiring flowers into wreaths, and making cakes, that is, when Davey hadn't underpriced them and done them out of the job! The rising voices set off both the children. They cried, and it gave her a headache. It was as though the teetering balance of Europe threatened also the delicate domestic balance of the home. 'Peace'! Huh! There was none in this house! Not with two great men arguing the toss!

'Peace at any price!' George bellowed. 'Even if the price is revolution?'

'It doesn't have to be a violent change, George!' Jack tried and tried to talk the old man round to his point of view.

'Tell the miners that!'

'The landed class don't want to give up their power, their money or their land. But it doesn't belong to them. Never did. It belongs to England.'

'Socialist!'

'I believe in a moderate line, George. If the Lords had passed the Parliament Bill . . . '

'How could they? It would have meant the end of the old order!'

'If there's a war, the old order, as you call it, will end anyway! It's time for negotiation, for compromise.'

'Rubbish! We'll be fighting in defence of order not against it!'

'Bang, bang! You're dead!'

'Sh, Os! Your Granda's talking!' Os glared at his mother, and went on with his game under the kitchen table.

'Who'll give the order to start the fighting? Who are the powers that be? The upper classes, George! And they have a vested interest. The people will only fight if their country's attacked. But the officers, they'll fight for arms profit, and to keep the workers down! They'll invent a war for their own ends! They're Empire-makers! They'll aggress. The people only defend.'

'Gerroff, Michael! You've smashed my army now!' There was a scuffle under the table. Frances rescued the baby from the attack of his brother.

213

'Michael, you've spoilt Oswald's game! Naughty boy!' And now they were both crying. The men raised their voices over them.

'Little orphan boy! You can't stand being the "have not", can you?' George shouted spitefully. 'Peace at any price, eh? Well, Jack, it sounds like cowardice to me! If I was young enough, I'd fight myself!' George stood tall, like a lion, his barrel of a body like John Bull. He raised his arm high in the air, 'For England and Saint George!' he cried patriotically.

'Hooray!' Os cheered.

George had given Os the set of toy soldiers, infantry and cavalry and he enjoyed playing with his grandson, hour after hour on the dining room table. And Frances was grateful, as she slaved in the kitchen over the ironing. At least it kept young Oswald out of the way. Maisie was nursing little Michael in the rocking chair, singing songs, to the rhythmic thudding of Frances' iron, while outside, in the yard, Jack was smoking. He never presumed to do so in the house. It was his one moment of peace in the long working day. When she'd finished the big pile of shirts, collars, table cloths and napkins, Frances took out her cup of tea, to sit with him, as usual, looking up at the stars. It was a cool autumn night. She shivered and Jack put his arm round her to keep off the night air.

'Happy?' he asked.

'I suppose so.' She sighed.

'If the government of Germany's as stiff-necked as your granda, we're in for trouble, love.'

'So you keep saying.' The moon was large; an amber orb looming over the roof tops.

'Have I told you I love you lately?' She giggled. It was a game they played.

'Now and then.' He smiled and waited for her to return the compliment. And she knew he waited. But she kept on looking at the moon, watching it sink behind the houses. Why didn't she just tell him she loved him too, and be done with it? But something was holding her back. What was it? The argument in the kitchen had upset her. The whisperings of discord stirred in her. She had caught it, like an infectious disease. And she was angry with herself for allowing it into her. She would pull herself together and say the words, 'I love you!' She took a deep breath, to speak. But Jack, tired of waiting, turned away to stub out the end of his cigarette on the window sill.

'You haven't forgiven me, have you?' he said. Frances' heart lurched. She looked at him abruptly.

'What do you mean? What for?'

'For bringing you back here.' She said nothing. Her mind was a welter of confusion. She didn't know what to say. What was he stirring it all up for? She had been about to tell him she loved him! It wasn't fair! She didn't want to think of whether or not she had forgiven. She had almost forgotten. Wasn't that enough? 'I'm right, aren't I?' She shrugged. ' "Scott and Sheridan" weren't all that good, you know.'

'Yes we were!' she retorted angrily.

'And even if we were, the music hall's finished.'

'Rubbish!'

'It is, love. We did better out of the Royal Command than Vesta Tilley herself!'

'What do you mean?'

'His nibs.' He nudged her, and she laughed, but he had raised the devil in her, and she could not stop herself. 'After the war, nothing'll be the same, including the theatre. We'd've been out on our beam ends, love!'

'You're scared, aren't you? Granda's right!'

'Of course I'm scared. Any man in his right mind'd be scared. I'm scared for you. I'm scared for Os and Michael.'

'You're scared for your own skin.'

'Yes. I'm scared for that as well.'

'Coward.'

'That's not fair, Fran!'

'Yes, it is!'

'If you were a man . . . ' Her voice was bitter.

'I'd've thought I'd proved that to you many a time!' He was trying to make light of the argument. But Frances wouldn't have it.

'Have you now! Is that all it is? Sex? I've proved I'm a woman, I know that!'

'Oh?'

'I've brought two bairns into the world, haven't I? Now it's your turn. And if you were a man, you'd want to defend your wife and children!'

215

'Of course I want to defend you . . . '

'Huh! I can just see you putting up your fists!' With that Frances went inside and left Jack, staring at the disappearing moon.

Both were shocked by the encounter. They made it up in bed that same night, but damage had been done. Jack himself had stirred up the monster of discontent and Frances was angry at him for doing it. But that same anger fed the monster, and it grew. Everyone seemed to be edgy these days. And yet fear was mixed with excitement. People talked of little else but Germany, Dreadnoughts and the like. The coming terror drew them like a magnet. It had excitement, glamour.

'Know what the English disease is?' Jack asked their customers in the shop. 'The English see disaster ahead, and then change course to make sure they meet it head on.' The laughter greeting this piece of wisdom was always strained. And yet, Frances knew Jack was right. Wasn't she doing the same? She fought against it. She loved Jack. He was a good husband and father. She was the luckiest lass in Shields. The very idea of him going off to fight made her shake in her shoes. She didn't want to lose him! And yet the voices whispered in her ears. They told her Jack had cheated her. They told her Jack had used her. They told her he was selfish and a coward to boot. And she could not shut them out. Oh, why had he stirred her up against him? He had gone on and on about the war, arguing with Granda, sowing discord in the family. He had said she had not forgiven him. It was his fault!

Blame shifted to Jack's side, and the voices grew in confidence.

The wily old barsket had got two free tickets for the boxing display at the old town hall in Market Square and Frances was, even now, sitting amongst the big wigs from the council, watching the taut, muscly man she had once called a 'pompous twerp', young Davey Lawson. Well, he'd got the last laugh! The tables had been turned. She was watching him on stage instead of the other way round, and he was the one with a future, not her! Frances' future was behind her. Jack had seen to that. She was still angry at him! She'd take a swing at Jack, if only she was a man! Sitting on his backside, pontificating, he was selfish

216

through and through. All he wanted was his own comfort. And by God he had it, on her back! George let out a roar of approval.

'The so-and-so's good! I'll say that!' George was a just man, and, watching the young upstart landing punches on the miner from St Hilda's colliery, brought out his sporting sense of fairness. Frances was amazed. She never knew Davey had it in him! Had she misjudged her one-time admirer? Watching him, she felt quite proud of having been his old flame. He'd come on in a lot of ways had Davey Lawson, and not only in the gentlemanly art of boxing. Lawson's confectioners had become a thriving caterers under his management. Of course, what he did wasn't fair. He undercut Beattie's, by subsidising the flowers with the catering and the sweets. And then, slowly, his satisfied customers becoming permanent clients, the canny lad raised his prices bit by bit, until now, he was doing very nicely indeed. The town of Shields was big enough for both of them, really. There were plenty of rich folk about. Perhaps, George had thought, Beattie's and Lawson's could come to a gentlemanly agreement; arrange a sort of truce.

'You used to know the lad, didn't you?' George had asked. Frances nodded.

'It was a long time ago, Granda.'

'Never mind. It's worth a try.' Frances had pulled a face. What was worth a try, she wondered? She cried out, as Davey's fist hit his opponent squarely on the nose. George gave her a disapproving look. She was supposed to avert her gaze, smelling salts at the ready, in ladylike distress. But she couldn't tear her eyes away. Davey was amazing, like a machine, hammering at the other man. The referee blew his whistle. The miner was finished. He reeled back against the ropes. Davey's hand went up in the air, and Frances clapped approvingly.

'I train with Indian clubs most nights, after the shop's closed,' Davey told her granda. 'I like to keep in good shape. Never know when you're going to need it, do you?' George murmured his agreement. They were standing outside The Glebe Chapel, after Sunday morning service. Davey still taught at the Sunday School. All the young lads looked up to him, tweaking their hats as they passed them on the street. Frances felt strangely shy with him, as you do with someone you once knew well and disdained.

'How's your mother?' George was asking.

'Well, thank you, sir.' George approved of the 'sir'.

'I wonder you can manage in the shop, with all that business.'
His eyes twinkled and Davey laughed.

'We've got a couple of good women working for us.' George
nodded.

'What you need's a wife!'

'True.' He smiled and turned courteously to Frances. 'But I'm
afraid someone else snapped up the most eligible lady in Shields.'

Frances blushed furiously and George laughed. Then Davey
nodded and made as if to go. But George stopped him, touching
him with his cane.

'Perhaps you and I could talk business one of these days,
young fellow-me-lad! We might do one another a favour . . . '

'We do seem to have cornered the market between us . . .'

'Exactly, Lawson. I have influential contacts, as you
know . . . ' Davey nodded. 'Instead of being in competition we
could . . . '

'You scratch my back, eh?'

'That's about it.' Davey nodded.

'Give me a ring some time,' he said airily then went, leaving
George, somewhat winded.

But the 'entente cordiale' between Beattie and Lawson was
shattered along with the entente between Britain and Germany.
The tide of war could not be pushed back. On the first of August
1914, Germany and Russia declared war. On the third of August,
there was war between France and Germany. And then Germany
marched into Belgium. At midnight on the fourth, Germany
having failed to respond to the British ultimatum to withdraw
from Belgium, England declared war on Germany. A kind of
euphoria, fed by patriotism, and dreams of heroism, gripped the
nation like a fever. It was a 'Land of Hope and Glory'. Mobilisation began at once and young men flocked in droves to
volunteer for the fighting. Davey Lawson was among the first in
Shields.

Hearing the news, George slapped him on the back after
chapel, tears in his eyes; 'I'm proud of you, son,' he said, in a

breaking voice. 'You set an example to the rest of the town. "Always Ready", eh? Good motto that. Let's hope Shields lives up to it!'

'They say it'll all be over by Christmas.' Davey smiled confidently. 'I wanted to get in on the fighting before it's too late!'

'I wish others thought as you do, son.'

'After that sermon you gave, sir, I'm sure they will.'

'Words, son. That's all. If I was a bit younger . . . Aye I'd be in there with you. In the thick of it.' He lunged with his umbrella and caught Frances' sleeve, yanking her backwards. Davey steadied her, as she readjusted her dress. 'What's your regiment to be, son?'

'Royal Engineers!'

'My, that's grand! Isn't it Fran?'

'It was the boxing swung it for me, sir.' But others were thronging to shake the hero's hand. The Beattie family gave way and Davey threw Fran a last cheerful wave, as they turned to go. George's sermon on the subject of righteous war had stirred the youth of the congregation, who were ready and waiting, outside the recruiting stations, to sign on, as soon as their doors were opened the next morning. But neither Jack nor Eddie had attended the service.

'Hiding in the lavatory!' George sneered. 'I'm ashamed of the pair of them. What about your young man, Maisie?' Maisie was startled. It was the first time her father had acknowledged his existence.

'I don't know, Dad. I've not heard from him, but I'm seeing him on Thursday, like.' George grunted.

'Now we shall see what he's made of.'

' "Rats and snails and puppy dogs' tails" ' Will commented wryly, when Maisie told him. But they were both cock-a-hoop, all the same.

'Don't let the old barsket force you into a position where you've got to sign up,' Jack warned his mate. 'He's a crafty old devil.'

'Oh I *want* to!' Will declared. 'I mean you've got to fight for King and country, haven't you? Eh? Look, Jack, if the Germans can overrun Belgium, they can overrun us! And God knows what terrible things they'd do here! Playin' havoc with all the women and children! Doesn't bear thinkin' of, man!'

Maisie was fairly worshipping Will with her big, shining eyes, and he loved it. He grew inches in her company that night. Jack smiled to himself. The pair of them were older than him but they were like bairns really. He hoped it kept fine for them.

'Don't believe all you hear about it being over by Christmas,' he warned. 'From what I've heard, Kitchener doesn't believe that, for one.'

'Hadaway wi' your bellyachin', man! The Hun won't last *that* long! Not with Geordies after him!'

'Well,' Jack laughed, 'stick our Maisie in a tank, and he'll run clean back to Germany. She's worth a dozen armies, her!' Their laughter was on the edge of tears. Maisie took out her handkerchief and wiped her eyes, as Will, gently, took her hand.

'Where's Frances tonight?' he asked, to change the subject.

'Stock taking!' Maisie explained. 'I was lucky to get away meself! We've been stocking up the business in case there's food shortages. We've got flour under the beds and sugar in the wardrobes! You can't get turned round for stuff!'

'Aye. It's the same at the pub.' Will suddenly got a wistful look in his eye. 'I think I'd like to fly, you know.' Maisie and Jack gasped. 'Do something other than the ordinary army, anyway. Aye, I'd like to fly in an aeroplane.'

'You know what the old barsket says about that?' Will shook his head.

'No. But I can guess. If God meant us to fly he'd have given us wings!'

Davey was off before they knew it. He and the first raggle-taggle mob of enthusiastic volunteers left for Newcastle Central Station and the south. A short period of training was ahead of them, before embarcation, and the western front. Crowds came to see them off. George, Frances and the two boys were among them. It was a great day for the town, to see the brave young men going off to war. Frances' heart burst with pride for them. Why, if she'd been a man, she'd have been among them! And George wept because he was too old. But Will, cautious as ever, wavered. What about the pub? What about his Dad? In September the lights of the town were dimmed. The shadows of the coming winter crept toward them. Unrelieved by the bright glow of street lamps, the gloom seemed deeper, the shadows longer. There was little news from the front. Surely their boys would be all right? Surely there was nothing to fear? The Almighty Father was watching over them, all through the long dark night.

CHAPTER THIRTEEN

The Almighty Father watched and did nothing. George watched too, as the little boy set up the battle lines on the Beattie dining table. The conventions of war demanded that the cavalry charge, like knights of old, the infantry bringing up the rear. Swift-moving action would bring about a swift conclusion, the enemy vanquished. The Battle of the Marne was fought in this way and the Germans were pushed back. All was going according to plan. Sitting atop the Ypres hills, the British army saw ahead of it occupied Belgium, and beyond, the great railway junction of Roulers, the tracks running on to the very gates of the Ruhr ammunitions factories. Behind them, the land gently sloped down to the ancient walled city of Ypres, a sleepy market town. Further back, beyond that, they could see the shimmering waters of the English Channel. But now, the Germans pushed the British, over the hills, and, down, down into the Ypres valley. Then, close by the Menin Gate, they paused to draw breath, before the 'last onslaught'. Most of the British ammunition had been used up and as, at last, volunteer reinforcements arrived from the training grounds of England, the regular soldiers looked hopefully to them for support. They came, like a local boxing team, surprised to have found itself transported from a village hall, into the middle of a real live war. So young Davey Lawson strode onto the scene, fists up, ready for battle.

War was a game played by gentlemen. The nation were willing spectators at home, and the young followed the sport eagerly.

'Bang bang you're dead!' Os cried. Jack looked up from his paper, observing his young son with his grandfather.

'That's right!' George encouraged the child. 'You see, son, we can't let that lot there get to the sea. Our soldiers have got to stop them.' The lad let out a rat-atat-tat of machine gun fire, mowing down the German lines.

'It's all right now,' he reassured his great-grandfather, 'they're all dead. The war's over.' George laughed.

'See, Jack? I told you! You'll be too late for the fighting!' Jack said nothing. He turned the pages of the paper.

'Looks like the line's holding anyway.'

Downstairs, in the kitchen, Ellen, Maisie and Frances were baking. The town hall were putting on a fund-raising do for the soldiers. Beattie's and Lawson's had both been asked to do the catering. It was a competition and Ma Lawson and her shop girls were also sweating over the stove in Ocean Road. But Ma Lawson had more incentive. Her lad was away doing his bit for his country. Back at number eighteen Victoria Terrace, the Beattie women fought on, fashioning guns out of marzipan, piping out the pattern of the Union Jack with coloured icing, ashamed of their menfolk.

'You know Baroness Orczy?' Maisie asked, as she stopped to clean the steam from her glasses.

'Not personally, pet. No.'

'Well, she writes them novels I like. Anyway, according to Aunt Harriet she's set up a League of Women. It's in the *Daily Mail*.'

'Eeh! Are we goin' to play football?'

'Don't be daft!' Maisie fished for the newspaper clipping in the pocket of her pinafore. She found it, coughed and began to read . . . ' "Pledge: I hereby pledge myself most solemnly . . . " '

'We've not got to take the pledge an' all, have we?' Ellen was dismayed.

'Not *that* pledge, man! " . . . . most solemnly in the name of my

King and country, to persuade every man I know to offer his services to his country, and I also pledge myself never to be seen in public with any man who being in every way free and fit has refused to respond to his country's call." There now!' Ellen was looking through the letter.

'Harriet says *she's* joined the league. Mind, she would! She says she's got a special badge for it an' all!'

'I think even Eddie would flee to the recruiting office with *her* behind him!' Maisie laughed. She picked up her knife and got on chopping the cherries, as the women slipped, each into her own thoughts.

If Jack wouldn't fight, then Frances would fight for him! Beating the butter and sugar with her wooden spoon, till her arm ached she worked on, into the night. Jack was going with her granda to the flower market in the morning and he was in bed, by the time she wearily climbed the stairs to their room. She undressed by the light of a candle and lay stiffly beside him, as the shadows flickered across the bedroom walls. Harriet *would* join the league. Just like her. Mind, she had to admire the old battle-axe! At least she was doing something! 'If women ruled the world it'd be a better place.' She was right as well. Look what a mess the men'd got us into! And now half of them wouldn't even go and fight to put it right! Marriage was a pointless institution. The men weren't up to it. It was all very well, loving, honouring and obeying somebody like . . . like . . . Frances pictured Davey Lawson, just before he left for the war. Now he was a hero! A real man! Whereas Jack . . . Michael stirred in his cot and began to cry. Frances sighed, lay listening for a few minutes, then got up to comfort him. His little arms reached out for her, in the glow of the night light, and she smiled, soothing him, holding him suddenly close. She was glad he wasn't old enough to fight; or Os either. How could women send their sons to be killed? Some of them were little more than children. She took the baby into bed with her, comforting herself. Suddenly she realised that Jack too was somebody's son, even if he didn't know whose. Jack, her husband, her own man. He wasn't so bad. He was kind and gentle. She was lucky. She loved him and she knew he loved her. Holding the baby close, her free hand reached to touch her husband's back. He shifted, sensing her, and as her arm slowly circled him, he settled into a deeper and more contented sleep. Frances lay awake a little longer. 'Men need their wives to show them they're loved,' her granda'd said. 'He's patient, but he's a man. Don't try him too much.' A man. Her granda'd thought a lot of Jack at one time. Well, she would be patient too. She'd wait and see what Jack would do.

Posters had gone up round the town, saying, 'Your Country Needs You!' George had put one in the shop window. Justice Mrs White had started up a local section of the League, in Westoe Village, and was pleased to see it, as she passed. Of course, these days, she tended to go to Lawson's who were cheaper, but she would gladly pay a higher price for her flowers, if it meant the old lion would lend himself to their cause and speak for them. With this in mind, she clanged the bell on the shop door in Fowler Street, one day, nearing Christmas.

'I wondered if you could show me what you have by way of Christmas wreaths, dear.' Frances called for her father, who came out of the kitchen, a cup of tea in his hands. Suddenly developing a limp Eddie hobbled into the shop. 'How awful for you, Mr Lidell,' Mrs White exclaimed. 'You must be champing at the bit to get into harness!'

'Pardon?'

'Join up.'

'Oh, yes, ma'am.' Eddie agreed at once. 'It's a real shame about me foot!' And he did a peremptory salute. It drove Ellen mad.

'There's nowt wrong with him!' she told the customer. 'Nothing that a bit of spud bashing in the army wouldn't put right.' Eddie's eyes reproached his wife. 'Huh!' she snorted, and went into the back shop for her own tea. Mrs White was shaken. Surely she could not have been mistaken about the Beattie resolution? Her posh voice had pierced the upper regions of George's office. His door opened. He strode out onto the balcony. 'Ah, Mr Beattie, just the man I wanted to see!' He smiled and came down to her at once. 'I was hoping to prevail on you to speak for us, in aid of the war effort.' Mrs White had a lot of influence in the village. Christmas was coming and the goose needed fattening.

'I'd be honoured, Mrs White.' He bowed graciously, the buttons on his waistcoat, straining.

'I'm sure that with your mighty eloquence, there'll not be a man in Shields out of khaki by Christmas!' she said. George was flattered.

'Nothing I'd like more, ma'am.' He stood up straight, almost saluting her. Frances pushed the catalogue towards the customer. Mrs White shook hands and turned to the selection of wreaths. Then Jack walked in, whistling. Mrs White was affronted.

'Sorry, ma'am.' Jack took off his cap in mock reverence.

'And what's *your* excuse for not doing your duty!' she challenged, looking him up and down. Jack shrugged.

'I'll do my duty if and when I'm asked,' he answered quietly. Mrs White shut the catalogue with a bang.

'Don't bother yourself about the war effort, Beattie. I daresay there'll be a man in uniform, home on leave, who could speak for us. Goodbye!' She stalked out, and the bell clanged joyously behind her. George's face was like a thunder cloud.

'What did you want me to do?' Jack asked. 'Limp?'

As the first volunteers came home on leave, the pressure to join up intensified further. The ditherers began to give way. But Jack was not amongst them. He had other ideas.

'Winston Churchill's asking for men for the navy!' Will said, during the interval at the Empire. 'I've half a mind to sign on meself!'

'The navy?' Maisie whooped. 'All the nice girls love a sailor . . . '

'Sh, man!' Frances hissed at her. 'Everybody's looking!' It was embarrassing being with two men in civvies. Everywhere they looked there was khaki. But Maisie was not to be put down.

'Do you think you might, eh?' Will nodded silently, and finished his tea.

'There's a recruiting ship in the Tyne and me Dad's got help now, so . . . '

'Well,' Jack raised his cup. 'Here's to you, Will. I wish you luck!'

'Why don't you come with's, man.' Maisie was looking hopefully at Jack. It would be nice to have somebody there to keep an eye on her sweetheart. But Jack was not to be drawn.

'No.' He shook his head. 'Anyway, I was thinking I might go down the pits.' Frances gasped.

'Why?'

'They're short-handed! There's a lot joined up. They need men to dig coal, and I'm an embarrassment in the shop, so . . . '

'Why don't you just go with Will!' Frances shouted. Many heads turned in their direction, among them, that of Davey Lawson. He waved, and came over, shaking hands with them all in turn.

'What's it like out there? Or haven't you been to the front yet?'

'Oh aye. I've been to the front. It's all right. Bit short of ammunition, mind.' It was bravado and they all knew it.

'What do you mean?' Will was worried.

'Well for the first few weeks we all just sat in trenches being shot at. We had one gun to the battalion. We used to take turns with it, just holding it like. We couldn't fire it because there were no bullets. But it was nice to feel it in your hand. We're holding the line, mind!' Jack shook his head.

'Fred Karno's army, eh?'

'It can't be true!' Frances insisted.

'Aye well.' Davey was turning back to his friends, 'Believe what you like. Most people do.'

'It can't be!' Frances was pale. 'It just can't.'

Jack touched her arm gently.

'I think I'll wait till they've got guns, before I join up, love,' he said. 'Meanwhile I'll just make do with digging coal.'

'What about you, Will?' Now Maisie was worried.

'I signed on yesterday, pet. It was a spur of the moment thing. I read what Winston said in the papers, and, well, I'll see the world, an' that . . . ' Suddenly Maisie was crying. Till this moment she hadn't felt it was anything more than a great adventure. And now, suddenly, the reality of it hit her, like a blow to the stomach.

'I don't want to lose you, Will,' she said. Then she blurted out, 'Oh, Will, why don't you marry me, before you go?' Jack and Frances laughed and started clapping. Maisie was smiling through her tears. 'Please, Will!' He reached out and held her hand.

'That wouldn't be fair, pet. What if I . . . ?'

'Don't!'

227

'Tell you what, though, just to make sure of you, just to show all the other buggers, why don't we get engaged, eh?'

'Go on, Maisie! It's now or never!' Frances urged.

'Oh yes, Will,' Maisie cried. 'Any time you like!'

They didn't go in for the second half of the show. Instead, they cracked a bottle of champagne in the Station Hotel. Laughing and crying, they bade Will goodnight, as they climbed into the van together. Tomorrow, Maisie would be back to buy her ring, and then she'd bring her sweetheart home for tea. Even George couldn't turn away a hero. They were home and dry.

'They're unlucky, you know!' Ellen was inspecting her sister's opal engagement ring. Maisie's heart missed a beat.

'Mam! Did you have to?' Frances said angrily.

'Is that true?' Jack asked.

'No, man!' Frances spoke emphatically. 'Opals aren't unlucky at all, not unless you forget to take them off when you wash the dishes. They dissolve in water!'

'When are you off, young man?' George asked.

'End of the week.' George nodded approvingly.

'It's up to each and every man to do his duty,' he said.

'Yes, sir. Mind it's dangerous down the mines an' all.' Frances kicked Will, under the table. But George was acting as though he hadn't heard. He reached into his pocket.

'I see you don't have a watch.'

'No, sir.'

'Perhaps this will fit the bill.' George handed him a gold plated fob watch on a chain. 'I was presented with two or three of these, in my time as Mayor of Shields. You might as well have one of them.' Will looked at the inscription on the back.

'I'd be proud to, sir,' he said reverently.

'Thank you, Dad.' Maisie's face glowed with joy. Will handed her the watch to look at, and smiling, she gazed at it, before handing it back. It was the happiest day of her life. George shook his head. His most unlikely daughter had come up with a good 'un. Who would have thought it? The ugly ducking, eh? He shook hands with Will, before he left, and Jack was reminded of the time in Birmingham, when he and the old man had also shaken on a deal. As though he had heard the thought, George murmured through his beard,

228

'I'm disappointed in you, lad. You've let me down. You've let your wife down and your country.'

'I'm sorry you think so, George.' Jack turned back into the shop, heavy-hearted. When he looked round to see if his wife was following him, he saw her, with her back to him, waving tearfully at the departing sailor, protected by her granda's arm.

Will was cheerful, and full of hope. One long last kiss, a blast from the station master's whistle, and he was off for his long period of training at the 'Crystal Palace'. Maisie went home, wept for an hour, cuddling Grace, and then felt better. After all, the Western Front was a long way from the sea, so Will wasn't in any danger, was he? He was a hero, but he was safe. Lucky Maisie! Frances resented having Jack's blackened clothes to wash, when he returned from the pit. And she resented the dirty looks she got from soldiers' wives. The dirt penetrated Jack's skin, and she had to scrub his back, like any collier's wife, in the bath tub after his shift. Os also resented his father. He was walking now, tottering about the house, chatting away to everyone he met, pointing his toy rifle at his younger brother, who cried when he shouted 'bang'!

'Takes after you, Jack!' George sneered, and Os laughed. Then news came that the Germans had attacked in the Southern Pacific and two ships, the 'Good Hope' and the 'Monmouth' had gone down with all hands. Maisie went cold with fear. And there was talk of a campaign in the Dardanelles! The war had spread like wildfire, covering the world and when, in mid-December a girl was killed by a Zeppelin attack, in Scarborough, cleaning her own doorstep, well, it brought it home to you, didn't it? Nowhere was safe, not even their own little corner in Fowler Street. Jack had been right. The war wouldn't be over by Christmas. But that didn't make them love him more . . .

Down at the 'Crystal Palace', Will thought 'If it takes as long as this to train recruits, the war won't be over this century!' He square-bashed, he rose early, he marched, he learnt to fire a gun, he stood to attention, he was bullied, and humiliated, he learned to be a number, dumb and unthinking. He had to obey, like an animal; he would have to kill like an animal and maybe die like one too. The instructing officers even used his name against him;

229

'Willie!' they jeered down the line, 'Little Willie! Can you aim that thing?'

Will got the bull in line, determined to hit it. 'Ready, aim . . . ' The instructor pushed down Will's rear with his foot. 'Do it by the book, if you please!' Will tried to readjust his aim, but too late, 'Fire!' and he missed the target.

'Little Willie missed. Now fancy that!' they scoffed. Will's hackles rose. But he knew better than to vent his anger against them. He would save it for the Hun. In full uniform, he smiled bravely into the camera, and Maisie cradled the photo to her breast, when it arrived home for Christmas. Then came six days leave, a whirlwind of delight, Maisie proudly on his arm, as he wore the khaki. They sparkled with love. It shone from them. Like innocent children, they played together. And when Will went again, Maisie sat bereft at the kitchen table, unable to get on with anything. Will's period of training was over. This time, inspected and passed by Mr Churchill and the King himself, he would be sailing into danger. She blew her nose and sniffed.

'I feel just like I did when I had all me teeth out!' she wailed.

Trudging home from the pit, Jack felt the first snowflake on his cheek. Cold and dark, the mornings, cold and dark the nights, freezing the atmosphere in the home. He came and went like a lodger. Frances was always too tired for him. He didn't blame her. She was doing the work of two. Lifting the latch on the back gate, he went in through the yard. There was a light in the midden. A puff of smoke oozed through the knot hole in the door. His father-in-law no doubt, looking at his dirty books. Jack went into the kitchen, and took the cup of tea Maisie offered. Ellen was still working in the shop. Frances too no doubt. He went upstairs to see his sons, tucked up in bed. But, on the first floor landing, Jack stopped, listening. There were voices in the office. Frances and the old barsket. And she was crying! Jack hesitated. A shadow crossed his heart. He stood, paralysed, wanting to comfort her, but his love was strangled by the silence with which she had bound him. He was tired. It had been a hard day. Michael, at least, would smile at him. His step moved on up the next flight of stairs, out of hearing.

* * *

'You said I should show him my love, Granda. And I do love him, you know, whatever he might be!'

'Does he love you, Frances?'

'Yes!'

'If you were attacked in the street, would he rush to your defence?' George looked hard at his grand-daughter. 'Think of your bairns, girl. Do you want them to grow up, knowing their father's a coward?' Frances sat miserably in the armchair, watching the fire flickering in the grate. George put his hand on her arm, and smiled at her gently. 'It was a bad beginning, Frances. It never works out, when two people are forced to wed. Look at your mother and father.' He sighed.

'But we weren't forced to wed, Granda!' George snorted.

'It was only a matter of time before you got pregnant. Look how quickly Os came on the scene. And in any case, do you really think another man, worthy of the name, would want shop soiled goods!'

'Shop soiled!' Frances' voice rose in anger. 'I was not shop soiled, as you call it! I was a virgin on my wedding day!' George went pale. He stared at his grand-daughter. She was telling the truth.

'But he told me . . .'

'I know! It wasn't true.' George hissed through his teeth.

'The bastard!' he exploded suddenly. 'There's nothing meaner than a man who marries for money!' Frances was crying.

'I don't believe that of him, Granda. He loves me!'

'How can he? He used you and you know it. Hah! And I thought you were in the wrong, shutting him out all those months. If I'd only known . . . I'm sorry, Fran. I've let you down. Forgive me.' Her anger fled. She reached out to comfort the old man, broken by betrayal, and he comforted her, in turn.

As the first daffodils arrived in Fowler Street, the Saturday shoppers were gathering in the market square of 'Wipers', when suddenly, all hell broke loose. The townspeople fled to shelter in the cellars, as walls crumbled, and towers fell, under heavy shelling. No one had ever seen anything like it. By dusk, as the last straggling refugees left the old town, there was little left of it but dust and ashes. Davey stared at the rubble that had once been Ypres. He could hear the distant rattle of light field artillery, in the lull. There was a gentle breeze, he turned his face into it, and gasped. It was coming from the north. He coughed, holding his arm over his face, watching as the thick yellow fog drew nearer.

'Stand your ground, lads!' the sergeant called. His eyes were streaming. The fog enveloped them, Canadians, Algerians, British, they all coughed, retching up their guts, lungs straining. Then, Davey saw the enemy. They were coming up behind the fog, in their hundreds, bayonets fixed, looming, in hideous masks, like creatures from another world. The Algerians broke ranks first. But the fog followed them and the guns fired. Horses reared in agonised terror, neighing, as their riders screamed and fell under their hooves. Soldiers, gasping, wounded, blinded, lay dying at the roadside. And the ambulances could not get through. Stunned by a shot in his side, Davey was dragged half-conscious behind what was left of the line. Then darkness fell, and the shelling began again.

The list of casualties shocked the nation. Tears streaming down their faces, the women of Fowler Street read out the list to George.

'We must not let those lads die in vain!' George's voice cracked. 'We have got to hold on to Ypres!'

'The Germans've got the key position, George,' Jack told him.

'Then we shall have to take it from them!'

'They aren't playing this war according to the Queensberry rules!' Jack shouted. 'We won't be able to just "take it"!'

Maisie clutched at the letter in her hand. It was from Will. It said 'On Active Service' on the envelope and it was stamped, 'Passed by the Censor'. Frances rose and took her aunt in her arms. Suddenly Maisie sobbed.

'He's going to the Dardanelles! He'll have to fight the Turks!' Frances gave her husband a withering glance. He sighed. It was his day off. He'd rather have been at work. 'I mean, what's the Turks got to do with anything!'

'The Russians can't hold them back, Auntie, so we must!'

'That's the spirit, Frances!' George approved. 'Chip off the old block!'

'Go on! Read his letter out! Unless of course it's too private!'

Frances teased. Maisie wiped her lenses and gladly read it all over again.

Howe R.N.D.
Polymedia
Cyprus

Dearest Maisie,

Just a few lines to let you know that I am in the best of health, hoping you are the same. From your letters I gather Shields is a lively place, most places out of bounds and no lights at night! But, I am worried that you are working too hard. Now, dear, I must tell you that if you make yourself ill I will declare war on you! It is not right to keep working day in day out from morning to night. Do write often, dear, because if there is too long a gap between letters, I will be swimming over to see what is the matter. The last lot took over four months to reach me. I still have your pretty picture with me. It will go with me wherever they send me, even if I have to leave my rifle behind! There is only one thing I am wishing for now, and that is for the next fortnight to be up, and then another letter from you.

Best love,
From Will

Maisie blew her nose in the sentimental silence that followed. George shook his head. Love was indeed blind.

It was only a 'blighty wound' and Davey's leave was not to last long. But his mother waited on him hand and foot and there was an article about him in the *Gazette*. He stood in chapel, eyes red and blistered, wheezing out the prayers. Frances wanted to cry for pity of him and, seeing her alone, he came up to speak to her, after the service.

'I suppose your husband's joined up by now?' She shook her head, unable to meet his eye. 'If I was in his shoes, I'd feel I had something to fight for.' She looked up at him, surprised. 'Sorry. Shouldn't have said that. It's just . . . the other fellahs've all got photos of their sweethearts and . . . '

'But surely there's some girl pining for you! There must be!'

'I've not had any time for girls. All work and no play, eh?'

Frances smiled sympathetically. She knew just what he meant.

'You should enjoy yourself while you've got the chance. I suppose you'll be going back soon?' He nodded bleakly. 'Oh, Davey . . . ' Suddenly her emotions were running riot. 'We're all so proud of you!'

'If *you're* proud of me, Frances, I'll go back to the front, singing.' She sobbed, her breath caught in her throat.

'If there's anything . . . '

'Would you let me have a photograph?' Frances was startled. 'I'm sorry. I had no right . . . ' He gave her a joke salute and went, leaving her staring after him.

At eleven o'clock on May 6th, Howe Battalion followed Hood up the Achi Baba Nullah. There was a swamp ahead. Under Turkish fire, the order came to cross. The first rush went forward. The men fell. The second rush went forward. The men fell. Then the third. And the fourth. On it went. Few ever rose again. It was as though the very rocks were firing at them. Will crawled out from under the bodies. A crack hit the ground just ahead of him. Dust hit his eyes. He lay still, then, as another rush came up behind, he made a run for it, and scrambled down behind a ridge to see another party of men felled to the ground. The sun blistered down. His tongue stuck to his mouth, parched. His chest hurt with fear. They were supposed to be making for the village of Krithia. But dead soldiers lay across the only gap in the stubbly ground. The survivors of the Howe Battalion bolted over the pile of bodies, and fell to the earth, hiding behind the very blades of grass till darkness came. Then, the Howes dug in. Next day came the attack. Starving, and without water, they fought. The Turks came on through burning scrub, falling amidst the flames. The stench was sickening. The heat was stifling. They slept. And when they woke, they were ordered on to another attack. Again night came. Gunfire continued through the darkness. Then the sun rose. Food was passed down from the French. Will had made pals with the survivors. It was as if they'd known one another all their lives. But they were mown down; there were now many gaps in the lines. The Australians and New Zealanders were engaged in support through the next day and the Marines came up to close the gaps. When finally the fighting died the youthful officer collected up the six remaining men of Howe Battalion. Then they 'rested'. They ate dry biscuits and bully beef, and the flies drank their sweat.

The letters came. But always months behind.

Z2097T
Howe Battalion R.N.D. Base.
Eastern Mediterranean Squadron,
C/O G.P.O. London.

Dearest Sweetheart,

As you will see from the above, I have left Cyprus and now am at Sidi Bishr, just outside Alexandria, on the edge of the desert. I don't suppose I will be here for very long. Note my address, dear. Squadron not force. The lads here, only a few, say our mob is in blue. So, you see, we are attached to the navy not the army. If I can get a pass to go to town, I will see about a birthday present for you. I hope I can, as it may be months before we can settle down again. I still have your dear little face with me. It does not matter what happens, Maisie, I will always love you. May this find you in the best of health and spirits. I will write every week, no matter what part of the world I am in. I now conclude with fondest love,

Will xxxxxxxxx

Maisie's birthday had been and gone. News from the Dardanelles was bad. If this was love, then it hurt like hell. The atmosphere in the house was tense. At last, George had found out about Ellen's drinking. He had gone mad. And when Jack went in to protect his mother-in-law, it had ended up in a fight.

'For God's sake, isn't there enough with the Germans and the Turks without us having a go at one another?' Frances bawled. Michael was terrified, screaming blue murder, and Os was clinging to her skirts.

'I'll stop, if he will!' Jack said, holding George by the throat. George snarled, and Jack threw him back from him.

'I'll not forget this me laddo!' George said.

'He's an old man!' Frances objected.

235

'What about her?' He pointed to Ellen, cowering behind her bed.

'She won't thank you!' Frances told him, and scurried the children away to safety. And she was right. She didn't thank him. It was a surprise to Ellen to find she had any pride left at all, and now even that had been humiliated. She hated Jack for it and whispered poison in Frances' ear, feeding the sleeping monsters of the past. And they spoke to her in her dreams. Jack listened, as Frances tossed and turned, moaning in her sleep.

'Stop the horses! Stop it! Granda! Help! Grandma!' He held her firmly in his arms, soothing her, and slowly she woke up. He lit the lamp by the bed. She was shivering. 'Come here. Let me warm you.' She cuddled in to him.

'I'm scared, Jack.'

'Sh. Sh. I'm here. Everything's all right.' Slowly the shivering stopped. 'It was about your grandma wasn't it?'

'Yes.'

'Reliving her death.'

'No. Not that.' She pulled away from him. 'No. I was on a roundabout; Grandma was watching; then a strange man came up and spoke to her, and she fainted, in a heap on the ground. And I couldn't get to her to help her because the horses kept on going round and round.'

'It was only a dream.'

'No it was real. I'd forgotten about the strange man. Why should I suddenly start dreaming about that now?' How could he tell? He could only comfort her, till like a child, she fell asleep again. And she woke, feeling sad and heavy. Only Maisie could cheer her up. She had had another letter from Will. He had got her present, but was soon to be on the move again.

Dearest of Sweethearts,

We may leave Sidi Bishr any day. All the R.N.D. have been called to base. 100 came from Malta last night, where they had a good time. Some were longer at Malta than we were at Cyprus, yet they got the privilege of leave today. Still, I can wait. Every dog has his day. Now, Maisie, I don't want you to send anything out but letters, until I say so. As you will know, dear, a bottle of wine, which has been corked up for a few years, goes off with some force . . .

'You never sent him a bottle of wine!'

'I was only trying to help!' The tension relaxed. Jack and Frances laughed till their sides aches.

'He's a patient man, Maisie!' Jack told her. But when the laughter had died down, Maisie fretted again. If only she could be out there with him! If only she could *do* something, instead of going on as usual in the shop. All over Shields, you could see what was happening elsewhere. Women were filling the gaps. Heads turned to see a female porter on the station. The trams now had women as conductresses. Farms were crying out for help, and women answered the call. Even the fire service was willing to take on female labour, especially after the June raid on Shields. Five bombs had dropped on the town, and the fire service was undermanned. Women were needed. Their hour had come. With the shop slack and money short, surely Maisie could do something now? She could drive, after a fashion! She'd not killed anybody yet! And it'd take her mind off things . . .

'Dad!' Maisie announced one day. 'I'm going to drive an ambulance!'

'Are you!' George laughed. 'And I'm the Queen of England!'

'No, but I am! I've signed on!' George reeled. Maisie of all the docile women in England, to have wilfully gone behind his back? What was the world coming to?

'You're lucky,' Frances told her. 'If it wasn't for the bairns, I'd join you! I could work in munitions! I wonder if me Mam'd look after Os and Michael?'

'Hadaway with you, woman!' Maisie told her. 'Your Ma's not fit! And *somebody's* got to stay in the shop!'

'Why's it got to be me?'

'Think yourself lucky you've got kids, pet!' And off she went, to the Ingham Infirmary, to take up her new post.

'She'll make more casualties than she saves!' Eddie sneered, as he took over driving the delivery van. Now George was in a cleft stick. What would people say if a fit, free man turned up, driving the Beattie van? Business would go from bad to worse. There was only one thing for it. Frances would have to learn to drive. She jumped at the chance. She enjoyed herself no end, careering about the town all on her own! Freedom at last! Ellen had to pull up her socks to look after the bairns, and the pressure on Eddie, to join up, was intensified.

Harriet, sent north by the League to rally 'the troops', stayed for two nights, and gave the men hell. She had a long talk with Frances who assured her aunt that Jack was definitely not 'getting his oats'.

'But it's your Dad that sickens me!' Harriet spat. 'At least Jack's doing a man's job, down the mines. What's your father doing? Apart from sitting on the netty and arranging flowers?' For two days she harangued the same wilting specimen of manhood. 'And that limp! It's put on! I'd swear it! Show me your foot!' Eddie was forced to reveal the unscathed limb for her inspection. Wrinkling her nose, she bent forwards, glasses at the ready. She prodded. She poked. Eddie winced.

'Nothing wrong with them!' Pronounced fit, he retired, crying to the greenhouses over the road. Then, taking up a spade he took a deep breath and chopped off his big toe.

'Now no bugger can make's go!' He limped home, weeping, his shoe swimming in blood. Maisie was called to take him to the Ingham, as Harriet left, bound once more for London.

'I'm ashamed!' Ellen wailed. 'So ashamed!' But Jack had no sympathy for her.

'That woman should be sent to fight in the trenches herself! How dare she drive men to the slaughter!'

Deeply shocked, Frances saw the truth of the statement. Harriet's hatred against men had, at last, found its true vent.

Lockjaw set in quickly and Eddie, slowly, painfully, died of his wound, his weeping wife at his bedside. Now she was sorry. Now she loved him. Now she would miss him. And now too, the pressure was taken from Jack. He was needed at the shop. But he wouldn't leave the pit for all that, and Maisie wouldn't leave the ambulance service either. She came home, one day, her skirt trimmed, showing her ankles. George was outraged!

'It's only sense!' she told him. 'I keep getting me heels caught in me hem, when I'm drivin'!' And Frances followed suit. The dandies of the old world had gone. They lay under white crosses in France. Those who were left were either wounded, old, or like Jack, the steady kind of man, the male kind. His turn would come. He looked at Frances' ankles and shrugged.

'It's no good complaining!' she told him. 'The land girls are wearing trousers!'

George slept uneasily. The shop was sinking. No one did as he told them. His lady customers wanted their own way with their flower arrangements, and wouldn't take his advice. And when he did them the favour of doing it his way anyway, because he knew it was best, instead of being grateful, and seeing the point, they were actually angry at him! Had he outlived his time? As he sank into the fitful sleep of dawn, he dreamt that he was on a big ocean liner. Anyone who was anybody was on it. It was the last word in luxury. The last word. Ballrooms, and chandeliers, beautiful gowns, luncheons and dinner parties, flowers, and red carpets; the old world; the old order. 'Unsinkable' they'd said. And like the 'Titanic', it was going down.

CHAPTER FOURTEEN

Deep in the sodden trenches of Flanders, with foot rot and lice, Davey's nerve began to fail. They had guns now, even ammunition, but what was the point of using them? It didn't get them anywhere. Now and then a new crater would be formed in No Man's Land, by a stray shell, and then each side would struggle to gain it. It then became a new outpost, in front of the front line, pushing forward the respective party a few more yards. They put up barbed wire, miles of it, deep as a road it was. And they dug trenches. Forward sap, latrine, front line, firing bays, communcation trenches, support line, reserve trenches, on and on and on, they stretched behind them, like a nightmare town. Davey had been in the front line now for twenty-nine days. It was his turn on sentry duty. He leaned against the fire step of the forward sap, his ears and eyes straining in the dark. Sickness crawled in the pit of his stomach. The stench was overpowering. He longed for a cigarette to cover up the smell of rotting vegetation, corpses and excreta. But the glow of the butt would attract the snipers. There was a light, metallic crack. Almost imperceptible, but the three sentries froze. Was it the shifting of a rifle? Or the sound of loose wire, blowing in the wind? It was Davey's turn. Praying to God, 'Our Father Who art

240

in Heaven . . . ' heart pounding, throat dry, he slowly raised his head till he was eye level with the parapet. His eyes swam. Everything seemed to be moving. An arm dangled from a corpse, enmeshed in the wire. A leg stuck out from a slimy pool. A sheet of corrugated iron flapped up and down. Was that a German? Or an Englishman, calling for help? He came down, shaking his head. The spell of duty was over.

Crawling back to his trench, Davey felt light-headed, glad he was still alive; or was he? Life was measured out in time. And time was passing, or not so much passing as . . . His brain seized up like an engine without oil. He sank onto the sandbags that made his bed, pulling his sodden great coat round him. It smothered him with its weight of rain and mud. But he didn't sleep. His eyes searched the blackness. Not so much passing as running out, time, like a serpent, had slithered from man's grasp. And now it ruled over him, coiling round him, holding him in its stranglehold. And the more he strove against it, the more it crushed him, hissing in his ear, 'A time to be born and a time to die, a time to plant and a time to pluck up that which is planted.' The old order. Outdated. 'To everything there is a season . . . ' 'Time gentlemen, please.' God was the Time Lord. Not man. God ruled the serpent. All man ever had was the free will to shout out, to fight against it. But what was the point? A faint light outlined the ragged cloth over the hole. Davey saw the pool of water in the trench beyond. His eyes flickered, then closed.

Then the shells came crashing down. Men urinated in their pants, turned to jelly by the continuous whining scream of shells, like banshees, vibrating the very earth. Pinned down by the paralysing sound, his bones rattling in his flesh, Davey danced the macabre dance of death. For when God danced, the moon, the stars and the earth danced with him, and no man could keep still; not even the general of a great army. And Davey's laughter was a high-pitched scream.

'Time, gentlemen, please.'

'Lawson's flipped.' A soldier down the trench remarked between his chattering teeth. Then there was a lull. Inspect the damage. Take the wounded back through the communicating trench. Let the bodies stay where they are, to rot.

241

Davey, hands shaking, was looking at the pictures in an old boys' adventure book. His eyes wouldn't focus on the word, his mind couldn't concentrate. The sergeant was asking for volunteers to make up a raiding party that night. He stiffened. Perhaps if he pretended he was dead, the sergeant would pass him by. And then light dawned. If he was dead, then no one would make him go over the top ever again. He would never have to do patrols or sentry duties. He would never have to suffer the helplessness of waiting for a shell to smash him. The thought flowed in him like honey, warming him, sweetening the air of the trench. His legs moved, as though they belonged to another man. His voice croaked. And he was in the party, automatically preparing for the assault. The other volunteers had been practising on dummy entrenchments behind the line. The replacements had to do without. They took off collar flashes, and regimental buttons, safety-pinning their jackets into place. If he'd had a photograph of Frances, he would have had to leave it behind. Frances. Did she exist? Did she know there was a war on? Did she know he loved her? He drank his rum ration. Then, like a man in a dream, he floated through the mud to the firing line. His face was blacked with cork. He carried his grenades, scrambling up the ladders, into the darkness. They made for the gap in the wire, silent footfalls through the debris of No Man's Land, stepping over the bodies. Davey followed on, skirting the shell holes in the dark. That was a death he did not want, sucked down and down until the mud smothered him. There was a half moon. They would be seen. It didn't matter. He was glad. Searching for a gap in the German wire, ten feet deep, they filed through. A stray bullet caught the man in front. Davey fell to the ground. Why? What did he care? He got up again, and pushed on. The leader halted, hand held high. It was blown off by a patrol, coming from the other side. Davey fell onto his belly, crawling like the enemy towards the centre of No Man's Land. The shapes loomed darkly in the moonlight. He pulled out a grenade and lit it. A German bomb flew clean past him, shaking the earth. His breath was short. His head swam. He stood suddenly and threw for all he was worth, and the fire flashed, and there were screams and all hell broke loose. His left ear went, as a grenade whizzed past, felling the man at his side. Davey sprawled in the mud, dazed. But he would rise again. He put his hand out into the mud and found something hard to push against. His hand slipped into the gaping mouth of a dead German. Davey stared at the livid face, green in the moonlight. Then he wrenched himself up into action. The bayonet men were finishing off the wounded Germans. Blood gushed darkly. They were near the German line. And then, firing started from the sentry post. Seven of the thirty men in Davey's party were still alive. Five of them ran. He stood with the other man. His name was Jim Walsh. Together they went forward against the fire. Jim lit a bomb, then fell, still holding it. Davey grasped it out of his hand, and threw it straight into the German sap. Screams told him he had hit his mark. His blood lust was up. He gritted his teeth. He would have more of the buggers before they finished him off! But the Brit was moaning. Ignoring him, Davey crawled forward. There was a German in the latrine. Silent as death, Davey took the rifle, bayonet fixed, from the body of one of the volunteers. He crawled on, slowly, slipping over the mud, trousers torn on the stray wire, legs bleeding. The bayonet slid over the top of the parapet, into the face of a German soldier. Trousers falling, the German raised his hands and came, easily, bare legged, back to the German wire. A sniper caught Davey in the thigh. He stumbled, but rose again, pushing the German on at the end of his bayonet.

Jim Walsh lay, moaning.

'Come on!' Davey hissed. 'Get moving.' But he knew he couldn't. He hadn't any legs. One of them was speared three yards off, on the fence. The other, Davey pretended not to see, as he walked through its remains.

'Don't leave me here to die,' Jim whispered. But Davey shoved on. And another sniper caught him in the shoulder, but now he was at the wire. He was getting through. He hadn't meant to. He turned in time to see the arm throw the bomb, and he fell to the ground. The bomb, caught in the wire, exploded. The German's bare legs were burned. Davey lost an arm. He pushed on. It wasn't enough. He wasn't dead yet.

'You're rotten shots!' he yelled behind him.

'Davey . . . !' The voice hissed out of the darkness. A cloud covered the moon. Davey scrambled back across No Man's Land, pushing the German through the gap, and down into the British Trenches. He was a hero. Sent back in an ambulance, to hospital, minus an arm, Davey was out of the war for good.

At home, the papers were full of the King's example. He was giving up all alcohol. George extolled the virtues of good King George, rubbing Ellen's nose in it as often as he could.

'Leave her alone, Granda,' Frances urged. 'She needs some consolation.'

'The country's going to the dogs with drink!' George roared, throwing down the paper. 'It's affecting war production!'

'Mam doesn't make shells!' But Ellen didn't drink so much these days. Eddie's death had shocked her, and now they'd had the news that Tommy the fishmonger, he with the kiss like a sink plunger, had died of his wounds in France.

'I'll not eat fish again,' Maisie said religiously, as she looked through the pile of letters from the morning's post. 'None for me?' she wailed. Then she picked one out, and looked at it carefully. It was a service letter, addressed to Mrs Frances Scott. 'Here, pet. For you!' Frances wiped her floury hands on a towel, and opened it quickly. She almost dropped it, when she saw who it was from. She sat suddenly. George looked at her curiously.

'It's from that Davey Lawson,' she said amazed. 'He's in the Kitchener Hospital at Brighton.' She read avidly. 'He says he's lost an arm, but he's fine apart from a few bullet holes.' She looked up at the shocked faces of her listeners. 'He's to be invalided out. And he says they're going to give him a medal.'

'Eeh!' Maisie whooped.

'A gentleman of the old school!' George stood to attention. 'His mother must be proud of him!' Maisie held out her hand for the letter.

'Let's see!' Frances held it back.

'It's private!'

'Huh! Why's he written to you, anyway?' Frances was blushing. Only Maisie saw, and she gave her a funny look. Thrusting the letter into her pocket, Frances went back to her baking. But later, when she had finished the deliveries, she drove down to the promenade. She coasted onto the little road beside the dunes, and got out her letter. The sea washed her thoughts. Swishing gently in and out, the waves calmed her. The letters stopped dancing in front of her eyes.

'Only the thought of you, dear Frances, kept me going. I know you will forgive the strange fancies of a soldier. War does funny things to you and, you might say, I am not myself. But, you see, I have dared to write to you, and God knows what else I might dare, to get what I want. I dared Fritz, didn't I? I only lost an arm over him, but I've lost my head over you. Lying in this bed, day in, day out, the old feelings have come back stronger than ever. Perhaps this letter proves to you that I am, like you said once, just a pompous twerp. Throw these few words on the fire if you like. I will not blame you, my own dear. I remain your affectionate friend, Davey Lawson.'

Frances looked up at the grey sea, then raised her eyes to the grey sky. You couldn't tell where sea ended and sky began. The boundaries were blurred.

Z2097T
D I Howe Battalion,
Eastern Med Squad
R.N.D. Details
C/O G.P.O. London

Dearest Sweetheart,
    After the best voyage so far, we have landed at Mudros. We have seen few from our Battalion here, and what a state they are in, like a lot of ragmen, while we are polished and our kits complete. I have made good friends with a man called Charlie Barford, from Yorkshire. He's a canny lad. You'd like him. Of course, dear, I have not received any letters, but Lovatt got one last night, and through him I know the folks at home are all right. I am not homesick, still I would very much like to give you these kisses, Maisie. What do you say? Conclude with fondest love,

Will XXXXXXXXXXX
XXXXXXXXXXX

'Romantic rubbish! Honestly, our Maisie makes me sick drooling over that letter!' Ellen was mopping up the blood from a nose bleed, and Frances, head back, gulped the words, uncomfortably.

'Keep still, Fran! I don't know what's got into you!'

'She was always daft over him. Huh! Wait till she gets married!'

'You didn't have to, you know! You had your eyes open and walked straight into it. Tut! You can't tell me you're happy, pet. I know better. It's not like you to be bad-tempered.'

'Mam! Not in front of the . . .'

'Why go willingly to your misery? That's what I say! Marriage's not all it's cracked up to be.'

'I'm sick to hear you say that! Anyway, it's not marriage that's up the creek. It's the blokes! Look at Dad!'

'Don't speak ill of the dead!' her mother snapped. 'I don't know, Frances, one minute you're all against marriage, then the next . . . eeh!' Ellen sighed. 'I know why it is, really . . .'

'Oh? Why?'

'You're jealous of our Maisie! I am an' all, to be honest! It's a lovely time, being engaged; romantic. It all changes once you're wed. Shattered dreams, eh?'

'Maybe Maisie'll be lucky. I hope so.'

'You've ruined your best blouse. That blood'll never come out!' Holding the cotton wool to her nose, Frances sat up gingerly.

'Ooh! I feel giddy!'

'You'll be anaemic again, I expect. You're working far too hard.'

'Who isn't?' Frances sighed.

'You'd best have a lie down for a bit.'

'Aha.' Frances looked down at the two small, interested faces, watching her. 'Do you know, I've not had a nose bleed since *I* was a bairn!'

'Will Auntie Maisie have to take you to the Infirmary now?' Os asked hopefully.

'Of course she won't!'

'You mean you're not going to die?' Os was disappointed.

'No! Now run along, you two! Your Auntie Maisie's making a cake! She might let you lick out the bowl, if you're lucky!' Frances watched Michael totter dangerously after his brother, down to the kitchen. 'Eeh, if it wasn't for them . . .'

246

'If it wasn't for them . . . what?' Ellen had a wily look.

'Nothing.'

'I thought as much!'

'What?'

'It's that letter, isn't it, Fran? That letter from Davey Lawson. By, you missed your chance there, didn't you?'

'Rubbish! At least Jack's got both his arms!'

'All the better to hug you with?'

'Mam!'

'He's doing well, is Davey Lawson. Cashing in on his war wound! Folk are flocking to buy from him, just so's they can take a look at a man with one arm!'

'That's horrible!'

'That's folk!' Ellen sighed, as she cleared the mess away. 'Well, pet, take my advice, if you've got to be miserable, far better be miserable in comfort.' Frances stared after her departing mother. Was she encouraging her into an affair? Her own mother? She should be moralising! Laying into her about her duty. 'For better or worse, for richer for poorer, love, honour and obey.' Or had she gone the way of Aunt Harriet? Like an invading mist, the old doubts insinuated into her. If it wasn't for Jack, Frances would still have the dancing career she'd dreamt of! In fact, she could be earning now, but for the bairns, even if it was only in munitions! The more she dwelt on it, the more Frances resented her husband for having cheated her. She'd always hated this house; the sickly sweet smell of flowers, that crept up the stairs, under the doors, into your dreams. And he'd dragged her back to it! The blood was caking inside her nose. She lay on the bed, staring up at the ceiling. Men, huh! Always thought they knew better than you what was good for you! Good for her? Hah! This house with its shadows? And talk about *her* running away from her responsibilities, indeed! What about Jack? He let men like Davey go to the war, while he stayed home! He wasn't a man at all! 'Do you take this man to be your lawful, wedded husband?' He wasn't a man! She had been cheated even in that! Suddenly Frances was gripped by a terrible feeling of loneliness. Why did these thoughts possess her? Where did they come from? They had driven a rift between her and Jack, between her and her family. She began to cry. Her arms ached to reach out for Jack. But he was down the pit, working. Unhappy and confused,

Frances dozed, as the afternoon light faded. And she dreamt. The old dream. Dancing all alone! And then the horse and the monster chasing it, attached by a thread so fine you can't see it. And the horse struggling to be free . . .

Frances woke, soaked with sweat. The bleeding had started again. She shivered, as she wrung out a towel in the wash bowl, and applied it to her nose. Blood. The past catching up on her. Family ties! Damn Jack! Damn him to hell for bringing her back here to be tied up in knots again! Anger made her cry. Tears and blood streaked her face. She was twenty-two years old and she looked more like forty! What life had she had? How could she have been so stupid as to be hoodwinked by Jack! Eyes open, she'd walked right into it, like every other women before her! Wrenching open a drawer of the dressing table, Frances felt under the pile of handkerchiefs and pulled out a pair of scissors. Then, resolutely, she began to hack at her hair. The long curls fell, one by one, to the floor. When she had finished, she stared at herself for a long time. Well, it was a beginning, anyway!

'I quite like it!' Davey said thoughtfully, then smiled. 'You look cheeky, somehow. Very young.'
    'Do you think so?' Frances was pleased. Davey nodded.
    'Boyish!'
    'No!'
    'Tomboyish! In the nicest possible way. Like an urchin!'
    'Ah. That's better. You had me worried for a bit. More tea?'
    'Don't mind if I do!' Frances squeezed the pot, and called the waitress to bring hot water.
    'Not a bit like a woman with two kids!' Frances frowned. Why did he have to remind her? But Davey was shaking his head, in delighted amazement. 'I never expected you to write back, you know.'
    'Why not?'
    'Should I be so lucky?'
    'You of all people, Davey! You deserve the thanks of the nation!'
    'A cuddle with you'll do!' he joked. Frances was shocked.
    'You used to be such a gentleman!'

'You hear a lot of coarse talk in the trenches, Frances. Much worse than that. Sorry.' He made her feel prim and stupid.

'It's all right! I'm not a child, you know!'

The waitress put the hot water on the table. Frances smiled, and poured it into the pot. But the waitress didn't go away. She was gaping at Davey. 'Thank you!' Frances said pointedly. The waitress jumped, and went. 'I bet you've got all the girls in Shields after you, now you're such a hero!' Davey smiled and touched her fingers.

'Not the one I want.' Frances pulled her hand away sharply. 'You're not just teasing me, are you?' Frances was nonplussed. How could he think such a thing? Her coming was an act of defiance! That was all! She hadn't meant to . . .

'My, you've changed, Davey! I don't know about *me* getting cheeky?'

'I love you.' Frances was looking out of the window at the passing feet of the pedestrians. It was raining, and their heels kicked up drops of dirty water. 'Did you hear what I said?'

'I heard.'

'Look at me!' His voice commanded her. She wanted to obey. 'You can't fool me, Frances. You might be able to fool yourself but . . . ' He had picked up her hand again and was kissing it in full view of everyone in the café. She was paralysed with shock. She liked it. It was what she wanted.

As she walked down Ocean Road, in the rain, Frances wondered at herself. What had got into her? And what had got into him? He wasn't the same shy young man who had gone to the war! She didn't approve of him at all. And yet, there was something exciting about him. Was it just the forbidden fruit that attracted her? Or something more? He put her in a dare-devil mood! Women all over Britain were going off the rails, why not her? Live now! Tomorrow might be too late! There was a defiant lift to her step, as she turned the corner into Fowler Street and strode up to the shop, every inch the 'new woman'. She grasped the door handle and pushed. But the door didn't budge. The notice had been turned to 'CLOSED'. She frowned. What was wrong? Perhaps her mother had had a turn? There had to be some calamity for her granda to close the shop! She peered through the window, and saw her reflection in the dim glass.

What a mess! The rain was still pouring down. Her felt hat, saturated, was dripping green dye down her face. Suddenly, she felt cold and realised her feet were sopping wet. Down from Cloud Nine, she ran round the back of the terrace, up the lane, and squelched into the back kitchen.

'There you are!' George was beaming, and her mother, Maisie and Jack were all sipping tea, just as if it was a Sunday!

'What's wrong?'

'Look at you!' her mother complained, dragging her to the fire. 'Get them wet things off at once!'

'Nothing wrong, Frances!' her granda said, his cheeks spreading over his whiskers. 'In fact, quite the reverse! I have to tell you Frances, that your husband has just made us all very proud.' Her knees turned to jelly.

'What?' she whispered, staring from one to the other.

'Where have you been?' Ellen was fussing with her shoes and stockings, stripping her before the fire.

'Jack?' Frances turned to question him. 'What are you doing home, at this time?'

'Why didn't you take your umbrella?' Ellen interrupted.

'Shurrup, Mam!'

'Hoity-toity!'

'Jack! What have you done?'

'I've joined up, love.'

Frances thought she was going to faint. Maisie steered her to a chair and sat her down.

'Why? Oh why?' she whispered.

'I thought it was what you wanted!' Suddenly she was shaking and crying. Jack crouched at her side and put his arms round her.

'I'll come back. Don't worry.' How could God have done this to her? He had turned her world topsy-turvy in a second! The 'new woman' had shrivelled, like a burst balloon. Fear and love for Jack, suddenly sprouted in its place. Guilt and shame consumed her. She threw her arms round his neck, and they hugged one another, watched by a tearful family. 'If I'd known it would have this effect, I'd have done it months ago!' he teased.

The crescent of the moon was swelling. Its pale light shone through the lace at the window, onto Frances' face, and her skin looked as though it had been blown by cobwebs. Jack touched her cheek, as if to brush them away.

'Thank you,' he said. She nestled in to him and sighed.

'The pleasure was mine.'

'Sounded like it!'

'I was only lying back and thinking of England!' She giggled.

'Tell that to the Marines!'

'By the way, what have you joined? The army, the navy or what?'

'Army. Durham Light. They came round the pit this afternoon. It seems they need miners.'

'What for?'

'State secret.'

'Oh!' She was cradled in his arm, head on his shoulder, lulled into peaceful contentment. But a question whispered in the distant places of her mind. She stirred, frowned and spoke it out. 'Why did you do it, Jack?'

'I told you. They wanted miners! Anyway . . . ' he sighed, 'They'll be bringing in conscription before long.' Frances' eyes jerked open. So that was it! Some hero! He yawned. Then, as though he read her thought, he said idly, 'I've no particular desire to be a hero . . . ' With that, he went to sleep.

It was a muddy autumn. The leaves turned to sludge in the rain, sodden heaps in the gutters. George went with Frances to see Jack off and her heart sank as the train pulled out of the station. Would she ever see him again? Or would he come back, like Davey, a different man? George held her hand tightly, and pulled her away from the barrier. His voice was gruff with emotion.

'I take back all I said about him. He's a fine lad.' Frances shook her head. His 'fine lad' had only volunteered to beat conscription, but, at least he'd gone, and he faced the same dangers as the others. She had to give him that. A lady porter skirted round them with her hand-cart. It was piled high with bags. 'Let me help you, my dear,' George asked, politely raising his hat.

'Gerroff!' the lady replied. George looked depressed all the way home. Had all the traditional values gone?

And now the moon had passed its peak and had begun to wane. While the children slept, Frances watched, alone, from her bedroom window. The calm of the night belied her spirits. It was odd being without Jack. Her life had revolved around him, creating stability through all the upheavals, both within and without. Freedom was a heady business. She missed him badly. She missed his warmth in bed. Hot water bottles were not the same! How long had he been gone? Barely a week! That was all? Dear Jack. She loved him, though she often wished she didn't. Why did he keep on cheating her? Perhaps if he hadn't told her about the conscription business, she would have gone on believing in him, in blissful ignorance. But no, he had to tell her he had taken her in, yet again, didn't he? The trouble was, she didn't trust Jack any more. Doubts echoed inside her brain, confusing her again. She couldn't hear herself think for them. She went across the passage, to the boys' room, and looked at her younger son. He was sleeping like an angel. Gently, she picked him up and took him into bed with her, snuggling down, the blankets round their ears, as if to shut out the voices.

But she could not shut them out. They had invaded her. They were all there now, loud and clear, all the voices from the past. Her grandma whispered, 'Promise me, Frances, promise me, you'll look after Hester. She's got the devil in her.' Frances shifted restlessly. In his sleep, Michael reached out and laid his hand on her heart. But the voice whispered on. And a man's, close to, muttered, 'the house built on shifting sands . . . ' Aunt Harriet's hurried words of discontent, formed the chorus. And her mother's, 'Don't do what I did!' cut across Maisie's longing sighs, while her granda intoned from the pulpit, 'Our sins never die. They take a form to haunt us, casting shadows on our lives. And by their shadows we know them. They grow into monsters, and one day, one day, they catch up with us!' Eerily echoing, she heard the monster howl, and her grandma's face peered, ghastly, green, out of the darkness, screaming silently.

'Frances, have you been down to the cellar?' She would put her hands over her ears. She would not listen. 'Frances!' This ghost was knocking at the door. She woke with a shiver, and sat bolt upright, letting Michael's hand fall from her. 'Have you done the flowers?' It was Maisie.

'Sh! Michael's sleeping!' Frances whispered.

'Sorry. Have you?'

'No. I forgot. I'm coming.' She sighed and threw back the covers. It was a job Jack used to do. Now she had to do it. She pulled on her wrap, and stumbled down the stairs, filling the pump with water at the sink, and on, down, down, under the house, into the dark cellars, her way lit by the flame of a single candle. Rats scurried round the feet of the statue. It loomed at her out of the darkness, huge and frightening; four arms, one of them pointing right at her, a whip in its hand. What had Jack said? 'Unlucky for whom?' A door slammed upstairs as a huge draught flew round the house. The candle flame went out. She was in pitch darkness. She began to scream.

In the kitchen, George stood, paralysed by the swirling cacophony of sound that seemed to come at him from beneath his very feet. He had just come in. He had been visiting his 'friend' Mrs Minto. His conscience pricked him as it always did, always had. What was this torment in the bowels of the house? Breathless with fright, he held onto a chair, gathering his senses. Then he wrenched open the cellar door and Frances fell out of the blackness, into his arms.

'Don't make me go down there again!' she cried.

'Sh!' George comforted her. It's all right. Your grandma always hated the cellar, just the same . . . I understand.'

'Grandma! Don't talk to me about Grandma! I hate Grandma!'

'Frances!'

'I do! I hate her. I hate all of you!'

'Now stop it, Fran . . . '

'I hate you!' She was clawing at him, screaming, like a banshee. 'I hate you! I hate the lot of you! The whole rotten family! May God damn you all to hell!' George's hand flashed across her mouth. Frances staggered back, holding her face with her hand and saw her son, Os, standing white-faced in the doorway.

She tried to explain, but he didn't want to know. The lad just turned his back on her, closing his ears to whatever she said. And he took it out on Michael, who was too small to defend himself. He stole his toys, tore the ear off his teddy bear, and pulled out its eyes. And he wouldn't be told! Her granda was no help. He said she'd brought it on herself, and she'd better deal with it herself. But the boy needed a man's firm hand. If only Jack was home! How could she fill his place? Then Michael cried, running to her for comfort. And she searched out her old toybox, from under the eaves, leaving him to find consolation in its contents. He pulled out her old worn top and whip and took it down to the yard to play. She had forgotten about the whip. It wasn't new when she'd had it. It had belonged to Maisie, and who knows who had it before her. She heard the top wheeling, singing on the stone flags outside, and then the lash of the whip. Memories. Or reality? Her granda whipping Hester! Her grandma screaming! Panic coursed through her. Her heart pounded. Voices. Was she going mad? Was that Hester screaming as the whip caught her flesh?

'Mam! Mam!' She struggled against the voices. No, no it wasn't Hester. This was reality. This was her son, Michael! She ran out of the shop, knocking over the chairs in the kitchen, and, through the window, she saw Os, whip in hand, scourging her youngest. Yelling with fury, Frances tore into the yard, snatched the whip from him, and took Michael in her arms.

'How could you!' Frances shouted. But Os glared back,

'I hate him! I hate you an' all!' Then he barged past her and ran upstairs to hide in his room.

Michael had long since gone to sleep in her arms, and now lay, peacefully, his face mottled from crying. Poor little soul. Her heart bled for him. She felt his pain, as though it was her own, as though the cord between them had never been cut. It had never been so with Os, her firstborn. It wasn't his fault. She blamed herself, but the harder she tried to put things right, the worse they seemed to get. 'Our sins never die. They take a form to haunt us . . . ' Dear God, was there no escape? Poor Os. Poor Frances. Poor everyone. She shivered. Winter was coming. The night air was chill with the threat of frost. She looked through the nursery window at the bright sliver of the dying moon. She was lonely, cold. She had to get out of this house, before it drove her clean out of her mind.

Her boots rang out on the frosted pavement. As though to reassure herself, she slipped her hand into her pocket and felt the rustling paper of Davey's note. Her step faltered. What was she doing? Jack had driven her to this. She'd fought against it, long enough. There was a pub ahead. She walked through the black-out straight into the bright lights, blinded for an instant. The men turned and stared at her. She would not be put off. She strode through the sawdust, up to the bar, and spoke to the landlord in her poshest voice.

'Do you have a telephone? I'm afraid I seem to be stranded.' He took her into a back room and left her to make her call.

'Well, this is a pleasant surprise!' Davey's voice crackled in her ear.

'I had to talk to someone. I hope you don't mind.'

'Flattered! I'm all ears!'

'Oh dear . . . I don't think I can . . . not on the telephone . . . '

'Where are you?'

'In a pub!'

'Good God!'

'I know.'

'What about the kids?'

'Mam's looking after them.' There was a short pause.

'Want to meet up?' His voice challenged her. She swallowed hard.

'Yes. Please.'

'Where do you suggest?'

'I don't know. It's a nice night. We could go for a walk.'

'Good idea. I'll meet you down at the Lifeboat Memorial, eh?'

'Yes.'

'I'll be about half an hour.'

'Yes. Bye Bye.' She put down the receiver, shaking. The land-lord appeared, as if by magic, at the door.

'All right, pet?'

'Thanks.' She nodded, and reached for her purse. 'Let me . . . '

'Why no! What d'ye take's for? Fancy a rum before you go?' She eyed the glass in his hand.

'No thanks.'

'Go on! It'll only go to waste! You look peaky!' She took it gratefully. The spirit warmed her stomach, and gave her strength. He was a kind man. He wouldn't take anything for the drink either, but escorted her out of the pub, setting her on her way, 'Mind, look after yourself, hinny! There's some funny folk about!'

He watched her till the blackout had swallowed her up, then

255

went back inside, shaking his head. Women weren't half asking for trouble these days!

The air was clear and sharp. The stars, hard points in the sky, glittered in the pale light of the crescent moon, as Frances strolled with Davey on the promenade.

'We'll look funny if there's a zeppelin raid!' Frances laughed.

'I'll look after you. Don't worry. I've been through worse.' She wished she had bitten out her tongue. A mist was coming in from the sea, enveloping them in its freezing vapour, and immediately, he was taking off his coat, and folding her in it. It was warm, heavy, comforting. One sleeve was pinned to the breast. The sight of the pin moved her and she began to cry. 'Poor Davey!' His arm had not left her. He pulled her in to him and let her cry on his chest. 'I'm all right. It's you I'm worried about!' She looked up at him, through brimming eyes. 'I can't believe my luck!' He laughed nervously.

'Come on. Let's walk,' she said. But he drew her over the sand, into the shelter of the dunes. The sea was whispering in and out and a fog horn blew far off in the mist. They stopped and stared into the inky darkness. 'I can't see a thing,' she said. Then she turned and faced him. 'Davey, you've got to help me.' He stopped her with his mouth. His kiss was hard and hurt her lips. She tasted blood. She pulled away, but he held her in the grip of his one arm and hissed fiercely into her face,

'I see! I'm too ugly for you, that it? Well take a good look!' He pulled his hair away from his face, showing the hole where his ear had been, and the brilliant scar alongside it. 'You want to think yourself lucky they left me my manhood!' He grasped her hand and forced her to put it on him. 'I love you, Frances! Don't deny me now.' Then he gripped her arm, forcing her against him, kisses falling on her, hard as hailstones, a storm of harsh passion, devouring her with his desire. And she wanted him.

Something in her responded to his need. Damn Jack! Damn him to hell! Davey was a man! A real man! He could command her! She would walk to the ends of the earth for such a man! But he was too quick for her. He left her out. And in the end, she wanted warmth and comfort. She wanted caressing, she wanted love. Afterwards, she lay back on the cold sand, surprised, feeling empty, and somehow rather dirty. Deeply asleep, Davey

256

held onto her hand. His grasp was hard. She tried to pull away without waking him, but he held on all the harder. It was cold. Silent. Far out at sea, in the mists, she heard the mournful blare of a fog horn. You couldn't see the stars, or the moon, or anything.

CHAPTER FIFTEEN

Chastened, Frances put it all behind her. Whatever it was, she had got it out of her system, for the voices had stopped. But Davey wouldn't leave her alone. He seemed to think he had rights over her now.

'You started it!' he told her, when she complained.

'I must've been out of my mind!'

'Thank you!'

'No. I didn't mean . . . ' Whatever she said, she was in the wrong. And then, having hurt his feelings, she ended up being extra nice to him, just to make up for it, which was what he'd wanted all along.

'Davey, I can't go on seeing you. You know I can't.'

'I don't see why!'

'What you need's a wife of your own.'

'Yes. You.'

'I'm married to somebody else!'

'He cheated you. You said so yourself.'

'I know.' She sighed. 'He did. But . . . he is my husband. Nobody's perfect, Davey, including me.'

'I see. So, you were leading me up the garden path, eh?'

'If you like.'

'I do not like!' His voice was fierce. It frightened her. He was strung up like a piano. 'Is that how you treat a hero?' Frances was taken aback. It was all very well people calling him a hero, but that he should call himself one . . . ! 'Anyway, you must think something of me. You still came to the café to meet me.'

'I feel . . . ' She dared not say 'guilty'. 'I feel I owe you something.'

'You're damn right you do!' Then, from intense fury, Davey suddenly changed, to pathetic grovelling. He grasped her hand, hurting it in his hard grip. 'Don't desert me, Frances. You're all that's keeping me alive. The only thing worth living for.' A weight fell on her. She could not shift it. He had been a hero, but it had cost him, and he was a hero no more. He was all used up. 'Tell me, please tell me you'll be true to me.'

'What do you mean?'

'Promise me. When Jack comes home on leave, if he comes home . . . ' Frances looked away in disgust, 'Promise me you won't sleep with him.'

'He's my husband!'

'You haven't slept with him for ages. You told me that. Why should things change now?' Frances looked at Davey, then down at her empty cup. 'You weren't lying to me, were you?'

'What about?'

'You haven't slept with him, have you?' His eyes pleaded with her, and yet, his pathos held a terrifying threat. She shook her head, and a tear dropped down her cheek. He sighed with relief. 'Thank you. Thank you, dear love. You don't know how much I love you, how much I need you . . . '

'You only think you need me, because I'm here, Davey. But it could be anybody!'

'I've always loved you, ever since we were children. I've been faithful to you, Frances, even when you weren't faithful to me.' She was in the wrong again. And she fell for it, every time. He was brilliant.

'I've got to go, Davey. Mam's on her own in the shop. Maisie goes out to work, you see, and . . . ' His grip tightened. She gasped with pain, then he let her go. Abruptly, he got up and walked out of the café before her. Well, she'd tried to put things right and Davey had been impossible. She could wash her hands of the whole business. So it was with a feeling of great relief, that Frances began to plan for Christmas, and Jack's first leave.

Then, she started being sick in the mornings. She could not, would not believe it. She stared at the calendar in the shop. She was two weeks overdue. Out in the kitchen, her mother was making the tea. She wondered if she could stomach it. Suddenly, she began to retch, and rushed to open the shop door, where she stood, gulping down the freezing air. Flurries of snow touched her face and hands. She shivered and looked up at the drifting flakes, falling out of the heavy sky. She opened her mouth, and put out her tongue to take one. It rested there an instant, then melted and she swallowed it down. Then a flake fell in her eye. Blinking, she put down her head, and saw Davey coming up the road. She fled into the shop, seized with panic and dropped down behind the counter, out of sight.

'Eeh! Where is she?' It was her mother's voice. Frances' head popped up and she saw the candle-lit cake, the family, beaming behind it, at the kitchen door.

'Happy birthday, pet.' Her Mam laid the cake on the counter.

'I'd forgotten it was me birthday,' Frances said, a puzzled look on her face. Michael was holding her round the knees. She touched his head with her hand.

'You can't fool us!' her mam said. 'We saw you glancing at the calendar all morning!' Frances flushed.

'I'm getting too old for birthdays.'

'Hark at her! Too old, if you please, at twenty-three! Tut!'

'God help anybody that misses my birthday!' George said, laughing.

'What were you doing under the counter, pet?' Ellen asked suddenly.

'Nothing! Just looking for something!'

'Come on, Fran! Cut the cake, man!' Maisie was hungry.

'She's got to blow the candles out first!' Os insisted. Frances took a deep breath, cheeks bulging, then the shop door clanged, Davey walked in, and she let out the air with a sudden burst.

'You've missed half of them!' Os complained and blew out the rest for her.

Davey was smiling as he approached the family group, every

260

member of which was watching him with curiosity. He held out a small parcel.

'Happy birthday!' Automatically, her lips twisted into a smile.

'How kind.'

'Well now! Isn't that nice,' Ellen said, over-enthusiastically.

'Open mine first!' Os insisted.

'Maybe Mr Lawson's got to go, pet, and I'd better not keep him waiting, had I?'

'Oh no! I've taken the afternoon off!' Frances' heart sank to her boots.

'How did you know it was her birthday?' Maisie asked suspiciously.

'We always used to keep each other's birthdays at Sunday School. Davey was in my class,' Frances explained. Then, she gasped. Inside the little box, was a gold locket and chain.

'My goodness!' Ellen exclaimed. 'Eighteen carat an' all!' She was inspecting it carefully.

'Nothing but the best!' Davey said proudly.

'It's too much.' Frances was thrusting it at him. 'I can't take it, Mr Lawson. Thank you, but . . . '

'I insist.' He pushed it back at her. The party was turning into a diplomatic nightmare.

'Have some tea, Mr Lawson?' Ellen asked, pouring him a cup.

'Don't mind if I do!' Then he made himself perfectly at home, sitting on the little chair, reserved for special customers. Frances made pleased noises over Os's drawing of a tram, then opened Michael's present.

'It's a special stone,' he said. 'I found it on the beach. It feels nice.' She felt it, weighing it in her hand.

'It's the nicest present I ever had,' she said, kissing Michael on the cheek. He was thrilled, jigging about with joy, while Os sulked.

'Cut the cake, girl!' her mother snapped.

'All right!' Frances slipped the knife through the thin icing, into the cake beneath, 'It's only a Victoria sandwich mind. We couldn't waste any fruit or eggs!'

'I'm glad you didn't!' Frances was busy opening the nightdress case made her by Maisie. It was shaped like a poodle. 'Eeh! Isn't it clever!'

'I hope Grace won't object!' Ellen laughed.

261

'That cat's past objecting to anything!' George snorted. 'She does nothing but sit by the fire the whole day long!' George's present was a new charm for her bracelet, and so was her mother's. She had a large collection now. Ellen was handing out pieces of cake, and Frances was putting away the waste paper. 'You're not finished yet!' George told her and handed her another parcel. Frances opened the little box with trepidation. It was a single strand of creamy pearls. They gleamed with such pure luminescence, they seemed to light up the space around them.

'They're beautiful.' Frances drew the card out from inside the box, and read; 'Happy birthday, dear love. Wear these as a reminder of my love for you. Pearls, it seems, like love, need human warmth to keep their lustre. In fact, the lady who sold them to me told me you have to wear them, even in bed, or they go black! A bit like marriage, really! (Live and learn, don't you?) Jack xxx'

Davey was furious. Desperate to distract him, Maisie began piling birthday cake onto the plates.

'How much do you want, Fran?' she asked loudly.

'Em . . . oh, I don't know I want any, just yet . . . '

'You've got to have a bit of your own birthday cake!' Maisie insisted.

'Just a little bit, then!' Maisie handed her a piece. Reluctantly, Frances picked it up and began to eat. Immediately, she started retching. She rushed out to the back yard to relieve herself, closely followed by her mother.

'I thought she was looking a bit drawn, like,' Maisie said. 'You shouldn't be such a slave driver, Dad! The poor lass is worn out!'

'Have you heard from Jack lately?'

They all turned to stare at Davey. He had a queer look on his face.

Hill 60, near Messines, was the objective. It was this ridge, held by the Germans, which was stopping the entire allied advance. There was no way over the top, so the army had decided to go underneath. After a short period of training in England, Jack and the rest of his battalion crossed the channel to Belgium. He had made some good pals in the few weeks they had been together. But there was a lad, just come from India, who took his particular attention. He was a half-caste and he was called Vijay Ridley. He'd sailed from Bombay with his father's blessing, only his father thought he was going to university. He was wrong. As soon as he'd arrived, all of nineteen years old, the lad'd made for the recruiting station and applied for the Durham Light.

'Why us?' Jack had asked him, warily. Vijay shrugged.

'My Father comes from that part of the country.'

'Gerraway!' one of the lads said, astonished. 'You don't half talk funny for a Geordie!'

'No! Really! He was born in a place called South Shields. Do you know it?'

'Do I know it?' Jack looked all amazement. 'I live there!' And at once he took Vijay under his wing. The lad didn't drink, being Hindu, which was all right with Jack. Like he'd said to Will, he could take it or leave it. But the Geordies, the real ones, thought they were mad.

'Why yer bugger!' Stew said. 'You should've been fightin' in Mesopotamia you! They're *all* heathens oot there!'

'Some Indian companies are fighting,' Vijay said. 'But they're fighting against Moslems, like in the Dardanelles. I didn't fancy that. God knows what they'd do to Hindu captives, like me.'

'Bloody hell!' Stew intoned. 'The silly sods! I mean, there's only one God! It stands to reason, like, eh? Doesn't it, eh?'

'Aye.' His friend Martin agreed philosophically. 'And he's fightin' on every bugger's side at once!' Jack grinned.

'There's nothing like a Geordie for having long discussions about the destiny of man,' he explained to Vijay.

'And God!' Stew objected.

'Him as well.'

'You Geordies seem to be like us Indians. You are used to God in many guises, none of them exclusive.'

'Eh?'

'Have you ever been doon a pit, Vee ja?'

'Vijay,' the Indian corrected.

'Why man, you don't expect us to be able to pronounce an outlandish name like that, do you?'

'All right. Call me Victor, if you like. That's what my name means . . . victory.'

'Well you bugger!' Martin shook his head amazed. 'With a

name like that, you can be our company mascot, son!' So Vijay was admitted into the Geordie elite.

But, arriving in Belgium, the tunnelling company had been held back at the coast. It was an unexpected reprieve for Vijay.

'I never have been down a mine, you know,' he confessed one night, as Jack smoked his evening cigarette by the canteen.

'You'll soon learn. I did,' Jack reassured him. 'You can be my "marra". Work alongside me. Keep you out of the firing line, anyway!' Both men fell silent, deep in their own thoughts.

'I suppose I'll have to write home to tell my father what I've done,' Vijay said at last. He sighed. 'I expect he'll be very angry.'

'How about your mother?'

'She's dead. Died when my younger brother was born. My father's hoping to keep Prajapati out of the war. He's very fond of my brother.' Jack couldn't miss the bitterness in Vijay's voice.

'Do you and your brother feel more Indian, or more English, if you don't mind my asking?'

'Oh, I don't mind, but I don't know the answer. I'm neither really. I know the Indian side of me, my mother's side, very well, but not the English. Not at all . . . ' The lad had a determined look about him, a look of implacable vindictiveness. 'That's why I came to England, really. To trace my father's family.' Jack was glad he had kept his silence. Every instinct now told him to tread as warily as on a minefield.

'I never knew my parents,' he said, easily. 'I was brought up in an orphanage. I look on my wife's folk as mine now.' Jack thought for a second. 'Did your father never speak to you about his family?'

'No. Never.' Jack dragged on his cigarette. 'But my mother, she knew something.' The smoke swirled up and the two men watched it, till it disappeared.

'If you don't mind me saying so, son, you sound quite bitter about your Dad.' Vijay gave him a sharp look, and walked off.

Frances met Davey at the café again.

'Me Mam knows,' she said.

'Soon they'll all know.'

'It makes no difference! They'll think it's Jack's.'

'And what will he think if he knows he's bringing up another

264

man's child?' She didn't want to think about that. 'What the head doesn't know the heart doesn't grieve over,' her mother had said. She had suspected even before the birthday party.

'Are you sure it couldn't be Jack's?' she'd asked. Frances shook her head. She'd had a period since Jack went. It was Davey's all right. 'Never mind, pet. You can kid Jack on. When it comes, just tell him it's late. He's daft enough to believe it.'

'Do you think so?'

'All men're daft, pet. I'd've thought you'd have learnt that by now, if you've learned nowt else!' But Frances loved Jack. 'He cheated you, didn't he? Now you can get your own back!' her mother sniped. Davey's voice brought her back to reality.

'What about me? It's my kid, you know! My flesh and blood!'

But she loved Jack. It was the one thing she kept coming back to. She'd do whatever Jack wanted. She'd tell him the truth. Yes. When he came home on leave, she'd make a clean breast of it and then . . . then God knew what. Meanwhile she hid herself away in her room, reading Jack's letters over and over. She was lucky. Maisie hadn't had any for ages. She was beginning to worry. Frances knew Jack's letters off by heart, but every time she read them over, a knife turned inside her. She put them away in her drawer. Lifting the stockings, she touched the old drawing of the elephant. Maybe someone in one of the photographs had drawn it. She pulled out the album her granda had shown her. There they all were in their stiff poses, and prim hair dos, the whole family. And there was her grandma, in family groups, and alone with her granda, and there was one of her with a young man. She looked little more than a girl herself. The ink had gone brown underneath. Frances screwed up her eyes to make it out. 'Jane Beattie and Robert Ridley.' Of course. The elder brother. There was none of Joshua, the youngest, nor any of Aunt Fanny. Frances sighed. Her grandma's family seemed to have disappeared, blown by the wind across the globe, America, India, and Fanny to her grave, a long time ago.

'Frances!' It was her mother.

'Sh! The boys are asleep in the other room!' Ellen was panting as she reached the top of the stair.

'Oh dear! I'm not as fit as I was. I'm not really.'

'You're getting thin, Mam.'

'I'm getting old.'

'Rubbish. Are you sure you're all right? I mean, have you seen the doctor about all this breathlessness and that?'

'Never mind me. Davey Lawson's here. He says he wants to see you. Best go down, pet, before your granda comes in.'

Davey was in the dining room. He had his back to her and was looking through the window, as she came in. He turned, smiling.

'I've come to fetch you home.' Frances thought she was going to faint. She steadied herself against the door.

'I'm at home now, Davey.'

'No, you're not. Get your things.'

'I think you'd better go.'

'Not without you!'

'Please, Davey! The children'll hear you! Please! Not here!'

'You can come quietly, or . . . ' He stopped, listening. There was someone downstairs. George had come home. They heard him sigh, as he trudged up the stairs from the kitchen.

'Please, Davey!' Frances whispered. 'If you love me, please don't say anything!' Her granda stopped on the landing.

'Who's there?' he shouted.

'Only me, Granda!'

'And me!' Davey emerged from the room, pushing Frances gently before him.

'Bit late for a visit, isn't it?' George asked, surprised.

'I've come for something that belongs to me.'

'Please, Davey,' Frances whispered.

'What's that?'

'My child. Frances' child.'

George staggered back. He caught the knob on the stair head, preventing himself from falling, just in time.

'Don't listen to him, Granda.' Now Ellen was in the passage with them. She ran to her father and supported him.

'What are you saying, man!' George bellowed.

'Frances is pregnant. I've come to take her home.' Frances wailed loudly, hiding her face in the doorway.

'I'm sorry, Granda. I'm sorry.'

There was a long pause. She turned, but when Frances saw him, she grew afraid. Her granda's face was white.

'Get out of my house!' he hissed. Frances stared, stupefied.

'Get out!' He fell forwards, but was held by Ellen. His colour had changed suddenly to a deep crimson.

'You'd better go, pet,' Ellen said. 'Who knows? Maybe it'll be for the best!'

'Mam!' They were all deserting her. Her mother was leading her granda into his room.

'Go on, Fran. Far better! Get out of his sight.' Where could she go? Davey stood, waiting, at the top of the stair.

A bleak wind wailed round the barracks. It was as cold as Christmas. Vijay picked up Jack's crumpled letter from the ground.

'Well, I don't think *I'll* be going home for Christmas! So if you'd any hope of tagging along with me.'

'Not to worry your head about me! I understand!' Vijay smoothed out the pages. 'But what are you going to do? That's the important thing.' Jack shook his head. He was at a loss.

'I don't know, mate. I honestly don't know.'

'Perhaps the child's yours?'

'She says not and she should know!' Jack sounded bitter. 'God knows how long it's been going on for!'

'She says in her letter, it was only the one time!'

'She says! She says! How can I believe what "she says", any more?'

'She asks for forgiveness!' Vijay thrust the letter in Jack's face. 'Look! She loves you!' Jack's throat tightened. He couldn't speak. He looked away into the biting wind. 'Look!' Vijay insisted, but Jack ignored him. In desperation, the lad began to read the letter out. 'I didn't want you to hear about it this way. I would much rather have told you to your face, when you were home on leave. But Granda forced my hand by throwing me out of the house, so I have had to write and tell you now.' Jack threw his cigarette to the ground.

'She thought she could get away with it, the bitch! She was never going to tell me! Never!' Vijay sighed. The man would believe what he wanted. Better leave it.

'What about your two boys?'

'They'll be all right. Maisie'll keep an eye on them.' Jack sighed. 'I'll stay at a place I know in London.' He jerked his head toward Vijay. 'You can come too, if you like!' The Indian nodded.

'Thank you. I'd like that,' he replied politely.

'Unless, of course you want to go up to Shields on your own. Follow up your family tree . . . ?'

'No. It's all right. My marra needs me. The parish records can wait.'

Yes, Jack thought, better let sleeping dogs lie.

Frances lay on the bed, in the flat above Lawson's shop, and stared up at the crazed ceiling. Why was there no reply from Jack? Perhaps he was dead. Dead to her, anyway. She didn't blame him. How would she have felt if the boot was on the other foot? 'Our sins never die. They take a shape and haunt us.' One moment, that's all, and it had changed her whole life. She would give anything to have her time over again. Poor Jack! He hadn't deserved this. He had cheated her, yes! But he had not deserved this! Her sobs grew louder. There were steps on the landing. Davey came into the room. He stood for a moment, looking at her from the doorway. Then he came and sat beside her, on the bed.

'Poor Frances,' he said, gently removing the stray hairs from the tear-streaked face. 'You'll never be happy without your children, will you?' She shook her head, crying loudly. 'There, there!' He held her, comforting her as best he could. 'I've been thinking . . . ' The sobbing stilled, Frances looked at him. 'Why don't you bring them here . . . for Christmas.' She stared.

'Could I?'

'Of course!' She still believed that either Jack would write and tell her what to do, or her granda would forgive her and take her back. The present arrangement was purely temporary.

'Just for Christmas?'

'If you like.' The temptation was great. She was desperate to see them, both of them.

'What about your Mam?'

'She won't say a word. I promise you. She wouldn't dare!' Quickly, Frances flung on her coat and pulled on her boots, running from the house without a hat. Mrs Lawson watched her from the shop window. She might not say anything, but she looked plenty. Her son had a heart of gold, taking in that little slut and her brood. He deserved better! Suddenly, she became aware of Davey, staring at her back. She turned uncomfortably, and returned to the counter, avoiding his unblinking eyes.

Once at Fowler Street, Frances hung about in the back lane, waiting. If only Maisie would come out, or her Mam. She could hear Michael, crying in the kitchen. She badly wanted to go in to him, but what if her granda should be there? It would hurt the child even more to see her, and be torn from her again. The crying grew louder. Never mind the 'old barsket'! She had to go to him. He was her child! She flung open the gate, and walked into the yard. Os was playing there with the top and whip.

'Hallo, son,' she said quietly. Os cracked his whip, sending the top spinning to her feet. She jumped out of its way and the child turned and fled into the house. But Maisie was at the door.

'It's all right. He's out. You can come in!' Relieved, Frances ran towards her, taking Michael and hugging him close.

'Mammy! Mammy!' he wailed.

'It's all right, pet. Mammy's here.' His little arms encircled her neck. He was crying as though his heart would break.

'I thought you didn't love me any more.'

'Of course I love you. I love you more than anybody in the whole wide world.' He cried for a bit, their tears blending on their cheeks.

'You won't go away again, will you?'

'Michael, I've come to take you with me.' Her eyes met Maisie's. Her aunt nodded.

'I'll get his things.'

'And Os's!' Maisie looked back, then went without a word.

Ellen came out and walked with her daughter, in the yard, to and fro, calming the little boy. Upstairs, they heard Os scream, 'I won't go! I won't! So there!'

Frances' heart felt full of stones. Her mother shook her head.

'Well, pet, you brought it all on yourself!'

'Thanks for nothing!' Frances spat.

'Hoity-toity!'

'If you say that again . . . I'm sorry, Mam. I'm upset, that's all.' Michael was calmer. Safe in her arms, he began to look around. Maisie came out with a little bag full of Michael's things.

'You'd better go now. He's due back any minute,' she warned.

Frances nodded, taking the bag in her free hand. 'Os won't come, pet. I'm sorry.'

'I heard. Poor little sod. He hates me, doesn't he?'

'He'll get over it. Go on now. I'll fetch the rest of his stuff over, when I can.'

'Thanks, Auntie. It's only for now, like. I'll be back!'

'Aye.' Maisie smiled bleakly. Nobody believed it.

'Have you heard from Will, yet?' Maisie shook her head. 'Letters take a long time from the Dardanelles.'

One last look at the old house. She'd always hated it and now she was seeing the back of it, she found it hard to leave.

'Go on now,' Maisie gently pushed her towards the gate.

'Where's Os?' Michael asked, alarmed.

'It's just you and me, pet. Is that all right?' Michael nodded slowly. He wasn't happy. But he wouldn't leave his Mam. The back gate closed behind them. Maisie stood staring at it forlornly for some time, then went inside, to write another letter to Will.

The fuse was burning. Will counted the seconds.

'One hundred-and-one, one hundred-and-two, one hundred-and-three.' Then he threw the jam jar bomb over the top of the parapet. Two seconds later, it went off just as it hit the ground on the Turkish line, thirty or so feet away. The blast was followed by a cry.

'Is it right what I heard about there being a tin of butter somewhere?' Charlie asked.

'Rubbish!' Will replied. There was a long silence. Charlie was getting ready to light his bomb. 'Watch out. This bugger's got a short fuse,' Will warned him. Charlie looked at it in disgust.

'They don't care who it gets, us or the bloody Turks, just so long as it kills some bugger!' He hurled it over the top, unlit. Seconds later, some Turk, finding it, a gift from heaven, lit the fuse to throw it back, and blew himself up.

'All's fair, Will!'

'Aye, Charlie. So they say.'

'Are you sure there's not a tin of butter?'

'You've been dreamin', man!' There was a long silence. Stalemate. The drive towards Achi Baba had been a disaster. But it had not been abandoned. The fierce heat of the summer had given way to the cool of autumn. The flies and maggots

270

burrowing at the bodies just beneath the soil, were getting more scarce. But deeper down, thousands of men crept, furtively, living like worms crawling about the labyrinthine galleries of Gallipoli. Emaciated, plagued by dysentery, targets of bullets and shrapnel, they lived a timeless existence. Tomorrow never came. Yesterday never happened. The paper from Maisie's letters lit many a fuse. Will read them till he knew them off by heart. Then, after tearing them into strips, he would kiss each one before lighting it and sending it on its way, with the words, 'Go on, Maisie! Get the buggers!'

He was living on borrowed time. Few survived more than a month in the carnage of the Dardanelles. Will was lucky.

'Reckon I'll get a bit of shut-eye, Will!' Charlie lay back on the shelf, his hat a pillow for his head. 'Nightie-night!'

Suddenly an officer was in the trench. He kicked Charlie with his boot.

'Don't you know there's a war on!' Will gritted his teeth.

'How long did I sleep?' Charlie asked as the officer ploughed on.

'Three minutes or so.'

'Damn!' But, then the officer was back.

'Prepare for advance. Enemy's suffered heavy shelling. Opinion seems to be that it's the right moment to take them!' Charlie remembered his bomb; the one with the short fuse.

'There's still a few of them left!' There was murmuring in the ranks, all along the line.

'We're going over in about one hour!' The officer checked his watch and went on. Will checked his rifle. In one hour it would be mid-afternoon, and the moon would rise, the crescent moon of the Moslems. It was quiet. No sign of life on the other side. Perhaps the officer was right. Will took out his watch and tried to see how much time had passed. It wasn't ticking. He shook it. George's offering had been battered to death. Will sighed and put it back in his pocket. Fifteen minutes to go. Ten minutes. Five minutes.

'Are you ready? Come on, men! Over we go!' Over they went into withering machine-gun fire. Charlie and Will made twenty feet, and fell to the ground, pulling the bodies of the fallen close, for shelter.

'By God! What happened to the shells?'

'Haway! Let's make a dash!' Will pushed away the sheltering body, and ran towards the Turkish front line. Charlie caught it in the throat, and fell behind him. Will leapt into the first trench. It was empty, bar the dead. A few of the Howe were advancing on the second trench, under the Platoon Commander. Will joined them and soon they were at the parapet. All the time the Turks were taking pot shots at him. He could see their flag, with its crescent moon, flying over the third trench. But Will would stay where he was. From here he could see what they were up to. Men were coming up behind, and heavy enemy fire came at them. Will's comrades split, and he crawled along the parapet to the right where the Hood were supposed to be. But where were they? Only a scattered few remained. And where were the Collingwoods, and the French? Something had gone wrong. Now the Turks were re-entering their trenches!

Encircled and fired on from all sides, Will knew he had no choice but to fall back. He stumbled over his own dead and dying. He had to leave them to their fate. But what about Charlie? Better finish him off. They said the Turks did terrible things to you, before they slit your throat. Where was he, though? Will crawled on. He had lost his friend and lost his bearings. He was within four yards of the first trench, when he discovered it was full of Turks. He was trapped, stuck. Nothing he could do, but wait, and hope. 'The Lord is my shepherd . . .'

For hours, Will lay low, not daring to move. 'Yea though I walk through the valley of the shadow of death . . . ' From the trench, he heard the Moslem prayer. 'Allah Akbar! Allah Akbar!' They were praying to the same God. Will grasped his rifle tightly. He didn't dare fill the magazine. His mouth was crammed with dust. He was choking with it, but he dared not cough. It was sunset. He had been there for hours. The chanting grew louder. His head swam. Maisie was standing on the parapet, in the Turkish sightlines. He shouted to her, waving, 'Get down!' What was she doing here? She just smiled and waved back at him. Dear Maisie, without her teeth, looking like a faun. She spoke to him.

'I wish this day could go on forever.' She smiled and he remembered the dappled sunlight on her flesh, the river water on his skin, her soft woman's eyes. He coughed, and spluttered, 'It will. In here.' His hand pointed at his heart. Then the bullet got him.

CHAPTER SIXTEEN

Maisie was at the door, a large bag in her hand. Mrs Lawson let her into the parlour and fetched Frances. The two women fell into one another's arms. Maisie was crying.

'It's all right, Maisie. He's being kind to us. You're not to worry.'

'I'm not crying for you!' Maisie snapped. Frances was stung. Her aunt was biting back her tears and when the flood gates burst, she wept uncontrollably.

'Auntie, what is it?' Frances asked. Michael was hugging his favourite aunt's knees.

'It's Will.' The words came out in little jerks, as though the effort to speak was much too much. 'He's dead. Or at least, they think so!'

'Oh, Maisie! No!' Frances was crying now. Michael looked from one to the other. Who was he to look after? He pulled at his mother's skirt, and brought her closer to his auntie, then he held the pair of them, as before, by their knees. After a while, the sobbing ceased and Maisie told her tale.

'His Dad wrote me a letter. Poor old man, he's all alone now! You're lucky having a bairn! I wish . . . oh I wish . . . '

'Auntie, stay with us here, just for a bit, eh?'

'Oh, I'm goin' to! Don't you worry! It's not just *his* things in here, you know!' Frances smiled, glad at last to have someone else to think about.

'I don't know what the old bitch'll say.' Frances laughed.

'She can't be any worse than the old barsket!' Suddenly the women were howling with laughter. The girls heard them in the shop and exchanged shocked glances. 'Do you know, our Fran, he's been like a bear with a sore head ever since Michael went. I think it was the straw that broke him. We all miss our little lad in Fowler Street.'

'How's me Mam goin' to cope with Granda, and the shop all on her own? Eeh, and Christmas is comin' on too!'

'She's a saint, that woman,' Maisie said, with real respect. Frances frowned.

'Me Mam?'

'Aha. Your Mam. She's really come up trumps. I don't know how she does it. It was her told's to come here.'

'Never!'

'Aye. And she's really wonderful with Dad. I never knew she had it in her. Honest I didn't.'

'Neither did I.'

'Sometimes it takes a crisis to bring out the best in folk.' Maisie said philosophically.

'Aha.'

'How's our Os?' Michael couldn't wait any longer.

'All right, pet.'

'Is he?' Frances asked.

'Same as usual. That kid's hard as nails. I don't know.' She sighed.

'It's my fault!' Frances looked away. 'Have you heard from Jack?'

'No. I'm sorry, pet. Not a dickie bird. Now don't you dare get maudlin', our Fran! I'm tellin' you, we're goin' to have a nice Christmas together, if it kills us!' The women whooped with laughter and this time, Michael joined in.

The children's choir were singing, 'Away in a manger', as Vijay stood looking at the nativity scene, in the corner of the church.

'I don't suppose you'll know what it's all about, eh?' Mrs Rosa said sympathetically.

'Oh yes! I've been to a church service before. I've even been to a carol service!'

'Fancy!' Mrs Rosa disapproved of heathens in a church of God. She went to sit in the pew, self-righteously folding her hands in her lap.

'You've put her out.' Jack grinned. 'She thought she was going to have the job of converting you.' Vijay laughed.

'Sorry! My father converted from Christianity to Hinduism.'

'Don't tell her that!'

'The story of Ganesha, your statue, with the elephant's head . . . does it remind you of anything? Immaculate conception, born to save the world, sacrificed by his Almighty Father, then resurrected!'

'Good God!'

'You see! You have the Trinity of the Godhead too. Father, Mother, Son.'

'Holy Ghost . . .'

'How can there be a son without a mother? Parvati, Mary, the Holy Ghost . . . call her what you will!'

'Are you talking that heathen talk again? And in a Church of God!' Vijay jumped. Mrs Rosa was breathing down his neck.

'No, ma'am! We were talking about football!'

'That's all right, then!' Jack jerked his head in the direction of the pew. Like good lads, they went and listened to the singing.

It was Christmas Eve. Snow was falling. Ice hung in columns from the gutters and the drainpipes. Jack watched Vijay, as he stared through Mrs Rosa's front window. A man in search of his family. They were both without family, and at Christmas! What had stopped Jack going home? Hurt pride? Fear? Jealousy? How could he have done it, not only to his children but to himself? And now it was too late, because the trains were stopping for the holiday. The day after tomorrow, he had to be back at the front. And Vijay had lost his chance of checking the parish records, up in Shields . . . not that that was necessarily a bad thing. Ridley, India, it was all too much of a coincidence. Jack studied Vijay, silhouetted against the light. His back had an invisible load on it and it bowed under the weight. What would he do, if he *did* trace his family? Vijay was close, but he had given away more than he knew. He was a potential troublemaker, and Jack was glad to have stalled him, until he had discovered more. At least some good had come out of it all. Why had Vijay's father never spoken about his family? And why was the lad so embittered against him, so jealous of his brother? Frances' words came back to him, uncomfortably. 'Grandma always seemed weighed down by guilt, as though she knew something much worse,' and his reply, 'You're trying to blame others for your own inability to accept what you are?' Wasn't that also Vijay's problem?

He walked over to Vijay's side, and put his hand on his shoulder. Together they watched the thickening flakes.

'There's a strange feeling in the air,' Vijay said quietly. 'Listen. How silent it is!' Jack stared out into the white street. Vijay was right. The snow fell like comfort, blotting out the ugliness, the pain and suffering, muffling the rumble of traffic, and the din of war. It was hard to think in the presence of such peace. It was a moment poised between past and future, separate from all other moments, and more real than anything Jack had ever felt before. The very gatepost seemed to take on portentous significance and Mrs Rosa's kettle whistled like a signal from the back kitchen. 'I've only felt anything like this once before, up in the Himalayas with my father, years ago. We arrived, barefoot and exhausted, after walking for days, at a huge cave, a cleft in the mountainside. We were among hundreds of others, crowding in to see the images of the Holy Family, Shiva, Parvati and Ganesha. Not, as you might think, statues carved out of the rock face, but made of ice. Every year, miraculously, they form themselves, and then, slowly they melt away again. Perhaps I was just exhausted from the long journey, I don't know, but, staring at the pure white glow of Shiva's icy linga, I felt a silent presence, so powerful that it could have moved the mountain and split the earth. I remember I cried with sheer joy. And I wasn't alone. Grown men, faces like leather, sobbed, and fell to the ground. It was like . . . it was like Christmas Eve.' Vijay faltered, then stopped speaking.

'What's Shiva's linga?'

'It's a sort of column, pointing straight up to heaven.'

'And Shiva?'

'The Almighty Father. That journey meant a great deal to me. My brother wasn't old enough to go. I was alone with my father for days. It was the only time I ever felt really close to him.'

Vijay was crying. 'I'm sorry. It's not very manly to cry, is it?' Jack shrugged, and watched and waited. 'I used to think my father hated me. He behaved just as though I wasn't there most of the time. And I tried hard to please him. But whatever I did, it seemed to anger him. My mother said, it wasn't me he was angry with. She said he was angry with himself.' Vijay looked at Jack, but Jack averted his eyes.

'Why? What had he done?' Vijay shook his head.

'Whatever it was, it had something to do with him leaving England.'

'Did he say so?'

'No. I told you. He never spoke about it. My mother said there'd been a row. He blamed himself. But . . . ' And now Vijay's voice hardened, ' . . . I don't think my father'd done anything at all! I think it was them! His family! They cheated him in some way! And when I find out how . . . !' Jack patted his shoulder thoughtfully.

'What about your brother?'

'What about him?' Vijay threw the words at him.

'You said your father loves him.'

'Yes. That made it all so much worse. I could bear my father's anger against me. But not his love for another son.' Like Os and Michael, Jack thought. Frances had been the same with them, and like Vijay, Os, the firstborn, was jealous. So many parallels. Two families, their history running blindly side by side. Jack was sure now he had been right. The family Vijay sought, was his own. But should he tell him?

Watching from the kitchen window, Maisie and Frances smiled.

'He's building a snowman! Ah!' The pile of snow was almost out of reach. But it wasn't tall enough. Michael looked round for something to stand on.

'Davey! Lend him a hand, eh? He'll fall off!' Davey pulled on his overcoat and went out into the yard.

'Time you gave him a head, eh?' He laughed. 'He'll be taller than me soon!' Michael looked quizzically at Uncle Davey.

'I want him to reach the sky!'

'Look, here's two lumps of coal for his eyes, and I'll lend you my scarf for his muffler! How about that?' The child stood by, watching, as the man finished the snowman for him. 'How about

277

that, eh?' Davey turned round, seeking approval, but the child had gone inside.

The shadow of the snowman fell across the yard in the light of the moon. Everyone was in bed but Frances. She sat by the dying kitchen fire, hugging herself close. Michael's stocking dangled from the mantelpiece. In the silence of Christmas Eve, she could see herself, and her life, with stark reality. What she had done, she had done. It could not be undone. She had hurt her husband. She had hurt her children and marred their lives. And now, here she was, in another man's house, and she was abusing him too. Oh yes, she was! Her belly swelled darkly in the firelight. She was carrying his child. She ate his food. She warmed herself at his fire. And she gave him nothing. He hadn't forced her. But she felt his longing. He deserved better than she, but she was what he wanted. Sighing, she rose and went upstairs. Michael woke as Frances crept into the room.

'Has Santa Claus been yet?'

'Not yet, pet. Go back to sleep.'

She began to undress. Across the passage she heard Davey stir. He was moaning.

'Poor Uncle Davey. He's having a nightmare, Mam!'

'Yes, pet.'

'Why don't you go in and comfort him?' So simple. She stared into the child's innocent eyes. They were unflinching. It was as though he knew.

'Do you think I should?' she whispered. Michael nodded slowly.

'All right. If you really think so.'

'Yes, Mam.' She went to the window and looked out at the white roofs. The moon was so bright. She wanted to cry. But the moaning from across the passage grew louder. She threw her wrap round her and went to the door.

'Goodnight, Mam,' Michael whispered.

'Goodnight, son.' The boy turned over and went to sleep.

'Davey! Davey! Are you all right?' Her voice fell like velvet on his sleep.

'Don't leave me to die! Oh, Jim . . . Jim . . . it wasn't me . . . it wasn't me . . . ' His cheeks were wet with tears. Her cool hands soothed them away, and his eyelids fluttered open. He swallowed hard, and stared up at her, as though she was a ghost.

'You were having a nightmare,' she told him.

'Frances . . . '

'What was it? Were you back in the trenches?'

'No Man's Land,' he whispered. 'I'm not a hero. Don't tell anybody.'

'No. I won't tell, Davey.'

'I wanted to die.'

'You?'

'Yes. I was scared. I wet my pants, Frances, I was so scared. I couldn't stand being frightened any more. But I needn't . . . I needn't have left Jim to die.'

'Jim?'

'I might at least have put him out of his misery. But I didn't. I left him in agony.' A wail wrenched up from deep inside. 'I'm not a man at all! I'm a beast, a heartless beast!'

'Sh, sh.' She took him in her arms like a big child.

'He called to me. He called my name . . . '

'Sh . . . '

'I had to tell somebody.'

'Yes.'

'I don't know why I left him, why I didn't finish him off . . . I don't know why.' He held onto her like a drowning man to a lifebelt. And she was so sorry for him; so sorry. The warmth of her pity fanned his need into a blazing fire, and she gave herself, at last, compassionately, out of a sort of love.

Sitting by the kitchen fire, George was making tapers out of old newspaper.

'Before long we won't have newspapers, never mind matches!' he said gloomily, as he picked up the front page of yesterday's *Gazette*. It bore the headline, 'The Charnel House of Verdun'. He stopped and glanced at it, before deliberately tearing and folding it. Maisie looked up from her mending and wondered whether to speak. She'd heard down at The Glebe about Mrs Minto's youngest, George's natural son.

'Dad . . . ' Maisie whispered. She wanted to tell him she understood, she was sorry. But he wouldn't let her. He kept his eyes glued to his menial task, ignoring her. George's secret life had its secret griefs. It gave him dignity in an undignified situation.

* * *

279

So, feelings were hoarded away, in Fowler Street, like the little van, dismantled now and laid to rest for the duration. Deliveries were made on foot, or bicycle, by Maisie, who had been forced to give up her job as an ambulance driver. George did the books, and Ellen ran the house and shop with Maisie's help, who also had little Os to care for. It was too much. Maisie threw down her mending.

'This tablecloth's holier than the Church.' She yawned loudly, but George said nothing. 'And it's too much for my eyes, Dad, we need help!' He looked up at last. 'If you won't have our Frances back, at least write to Aunt Harriet.' George made one more taper and placed it in the little tin on the mantelpiece.

'Sufficient unto the day is the evil thereof,' he said, and went up to the office to prepare his sermon for the following Sunday. Harriet would have brought them out of themselves. But, George feared such intrusion on his privacy. The household might exist under one roof, but each member of it lived in isolation from the rest, the natural expression of their feelings gagged. Deviously, the feelings sought new outlets . . .

George slowly transferred his love for his lost son, to Os; he was too young to fight in any war, so it was safe to love him. And the lad finding himself, so suddenly and unexpectedly, the centre of attention, was soon a fair way to being spoiled rotten. He soaked up George's disdain for his mother, and began to play the part of the poor little orphan boy, self-pity making him loud and bossy, unpopular with the other children in the street. And so, he played alone, the chip on his shoulder growing larger with every month that passed. The women had neither the time nor the energy to deal with him, cocooned in their own deep griefs. Then, Maisie was dealt another blow; one which seemed to floor her more than all the rest put together.

Coming down to make the tea, early one morning, she found Grace, her little cat, dead on the hearth. She had died, finally, of old age, passing away in her sleep. The tiny death affected the whole family, and Maisie was inconsolable. Ellen couldn't understand it. She hadn't cried as much as this over Will, why over a cat? But unable to have children of her own, Grace had been Maisie's baby, a constant, loving companion, for eighteen years, and, besides, the death of the animal had released the pent up grief for Will. No wonder then, the loss tore at her heart so painfully. And now she sought consolation. She sought it in her prayers, and in the services at chapel. She had no doubts about eternal life for humans, but what about God's creatures? If Maisie could only believe that one day, when she also died, she'd see Grace again, just like Will and her mother, then, she felt she could bear it. But how to tell? She sat, twisting her handkerchief in the pew, as George spoke out against the current fashion for Spiritualism.

'We have all suffered great losses in this terrible war.' George paused, and the sincerity of his struggle to control his emotions drew respect from the congregation. 'But, if there is anything that I have learnt through it all, it is that each one of us has some-thing divine within; that spark, that spirit, which is part of God, and absolutely free. We cannot possess one another. If we truly love, we have to let our loved ones go. On the Western Front, our boys are fighting for freedom. Have we then, here at home, any right to hold onto them, when they have gone? Have they not earned their rest? What reason have we to trouble them, by calling on these misguided men and women who call themselves psychic mediums? Many of them are mere charlatans and will take from us nothing but our money. But what of those who have real powers? Fools rush in where angels fear to tread. My friends, when we open the doors of our houses, who knows who may walk in? Not only our dear departed perhaps, but malevolent entities, preying on our weaknesses and griefs. Danger lurks in the crystal ball . . . ' George's voice grew in strength and fury. Many women, who had indulged in spirit communication, cringed before him, but Maisie knew her father, and had lost her fear of him long ago. Her mind wandered, remembering her old belief in her 'own powers'. There were such things as mediums, she was sure. And many women had been comforted by them, why not she? If her father had not spoken out against it, the idea might not have occurred to her, but now he had, well, surely, she persuaded herself, it couldn't hurt to try it, just once? The following day, scouring the personal columns of the paper, as usual, Maisie found an advert for psychic sittings. Then, without telling a soul, she wrote in and secured 'an interview for a reading'.

The woman, whose name was Nelly Lawrence, had a room over a shop in Laygate. It was a warm, cosy room, if rather shabby. The bed in the corner was covered with old dolls and teddy bears, while the old-fashioned chairs were festooned with shawls and rugs. She had the fire on too, but it was hidden by a clothes horse, draped in wet washing. Dampness steamed up the windows, and hung, like an invisible cloud, heavy, on the air.

'Sit down, pet,' Nelly said cheerily. 'Make yourself at home!' Maisie sat, looked warily at the crystal ball on the table in front of her and began to wonder uneasily, whether she was doing the right thing after all. But Nelly's mind was on more material matters. 'Have you got the er . . . wherewithal?' Maisie nodded and handed her a sealed envelope. Then, Nelly disappeared behind a curtain into her kitchen and counted the money, which she slipped into her tin above the gas ring. It was too late for Maisie to change her mind now, but, at least she could test the water before giving her trust. 'Well now,' Nelly came back in, rubbing her hands, and looked at the bleak face before her. 'Would you like a cup of tea?' Maisie accepted gratefully, and, she relaxed a little. Surely this unassuming little body meant no harm? 'You've lost somebody, haven't you? I can tell,' Nelly said sympathetically. Maisie nodded. 'And you want to make contact, eh?' Again Maisie nodded. 'Tell me, dear, what's the name?'

'Grace.'

'Grace . . . ' Nelly shut her eyes, threw her head back, and began to go into a trance. 'Grace . . . are you there dear?' There was an ominous pause. 'Ah yes . . . I can see her now. She's old, very old . . . a grey old lady . . . ' Maisie nodded. 'She can't understand what's happened to her . . . she thinks . . . she thinks you still need her. She's telling me there's something in the cellar of the house . . . something very important . . . '

'Mice,' Maisie said. 'Grace was a very good mouser.'

'Pardon?' Had Maisie caught her out? Then the 'medium' suddenly screamed. 'Ah!' She seemed to be in pain. 'Someone desperate to reach you.' She gasped. 'I see . . . I see a man, a young man, with a kind face. He's . . . he's holding a bottle of beer in his hand.' Nelly put on a theatrical Scots accent,

' "A man may chafe at fate and a man may criticise,

But there's aye a way to the gates o' Paradise."
Is he Scottish dear?' Maisie shook her head. Then, suddenly, the
medium's voice changed, growing low and dark, ' "I wish this
day could go on forever . . . " ' Maisie sobbed. There could be no
doubt about it!

'It's Will! Will, where are you?'

' "Question why and you're not trusting any more . . . " '

'I love you, Will. I miss you! Oh, Will, why didn't we get
married?'

' "What difference will any of it make in a million years
time?" '

'Will I ever be happy again?'

' "Happiness, unhappiness . . . " '

' . . . "live side by side", Will . . . '

' "Go on forever . . . ' " Suddenly Nelly's voice changed back.
'He's gone,' she said, sitting bolt upright. Maisie was sobbing
violently.

'What did he mean?'

'I don't know, dear . . . the messages are often cryptic. That's
how they talk over on the other side.'

'Can't you try to get him again?' Nelly shook her head.

'If you want to book another sitting, dear, I will gladly oblige.
For the usual fee, of course.' She rose and showed Maisie to the
door.

Walking home, Maisie pondered Will's message. 'Happiness,
unhappiness . . . go on forever . . . ' That's what he'd said. It was
cold comfort. She had to know more. There was nothing for it.
She would have to book another sitting. But, brooding by the
kitchen fire, that night, Maisie considered her own powers. She
had always felt she had them. And now, suddenly, as if
answering a need, at dead of night, she felt her mother's presence
coming near. The flames flickered in the grate, the coal settled,
and the rats scurried, down in the cellar. Perhaps Grace was still
chasing them . . . perhaps . . . perhaps . . . she closed her eyes,
and listened. There was something scrabbling . . . gnawing . . .
eating at her heart. Something . . . someone . . . anxious, restless,
wanting to be heard. But, try as she might, Maisie could not
hear. Suddenly, there was a draught, and the box of tapers fell
from the mantel, spilling all over the hearth. She watched them

take light, curling into little flames at the ends, dancing at her feet, black smoke issuing from the hollows inside. Shaking, Maisie stamped out the flames, and looked at the ashes. They formed the letter 'H'.

Upstairs, in the office, George was slumped over his books. The pen had slipped and slithered haphazardly through the list of figures. His mouth hung open, slavering on the page.

Deeply troubled, Maisie crept past his room, on her way upstairs. His light shone from under the door, but it didn't register. She went on, brooding, to undress and take out her teeth. 'H'. Was it an initial? Whose? Harriet? She turned and looked at the dark window. Was it 'H' for Harriet, sitting in the twilight, out in the yard, whispering with her mother . . . ?

'I'm glad you've told me, Jane.' Or, was it 'H' for Hester?

'Hester needs to be kept out of trouble.' What had become of Maisie's little sister? Aunt Harriet had promised to watch over her. But, where was she? What was her mother trying to tell her? What did she want Maisie to do? Or was this a warning? A chill spread across her heart. 'Fools rush in . . . ' Was she a fool, after all? Just simple Maisie Beattie with the hump back? She put out her lamp and in the sudden darkness, she remembered the light under her father's door. Her father often sat up late, but, tonight, there was something different, something she could not pin down. What was it? Relighting the lamp, she stood, for several moments, before her dressing table mirror. Her hair waved in the fault of the glass and her breasts curved. She saw her image, metamorphosed, and brooded on the fact she was a woman. Not a mother, nor a wife, she was, nevertheless, both a sister, and a daughter . . . she still had a role to play. There were still people to look after. That light from the office . . . suddenly, without waiting to throw on her wrap, she ran down and threw open the office door.

George had had another stroke. Alerting Ellen, who went to sit with him, Maisie dressed, then disappeared into the blackout in search of the doctor.

At midnight, the dim lights of the town had been extinguished. And now, a natural curfew reigned, in which only the desperate and the ill-intentioned lurked, under the dark face of the moon. Flying down the street, Maisie's footsteps echoed back, from the walls of houses, windows thick with concealment. Dark wings hovered. An owl hooted, swooped, seeking out its prey, and the invisible cat stalked, stealthy in the night. Reeling with fright, Maisie pulled on the doorbell of the doctor's house. The clanging resounded through the sleeping rooms. But the doctor was dead to the world. A sound, close to her heel, made her turn in fright. But she saw nothing. She rang the bell again, more urgently. It sounded out like the alarm on the Groyne Pier. The doctor surfaced, pulled on his dressing gown, and came down to open the door.

'Who is it?' he whispered through the crack.

'Only Maisie Beattie.' The door opened wide, and in the sudden light, Maisie's shadow, seen for an instant, swept down the street, and was gathered, with her, into the house.

Would he never come? Ellen stared at the still face of her father. The gas flame flickered, curling tall, and smoke poured from the mantle. She would have to turn it down. Eerie, in the dimming light, the livid gas cast shadows in the corners of the room. Was her father dead? His great form lay still. She had never felt so alone, so defenceless. He had been a bulwark in their lives, and now he had fallen, what would become of them? She and Maisie were not strong enough! There were the children to think of. He surely wasn't going to desert them now? A sob caught in her throat, and Ellen fell on her father's huge chest, wailing, 'Dad! Dad! Come back! Dad! We need you! Please don't leave us!'

And George, slowly, unwillingly, emerged from the deep blackness. He was tired, so very tired. Why did she call him back? Wearily, he stirred. Had he not left his books in order? His books. His eyes sprang open. Ellen stepped back in surprise. Harriet May! His brain was clear. He remembered now what he had left undone. Harriet owned fifty per cent of the shop. He had to buy her out before he died, buy her out, or see that she made a will. Os must get her share. Yes. Os. It must be cut and dried, no loopholes to trouble the legitimate bloodline; his own descendants. And he would not depart this life until he had made sure of it. His breaths came in loud rasps. His lips moved. Ellen

285

bent her ear to listen. What did he want to tell her? The look on his face was urgent. But she couldn't understand. He tried again, battling within, straining and struggling with the words. All senseless gibberish. Ellen shook her head and a look of dark despair tortured her father's face.

CHAPTER SEVENTEEN

There was deadlock on the Ypres salient. Above ground, the battle raged on senselessly, the night ablaze with the fire of exploding shells. But, deep under the earth, in a hidden labyrinth, the tunnelling companies drove on, unseen, towards the Germans on the ridge. There, in deadly silence, the distant dynamo hummed monotonously, generating the dim electric light, by which Jack and Vijay laboured, wearily scraping at the clay, filling the sandbags, and sending them on bogies, softly sliding, back along the shaft. When they had to speak, it was in whispers. The slightest sound, a tap, a knock, a drip of water, and they stopped to listen. Was it the Germans? Had they laid a mine, inches away, on the other side of the clay. Any second and they could be blasted to Kingdom come. Another drip. Breathing deeply, they worked on, stifling, in the dark heat. They had tunnelled eighty feet or more under Hill 60. But, the Germans sought them underground, countermining, till the earth was riddled with secret passages, and they were in constant danger of breaking in on an enemy shaft. There was another, almost imperceptible sound, but the men, senses strung to the pitch of animals, froze, alert, waiting.

'Get the sergeant,' Jack whispered. Vijay crept back along the tunnel, leaving Jack at the face. Sweat poured down his back. His lips were dry. He licked them. A dull thud. The sergeant came and put the ball of his geophone against the clay wall, listening. The men watched intently. He had heard something. He waved them back along the tunnel. He would lay a mine, to blow up the Germans on the other side. Kill or be killed. Better get in first.

Vijay and Jack stopped close to the shaft entrance. It was still dark, and there were five hours left of their shift. So there they sat, encamped under the intertwining roots of a huge tree. They pulled out some biscuits and the rum ration, then made themselves comfortable in the mud. A blast flared fiercely, momentarily lighting up the entrance to the shaft. Vijay yawned, looking up at the entangled roots, in the flashing light.

'Amazing, aren't they?'

'Mmmm?'

'Roots! You can trace them back and back. I came to England to trace mine,' he laughed ironically. 'And here I am, up to my ears in mud instead!' It annoyed Jack, the way Vijay went on and on about his roots. It put pressure on him, to tell him what he knew. His voice betrayed his irritation.

'Nobody forced you to join up, me laddo!'

'You have to fight for King and country!'

'Jingoism!' Jack snorted. Vijay shifted uneasily, as another blast lit up the overhanging roots. Had Jack struck, accidentally, on some new truth? 'You could've put off joining up, till you'd looked up your family! Why didn't you?'

'Never put off till tomorrow . . . ' Vijay was hiding behind clichés. 'Duty comes first.'

'Have it your own way!' Jack sighed, closing his eyes against the flashing sky. Of course, Indians did have a very strong feeling for duty. They had a lot of funny ideas. Mind you, there was sense in some of them, when you thought. They laid a lot of store by family. Drawing on your roots, gaining strength from them. Yes. Perhaps not having roots had made Jack . . . . He tried to hide from the word, but it flashed like an exploding shell in his brain. 'Weak'. Yes. He was weak. He opened his eyes and drank down a mouthful of rum. He had cheated Frances. He had watched her grandfather jumping to the wrong conclusions, and then benefitted. Jack had a tendency to sit on the fence, on his backside. He had been like that about the war, and Frances had lost respect for him because of it. Would he protect her, in her need? Vijay was staring up at the branching roots, his eyes tenaciously searching out the junctions.

'In India, tradition's important. Even if you haven't got a family, like you, the old traditions provide a framework for life. It makes it easier to grow. Like having roots.'

'Frances always wanted to cut off from her roots. She said they were dragging her down.'

'My father wanted that. But now he has the air of a man who lost himself somewhere along the way.'

'Traditions, eh?' Jack yawned. He was tired. In the safe shelter of the tunnel, he could just drop off. 'Tradition . . . ' He sighed. 'What price tradition after this war . . . ? We're all going to be wandering about like your Dad. Lost souls . . . '

There was a dull thud deep under the hill. The earth around them shook, and pieces of clay fell onto them from the quivering roots. A shiver above their heads sent them sprawling to their feet, and they ran from the tunnel into the shell-shocked night, as the great tree fell, branches splintering into the firing line. They would have to start digging all over again.

Frances tossed and turned uneasily. Alert to the slightest sound, she jolted out of sleep, as Davey moaned, heart pounding and damp with perspiration. It had been a bad night. He had been in a foul mood the entire day, taking it out on everyone. Michael had left a toy on the stair. It was only his wooden sword, the one from the set his father had sent that Christmas. Davey had hurt his knee, falling against the rails of the banister to save himself. He had screamed, as though in agony.

'Haven't I been through enough . . . ' he shouted, ' . . . without my own, so-called family trying to do what Jerry couldn't and cripple me?' Frances had been out, taking the air. The baby was due in little more than a month. So Michael had run to Ma Lawson for protection, hiding behind her skirt, in the shop. But Davey came after him, waving the sword in his hands, and then, right in front of his eyes, he had put it across his knee and snapped it in two. The little boy wept bitter tears, making matters worse, for Davey's anger exploded into a rage. Coming back in the thick of it, Frances had sized up the situation at once. The shop girls had gone home in fright. Ma Lawson, arm protectively about the little lad, cowered, white-faced behind the upturned pails of flowers, petals strewn all over the swimming floor. There were tears in the old lady's eyes. But they had been opened at last. Frances began the long slow job of calming her son, and soon, Davey was smiling again, handing out sweets as compensation.

Michael forgave him, and suffered him to pin the two halves of the blade together, pretending to be pleased at the result.

That night, Davey went up to bed early, saying he was tired. But his mother kept Frances back, on the pretext of work still to do in the kitchen.

'I've done you an injustice, Frances.' She wept bitter tears. 'Can you forgive me?' Frances put her arm round the mother, comforting her as best she could. 'He needs you. I can see that now.' The sobs grew louder. Frances tried to hush her, afraid that either Michael or Davey would hear, and more trouble would result. 'Promise me, Frances, please, promise me you'll never leave him! On my bended knees . . . ' Distressed, Frances quickly promised, and escaped to her bed. She had been here before! Hadn't her grandma made her promise to take care of Hester in just the same way? Out of the frying pan into the fire! Exhausted with emotion, she drifted off to sleep.

She and Michael were at the fair. They were having a grand old time, playing truant. They rushed from one ride to another, sampling all the fun, and then, hand in hand, they embarked on the ghost train. Holding one another close, they giggled, at first, as they entered the dark tunnel. Unseen wisps, like cold fingers, touched their faces. Skulls, lit by a green lamp, glared at them from the pitch blackness, then disappeared. Voices cackled. White draped ghosts took them by surprise as they quickly rounded a corner. Wolves howled. And they heard the pounding feet of something coming up behind, closer and closer. Screaming with fright, Frances snatched up her son, and ran from the train, running, running, as fast as she could. She had to find her way out of the tunnel. But it was dark and she couldn't see. The beast was getting closer. She screamed and ran faster still, looking behind at the orange glow from its devouring flames. And then, something right in front of her caught them! She screamed in terror. Its arms were everywhere, and she lashed out, with Michael's wooden sword, cutting off its head. But it wouldn't die. And in the dim light she saw that the creature had six more heads. It was moaning, crying, and they were beginning to drown in its tears . . .

Frances struggled back to consciousness. Davey crying in his sleep . . . that's what it was. Heart pounding, she lay, as the sweat grew cold on her. She put a hand on him, to calm him. He stopped crying. But there was a sound across the passage. Was Michael awake? The electric light shone brightly, to comfort him during the night. And the doors to the two rooms were left ajar, in case he needed her. She lay stiffly, listening, not daring to sleep for fear the nightmare would begin again. But she was tired. She closed her eyes to rest them. Another sound. Her eyes shot open. But it was dark. Had someone put out the light? No. No, she could see its dim glow against the ceiling. It was on. But the light it cast was a dark light, and the darkness of the room was thick, tangible, like a black cloud engulfing them . . . Her throat was dry. But she wouldn't give in to fear. She had to see if her son was all right. She threw back the covers and floated out of bed, clean through the wall of her room, across the passage, and in through the wall of Michael's room. It was quite a nice feeling, but it was so dark! She reached for the light switch on the bedside lamp, and the electric lamp glowed, as before, casting no light. Terrified, she looked at Michael. He slept, his face damp against the pillow. She touched his soft cheek tenderly, and crept in beside him, to fall asleep almost at once.

Next morning, Davey was annoyed. Someone had been putting on lights all over the house! Burning good money! And then, the telephone rang in the shop. It was Maisie Beattie. Anxiously, Frances took the call. Her granda had had a stroke in the night. Frances was shocked. She loved her granda, even though he'd thrown her out. And then, in the afternoon, the pains began. One of the girls went to summon the midwife. The baby was expected in June, and it was only May! Brought on by the shocking news, no doubt. Davey sat on the stair outside her room, in a state of contradictory emotion, at one moment fearful, because the child was early and would surely die, and the next, euphoric with excitement, because the woman he loved was about to produce his child. Pushing down and down again, Frances strained to see the baby, as the midwife eased out first its head, and then the shoulders, the rest slithering onto the sheet between her legs.

'It's a fine healthy girl!' the nurse shouted in triumph. Frances looked. 'See? Absolutely normal! You must have made a mistake with your dates!'

'You mean, it's not premature?' Frances gasped, dismayed. The midwife shook her head.

'Not in this world!' she said. She placed the child in its mother's arms, and Frances lay back, staring at the surprised expression of her little daughter's face.

'I don't believe it,' she breathed at last. She shook her head, not knowing whether to laugh or cry. 'I don't believe it!' And then, in spite of everything, Frances laughed.

Maisie was all for writing to Jack to tell him, but Frances knew better.

'He'd never believe me! I mean, if you were in his position, would you?' Maisie shook her head. Besides, Davey would go out of his mind if anybody tried to take 'his' baby daughter away from him.

He was tormented. Sometimes, he thought his comrades had left him wounded, in No Man's Land, dying in agony. Then, Frances had to soothe him till he slept. But when he woke, in his right mind, in many ways it was worse. For then he remembered he was the one who had walked away. 'Don't leave me here to die . . . ' And he would lapse into a maudlin mood of gloom and self-pity, or work himself up into a temper which sent Michael running into a corner to hide. The slightest thing would sway the precarious balance of his mind. A few words, read in a newspaper, the sound of a child's laughter, anything could set him off. If the girls in the shop whispered and giggled together, they had to be talking about him! Frances had told them what he had done in the war and now they were laughing at him! Frances laughed at him behind his back, so did Michael, everyone laughed at him! And it was no good setting Davey right. Frances may have kept his confidence, but he had no confidence in her.

'Trust me, love!' she pleaded. He wanted to, and for a while he allowed himself to be reassured, but, inevitably, the doubts crept in again, and then he told her his impotence was all her fault. She was an unfaithful slut. She had gone with him, why not others? She had slighted his manhood, and this was the result! Again she had to soothe him, persuade him of her loyalty, and he cried, cuddling up in her arms, for comfort. But, if she failed, he would go into a rage so fierce, his face was not just white, but livid with hate, and he destroyed anything that got in his way. Cursing blindly, he would catch hold of Frances by the throat, his fingers hard on her neck. She never resisted, but waited, looking up at him, till he remembered himself, and his hand dropped away again. At times like these, Davey recovered his virility, and he made love to her, fiercely, possessively, as though putting his stamp on her. Afterwards he gave boxes of sweets to 'make it up', and thought all was well. They were surely the happiest couple in the world. And the world believed it. For, in public, Davey was the life and soul of the party. He grinned jovially. He cracked jokes, and was full of cheerful bonhomie. He was like two people, and Frances didn't believe in either of them.

She did what she could to hide the worst from her children. She had considered sending Michael back to Fowler Street for his own sake. But when she suggested it, he cried, pleading with her to let him stay. And it seemed a pity to part Eve from her brother. Michael loved playing with her. He would chat to her and entertain her for hours on end, and, if she cried, he had the knack of making her smile again. The children had a separate world, providing security for one another, sharing a secret kind of joy. So, Frances gave in, and next considered whether to run away. But where could she go? A woman with a babe in arms, a toddler, no qualifications, no money, and all in war time? It was unthinkable. Besides, in her heart, Frances knew that if she left him, Davey would go permanently out of his mind. And it wasn't his fault. He was a hero, whatever he might have done. They were all heroes, all the men who had gone to fight in this war. She had made her bed. Now she would lie on it, come hell or high water. No good running away. Look what had happened to her last time! Better face things! Better grow up. Yes, she had made her bed. So Frances stayed. And Jack? Jack had made it perfectly clear, by his long silence, that he didn't want her any more.

Jack slipped, and Vijay, holding onto his arm, steadied him from behind. A shell screamed overhead. They ducked. It fell beyond, exploding, killing, maiming. The barrage was continuous. Their legs were unsteady, from the long hours of toil, deep in the tunnels, and it was treacherous on the muddy duckboards, which formed a path through the sodden labyrinth of trenches, on and on, to Hellfire Corner. Rest? They would rather have stayed in the tunnels! They felt safer there. Was it worth it for four days, only to go back again through the screaming shells, pelting down without cease? No wonder men deserted, running away into the woods, to forage like animals; running away, like Vijay's father, like . . . like Frances. She had run away to go on the stage, to marry him . . . and he'd brought her back to her roots. Now she'd run away again. *He* sat on the fence. *She* ran away. There was a pair of them, no better than each other. From bitterness and hatred, Jack's feelings for Frances had mellowed to compassion. Would he protect her? Now? He half-turned, to see Vijay duck, missing a passing shell. There was a dug-out coming up on the left. Jack jerked his head towards it. Vijay nodded gratefully, and they slithered on towards it, for a breather.

Jack lit a cigarette and gave it to Vijay.

'To what do I owe the honour?'

'Must be feeling guilty.' Jack laughed uneasily. Vijay drew on the cigarette and coughed. 'Nasty Western habits!' Jack took it back to smoke himself.

'I am *half* Western!' Vijay complained.

'Which half?'

'Now you're being silly.'

'No, I'm not. It seems to me, lad, that your problem is, you can't accept yourself for what you are! You want to blame some-body else . . . that family your father left behind in Shields. You want to make them the scapegoat, pay them back, for all the hurt your father gave you! I'm right! I am, aren't I?'

'In that case, why did I join up? Why didn't I go straight up there, and find them!'

'I'm not sure.'

'Hah!'

'Perhaps . . . yes, perhaps it was to spite your father. Yes. Another way of paying back. You knew, if you joined up, if your life was in danger, he'd be sorry! And if you were killed . . . !'

'Pull the other one!' Vijay looked angry.

'Or, perhaps you were scared of what you might find?'

'No!'

'You signed on for the army rather than face the truth!' Upset and confused, Vijay just went on shaking his head.

'All right. What is the truth about you, Vijay? Come on. Tell me. Because it seems to me, you're just a great big sham!'

Vijay felt cold. He huddled into his greatcoat and stared at the rain, splashing on the duckboards beyond the dug-out. Vijay was cornered, and he knew it. Jack almost felt sorry for him. He inhaled deeply on his cigarette. 'You know, I think it's much harder if you don't face things. At least, once you know the worst, there's nothing left to be afraid of.' Slowly, Vijay stood, easing his body out into the trench. Jack, throwing the butt end of his cigarette into the mud, crawled out after him, slinging his luggage on his back. He was disappointed. Vijay hadn't given himself away after all. And then the lad turned, half-smiling, and said,

'I think you and I were brought together for a purpose. Yes, Jack, I'm grateful. You've shown me the way. Why should I kill myself to hurt my father? I'm a big boy now. It's not him I have to pay back. It's his family. And I will. Whatever it costs me, I'll come to Shields, next leave, Jack. And I'll find them out.'

Vijay grinned and held out his hand. Jack took it. He heard the menacing whine, and suddenly he pushed. Vijay staggered, as the shell fell, exploding right behind him, throwing Jack back across the entrance to the dug out. Smothered in mud, Jack lay, stunned, for some seconds. The smell of cordite was overpowering. What had he done? Where was Vijay? Had it got him? There was something sticky on Jack's face. More mud. He pulled an arm free, and wiped his hand across his cheek. He looked at it. It was red. This was no mud. This was Vijay, the bit of him that wasn't lying, shattered, in the trench. As he looked, the rain fell, and the blood ran, thicker than water, pouring down his hand, flowing down his arm, over his body, under the duckboards, into the earth beneath. All that was left of a man; water streaked with blood; and it ran, thinner and thinner in the pouring rain.

'Why don't we let bygones be bygones and have our Fran back?' George glared at Ellen fiercely and began beating the arms of his chair with his fists.

'We've got to have somebody, Dad! We can't cope, on our own! Can we, Maisie?' Maisie shook her head. 'What are we going to do?' Then, the old man seemed to lapse into a daze. They shook their heads. His brain had surely gone. But, as they turned to leave, he made a noise, calling them back. Pointing and grunting, like a primitive, slaver running down his chin, George was asking for pen and paper.

'What is it, Dad?' Maisie asked gently. 'Is it somebody to help us in the shop?' George nodded.

'Eeh, our Maisie,' Ellen was astonished. 'He's not as daft as he looks, you know!' Maisie brought the pen and paper and helped her father hold the pen in his hand. The effort was terrible. Tears of despair fell down George's cheeks. But he would not give up. Slowly, shakily, he drew the lines of a letter, the upright, the second upright, the bar across the middle . . . Maisie went cold as she stared at the page. It was the letter 'H' . . .

Harriet looked at her stepfather, wondering whether the old barsket was as far gone as he looked.

'He has his good days and his bad days,' Ellen explained and Maisie nodded in doleful agreement. George extended a drooping hand. 'There! Look! He wants to shake hands.' Then he grunted and tried to speak, the words coming out all wrong, in meaningless gabble.

'Do you want something, Father?' Harriet spoke as though to a child and Ellen nudged her out of the room as George roared with helpless fury. Tears trailed down the old man's face. He knew what he wanted to say. He had the words right in his head, and he understood what other people said, so why couldn't they understand him? Were they all mad? There was nothing for it, he would have to write Harriet May a letter. His heart sank at the prospect. He could hardly hold a pen. His hand reached out to his desk, but the fingers only pushed the pen further away. He couldn't grasp it. He sank back, exhausted. Harriet was only staying till they got paid help. He hadn't much time. He would have to work at his recovery. He set his mind to the task. If anyone could do it, it was George Beattie!

Harriet worked hard in the shop with Maisie, leaving Ellen free to run the house and bring up Os. She made out, of course, she was there under sufferance; but, in fact, Harriet had been glad of the excuse to get away from London, where her life had fallen into the doldrums. She had even taken up tapestry, and now sat, of an evening, 'baby sitting' George, while Maisie minded the shop till closing, and Ellen cooked. The tapestry was a tasteful design, in the new mould, a stark geometric piece, in browns and beiges, hard on the eyes in the old-fashioned gaslight.

'Mean old barsket!' she muttered. 'Why couldn't you have got in the electric? God knows I gave you enough money! Lost it, I suppose. You couldn't run water, never mind a shop!' Then she looked at him, staring back at her, fists opening and closing rhythmically. 'Like to hit me, would you?' she sneered. 'Some hopes! Helpless as a baby!' Then she laughed, but George kept on, working his hands, even as Harriet wiped the slaver from his chin. Yes, Harriet had been glad to come. The war had been getting too close for comfort back in London. In August she had heard the distant rumble of guns, from her flat. The bombardment of the Somme had begun. Her clarion call had sent thousands upon thousands of men to fight for their country. But now that work was done. Conscription had come in, and she had grown bored. Too old to be a nurse, or driver, Harriet May had had to stay at home, helping to run tea parties for the troops! She hated it. Wounded soldiers were ugly, pitiful creatures. And they were so grateful! She despised them for being grateful because some woman in a nice dress gave them a cup of tea and a biscuit!

At least George wasn't grateful. She looked at the fierce expression in his eyes and smiled. How she loved to take a rise out of him, and no fear of him getting his own back. 'It's the women running the country now, Father!' she said loudly, as though he was deaf. George growled, and she laughed, delighting in his discomfiture. 'I've waited for this moment for many a long year! Got you where I want you now, haven't I?' George ground his teeth, but his hands were still working. One by one, he raised the fingers, stretched them, then released them again. Harriet watched him, amused. 'You've developed a twitch! Don't know what you're doing, do you, silly old barsket?' Her eyes brightened. 'Would you like a cup of tea and a biscuit, dear?' she asked, shouting into his ear. George winced and nodded, assuming an air of gratitude; anything to get rid of her for five minutes! Harriet May smiled smugly. Yes, it had taken a war to bring it about. But now the women ruled. Serve the men right! They had commanded the world, and now, all they could command was a cup of tea and a biscuit!

Maisie went down to Ocean Road, after chapel on Sunday. She looked forward to her gossip with Ma Lawson and Frances, all week, and she doted on the bairns. Michael had always been her favourite, though she was ashamed to admit it, and Fran was always keen to hear the latest about Os. But, it was with a sinking heart she rang the bell at their door today. In her pocket, she carried a letter. It was addressed to Frances, and it was postmarked 'The War Office'. Why had she to bear such news? Hadn't she enough troubles of her own? Poor Jack! She had loved him. He had been a good brother to her and Will. They'd had good times together, and now . . . ! She was close to tears, as Mrs Lawson opened the door. Automatically, Maisie looked past her, up the stairs, to see if Davey was there. But Mrs Lawson whispered,
   'It's all right. He's in his room, sleeping.' Reassured, Maisie followed her in. Davey's lost arm still gave him pain. It haunted him, like a ghost. Sometimes the pain was so real that looking down, he was surprised to find nothing but an empty sleeve, pinned to his chest. But he used the arm as an excuse. Sick of nightmares, he looked forward to the nights when the pain was bad, and the drugs took him down the long black tunnel, to sweet oblivion. Peace at last. Peace for Frances, too. He knew he drove her, and he hated himself for it, for he loved her, in his way. Poor Frances. She couldn't win. If she went pale, without rouge, she was making out he was a slave driver, exhausting her. If she did wear rouge, she was trying to attract other men. Half of him enjoyed torturing and taunting her in this way, the other hated it. But he was helpless to stop himself. So the drugs were not only an escape from pain and nightmare, but also a way out of a

dilemma. As Mrs Lawson said, her son worked hard, and it was not surprising he needed a nap of a Sunday afternoon.

Frances was pleased as ever to see her aunt. She sat her down, making much of her, as Ma Lawson went to get the tea. 'Michael's in watching the baby. Honestly, he's smashin' that lad! I don't know what I'd do without him!' But then, she noticed Maisie's anxiety; 'Why the long face, Auntie? What's Harriet done now?' Maisie shook her head.

'It's not Harriet.' Then she sniffed back her tears, and fished the envelope out of her bag. 'It's for you . . . ' Pale with apprehension, Frances took the letter and tore it open. Maisie was crying, rocking to and fro in her chair. 'I tell you what consoled me, pet . . . it was a visit to a spirit communicator. She had a message for me, from Will . . . '

Then Frances, the colour flooding back into her cheeks, laughed out loud, throwing the letter high up into the air.

'He's been invalided out!' Maisie stared at her in amazement.

'Jack?'

'He's coming home . . . ' But then Frances realised, she wouldn't be there to see him and a new pain caught at her heart.

'What does he say?'

'He got hit by shrapnel. It went straight through his right arm, and lodged in a train ticket in his wallet!' She laughed, wiping away her tears with her apron. 'He's severed a nerve and can't use his hand, so that's why you didn't recognise the writing. He had to get somebody else to write for him.'

'Eeh!' Maisie cried. 'Eeh!'

'I quite agree with you, pet!' Frances laughed. But there was sadness in her eyes.

'Maybe he'll have forgiven you, Frances . . . we'll wait in hopes, eh?' Maisie said softly. Frances sighed.

'It wouldn't make any difference now.' And then, Ma Lawson came in, the tea tray in her hands.

'I heard you both laughing and carrying on, down in the kitchen! What's happened?'

'It's Jack. My husband,' Frances said softly, taking the tray from her. 'He's been invalided out. He's coming home.' Mrs Lawson's hand went straight to her chest.

'You promised me, lass . . . ' she pleaded. 'You promised me . . . '

'I know. It's all right. I'll not let you down . . . ' Frances' voice broke, as she said the words, 'I'll be staying.'

Poor Frances. Maisie's heart went out to her. What had Will said? 'Happiness and unhappiness go on forever.' Aye, on and on and on, world without end, like a wheel going round. You were up one minute, and down the next, like a child on a carousel. Still, her Dad was looking better. He had a bit of colour in his cheeks these days, and his eyes were more alert, she was sure. She fluttered the letter at him, when she got home.

'It's about Jack!' she said. George stopped his 'twitching' and looked at her intently. 'He's been wounded. He's in hospital now. But he's going to be all right. He's coming home!' And he smiled! Her Dad smiled! My, this *was* a red letter day! She grinned back and kissed him on the cheek, a proper smacker, and that seemed to please him too. There were tears of joy in the old man's eyes. He tried to speak, his hand reaching out to touch her. He wanted to tell her he was sorry about Will, but, as usual, she didn't understand, and sadly, he shook his head. 'Never mind, Dad. You're coming on,' Maisie said. 'You'll soon be down at The Glebe giving your sermons again, don't you worry!' George was hurt. Why did people talk down at him, as though he was a fool? Even dear Maisie! She meant well, but . . . He sighed and looked at the writing paper and the pen. 'Do you want them?' He nodded and Maisie put them by his hand. He reached out and grasped the pen, holding it perilously in his hand. Maisie gasped. 'Eeh!' she shouted. 'You really *are* coming on, aren't you?'

Slowly, laboriously, George wrote. It was like a child's hand, hesitant, shaky letters, some large, some small, but they fitted together, and they made sense. Late at night, when the women were in bed, he worked, till, at the end of a week, he had finished. Then he rang his little brass bell and Ellen came, tired and dishevelled up the stair from the shop.

'What is it, Dad? Do you want another cup of tea?' George shook his head and held out the letter. Ellen frowned, and read the higgledy-piggledy name on the front, 'HARRIET'. 'Eeh! A whole letter! Fancy! What a good boy you are, then!' George winced. 'You want me to give this to Harriet, I know!' She was trying to take it from him, but he held onto it, shaking his head and beckoning with the envelope. 'Oh! You want me to bring her to you, eh?' At last, she'd understood. George nodded, and Ellen went to fetch Harriet May.

As soon as she entered the room, Harriet knew there was something afoot. George was different somehow. Previously, it had been as though she was sitting in a vacant room, but now, suddenly, she felt her stepfather's old presence again. His eyes pierced her, and his hand, no longer drooping, indicated a chair in which she sat, obediently. The slaver still leaked from the corner of his mouth. That, at least, was reassuring; and clumsily, his hands grasped at the envelope he was holding out to her. She took it, smiling at the childish letters on the front.

'For me?' she said, as though receiving a present from a child. George watched and waited till she had opened the letter and begun to read. Then, her expression changed. He saw anger first, then fear followed. The lines of her mouth hardened, and when she spoke she was hard and bitter. 'You stupid old fool! Even if I still had the shares, I wouldn't will them to Os! I'd rather leave them to the Cats' Home!' Her laugh was like a crow, screeching triumphantly over him. He howled, desperate to know what she meant. And then Harriet leaned in close. She spoke in cold, clear tones. 'I transferred the shares to Hester, years ago. So put that in your pipe and smoke it!' She dusted her hands, and went up to her room, to begin packing for London.

Neither Ellen nor Maisie could understand it. George had gone right back, no doubt about it. He had a hopeless, helpless look, worse than straight after the stroke, and Harriet was suddenly acting as though she couldn't get away fast enough. But she *wouldn't* tell them what was wrong, and George *couldn't*. Then, as the cab arrived to take her to the station, Harriet held out a slip of paper.

'If you still need help, this address might find your sister!' she said. Then she got in and sped away, back home to London. It was an address in Streatham; a Mrs Fairbairn.

'But I thought our Hester was in China!' Maisie said, in surprise. Ellen shook her head, mystified.

'Still, it's a thought! Our Hester'd be better than nothing. I mean, I can't see us getting paid help in the shop till the war's over! The munitions factories pay far too well!'

'I don't know, Ellen. I don't like it.'

'Why not?'

'I don't know why not. I just know I don't like it!' Maisie snapped and went back into the shop.

As her train trundled south, Harriet began to smile. She'd *really* put the cat among the pigeons! Her smile broadened into a grin. Hester! Back in the shop! Back in the family! God knew what ructions she would cause! The passenger facing her was alarmed by a sudden fit of uproarious laughter from the staid old maid in front of him. Tears were running down her cheeks. And the best of it all was that it was George's own fault! He had rubbed salt into Harriet's wounds, spurring her to do it. Really, when you thought about it, she couldn't help herself! Yes, the Beatties had brought fate down on their own heads. And now Hester would do the rest for her. She would wreak vengeance for the woman she had spurned. The memory of pain killed Harriet's laughter, and other memories came crowding in. What of her promise to Jane? Quickly, and for the last time, she thrust all doubt aside. Jane was dead and buried, along with Harriet's conscience. She'd never know a thing about it. Yes, as always, her agnosticism was a great comfort to her. She would put the whole affair out of her mind and start planning the redecoration of her flat!

George's daughters looked to him for guidance but, struggling through a gloom as deep and muddy as the trenches, he gave none. In desperation, Maisie suggested they ask the spirits for advice. And, one night, after the blackout had gone up, hearts beating with excitement, they lit a candle and set out the letters of the alphabet in a circle on the kitchen table.

'We need a glass,' Maisie whispered. Ellen fetched one from the sink, drying it on her pinny, and set it, upside down, in the middle.

'Touch hands.' The sisters put their hands on the table, fingers touching, and the circle was complete. In silence, they stared at the glass. At last, Maisie whispered.

'Is there anyone there?' Nothing happened. She repeated her question, more loudly. The candle flame lengthened. 'Is there anyone there?' Suddenly, the glass started moving, in little jerks, at first, then, all by itself, it began to whizz round the table. 'It's finding its way about.'

'Who is it?' Ellen gasped. And then the glass slowed, deliberately picking out the letters. 'JANE' it said. Then it jiggled about a bit, as though laughing up its sleeve.

'Ma . . . ' Maisie whispered, 'If it's you, tell us what to do.' The glass went straight to the letter 'H' and stayed there. Ellen and Maisie waited for a long time, but it didn't move again. 'Hester?' Maisie asked. The glass jiggled, on the spot. 'What about Hester?' The glass spelled out the letters, 'S.O.S.'

'Mam means we should send an S.O.S. to our Hester!' Maisie frowned.

'She would never use a word like S.O.S!'

'How do you know what she'd say, now she's a spirit?' Maisie sighed. She had hoped for enlightenment, but when it came, everything felt darker than before. Suddenly, in the silent house, they heard something move. They froze. There was a loud bump, then the sound of something dragging. The sisters held on to one another's hands. It was getting nearer. 'Are you not supposed to tell it to give two knocks for yes, or something?'

'If you are our mother, give two knocks,' Maisie said tremulously. There were two sudden, loud bangs. Ellen screamed. Then the door flew open, and George Beattie stood, panting in the doorway. The sisters rose in horror, as he dragged himself forward, picked up the glass and smashed it against the hearth. 'I'm sorry, Dad,' Maisie blubbered. Ellen stood silent, white as a sheet. From upstairs, they heard the sound of Os crying, as George crumpled to the floor. 'This puts the tin lid on it,' Ellen said, as they and the doctor got him back into bed. 'I am definitely writing to Hester tonight!'

As the children rose to sing, Frances looked across the line of pews at the gem-like colours of the new window. Saint Michael and All Angels had been a sanctuary to her ever since her banishment from Fowler Street and The Glebe, and Michael had taken to the Sunday School. He'd been so excited this morning; to be actually singing in the childrens' choir! Frances had put on her best hat, and he'd let her brush his hair till it gleamed. She smiled. It was a beautiful window; a triptych, Christ in the centre, a fallen soldier at his feet; on the right, a Roman legionnaire, and on the left, Saint George, with his red crossed banner. She would have to take a proper look at it before she went. The organ started up. She brought her attention back to the choir, and looked for her son, amongst the little ones in the front row. She laughed and shook her head. Michael was nervously pushing back his hair with his fingers. It was standing up on end, like a scrubbing brush! Ah well! She'd tried! And what did it matter? His face was gleaming with pride as he sang;

> 'Come forth dark night, your starry mantle spread.
> Arise Saint George, Champion of valour true;
> Restore our faith and raise our hearts anew
> Upon the field where hope was left for dead.
>
> 'Dragons abound where angels fear to move.
> Virtue besieg'd calls for her cares to end.
> With steed and banner white her plight you mend;
> One hero only, conquers all by love.'

Saint George was like an old friend. Her eye strayed back to the window. The saint had a childlike quality, quite unlike her own early imaginings. His fair hair curled, just above his shoulders, and he had a happy look, not at all like one who had been in mortal combat!

> 'Nobler the breed that seeks a higher prize
> With tempered steel in valiant enterprise.
> Be thou our fence against an army wide:
> With thee before, can England be denied?'

She almost clapped as the children sat, and could hardly wait for the service to be over, so she could hug him. Embarrassed, Michael struggled in her arms After all, he wasn't a cissy! He was a knight in shining armour! So, chastened, Frances put him down and accompanied him to inspect the window. There was quite a crowd, milling round it. One woman, in particular, seemed to keep getting in their way. Her black hat bobbed about like a will o' the wisp! Michael tugged on Frances' skirt, and she picked him up. Then the woman started to make her way out of the crowd. That walk was familiar. Who was she? Michael was pointing at the window; 'Look Mam! There's the dragon!'

'It was Hester! She'd come back!

CHAPTER EIGHTEEN

'Of course, my husband went to China. He's a missionary, you know.' The ladies of the church of Saint Michael nodded, over their cups of tea. 'I wanted to go myself, but Tom simply would not have it. "China is no place for a woman with a baby," he said.'

'How long's he been gone?' Mrs White, wife of a local magistrate and pillar of Westoe Society spoke in hushed tones.

'Since just before the birth of his child.' Hester inclined her head in sacrificial gesture, as the gasps of the assembled company expressed sympathy. 'When the Good Lord calls us, we have to go,' she added reverently, accepting the proferred rock cake. Mrs White shook her head in admiration, as the black garbed figure finally departed.

'Such dedication deserves its rewards,' she said. 'In future, I shall be placing my orders at Beattie's shop.' The hums and hahs of the other ladies ensured an upturn, in the dwindling fortunes of the reverent lady's family.

But the family were less enthusiastic than might have been expected, at the advent of Hester and her little daughter amongst them. Hester worked like a Trojan, no doubt about it. She scrubbed floors, with the air of a penitent, and wired flowers into wreaths, pricking her fingers till the blood ran and her flesh was raw. And she was always the first up in the morning. At five o'clock precisely, her little cambric nightcap could be seen bobbing down the gloomy stair to the kitchen, where she cleaned the grate, and lit the fire, before making so much as a cup of tea. Then, she would dress, and at half past five on the dot, she would reach for the baton and clang the dinner gong with all her might. On the first morning, the din resounded through the house, and Os dashed excitedly downstairs, behind the two shaken females, demanding to know where the fire was. Anna, of course, was more accustomed to her mother's behaviour, and took it as the norm. She drank her milky tea, and got down on her knees to pray, the other members of the family following suit in shocked obedience. But on the second morning, Maisie spoke up.

'What gives you the right to boss us about, I'd like to know?'

'Maisie, dear,' Hester began in patient manner, 'I am your spiritual superior.' Maisie's jaw dropped to her boots in astonishment. 'And I consider it my duty to watch over the moral welfare of those God has put in my charge.'

'What do you mean "put in your charge"?' Ellen objected.

'Well, you are in my house . . . '

'What?'

'Oh, didn't father tell you? How remiss of him! I own fifty per cent of the shop and the house.'

'I don't believe you!'

'I have the papers to prove it, if you'd like to peruse them.' She smiled sweetly and insisted on sending off for them, so that Ellen and Maisie could see for themselves. When the documents arrived, the sisters read them in stunned silence. They deeply resented the underhand way in which their father had transacted the business with Harriet and Hester, leaving Ellen and Maisie to work on in the shop, in ignorance. But what could they do about it? It was all legal, and though they might fret and fume, they were stuck with it! They were stuck with Hester too and if they asked her, delicately, when she thought she might be going to join her husband in China, she just shook her head, and said in a plaintive tone, 'Not as long as my family need me . . . '

And they couldn't pretend they didn't! After all, nothing had changed since Ellen sent her S.O.S., had it?

The hero of the hour, returning soldier Jack Scott, was dumbfounded to find Hester in residence, and an air of gloom hanging over the place. The house should have been sparkling with laughter, with them two little 'uns running about the place! What was the matter with them? Sitting down to his first meal, he rubbed his hands together, picked up his knife and fork and . . .

'Jack!' Maisie warned, head bowed. She was looking sideways at Hester.

'Oh sorry!'

'For what we are about to receive may The Lord make us truly thankful.'

'Amen.' Jack had nothing against grace, of course, but once that was over, surely they could dig in, and talk and so on? But no. Hester opened the bible and began to read a lesson from the Epistles of Saint Paul. Her voice droned on over the bland supper of white fish and boiled veg. Struggling with his left hand, Jack dropped a potato on the cloth.

'Damn!' he swore. There was a sudden silence. He looked up to see Ellen, Maisie and the two children, looking fearfully towards the first lady of the house, Hester Fairbairn.

'Language!' she hissed. 'You might show a little more reverence for the holy scriptures!'

'Holy? Saint Paul? The man was a fanatic! First of all he persecutes the Christians to death and then he swings the other way, getting all holier than thou and telling us that natural instincts between men and women aren't nice, making people feel guilty and generally creating an atmosphere of gloom and repression! Christ never said anything like that! The man was a pompous crackpot! You've only got his word for it that he ever saw the light at all!'

'You may get down from the table!' Hester commanded.

'And you, madam, may get down from your high horse! Because, I'm telling you that I, for one, am not going to put up with all this carry on for much longer!' Hester's bottom lip began to quiver.

'I am mistress here!' she said in a wavering voice.

'You're not *my* mistress, dear!' Maisie splurted her fish over the table, then choked. Ellen smacked her hard on the back, sending her teeth clattering into her plate, and Hester ran from the room weeping at such an irreligious state of affairs. Ellen and Maisie kissed Jack on both cheeks.

'Eeh, pet! I'm glad you're home!' they shouted with glee. And Frances relished the tale as told by Maisie, the following Sunday afternoon.

'He's come back that masterful!' Maisie told her niece. But Michael was quiet. He wanted to see his dad, yet dared not say so for fear of upsetting his mother. If only there was a way of bringing them back together . . . Maisie sighed romantically over the possibilities, as she lay in bed that night surveying her soaking teeth. They still loved each other. She was sure of it. Aye, it was a pity about Davey Lawson. The war had made one man and destroyed the other.

And the ruined man grew jealous and fearful. It hadn't mattered while Jack was away, but now he was back, Davey felt threatened and began to press Frances to sue her husband for divorce.

'On what grounds?' she asked.

'Desertion.'

'You can't sue a man for desertion, when he's gone to fight in the army, man!'

'Don't laugh at me!'

'I'm not laughing, love, only . . . '

'Then he'll have to divorce you!'

'How do you know he would?'

'Ask him!'

'I'll have to see him then . . . ' And that put Davey in another spin. If she saw Jack, she might fall for him again, and then where would he be? So the subject was dropped, for the moment.

Jack, meanwhile, spent long hours sitting with George, in his room. It was the only peaceful place in the house, where Hester never ventured. George sat, withdrawn, brooding or sleeping. Sometimes Jack read poetry to him, or told him tales about the war. But he never mentioned Vijay. His head burst with questions, but his mouth was stopped. He had killed a man, to protect his wife and her family, to protect his sons; yes. But he

309

had killed all the same. He had come down from his fence and committed an action, which involved him in the drama forever more. And he would always now be in doubt as to whether he had done the right thing or not. What would have happened if Vijay had come to sit where Jack was now sitting, face to face with George Beattie? He would never know. Jack had done what he had done. And if the true story of Robert Ridley and his sister never came to light, then so be it. Jack had interfered in the natural course of events, but he would interfere no more. He had a man's blood on his hands. It was enough.

So, as the old man slept, Jack took up a pen, and busied himself with the long task of learning to write with his left hand. He was deep in concentration, when he heard a grunt and looked up to find George's eyes fixed on him. The old man clenched his fist and opened it. Jack frowned. What was he getting at? He did it again, then, he began exercising his fingers. Jack smiled.

'Exercises, eh? Think that might get the hand moving again?' George nodded and, together, they set to work on a programme of exercise and massage, slowly, over the weeks, strengthening the muscles, until eventually, Jack was able to move every part of his right hand, except his little finger. And then, they began work on George's speech. 'It's a bit of your brain that's gone, George,' Jack told him. 'So, what you've got to do, is to try and think with a different part! Go on. It's worth a try.' George tried and tried and Jack sweated with him through the last, dragging months of the war.

The fighting finally came to an end amid hysterical rejoicing. But, soldiers coming back from the trenches brought with them a new and virulent virus, a killer form of influenza, and soon, households who had believed their period of mourning was over, were plunged into another misery. Saint Michael and All Angels closed its Sunday School, as the epidemic raged. But it was too late. Little Michael Scott had already contracted the disease, and in a matter of five days, from the first signs of illness, he lay dying in the house in Ocean Road. Maisie flew home with the news.

'It's God's judgement on the child's mother!' Hester pronounced.

'Shut up, you silly bitch!' Jack shouted, and, reaching for his jacket, fled with Maisie to his son's bedside. But Mrs Lawson met Jack at the door. Her white face told him everything. Still, Davey wouldn't let him in the house, and the wounded soldiers almost came to blows on the pavement outside the shop. Then, Frances appeared.

'Stop it! The pair of you!' The men stood, shamefaced, before her. She looked at Davey first. 'If you don't let Jack in, to see his own son, I'm going to pack my bags! I'm warning you!' She meant it. Terrified of losing her, Davey swung out into the street, walking God knew where, as the husband entered his house. How could he bear it? He could not. He took refuge in a pub, where he got blind drunk.

'I blame myself,' Frances whispered, as she looked down at the dead face.

'You shouldn't. It's got nothing to do with you. It's an epidemic. It would have happened if you'd been at Fowler Street, just the same.' Frances choked on her tears, and Jack took her in his arms, to comfort her.

'I'm sorry, Jack. I don't know what got into me. But, I tell you this, by God, I'm paying for what I did!' Jack stroked her hair, as he used to, fondling her ears, her cheeks, then kissing her on the mouth. She drank in his affection as one thirsting for the comforts of love. 'The stupid thing is . . . ' she sobbed, 'I know you won't believe me, but . . . Eve, the baby, she's yours!'

The hand stopped its stroking. Jack swallowed hard.

'Do you remember that night, after you'd signed up?' He laughed and nodded. 'That's when it happened. It was after that that I . . . ' she sobbed. 'I got the dates all wrong.' She looked at him, through her tears. 'Do you believe me? I mean I won't blame you if you don't, but it's true all the same.' They stood, in the presence of the dead child, holding one another silently. At last, Jack coughed.

'What are we going to do?'

'I don't know, Jack . . . that's the trouble.' She began crying again. 'It's all such a mess.'

'Do you love me?'

'Yes.'

'I love you too.' But her crying only grew louder. 'You're stuck, aren't you?'

'He'd go mad, if I left him. I daren't tell him Eve's not his!'

'Frances, look at me . . . tell me, does he ever hurt you?' She looked away and sighed.

'Not really.' Absently she touched her throat.

'Are you sure?'

'When he's in one of his moods, he'll throw things and . . . well, he threatens to hurt me, but he never does. Not really.'

'Because if I found he'd laid a hand on you, I'd kill him.' Frances looked at him steadily.

'I do believe you would.'

'I've changed, Frances.'

'So have I. Older and wiser in my case.' She laughed bitterly. 'I can't walk out on him now, can I?'

'Do you want to?'

'I don't know.' She sighed. 'I'd rather be home with you and Os and everybody but . . . '

'I thought you hated Fowler Street!'

'I used to think it was hell on earth.'

'And now this is, eh?'

'The same but different . . . if you know what I mean.' She laughed. 'I think hell's inside you. And that's why . . . why . . . '

'You're not going to leave Davey.' She shook her head. Jack swallowed hard. 'I'm glad.' She looked at him, surprised.

'Glad?'

'Yes. I am. Because it means you've stopped running away.'

'I feel responsible . . . '

'Yes. I understand.'

'As long as Os . . . '

'He's all right. I'll make sure of that.'

'And I'll make sure of Eve.'

It felt like goodbye. They looked at one another for a long time.

Michael's funeral was short and simple, attended by Mrs Lawson, the parents and the aunts. Davey had gone to bed with a cold. But, to Frances' surprise, George turned up, supported on the arms of his daughters. His speechless sympathy found its way to Frances' heart. He hadn't said anything. But, she felt, somehow, that she had been forgiven. After the service, they stood for a while at Jane's graveside and then they parted at the gates, Frances going one way and Jack the other. Was this really happening?

The familiar had a strange air of unfamiliarity, as though they were dreaming. Each one of them, Ellen and Maisie included, felt a stranger in the world. Certainly it wasn't the world they had been brought up in, the pre-war world. They had the vote now, for one thing! And for another, there was no cheap help to be had in the shop, nor work for Jack, beyond the confines of Beattie's business. A wall of loneliness enclosed them, and their hearts reached out for something, someone to restore them to themselves. Davey's cold developed into flu but, as he recovered, Mrs Lawson went down with it and died, a week after Michael's funeral. And, to everyone's surprise, Davey rallied after his mother's death. Suddenly, he launched himself back into the business, immersing himself in the latest techniques and fashions.

Beattie's florists had stuck to the old ways. They were still without a telephone, though Jack did get the van back on the road, and business dwindled further during the hard times after the war. The women were too preoccupied with the children, to do much about it and, it was felt, generally, that big changes would upset George. But something had to be done. And, one day, the three sisters held a war council with Jack, in the kitchen.

'Lawson's is taking away all our business!' Hester complained bitterly, chewing her thumb nail. 'It's your wife's fault, Jack! She's stolen all our customers!'

'Rubbish!' Maisie grew red in defence of her niece. 'People were leaving us for Lawson's years ago!'

'And why's that, I should like to know, if not because that little madam was already flaunting herself with her paramour, giving away trade secrets?'

'What trade secrets? If you mean the toffee, our Fran never knew the recipe in the first place!'

'That's all you know.'

'Cat!' Ellen hissed.

'Ladies, ladies!' Jack thumped on the table.

'You're too soft, Jack. That's your trouble!' Hester informed him. 'She was always a wayward wanton, was Frances!'

'*She* was!?' Maisie's jaw hit the table.

'Oh yes, butter wouldn't melt in her mouth, when she was with you, but I heard things I wouldn't like to repeat in mixed company.'

'Liar! You were the whore of this family!' Hester went white and bit down into the flesh beneath the nail.

'Let's get back to the point, for God's sake.' But Hester was not to be put off.

'If we're in trouble now, it's her fault! Now I've got Anna's inheritance to consider . . . !'

'And we've got Os's!' Jack snapped back. 'Your attitude to the customers isn't helping any, Hester! You boss them about! You always know better than them what they want, and God help them, if they argue about it!'

'I'm only trying to help!'

'And she's as bad as Dad, sticking to the old fashioned flowers and that . . . '

'It's a matter of taste!' Hester insisted.

'Taste's a matter of fashion!' Ellen gritted her teeth. 'And you're behind it! Why can't we do block setting for a start! We're the only florists in Shields *not* doing it!'

Hester's lip began to quiver, whether with anger or distress, it was hard to tell.

'Fashion's the work of the devil!' she spat.

'Why don't you just bugger off to a convent, and be done with it!' Jack shouted.

'I know where I'm not wanted,' Hester wailed and ran to the throne room for sanctuary.

Anna and Os were playing in the back yard and Anna looked up, flinching, as Hester passed, hanky to nose, on her way to the midden. Os put an arm protectively round the little girl's shoulders.

'She's too strict with that kid, by half,' Jack observed, watching the mother disappear behind the midden door. Ellen nodded her agreement.

'She's got that closet habit from Harriet,' she said. Maisie nodded solemnly, and Jack, finally, brought the meeting to order.

'I move that we close down the catering side of the business and push all our resources into the flowers.'

'Here here!' said Maisie. 'I'm sick of mending them old table-cloths, anyway!'

Hester sat in state, chewing her nails, as the children played on in the yard. She could see them through the crack in the door. Her little girl. She loved her so much, she could eat her up. Such a pity she had to grow up, to suffer, one day, the trials and tribulations of a woman. And she was frail, both physically and spiritually. How would Anna resist the terrible temptations of the flesh? Even now Os had his eye on her. She watched him, winding the whip around the top and setting it to spin for her. Proper little gentleman he was, now . . . But later . . . And look at the example his mother set him! Oh yes! She'd have to watch their Anna! She'd have to be very strict with her, if she was to strengthen her resolve against her weaknesses. A fly passed through the gap at the top of the door and buzzed round her. Distracted, Hester looked at it, as it swooped and soared, and her eye was caught by some paper, sticking out from under a brick in the wall. She moved the brick, pulling out the faded covers of a book. Some forgotten reading, no doubt. Whose? She flicked through the pages. Such pictures it had! Disgusting! Naked women and men doing . . . Oh dear, oh dear, oh dear! She bent to concentrate, gasping and groaning till, hearing her, the children wondered whether they should run for help.

The meeting over, Jack and the sisters stood at the kitchen window, watching the children play.

'Eeh, aren't they canny!' Maisie said indulgently. 'That little lass has the power to tame our Os!'

'I'm glad somebody has!' Jack laughed. Os had set the top spinning, and now he handed Anna the whip. She whooped with delight, as the top scattered and spun at her bidding. Suddenly, without reason, Jack felt compelled to ask, 'You know Robert Ridley . . . ?'

'Robert Ridley? What on earth made you think of him, Jack?' Ellen asked, surprised.

'I don't know really,' Jack said idly. 'He was your uncle, wasn't he? Jane's brother?'

'Yes. What about him?'

'He went to India . . . '

'Did he? Maisie . . . ?'

'Aha. Do you not remember, it was your wedding day, Ellen, when that great statue came . . . the one that's down in the cellar.'

'Oh yes. So it was.'

'I suppose Robert must have sent it?'

'I suppose he must've.' Ellen frowned, trying hard to remember. 'What's so interesting about him, anyway?'

'All this mystery, surrounding his disappearance!'

'Mystery? What mystery?' Ellen protested. 'He ran away, in disgrace, after robbing the till!' Jack's heart lurched.

'Is that all?'

'All? I should've thought it was quite enough!' So, that was what it was. And Jack had killed for it! He didn't know whether to laugh or cry. Out in the yard, Anna suddenly collapsed in a paroxysm of crying.

'Go on out, Jack. You're always good for her when she's having one of her tantrums.' He dashed out, reaching the child before her mother emerged from the midden, white-faced and ready to strike. The sisters watched the drama from the window.

'Look at our Os,' Maisie said. 'It breaks his heart to see her like that.' Ellen nodded slowly. 'What are you thinking of?' Maisie asked.

'It would sort out a thing or two, if them two kids ended up wed!'

Jack and George continued to work at the speech exercises. George had to concentrate very hard, slowly forming words, into sentences which all too often ended up back to front. 'H . . . o . . . w . . . c . . . ooo ww . . . ' The sun was pouring in, through the bedroom window. Jack was lost, watching a butterfly flutter in the dappled light, through the open frame. As though reading his thought, George said, 'H . . . oo www iss Fran?' Jack was jerked back into the present.

'Sorry, George. I was miles away.' The old man waited for his answer. 'Did you ask about Fran?' George nodded. 'I haven't seen her since the funeral.' George pointed at his own chest.

'Bl . . . a . . . me,' he said.

316

'How could you be to blame, old man?'

'Hyp . . . o . . . cr . . . ite,' he said, snapping his teeth together as he delivered the word. 'I . . . sent . . . her . . . away!' He shook his head. 'Wrong!'

'She says the little girl's mine, you know,' Jack told him. A tear squeezed from the corner of George's eye.

'Davey!' George put his thumb down to express his feelings.

'It's not his fault, George. The war damaged a lot of us.'

'Fran . . . n . . . eeds . . . ' He pointed at Jack.

'She's as good as married!'

'You need . . . !' George grinned.

'Now that's enough of that!'

'Hol . . . i . . . day . . . '

'Let me get this straight. Are you saying that Frances needs a holiday, or I do?' The old man nodded enthusiastically. Light dawned. Jack laughed. 'You mean . . . we both do?!' Down in the yard, the boy and girl heard the raucous laughter of the men and stopped playing, to look up at the open window.

Davey's renewed zeal for business during hard times, was paying dividends. He had cornered the upper end of the catering market completely; and having found an outlet for his energies, he became more stable, reducing his intake of drugs. Frances had grown resigned to her lot and was, in any case, preoccupied with bringing up Eve. But Eve had a small problem. She was always getting tonsilitis. Maisie passed the news on to George. The local doctor had recommended the removal of the tonsils, and George knew of a very good specialist in London. Davey, who considered that nothing but the best was good enough for his daughter, agreed to the trip. And when Maisie passed the news on to Jack . . .

Faded blossom scurried about their feet in the wind, as they walked, side by side, on the afternoon of Eve's operation. In the distance, they could hear a band playing rag time. Frances' step skipped on the path. She bit her lip and tried not to smile. It was dreadful to feel so light-hearted. She was quite ashamed of herself. Jack glanced at his watch.

'I think we might wander back now,' he said.

'I hope she's all right!'

'Course she is. She's got the best surgeon in the country. And it's only her tonsils!'

'All the same, you can't help worrying.' But there was nothing to worry about. Eve was still asleep, when they went up to the ward. The sister took them to her bedside, and Frances wept with relief.

'You great softie!' Jack put his arm round her, and the sister whispered, 'Come back tomorrow morning, Mr Lawson. She'll be wide awake by then!' Frances and Jack dared not look at one another. They left the ward, desperately trying not to laugh and made their way back to the hotel.

Mrs Rosa had long since given up her lodging house, and gone to live with her widowed sister down in Kew and, in any case, Davey had booked Frances into a little pension in Earl's Court. So they took the tube back there, in time for Davey's daily telephone call. Jack didn't like the place. It smelt of carbolic and boiled cabbage, and the wallpaper had a dingy down-at-heel look to it. As they sat, drinking tea, he remembered, with nostalgia, Claridges Hotel and that marvellous big bath. He turned to mention it to Frances, but just then the phone rang. It was Davey.

'She's fine, pet. Don't worry. Apparently it all went very well . . . they're keeping her in for a week, so I'd better stay, hadn't I? . . . no, don't worry, I'll be all right on me own . . . I think I'll just have a nice bath and an early night. It's been quite a day . . . Aha . . . Tomorrow at the same time. Right you are . . . Tarrah, pet.' She put the phone down with relief, then went to sit by Jack, as before. 'Well!' she said.

'Well!' he mocked.

'What now?'

' . . . I thought I heard you say something about a bath . . . '

'Eeh, well, that was just for . . . well . . . something to say, like!'

'That's a pity. Because I think a bath would do you good.'

'Eh?' He took her arm and, unseen by the landlady, they slipped out into the twilit street.

'Let's go shopping,' he said.

'What for?'

'Well, I need some pyjamas, you need a nightie, and do you

318

mind sharing a toothbrush?' She grinned, and, like the spend-thrifts they were, they took a taxi into the west end.

The porter took up their one small bag and they followed with as much dignity as they could muster.

'They think we're, you know . . . '

'I know,' Jack said. 'Funny, isn't it?' She nodded, not quite sure how she felt, as the door closed behind them, at last.

'I'll run the bath, shall I?' Frances busied herself in the bathroom, scouring out the bath, which was already perfectly clean. Jack came in and, as she worked, he undid the back of her dress. She stood slowly and turned, unable to meet his eyes.

'I don't half feel naughty,' she said.

'I know. Isn't it nice!' He laughed at her shocked expression. 'But it's all right. We're married.'

'I know. That's the funny thing.' He pulled her dress away from her shoulders and groaned with delight.

'Do you really want a bath?' he asked.

'Perhaps later on, eh?'

'Good idea.' They stood, staring at one another, then firmly, he pulled her close and kissed her, his mouth searching for her answering love. And it rose to meet him, like the fragrance of flowers, warm and welcoming as a garden on a summer evening. They were no longer romantic boy and girl. They were a man and a woman, secure in the knowledge of one another's love.

Ambling through the gardens at Kew, Frances felt the years easing away.

'Let's go somewhere on the river, for tea,' Jack suggested.

'I can't, love.' She looked at him. He seemed content in their make-believe, holiday world. 'I've got to get back for Davey's trunk call.'

'Damn.' She was right. The real world was like an unwelcome guest at a private party.

'I know.' She sighed. 'I wish . . . ' He looked at her, met her eyes, but looked away again.

'You said, you wouldn't leave Davey now.'

'I did. Yes . . . ' She agreed doubtfully. Jack sighed. Why did he find it all so difficult? Why didn't he just take the decision out of her hands, and reclaim her for his own?

'I'm glad,' he said. Frances thought she was going to cry. She couldn't understand. Didn't he love her, then? A chill breeze made her shiver. Jack put an arm round her and guided her towards the conservatories.

'Want to have a look inside?' he asked. 'It'll be warmer.' She nodded, and followed him in. The light spring air was exchanged for the heavy, humid atmosphere of the glasshouse.

'I wish Granda could see this!' she said.

'He's hanging on there! I'm amazed at him. Strong as an ox, that old lad.'

'Us Beatties *are*!' Frances grinned, through her tears.

'We'll hang on, as well,' Jack said.

'Hang on? How? What do you mean?' She was weak at the knees. He held her up, now, at last, looking into her eyes.

'Something happened to me, in the war, Fran.' She waited, as he struggled to get it out. 'I killed a man . . .' Frances snorted,

'In a war . . . !'

'No. He was on our side.' She frowned, wanting to know more. 'I can't tell you much about it. I thought I was doing the right thing. But, I wasn't. And now God knows what it would do to Davey, Eve, Os . . . us! If we took the law into our own hands . . .'

'Us?'

'Yes. It would damage us, Fran, if we snatched our happiness at the expense of other people. I don't think it would work out, somehow. I think we should let events take their course. See what happens.' Frances stared at him.

'I do believe you like it! You do, don't you? It gives you some perverse sort of a thrill, to have me like this . . . your bit on the side!'

Jack bit his lip and shrugged. 'Well, you can't have your cake and eat it, Jack Scott!'

This was hard. What was he to do? The old familiar pressures were building up. It had been the same when he'd refused to volunteer for the war. She was trying to force him into action. But look where action had got him? He had a man's blood on his hands.

Frances watched his jaw stiffen. She knew that look; that old, familiar look. He wasn't going to give in. She started crying.

'Oh no! No, Fran! Don't do that to me!' Then Jack's face softened, as she tried hard to suppress her tears. 'All I'm saying is, let's not rush into doing anything just yet.'

'And meanwhile . . . ?' she asked bitterly.

'How do you think I feel about my own daughter, calling another man, "Dad"?' Frances hung her head. 'You see, it's not all cake for me, either.' It was true. She was in no position to criticise Jack. And perhaps he was right, after all. She looked up at him, a new trust in her eyes, and saw a strength, she hadn't seen before.

'Meanwhile . . . ' She let him take her hand, and he walked her slowly towards the pool at the centre of the hothouse. ' . . . I'm not going to give you up.'

'Then you'll have to wait for me,' she said blankly. 'And you might have to wait for a very long time.' They sat on a seat, overlooking the pond. It was filled with flowers.

'What do you think they are, Jack?'

'I don't know.' He bent to read the label. 'Lotus. Northern India.'

'They're lovely.' The fragrance of the flowers sharpened her pain. Frances sobbed, 'Some time, somehow, there's got to be a way out of all this mess.' Jack was still looking at the label.

'It says here the blossoms grow straight out of the mud . . . '

PART THREE: 1933

Is there a doctor to be found
All ready, near at hand,
To cure a deep and deadly wound
And make the champion stand!

CHAPTER NINETEEN

Slowly, Eve turned the kaleidoscope and the pattern broke. She frowned. She had liked the star. But perhaps, if she turned the thing again, it would reform. Carefully, she placed her fingers on the drum, but the distant sound of an approaching brass band distracted her. She sighed. She should have gone and watched her Dad, standing stiffly to attention at the cenotaph. But she hated all parades. And anyway, Remembrance Sunday was a day for the dead, not the living, and Eve was very much alive, thank you very much! She screwed her eye up tight and turned the barrel slowly, hoping to surprise the pieces into reforming in the old order. But, try as she might, the thousand coloured shapes, reflected in the fractured glass, spilled willy-nilly, never to be the same again. Disappointed, Eve put her toy down, and blinked in the light of the window.

The band blared in the street below, where her father marched, head high, medals gleaming on his chest. Why had she let him down? She was proud of him really. He was a hero, even if he was a bad tempered old sod. And he had feelings. Oh yes. He had feelings all right. He would be hurt she hadn't gone. He'd probably go and drown his sorrows in the pub, come home 'palatic', and then she'd be sorry too! Not half she would!

Putting her hands on her ears, to shut out the maudlin sound of the band, Eve launched rebelliously into the refrain of, 'We're in the money . . . ', and tap-danced her way downstairs to the kitchen, where she vented her feelings, peeling spuds for the dinner. Mind, her Mam was well out of it and no mistake!

But it was hard to 'get out of it', even in Maisie's little haven in Keppel Street, where Frances waited. She checked her watch. It was half past ten. Where was Jack? Eeh, it would be just their luck if Davey's procession just happened to be passing down Fowler Street, as Jack turned into Maisie's road! And if Davey was to see them and put two and two together . . . ! For years, they'd held out, her and Jack. He'd had his hands full in the shop, steering it on its precarious way through the Depression with Ellen and Maisie's help, and always with a backward glance to see what Hester was up to. She couldn't be trusted. Either she was playing some underhand trick with the business, or she was laying into Anna, who, for the sake of peace and quiet had followed her mother into the bosom of the Roman Catholic Church. Thank God religion took up so much of their time! Jack was grateful to the Pope for that, and suffered the early morning incantations with philosophical forbearance, as he was shaving in his room, upstairs. Then, suddenly as it seemed, Os had grown into a young man, and was demanding his place in the business. Immediately, Hester tried to bar his way. And then, Maisie stepped in with her bombshell. She was leaving the shop! Will's father had died, leaving her a little nest egg; not much, but enough to buy her an annuity. Independence at last! Maisie of all people! She waltzed off, to set up home, a few streets away, in rented rooms, watched jealously by Ellen and Hester. But Maisie's departure had left a gap in the shop, which Anna was too frail to cover, and Hester was forced to allow Os to take her place.

Jack hadn't forgotten Frances. He was a man. He had his feelings. And his eye roved from time to time. But it was usually nothing too serious. News of his 'goings-on' reached Frances in Ocean Road, where life was far from rosy. Davey had turned from drugs to drink, and Frances was running Lawson's almost single handed. Eve helped, of course, when she wasn't off at her dancing classes, or socialising with her friends. Watching her daughter, Frances could see herself, when she was young. She would have been tempted to live through her, if Eve had let her. But she was different, after all. She seemed a tough nut, typical of the bright young things of the post war years, troubles falling from her, like water off a duck's back. It was hard to get through to her. And Frances felt increasingly isolated, her thoughts straying more and more often to the husband in Fowler Street.

'How is he, Maisie?' she'd ask with transparent carelessness.

'Oh fine, pet,' Maisie would say. 'He's got himself a new lady friend. One of the nurses at the Ingham Infirmary. Do you remember when Anna broke her arm? Mind, when I say broke it, I'm not sure it wasn't broken for her,' Maisie said darkly. 'By, I was glad to get out of that place. Aye, and I don't blame Jack for seeking his comfort elsewhere.' Frances was jealous, just as Maisie had hoped. Yet, even if there hadn't been Davey to consider, she wouldn't really have wanted to go back to Fowler Street. Not with Hester there. And then, there was Os . . . But Maisie watched and waited, papering her room, making it cosy. The nurse came to nothing, and a mood of rebellion touched both Jack and Frances, both of them fed up with their lot. Maisie seized the moment, invited them to tea, and left them to it. The 'tea' was repeated, and a pattern was soon established, which kept both Jack and Frances going in the doldrums of their respective lives.

Maisie loved it! Real life romance! She relished her part in it all, thrilled by the secrecy, the danger. She was living life at second hand, but it was better than living it through her magazines! Yes, the arrangement kept them all happy. But Frances felt guilty, which was daft, as Jack pointed out, over and over. They were, after all, still married! Fancy having an affair with your own husband! It was crackers! But Jack liked it that way. And Frances knew he did, deep down. She wondered if he would have continued to feel the same way about her, if they'd been living together, as man and wife, all that time?

Waiting for him now, Frances sighed and shook her head. Aye, the men always ended up having their cake and eating it. Look at her granda! They were all the same, given the chance. Men! There was a sound at the front door, downstairs. Frances heard it and froze. Outside, Jack Scott looked this way and that, then slipped his key in the lock and crept upstairs. Frances called out nervously,

'Who is it?'

'Who d'ye think?' Jack laughed, coming into the room.

'Where've you been?'

'The old barsket was in a bit of a state, this morning. Put the kettle on, eh? I'm parched.'

'There's some in the pot . . . haway! Give's a kiss! I've been dying for a cuddle.' Jack obliged enthusiastically, hurling her on the wheezing bed, before she had time to pour him a cup of tea.

But the distant strains of 'Abide With Me' cooled their ardour. The wreaths were being laid at the cenotaph. Jack went to switch on the radio, to drown it out. 'How *is* Granda?' Frances asked.

'Well, he didn't get much sleep last night . . . his legs are filling up with water now.'

'Oh dear. That doesn't bode well.'

'I don't know how he hangs on, I don't really.' The radio was warming up. The melancholy tones of the Dead March filtered across the air waves. 'No peace for the wicked!' Jack commented as he switched it off again.

Line upon line of red poppies honoured the dead. A tear oozed from the corner of Davey's eye, as he stood, staring at the wreaths, remembering. What had it all been for? Who cared? It was all past now. Forgotten. The new generation didn't want to look back; didn't want to know. All they wanted was to escape into their dream world of films and music. And who could blame them? The one they'd been born into wasn't up to much, when all was said and done. 'A land fit for heroes' . . . Aye well, if T.B. and unemployment were what made it fit, then Tyneside was just the place. The shipyards had died, or had been murdered . . . it was the beginning of the end. The mournful notes of the Last Post tore at his heart. What was there left to live for? 'Don't leave me here to die . . . ' But old soldiers never die. The ghosts remained in the new and alien world, unsatisfied, demanding their due. They wanted vengeance. They could not understand young people, like Eve, who preferred to stay at home playing records. They were unfeeling! But they should be made to feel! They should be sorry for what had happened. Davey rose to the task. 'I'll make them sorry, Jim. I promise. I'll make them sorry.

328

Then will you be satisfied?' The living broke ranks and made for the pubs, leaving the ghosts littering the streets, their voices carried on the breath of memory. 'I'll keep you to that, Davey! You left me in No Man's Land, to die. I'm still there, Davey, still in agony, still waiting for you to come back.' Davey downed his fourth scotch and looked at the bleak faces round the bar. Old soldiers never die. It was a curse laid on them by a merciless god. Look at them all. Anachronisms. They should have died with the rest of them. 'Come back. Don't leave me here . . . '

'Shrrup, Jim!' The men at the bar turned in surprise to look at Davey, temples working, jaw clenched. The landlord shook his head. Best not to ask. Respectfully, they looked away again, and Davey ordered another scotch, before making for home.

The mashed potato stood cold, in the plate, the fat congealing round the edges. It was a pity to waste good food. Eve covered the plate and put it in the larder. She would heat it up for her mother when she got home from auntie's. Waste not want not. She sighed. It was coming in dark already. She switched on the light and reached for her film magazine. Sequins and gauze paraded before her eyes. That was the life! Hollywood, where you bathed in bubbles, and drank champagne and 'lived'! Eve had relations in America. Her grandma had told her so. They had a ranch or something in California. Wasn't that near Hollywood? She lay back, dreaming. She was dancing down the street, like Ginger Rogers, in a long floaty dress, when this gorgeous young man, in a top hat, suddenly steps out of the crowd, dazzled by her dancing. He smiles with all his teeth and holds out his hand to her, commandingly . . . There was a bump upstairs. Eve jerked back into reality. What was that? She frowned, then shrugged. Probably nothing. Her eyes fell on the magazine. Yes, and she took his hand, and he reeled her in to him, and they danced, gliding, cheek to cheek down the street, the passers by waving and smiling at them . . . It was funny that bump. It bothered her. What could it have been? Sighing, she closed her magazine. Only one way to find out. She swung upstairs and knocked gently on the door of her father's room.

'Dad . . . are you all right?'

* * *

'It's getting dark, Jack.' Frances yawned and stretched. Jack moaned, drifting out of sleep.

'Mmmm?'

'It's getting dark. I'll have to go soon.'

'Ah . . . let's have another cuddle.' She wriggled close and smelt the warmth of a sleepy afternoon on his skin.

'Oh, I do love you . . .' She sighed blissfully.

'Ditto,' he said and grunted contentedly.

'Maisie'll be back soon. We've got to get up.'

'Not yet . . . she won't mind.' He rolled over, entwining her in his arms, and kissed her indulgently to the chorus of a wheezing bed. A loud bang on the front door made them jump. They lay still, listening. Mrs Fry, downstairs, went to answer it. 'It's not Maisie.' Jack resumed the kiss, their bodies moving on the groaning bed.

'Auntie Maisie?' Eve's voice rang out.

'Oh my God!'

'Keep still!' Jack hissed. But Eve ran upstairs, flung open the door and surprised her mother in bed with Jack. All three stared in silence for some seconds. Eve turned to go, then stopped in the doorway. She was crying.

'I came to tell you . . . Dad . . . Dad . . .' Frances got out of the bed and started dressing.

'Wait for me. I'll not be a second. I'll come back with you. It's not what you think . . .'

'You sound like a film, you two!' Eve said bitterly, then glared at Jack.

'How bad is he, the drunken devil!' Frances was pulling on her stockings.

' "It's not what you think." Huh! The heroine always says that when she's caught out with her fancy man!'

'How dare you speak like that about your father!'

Eve went white, and stared at her mother, who was biting her tongue in anguish.

'What did you say?'

'Nothing. How bad's your dad?'

'He's dead.' One hand on a stocking top, Frances froze.

'What?'

'He's dead. The neighbour's in with him.'

'Are you sure?'

330

'Well he's not breathing, and he's very pale, and he won't answer when the doctor asks him to, so . . .'

'Don't speak like that to your mother!' Jack put in, at last. Eve shot him a contemptuous look.

'The poor bairn's had a shock, Jack? Leave her be.' Jack, naked in the bed, was helpless.

'Will you just do me a favour, Eve, and wait outside the door for a minute,' he pleaded. Eve howled with rage, turned and fled, dashing down the stairs, followed by her mother, who yelled something to someone on the stairs.

'You've dropped your poppy!' Jack shouted. Forgetting himself, he leapt out of bed, to pick it up. The door opened.

'Here it is . . .' Maisie's jaw dropped. Confronted by a naked man, holding out a poppy, she had to laugh.

'What on earth's happened?' she asked.

'Davey Lawson's dead,' Jack said, running his hands through his hair. 'What a bloody fiasco!'

'All these years and she had to find out now!' Maisie shook her head at Frances, then burst out laughing. 'Sh! Have you no respect?'

'I'm sorry, but if you'd seen Jack with that poppy!' She wheezed with suppressed laughter, and Frances smiled in spite of herself.

'What is it about funerals that's so funny?' Frances asked. 'I've not been to one yet where I haven't wanted to laugh. I mean, you feel such a fool, don't you, dressed up in your black, standing at the graveside, rocking with laughter.'

'True.'

'I wonder why our Eve threw that poppy onto his coffin . . .'

'It seemed right somehow.'

'Aye.' Frances sighed. 'He wasn't a bad man, Maisie. The war's got a lot to answer for.'

'He left you all right, anyway.'

'Aye. He did.' She paused, considering her situation. 'More or less.' Maisie's ears perked up.

'What do you mean, "more or less"?'

'Well, things haven't been going that well for us, either, you know.' Maisie nodded. 'We're a luxury trade, flowers, catering, sweets . . . folk can't afford luxuries these days.'

'True.'

'I don't know what I'm going to do . . . I mean, I've got our Eve to think of.'

'She'll work in the shop, surely?' Frances shrugged.

'She doesn't like it. You know her.'

'Oh aye. I know her!' Maisie pulled a face and smiled.

'Got ideas above her station!'

'Takes after her Mam!' Frances looked up slyly.

'Aye well. I daresay you're right, Maisie. Like mother like daughter, eh?'

'That's about the top and bottom of it.'

'But I can't run the place on me own, and I can't afford to take anybody on . . . so . . . '

'So . . . ?' Maisie was looking hard at her niece. 'Has Jack not said anything?' Frances shook her head. 'Well, it's not for me to poke me nose in.' Maisie stood, ready to go.

'Stay a bit, Auntie,' Frances pleaded. 'It's awful sitting in of a night. Our Eve still won't speak to me, you know. I thought maybe if you . . . '

'She's *your* daughter!'

'Yes. She is. All right. Off you go home. Thanks for coming to the funeral.'

'Least I could do. I know you loved him, in a way. You put up with more than most. You've got nothing to reproach yourself with on that score.'

'Not on that score, no . . . ' Frances sighed.

'Not on any, pet. You've paid.'

'Have I?'

When Maisie had gone, Frances braced herself and went up, to knock timidly on Eve's door. There was no answer. She pushed it and went in. Eve was lying on the bed, face down. Frances looked at her for a long time.

'Are you asleep, pet?'

'Huh!'

'Look, love, I know how it must look, but . . . '

'You're a tart!' Frances swallowed the hurt and sat beside her on the bed.

'I want to tell you what happened, Eve. I was very young, when I married Jack . . . ' Eve turned to stare at her mother. 'You

332

know he was a music hall comedian . . . ' Eve nodded. 'Well, I was like you, when I was younger, all starry-eyed and stage struck.' Eve pursed her lips. She took her own talents far more seriously than that! 'I ran away from home to go on the stage as Jack's apprentice.'

'Then why were you so daft as to get married and let yourself be dragged back to work in a flower shop!'

'Women did what they were told in them days! It's different now.'

'I'd have paid him back, if he did that to me!'

'Yes, pet. I'm afraid you do take after me. More's the pity! And I did pay him back! I . . . it's hard for me to tell you about this!'

'Is that when you took up with me Dad?'

'Davey Lawson was not your Dad.'

'I don't believe you.'

'I went with him, partly to spite Jack, I suppose, but I was sorry for Davey as well. I don't know.' Frances sighed. 'It was only the once. The good girls always get caught, you know. It's the bad ones get away with it.'

'You got pregnant, with me?'

'I thought I did. I got me dates wrong. You're Jack's child.' There was a long silence.

'I don't believe you.' Eve was crying. 'I mean, why didn't you go back to him, if that's true.'

'Because . . . because I couldn't. I was stuck. I'd got meself in a position where whatever I did, it was bound to be wrong. I'd made my bed. I had to lie on it. Jack agreed, and after all, he was my husband.'

'Do you mean . . . did you never get divorced?' Frances shook her head.

'Davey wanted me to, but I wouldn't. He never knew about me taking up with Jack again.'

'I think he did! I think that's why he did it.'

'Your Dad, I mean Davey, did not commit suicide, Eve. He drowned in his own vomit, after drinking himself into a stupor!'

'But why did he drink? Wasn't it because he knew about you and Uncle Jack?'

'He's not your uncle!'

'He always will be to me.'

'And no . . . I swear he didn't know. We were very careful. You didn't guess, did you?' Eve shook her head bitterly, then slowly her expression melted into tears.

'I don't know who I am any more. . . . I don't know who to believe. Who is my Dad?' The mother took the daughter in her arms, and held her close.

'I'm sorry, pet. I've done you wrong. I've done wrong by my sons, by my husband, by my family. But I've paid, love. I have really. It hasn't been easy all these years, and I've done my best. Life's not always as cut and dried as you like to think it is, at your age. Try and forgive me, pet.'

'I'll never forgive *him*!'

'Jack? Why? What's *he* done?'

'Carrying on . . . '

'He is my husband, you know.'

'What a mess!' Bewildered, Eve looked away, and began fiddling with the quilt. Suddenly, she stopped and looked up at her mother, alarmed. 'What's going to happen now?' Frances looked away and sighed.

'I don't know, pet. I can't manage here on me own . . . '

'You're going to go back to him, aren't you? Uncle Jack?'

'He's not your . . . '

'He is to me!' Frances stroked her daughter's hair, lovingly.

'Sh . . . pet . . . there now.' Eve picked up her kaleidoscope and turned it, trying in vain to get back her star. Then she sighed and flung it on the bed, in disgust.

'Well I'm not coming with you!'

'He hasn't asked me, yet! Look, do you want me to stop here on me own! I will if you want.' Eve shook her head, miserably.

'Does Os know?'

'Some of it. Not all . . . '

'And Anna?'

'No.'

'You do what you like, Mam. I'll go me own way.'

'Talk sense! You're only seventeen!'

'I don't want to work in any flower shop! So there! Ah, Mam, your family spoiled your chance of being on the stage, you're not going to spoil mine, are you?'

'Eeh, pet. Times are hard. The theatre's a difficult enough life at best . . . I mean they've just closed down the Palace Empire! It's not a good time to launch yourself on a career like that!'

'Not here, maybe.'

'Where then?'

'America.' Frances drew in her breath sharply. 'Films are the thing now. Not the theatre. I want to be in films.'

'So does every lass in Shields!'

'Aye, but I'm different!' Frances retorted. 'Give's a chance, Mam! I can make it! I know I can! I can tap better than Ginger Rogers any day of the week!'

'You talk like a film yourself!' Frances snorted. ' "Gold Diggers of 1933", if you please!'

'Mam . . . !'

'If you think I'm going to let you gallivant off to Hollywood all on your own, you've got another think coming!'

'We've got family over there, haven't we?' Frances' heart skipped a beat. Life! You never knew what was round the corner, did you?

Maisie shut the door of her haven, and sighed. Home Sweet Home! The place had been a godsend. She didn't know how Jack and Ellen stood it in Fowler Street. It might not be much but at least this one room and a cupboard were hers! She could bless Will's Dad forever, for making it possible. God rest him! Maisie Beattie, no teeth and a hump back, not very bright, a woman of independent means! Well now! Didn't it take the biscuit! She pulled off her boots, wincing. Then she undid her stays, took out her dentures, and sprawled before the hissing flame of her gas fire. Bliss! What was on the radio? Should she bother to get up and turn it on? There were steps on the stair. Maisie's heart sank. Now what?

'Maisie, are you in?' Jack. She might've known.

'Come in, lad. You'll not have to mind . . . ' She indicated the dentures in the glass. 'I'm not puttin' them back in, even for you.' Anxiously, Jack sat in the chair opposite. He looked pale and nervous. 'How was the funeral?'

'All right.' Jack thought for a moment. 'I suppose.' Maisie eyed him, suspiciously.

'Have you said anything to her?'

'Who?'

'Frances! Who else?'

'Oh.' There was a long pause. 'You mean about . . . '

335

'Why aye, man! Oh I see! I might've known you'd try to wriggle out of it! Men!'

'I'm not trying to wriggle out of anything, Maisie!' Jack protested. 'Only it's a big step, you know.'

'Big step, my aunt Fanny! Why, you're married already! She *is* your wife!'

'I know!' Jack frowned, rubbing his hands, as though he was feeling the cold. 'It's just, well, it'd be a shame to spoil things . . .'

'Eeh!'

'Give me a chance, Maisie! All I'm wondering is, would it work as well, between Frances and me, as it does now, if we were living together?'

'You want to start asking yourself if it *is* working for her, me laddo!' Jack looked guilty at once. There was a moment's silence.

'I *want* to be fair to her . . . ' Maisie forbore speaking. 'I mean, she'd have our Hester to deal with, for a start!' That *was* a drawback. Even Maisie could see that.

'Well!' she said at last. 'In my humble opinion, it's up to Frances to say whether she wants to come back and live at the shop, or not. You do, at least, owe her the dignity of asking her.'

'Yes.' Jack nodded slowly. 'You're right, Maisie. I do.' Maisie shook her head at him.

'Jack, lad, isn't it time you grew up? Accepted your responsibilities?' He smiled sheepishly. 'Why, man, you might even get to like it!' He grinned. 'You're a rogue, Jack Scott! Eeh, but I like you!' Then, she bared her gums and roared with laughter.

But, there was a lot of sounding out to do, before Jack dare approach Frances. First there was George, who seemed relieved at the prospect, and then there was Hester.

'I am not having that trollop in the house!' Her face was white and fierce.

'Dad says she can come back, and he still owns half the business, you know!' Ellen said. Hester's eye twitched.

'He's senile!'

'How dare you!' Jack shouted. 'He's got more sense in his little finger . . .'

'Shouting won't help, Jack.' Maisie put a restraining hand on his arm.

'If Frances Lawson comes back here, it'll be over my dead

336

body. I have a daughter's morals to protect!' Anna, pale and cowed, looked up from the corner, where she sat next to Os.

'It isn't Frances she needs protecting from, it's you!' Jack couldn't help himself.

'And what do you mean by that?' Maisie cast a sidelong look at Anna, who was looking more anxious than ever. But Jack was in no mood to back down now.

'Look at your daughter! Go on! I'm sick of seeing her, bruises everywhere, shaking in her shoes! The number of times I've had to come between you and her . . .'

'You've no right to interfere! She's my daughter!'

'Jack . . . shush!'

'It's no good! It's got to be said!' But Anna was crying now. Jack sighed, stumbling to a halt.

'Now look what you've done!' Hester spat.

'What I've done! You hypocritical . . .'

'Making out you care!' Hester sneered. 'Huh! What did any of you ever care about *me*!'

'You?!'

'Please, Uncle Jack! Please stop it!' Jack turned his back, walking to the window, to stare out into the yard.

'All right,' he said. 'I'll stop . . . for now, Anna. On one condition, that Hester holds her peace about my wife!'

'Your wife?' Hester jeered. 'Yours and who else's?' But now Os stepped in.

'Now look, Auntie. I can't say I'm overjoyed at the prospect of having my mother here, but she is my mother, all the same, and I can't sit by and let you call her names. As for Anna's morals, they're quite safe in my hands.'

'You're all heathens, the lot of you!'

'And you're crackers!' But Ellen raised her voice above Jack's.

'Now, look here, Hester!' Her voice carried authority. 'Let's keep things on a business footing, shall we?' There was general assent. 'The thing is, there's not room for two florists in this town, in the present state of affairs.'

'True . . . true . . .' There was murmuring agreement.

'And if Frances was to come here, amalgamating the two businesses, it'd make a lot of sense!'

'There's more to life than sense!' Hester screamed.

'Calm down, woman!' Jack commanded. 'They'll hear you over the river, if you go on like that!'

'Let them hear me!' Hester stood, her hand raised as though speaking to a crowd. 'None can silence God's messenger!'

'I tell you, she's crackers!' Jack shook his head.

'And then there's the money,' Ellen went on undeterred. 'If Frances sold the premises, with the flat above it, it should make a few bob.'

'Yes.' Jack nodded, suddenly smiling. 'As long as she doesn't think I'm marrying her for her money!' Even Os laughed, but Hester banged her fist on the table, to silence mirth.

'You must admit, it's got its funny side, Hester,' Maisie said placatingly.

'I am in a nest of iniquity,' Hester said, sniffing back the tears.

'Hadaway, man!' Ellen retorted. Hester rose in silence, washing her hands of the business, and went up to her room, to pray.

George opened one eye, as a head peeped round his door. It was Os.

'I thought you might be asleep.' The old man shifted uncomfortably and indicated the stool next to him, where Os sat, obediently.

'Well? What happened?' George's voice came in rasps.

'Dad says you want me mother to come back here.' The old man nodded. 'I see.' Os sighed. 'It'll change things, Granda.' George was panting to get breath enough to speak.

'Good,' he said at last. 'My fault she went in first place.'

'It'll make things difficult.' George's colour deepened. 'Aunt Hester hates Mam, and, well, it'll make things awkward for Anna and me.'

'How is Hester?'

'She's getting worse . . . ' George nodded.

'Frances make things better.'

'I see.' Os fidgeted, wondering whether to speak, then blurted out, 'Granda, I want to look after Anna.' George sighed and shut his eyes. Os watched him, waiting, then realised the subject was closed. He rose to go, and then remembered himself. 'Is there anything you want?' George groaned, and shifted, miserably. His hand reached down to his knee. Os held the rug away from the legs. It gave George obvious relief. 'I'll rig up something for you, to take the weight off,' Os said thoughtfully. George nodded and let the lad go.

Out in the yard, Os sawed and hammered, experimenting with pieces of spare wood. Jack came out and watched him, silently, until, exacerbated, waiting for his father to speak, Os laid down his tools and spoke for him.

'It's all right, Dad. I'll not stand in your way.' Jack looked uncomfortable. 'If you want me mam back, good luck to you.'

'Thank you, son.' Os shrugged, and got on with his hammering again. 'It's funny. I'd got cold feet about the whole thing, till your Auntie Hester started having a go about her. And now I can see how much I want her. Having your mam with us'll be good for us all.'

'If you say so.'

'I do. Look at Anna for a start. Fran'll be a big help there, keeping the old dragon at bay!' Os laughed. 'The trouble is, your Auntie Hester's not so funny any more. I'm getting really worried about her. Ellen and Maisie still treat her like a big joke, but I'm not so sure.'

'What makes you think me mam'll bother with Anna at all, even if she does come to live?' Jack frowned. A tone of resentment had come into his son's voice.

'She's a mother!'

'Is she now?' Os sounded angry. 'I never knew much about it. She never cared for me, when I was a kid. It was always Michael this and Michael that . . .'

'Aye well.' Jack flared for a second, then sighed. 'She's not perfect, I grant you, but then, son, neither am I? Give her a chance, eh?' Os looked at his father thoughtfully.

'Do you love her, Dad? I mean really? After what she's done?'

'Yes. I do. And I tell you, son, the fault wasn't all on her side . . .' A shape moved at the kitchen window. Both men turned to see Hester's face, staring out at them. Jack changed the subject. 'What's that you're making?'

'It's for Granda . . . to keep the rug off his sore legs . . .'

Watching Os, as he hammered the frame together in the yard, Hester shook her head.

'What's wrong now?' Ellen asked, coming up behind her, to look out of the window.

'I don't know why he doesn't just die and be done with it!' Hester muttered. Ellen smiled as she saw the frame taking shape.

'He's a good lad, is Os.' But Hester was obsessed with the man upstairs.

'It's not decent, hanging on like this. It's an insult to God Almighty. Doesn't he want to go to heaven?'

'He's maybe afraid of going to the other place,' Ellen observed, lightly.

'He's in pain all the time. His legs are blown up like great balloons . . .'

'He's got the will to live! You've got to give him that, Hester!'

Hester stared out of the kitchen window and watched, as her daughter wheeled her bike in at the back gate. She and Os began talking, with Jack as bystander. Os was patient, kind, smiling on Anna, as she chattered on about all the deliveries she'd done on her bike, dying for his approbation.

'Dad should make way for the new generation,' Hester commented.

'Them two?' Ellen looked at Hester, surprised. 'I thought you couldn't stand the sight of our Os!'

'He's going to come into fifty per cent of the business . . .'

'Oh! I see! So, you're plannin' a dynastic marriage, like?' Ellen's light, mocking tone was lost on Hester. The shop door clanged. Ellen sighed, leaving her sister to go and serve. Still as a statue, Hester watched on. Frances! Her lip curled in disgust. She could not be allowed to come back! Spoiling everything, putting her oar in, flaunting herself! Which room would she have? She wasn't going to have hers, that was for sure. Then, Hester paled, remembering. She'd share Jack's of course. She shook her head. She wouldn't be able to bear it, living in the same house as them, and their 'goings-on'! She shuddered. She might even hear them! Tears came into Hester's eyes. Feverish thoughts flooded her mind. Frances was the door by which they would let in the devil! She was Jezebel! Surely, God would not want his handmaiden, Hester, to stand by and let such a thing happen? She bit back her tears, as Maisie came into the kitchen, poured a glass of water, and set up a tray for her father.

'Time for his water pills!' she announced, and went upstairs

340

with them. No. God would not want that. And if her own father
took the part of the devil . . . If he opened the door . . . why, it
was Hester's bounden duty to stop him! She looked up at the
bottle of pills on the shelf. It wobbled dangerously. Had Maisie
been careless, putting it back? Or was it a sign from God?
'Jack . . . !' Maisie was shouting, as she came back down the
stairs. She looked into the kitchen. 'Have you seen Jack, Hester?
Dad wants him.'

George sat, up to his waist in water, refusing to die. He
couldn't sleep. He dared not. For Death might take him
unaware, his task unfinished. So he sat, night and day, watching,
waiting, and the time had almost come, at last, when he might
hand on his burden. And then, like Simeon, he could depart in
peace. Peace . . . the word flowed through his brain like a
quenching river. But not yet. Not yet. There was still something
left undone. Where was Jack? He had to talk to him, about Os,
and Anna. The door opened. George's heart leapt. It must be
him. But Maisie walked in with his pills and a cup of tea.

'That's the third dose down the hatch!' she announced
cheerfully, dropping them in his mouth. He swallowed hard.
'Are they doing you any good?' George shook his head and
Maisie lifted the rug to check his legs. They were worse if
anything.

'More pills! Not enough!' he gasped.

'It does say up to five, on the bottle. Shall I fetch you the other
three?' George nodded. Doctors were always overcautious. He
had a good constitution. He could take it. Better than his lungs
filling up and drowning! So, Maisie hurried down, fetching the
bottle back up with her, and George downed the extra pills with
his tea. 'Anything else?'

'Jack!'

'He's not back yet. He went down Ocean Road to see our
Fran.'

'Good.'

'I'll send him up, soon as he comes in. Why don't you get forty
winks in the meantime?' She reached for the switch on the table
lamp, but George growled.

'Light on!'

'Have it your own way . . . ' Maisie sighed and left the old man to it. If only he didn't feel so tired. Perhaps some poetry would keep him awake. Slowly he reached for his book. The sun was setting. Its red light glowed on the page. And the words glared up at him.

> 'Our noisy years seem moments in the being
> Of the eternal silence:'

'Eternal silence' . . . He would drown in its ocean soon enough. But not yet . . . not yet . . . His eyelids drooped. He was so tired. If only he could close them; just for a moment. They fell heavily, and a haze seeped through his brain. He mustn't give in to it. He forced his eyes open and read on.

> 'The clouds that gather round the setting sun
> Do take a sober colouring from an eye
> That hath kept watch o'er man's mortality.'

'Sober' . . . Yes. The page was growing dark . . . His breath sank in his chest. If only he could sleep! He must concentrate; words swimming on the page. He was falling asleep. He clenched his hand, digging his nails into his palms, using the pain to keep himself awake. But the heaviness dragged him down . . . The pills. Had he taken too many? Suddenly his brain was clear and alert. The pills. Yes. They had tasted different! Why? Who? The door creaked open. George could barely lift his head to see. A step, light, a woman's, came into the room. And Hester crouched at his feet, looking up into his face, smiling. Hester! Her eyes glowed with expectation. What had she done? With a great effort, George lifted his head and his eyes burned into her. She sat back on her heels, in surprise, then smiled again, as saliva dribbled from the corner of his mouth.

'Feeling sleepy, Dad? Why don't you drop off, eh? Do you good!'

'Never!' His voice grated like a tombstone. 'You changed pills?'

'Yes!' Her laughter rang round the room.

'Your own father!'

'You were never a father to me! You always hated me! You never really tried to help me! Not you nor my mother! You denied me everything. Love . . . ' She was crying bitterly. 'You palmed me off . . . on that perverted old hag, Harriet!' Her face screwed up with pain. 'You never asked me what I wanted. Never tried to get to know me . . . All my life I've been a square peg, a square peg that other people have tried to shove in round holes. And it hurt! It hurt, Dad, every time! It still hurts! I never became round. I'm still square, only I've got bits hacked off me! Wounds!' She tore her bodice open, pointing at her heart. 'Wounds!' George's head drooped. She wrenched it up, with her hands, and made him look at her. 'I've tried! All these years, I've tried to be a good woman! And now, you want to bring that bitch back into the family! Well, I won't let you! I'd rather kill you first!' George struggled to free his head, but Hester hung on, her grip like iron. 'I'll see my daughter mistress of this shop! She'll marry Oswald, and her children will inherit after her!'

The old lion wrenched himself free, lifted up his head and roared. Down in the kitchen, Jack heard. He put down his cup of tea and raced up the stairs, falling into the room, as Hester departed, in a flurry. George's face was scarlet, and his breath came in long, low rasps.

'What's happened?' Jack shouted.

'He . . . st . . . er . . . ' the old man hissed. 'Pill . . . s.'

'What pills?'

'Po . . . st . . . mort . . . emmm . . . Musssst.' Jack went white.

'Come on! You've got to be sick!' But darkness was invading the world.

George, tears running down his cheeks, struggled against it, shaking his head from side to side in agony. 'Os . . . not marry Anna! Ask Harriet . . . Sh . . . ad . . . ow . . . of . . . the . . . eleph . . . ant.' He was dead. Jack could not revive him. They sent for the doctor and Jack insisted an autopsy be performed.

CHAPTER TWENTY

Jack leaned forward and wiped the mist from the windscreen. Beyond the rain-soaked beach, he could see the sea, grey and choppy. Frances stirred, smearing the tears from her cheeks, with her sleeve. She'd loved her granda, in spite of everything. How could Hester have done such a terrible thing?

'Are you sure she's not just making it up? There are such things as false confessions, you know. I mean, if, as you say, she's not in her right mind . . .' Jack shook his head.

'If you'd heard his last words . . . ' A lump came to Jack's throat. The pain of George's death had surprised him. Was it losing him, or was it something else that hurt so much? 'The shadow of the elephant.' He swallowed hard. 'Do you remember, I told you once I'd killed a man . . . in the war?' Frances nodded and looked at him, surprised at this departure.

'You don't mean to say you actually sympathise with our Hester?!'

'Don't be so bloody silly!' Rebuked, Frances sank back in her seat, to watch the mist clouding the windscreen, where Jack had wiped it. 'I'm sorry.' Jack took a deep breath and tried again. 'That story your Mam told you, about Robert stealing the takings and running off. Do you believe it now?' Frances frowned. She hadn't thought much about it; not in years!

'I don't know.'

'Because, I don't.' Frances started, a strange feeling clawing at her heart. 'Not now.' This was too much. Hadn't she had enough shocks for one day? Did he have to dredge up the old nightmares, all over again? 'Your granda's last words were, "The shadow of the elephant . . . " What did he mean by that?'

The direct question surprised her. She shook her head, then suddenly remembered the statue in the cellar.

'Oh! I know. That carving, with the elephant head. Is it still there? It used to be . . . ' Jack nodded, looking at her, waiting. 'It belonged to my Grandma. That's all I know.'

'Not your mam?'

'No.'

'According to her, it was sent as a wedding present to her and your father. She thought Robert must have sent it.' Frances raised her eyebrows but said nothing. 'It represents innocence. It's a Hindu God.'

'Yes. You told me.'

'Now, why would Robert send it on your mam's wedding day, and why would Jane claim it as hers?' They listened to the rain clattering on the van roof. Finally Jack spoke again. 'Can you remember what Jane told you, when you asked her about her brother?'

Frances sighed, thinking for a moment: 'She didn't say much. She said it wasn't true Robert had stolen. But she never said what it was he *had* done.' Jack was pale. He cleared the window again and stared out at the rain. You couldn't tell where sky began and sea ended. Everything was blurred and grey.

'The man I killed . . . ' Jack swallowed hard. 'He was Robert's son.'

Frances gasped, tears welling up inside her from God knew where. 'He was very bitter. He wanted to get his own back on the family, for what they'd done to his father.'

'What had *Robert* done, to deserve it?'

Jack laughed bitterly.

'He didn't know.' He turned to look at Frances. 'But, I think I do.' Frances' heart sank. She didn't want to hear. 'What crime could a brother and sister commit, against innocence, that would drive the brother to exile, the sister to suicide, and, in later generations, leave behind it a trail of madness and murder?'

345

'A brother and sister . . . ' Frances whispered. 'Oh my God! And you think our Hester is . . . No wonder! If you're right . . . And Anna too!'

'George, the poor old sod, did his best to stop Hester having children.'

'Grandma said once, our sins took a form to haunt us. Did she mean Hester?'

Jack shrugged.

'Of course, this is all conjecture. It might not, any of it, be true!'

'It all falls into place, Jack!' Then a new thought struck her. 'Is our Os serious about Anna?' Jack shook his head.

'If only we knew for certain, what really happened . . . '

'Aunt Harriet. I bet she knows. Grandma was very thick with her at one time.' Jack nodded.

'Well . . . She's coming up for the funeral . . . ' There was a long silence. Frances drew Jack's arm round her. He smiled down at her, warmly. 'Well? Have you decided?'

'What?'

'Whether you're going to marry me, or not!'

'I am married to you, you clot!'

'Only in name!'

'Huh!' For a moment, Jack thought she was going to refuse him.

'I don't blame you,' he said. 'If we could only start again, somewhere new. It'd be different.' Frances laughed.

'No, it wouldn't! I've tried that. It didn't work. No! I'm coming back, Jack! To you, the shop, the whole can of worms! I'll stand by you, if you'll stand by me.' He hugged her, groaning with relief.

'It's more than I deserve.'

'Me as well,' she said ruefully.

'I love you.'

'I know. And . . . if it doesn't sound funny like, I respect you, Jack. I mean, I do love you as well, but I respect you.' Jack thought he would burst with pride.

'We'll make a go of it. We might even be happy.'

'Don't tempt fate, pet!'

They held onto one another, listening to the rain and the sea, faces wistful, hopeful, fearful, all at once.

346

'What'll the kids say?'

'Os is prepared to tolerate you.'

'Huh!'

'What about Eve?'

'I don't know. And that's the truth.'

Ellen had engaged a young girl to help in the shop. She was called Mary Jean Hodgson, and she was thrilled to the marrow to be at Beattie's, of all places in Shields, at the centre of a real life drama! Eve too had been roped in, purely as a temporary measure, of course, to help, over the crisis. The two girls chirruped like sparrows, as they worked on the wreaths and sprays.

'Have you seen "Grand Hotel", Eve?'

'Aha. But it's not me favourite.'

'Oh, I love it. Leslie Howard's nice too. "Smilin' Through" had me in tears most of the time.'

'I thought it was soppy. No, I like . . . '

'I like the scary ones an' all. "The Mask of Fu Manchu" was good for that.'

'I like "Million Dollar Legs", and "Red Dust" best. Have you seen "Red Dust"? Clark Gable's smashin'. I've seen lots of his stuff. He's not much of a dancer, mind.'

'What do you know about it?'

'I'm only the best dancer in Shields!'

'You're never!'

'Right! Stand back! I'll show you!' And Eve started tapping her toes, launching herself into a routine that made the shop shake.

'What's going on here?' Os glowered at them from the kitchen door.

'Eve was just showing me her tap! Mind, she's marvellous, Mr Scott. She should be in the films!' Eve's smile was quickly wiped from her face.

'Oh yes? And have you finished that wreath yet, eh?'

'Give me time, Os. I've had to teach Mary Jean everything!' Os was inspecting their work.

'You've blocked it, I see. Well me Granda didn't hold with blocking. And it's for his funeral. So, you'd better do it all over again.' Mary Jean groaned, and Os gave her a sharp look. But Eve grew hot under the collar.

'That's how we do wreaths in me Dad's shop!'

'Which dad?' Immediately, Os wished he'd bitten out his tongue. 'I'm sorry,' he murmured and backed away. Mary Jean looked after him, with widening eyes.

'What's he mean, Eve?'

'Nothing.'

'Isn't he stern? But gentle an' all. Just like Leslie Howard.'

'Rubbish! He's more like Tarzan . . . or the apes!' Mary Jean laughed and the two girls began whispering, and giggling, as they took apart George's wreath.

'Where's the missus?' Mary Jean whispered, glancing back to the door.

'If you mean me grandma, she's gone out. She's meeting a woman come up from London for the funeral.'

'London! Eeh!' London was on the other side of the world.

'I've been to London, of course,' Eve swanked. 'I had me tonsils out in London, when I was little.'

'Never!'

'I'll show you.' Eve opened her mouth wide and Mary Jean stared into the yawning cavity.

Os was blushing as he went upstairs. 'Leslie Howard' indeed! That lass was going to be trouble and no mistake. If only Anna would pull herself together, and get back to serving in the shop. For the umpteenth time, he went up to her room, where Maisie sat, knitting at her bedside. Anna's big, black eyes stared beseechingly at him, from her thin, white face. He smiled encouragingly, fighting back the old, trapped feeling. It felt like chains around his heart.

'When's the train due?' he asked Maisie.

'Should be in by now. By, I wonder what her Majesty'll have to say about all this!'

'How's me mam?' Anna's voice was plaintive. Os and Maisie glanced at one another and the sick girl, eyes like a hawk, saw. 'What are you hiding from me?'

'Nothing!' Os reassured her.

'Will she be well enough to come to Granda's funeral?'

'I doubt it, pet.' Anna's brow creased with vexation. Os wished he could run. He hated telling lies. But, after all, what else could he do?

* * *

At Newcastle Central Station, Ellen waited, wondering where her auntie had got to. Nearly everyone had got off by now. And then, just as she had given her up, a black behind edged through the door of the first class carriage. A man, in his forties, blond, a patch over one eye, watched helplessly, wondering which part of it he could hold, in order to assist its owner. It squeezed itself further through the door, then, like a cork out of a bottle, Harriet May Lovely emerged, red-faced and panting, onto the plat-form.

'There you are, at last!' Ellen squealed, running down the platform towards her.

'I blame the Kaiser!' Harriet blurted out indignantly.

'What for, Auntie?'

'He used up all the metal for guns, and now there's not enough left to make proper trains! It's all skimp and scrape, little seats, little doors! I mean, folks aren't midgets, are they?'

'No, Auntie.' Ellen gave the stranger a sidelong glance. Immediately, he put out his hand to her.

'Tom Fairbairn, at your service, ma'am.' Ellen's jaw dropped.

'But you're in China!' she objected.

'Oh dear, Miss Lovely. I'm afraid we must've got on the wrong train!' His eyes sparkled. Ellen's hand reached up to her mouth and she burst out laughing. Harriet slapped her across the face.

Stunned, Ellen fell back. By God she'd forgotten what the old faggot could be like!

'I want to go to the gaol first!' she said.

'But Auntie . . . '

'I'm used to gaols. They don't shock me. Not any more.' Ellen glanced at the stranger. His face was pale.

But the warden was not interested in Harriet. It was the husband they wanted to see. Ellen waited in the corridor with her aunt, as Tom Fairbairn was ushered in to see the prison doctor. They could hear low voices, murmuring, through the door. Ellen strained to hear but couldn't make out the mumbled secrets.

'Aunt Harriet, what do you know about Tom?' Harriet turned a sharp eye on her. 'Did he ever go to China?' Harriet shook her head.

'No. He lost his faith and joined the Labour Party. He says it

349

was Hester's fault. He said she was enough to drive an angel to agnosticism.'

'I'd second that!'

'He said she might as well have been a nun . . . if you take my meaning.' Ellen stared at her aunt.

'Oh dear. No man can stand that.'

'Hester should never have left me.' Harriet pursed her lips, remembering. 'If she'd stayed with me, she'd have been all right. We're two of a kind.'

'You're not a murderess!'

'Aren't I now!' Ellen looked at Harriet May. The old lady stared straight ahead of her. 'I'm a killjoy,' she said. 'But then, why should anybody else be happy, when I'm not?'

Tom Fairbairn braced himself as Hester was shown into the room. Her face shone with feverish intensity, and her eyes were bright. She sat facing him, a victorious look on her face.

'I stood firm at the side of the Almighty!' she announced. Tom glanced nervously at the doctor, who shrugged. Tom looked back at his wife.

'Why did you do it, Hester?'

'My voices told me to! I had to obey! I am the handmaiden of God. His laws are above the laws of man. He can turn the night into day and day into night. When He wills it, sin becomes morality. Do what you will with me! Bind me in chains! Blind me! Burn me! I shall die a martyr in His cause and you will all rot in hell for abusing His Handmaiden!'

'She's crackers,' Tom blurted out the words before he could stop himself.

'I am not crackers!' Hester screamed. 'I am inspired!'

'Not by God, I doubt.' The doctor observed quietly as he drew the drug into his syringe.

'You will not silence me!' The wardens held her, while the needle went in. Hester slumped and the two big women took her by the armpits, dragging her back to her cell.

'It won't go past the coroner,' the doctor said gently. 'She's not fit to stand trial. Your evidence will help to commit her.' Tom dropped his head into his hands and cried like a baby.

After many delays, at last George Beattie could be laid to rest.

It was snowing hard on the day of the funeral, but a crowd had gathered in the street, dark figures, huddled in scarves, drawn from their firesides by the drama. For the newspapers had been full of it. A past mayor of Shields, murdered by his own daughter! And hadn't he had trouble in the past? Hadn't his wife, Jane, once been in court over the murder of a lover? Wasn't there some tale of rape? Tongues wagged, gossips whispered, and the town turned out agog to see the 'Fated Family' on parade. But they were late. Outside, the horses snorted steaming clouds into the cold air, waving the black plumes on their heads. And the ushers stood, freezing in the thickening snow. What was keeping them? Had there been some new drama in this 'house of tragedy'? The journalists sharpened their pencils, licking the phrases into shape, even as they watched and waited, huddling in the shop door. 'Daughter of murderess speaks out.' 'I can stand it no longer. I must tell my story to the world.' If only she would, if only . . .

Inside the house, the family also huddled, in little groups. Os sat with Eve in Anna's room.

'Of course you know why I've got such little feet . . . ' The bright black eyes sparkled up at them.

'No . . . ' Os said gently. 'Why?'

'Well, when I was very little, they bound them. They do that to all the little girls, in China, to stop their feet growing. They like women to be dainty there. I'm dainty, don't you think?' Os half smiled. Eve couldn't look at either of them. For a lass born in Clapham and brought up in Shields, Anna Fairbairn had a lot of imagination!

'Aye well . . . ' Os searched desperately for something to say. 'Let's hope they start growin' again, now you're back in Shields, eh?'

Downstairs, in the kitchen, Tom sat drinking sherry with his sisters-in-law, Ellen and Maisie. The poor man was in a state of shock. It wasn't so much seeing Hester, and knowing what she'd done that had upset him, it was the sight of his daughter. Suddenly she bad become real to him, and he blamed himself bitterly for the nervous state he found her in.

'We've done our best!' Ellen told him, between pursed lips.

351

'And mind, it wasn't easy.' Tom didn't blame the Beatties. Hadn't he run away from his responsibilities?

'I don't know.' He gulped down a mouthful of alcohol. 'Till I came up here, I thought I was doing great work! Trade Unions, the Labour Party. I've just been elected to the L.C.C!'

'Fancy!' said Maisie. 'You never said you played cricket!'

'Pardon?' Tom was mystified.

'He said L.C.C., you silly faggot!' Ellen snapped. 'Not M.C.C.!'

'Oh?' Maisie answered back. 'And what's that when it's at home?' Ellen flushed and looked accusingly at Tom.

'The London County Council,' he explained, smiling, in spite of himself.

'Oh? You're on the council, are you?' Ellen said graciously. 'Dad would have appreciated that. He was Mayor of Shields, you know.'

'Oh really?'

'Of course you've got a long way to go before you reach that pinnacle, but still . . . '

In George's office, Jack and Frances were grappling with an obdurate Harriet May.

'Look, Harriet.' Jack was doing his best to be reasonable. 'I mean it's no skin off your nose, is it? Why don't you tell us, eh?' Harriet sat silent, glaring at them.

'It could be very important,' Frances pleaded. 'You must see that. People's lives are at stake. I mean, look at Os and Anna. If we only knew, we'd know what to do for the best. Please, Auntie. Tell us!'

'Why the hell should I?!'

'You must have some family feeling!' Jack exploded at last.

'Oh? And what makes you say that?' Frances gasped.

'Well . . . you took our Hester in . . . and . . . well . . . you've come up for the funeral! I mean, why would you come all the way up here, if you didn't care?'

'I wouldn't have missed George Beattie's funeral . . . ' Harriet laughed suddenly, 'For all the rice in China! It'll give me supreme satisfaction to see the old barsket put underground at last. I'm grateful to Hester for that, at least!'

'How can you say such things! Hester's going to be put away

for it, woman!' Harriet nodded, smiling grimly.

'I think it's time we went. This funeral's been delayed for long enough!' With that, Harriet left the room.

Jack and Frances sat on for a while, in silence.

'Well!' Jack snorted. 'That would appear to be that!'

'What are we going to do?' Jack looked at Frances, a question in his eyes. 'About Os and Anna, I mean?' Jack sighed.

'We daren't risk it.'

'What will you tell him?' Jack shook his head.

'I'm not going to tell him anything. You are!' Frances was horrified.

'But he resents me enough as it is! What's he going to say if I part him from his sweetheart?'

'You're his mother. You've got to!'

'You're his father.'

'I've proved that.'

'Oh I see.' Frances sighed. Jack looked steadily at her.

'Don't fail him, Fran,' he said quietly. Frances bit her lip, swallowing down the tears.

'I thought I'd finished paying!'

The crowd shuffled back, as the shop door opened, and the family, swathed in black, crowded into the waiting carriages. From upstairs, they could hear the strains of 'The Moonlight Sonata', played on the piano. It was Anna's way of shutting out the nightmare world. Tom, the outsider, stayed behind, to keep a watch over her. Outside he was a man of the world, confident, successful, debonair. Inside, like Anna, he was a welter of confused emotions. Anna turned to him, her hands poised on the keyboard, 'Do you think we might go back to China, one day, Father?'

'We were never there, dear,' Tom said, looking straight at her. Anna looked puzzled.

'Don't be daft! Anyway, my mother's gone back. We ought to go and join her!' Tom was desperate. There must be some way of getting through to her. But it would take time, a lot of time . . .

The Glebe was packed. Frances lifted her veil to look round. Her granda had been a great man. He'd made his mistakes, but he'd done his best, according to his lights, not caring whether his family loved him for it, or not, not caring even whether they understood. And they'd judged him for it, in their arrogance. And if she and Jack were right, he'd carried a burden, all these years, that must have weighed him down. And now, they carried it, she and Jack . . . If they were right. Frances sighed, brushing aside her tears. She couldn't blame her granda for taking his comfort with Alice Minto. There she stood now, with her remaining children, weeping openly, like the stricken widow. Ellen and Maisie bristled at the offence. Harriet, standing beside them, was stiff as a ramrod. Was she enjoying her pound of flesh? Her face was blank, her eyes dead. Os stood next to Eve, his back bowed with grief. As they searched their hymn books for the place, Os turned to help her, but Eve swept his hand away brusquely. Poor Os. He looked quite put out. He was a gentleman, old-fashioned, he liked to look after women . . . women like Anna. Poor Os. How could Frances bear to hurt him, as she knew she must? How could she bring herself to do it? It was George's favourite hymn, 'Love Divine.' Frances held up her head and sang.

The next day, Frances told Os she was sending Anna away. His reaction was swift and violent.

'I know what you're doing! You're getting rid of her, because you want her share in the shop!'

'How can you say such a thing, Os?'

'It's not her fault her mother was mental. If you ask me, we should all be sorry for her, not hound her out like this!'

'Look, Os, if you've got any ideas about marrying her . . . '

'Why shouldn't I?'

'You're cousins for one thing . . . '

'So?'

'And for another, what would it be like for her, eh?' Os looked puzzled. 'Shields is a small town. People've got long memories. Do you think, that if she stayed here, they'd let her forget her mother was a murderer? That she was put away in an asylum? It's no good, Os. The poor lass needs to get clean away from this place, away from the memories, and put the past behind her. I know you mean well, but you won't help her by keeping her here.' Os was thoughtful. In spite of himself, he knew his mother was talking sense. Suddenly a new thought occurred.

'I could go with her!'

'No, Os.' Frances put her hand firmly on his arm. 'You wouldn't be happy. For both your sakes, let her go!'

Os hated his mother at this moment. He would have done anything to go against her. And, the worst of it was, that in his heart, he was relieved. He didn't love Anna. He was sorry for her, but he didn't love her. Did Frances know that? He hoped not. Because he wanted to punish her for his own default. 'And what about the shop? You've a duty to your family, Os.'

'You talk to me about duty?' he sneered. Frances sighed, looking on the son she had deserted years ago.

'I'm doing it now, Os,' she said gently. 'If I didn't do it before, I'm doing it now.'

Frances felt sorry for her son. He was such a softie! He didn't know what love was really. But, Frances, at least, was beginning to learn, and she continued her work, without corrupting sentimentality. Taking Tom aside, she broached the subject of Anna. Should she tell him her suspicions about Hester's birth? Frances hesitated on the brink. If only she knew for certain! But Tom, in any case, was deeply shocked by recent events, and struggling with his own feelings of guilt. He saw, at once, that a marriage with Os wouldn't work out, and Frances encouraged his plan to take Anna back with him, to London. Perhaps she needn't tell him yet. The immediate danger had been averted. So, Frances let it go, for the moment, and Tom Fairbairn left, with Anna, in ignorance.

Sorting her father's effects in the office, Frances searched for clues. Piles and piles of papers had to be sifted through, mounds of letters, books and documents. Sitting alone, in the silence, Frances felt the gravity of the man who had gone. He had carried the burden alone, resentful eyes following him, as they followed her now, from Os, Eve and Anna, dubbing him 'the old barsket'. And now she'd taken his place. What would they call *her*? Frances wept bitter tears. Yes, the burden had been passed on, and now she was feeling the weight of it. Letters . . . from his time as mayor; a box that had belonged to Jane Beattie; letters from her brother in America; an empty ribbon, containing nothing, the contents destroyed perhaps . . . Frances was a child again, knocking on a locked door, because she could hear her grandmother crying.

'I've been having a clear out. Just burning some old letters.' Letters from Robert? Frances sighed. No clues there. So many books . . . the favourites well thumbed, Blake, the Bible, markers in place. 'Revelations'. The lines well scored underneath.

'And I stood upon the sand of the sea, and I saw a beast rise up out of the sea, having seven heads and ten horns . . . and the dragon gave him his power, and his seat, and great authority. And I saw one of his heads as it were wounded to death; and his deadly wound was healed; and all the world wondered after the beast, saying, Who is like unto the beast? Who is able to make war with him?' Saint George? She remembered the old school play; she had taken the part of Father Christmas! 'Is there a doctor to be found, All ready near at hand, To cure a deep and deadly wound, And make the champion stand!' It never stopped! The fight was never won! 'You'll be the saving of this family,' her granda had said that about Frances. But for how long? The dragon would rise again to fight another day. They were all wounded, the whole family, and she had to heal them. But where was Saint George?

'There's not many men answering that description in Shields!'

'You're called George and you're fierce, Granda.'

'Aye, but I'm no saint, pet.'

Saint or not Frances wished her granda back! She felt so utterly alone.

And where was Jack? Standing, in front of the shop, with Eve, he was admiring his handiwork. 'Scott and Sons. Nurserymen, Seedsmen and Florists.' He was full of beans, chattering away to Eve about the old days, showing off some old, remembered dance steps. Well, it was good they were making friends.

She went down to her mother in the kitchen, for a reviving cup of tea. Eve and Jack had gone back into the shop, and a row was brewing with Os. Frances listened to them, through the dividing door, and sighed.

'No peace for the wicked!' Ellen commented wryly. Then Eve barged in, followed by Jack.

'If Os tries to stop me climbing up ladders and that just once more, I'll thump him! I swear I will!'

'He's only trying to help, pet,' Frances explained gently.

'I don't need his help!'

'Oh I see!' Jack laughed. 'Mary Jean doesn't seem to mind it!'

'She's soft on him, the great nit-wit!'

'You should think yourself lucky you've got a job at all!' Frances reprimanded her daughter. 'Never mind complaining about it. There's plenty haven't, you know! Men with families to support!'

'Oh, I'll get me violin out in a minute!'

'How dare you talk to me like that!' Frances was shocked at Eve's behaviour. She was so glib, so . . . hard-boiled! She took nothing seriously, apart from her own selfish desires. 'I don't know what the next generation's coming to!' Then they all laughed at her.

'You sound just like the old barsket!' Jack told her. Frances glared at him. He shrugged, and withdrew from the discussion.

'I'm sorry, Mam,' Eve said indulgently. 'But, I've had enough of helping out here. I'm not cut out to be a shop girl!'

'My, don't you talk big?' Frances was upset. 'Times are hard. You want to be glad you've got a family to take you in!'

'Well,' Ellen said casually, 'We do have family elsewhere.' Frances started. Eve was slyly trying to shush her grandma, and Jack had faded from the room.

'And what's that supposed to mean?' Alarmed, Frances looked from her mother to her daughter.

'Nothing, pet. Just a silly remark. That's all.' Ellen smiled, and handed her her cup of tea. 'Drink up, pet. It'll do you good. You're overwrought!'

The shop in Ocean Road still had to be sold, and it was a buyer's market, for there weren't many people with money to spend, and a lot of businesses were going broke. Besides, Eve refused to move out of her old home, so Frances found herself living half in one place and half in another, keeping her eye open for the chance of a sale. They had just shown a prospective buyer round the premises, and, as requested, were sitting down to write an inventory of contents when Eve dropped her bombshell. She'd

357

been chatting on brightly about dancing classes, the next show, sneering at the local audience,

'I mean, they're not what you'd call sophisticated, are they, Mam?' And Frances was gritting her teeth against the onslaught. Then Eve said, gaily,

'Jack thinks I'd do well in America!' Frances looked up from her work.

'Who?'

'Jack.'

'Who told you you could call him that?'

'He did, as a matter of fact!'

'Did he now?' Frances shut her mouth, for the moment, and got on with her work.

'Anyway, he says I've got a lot of talent and that's the place to go, if you want to get on.'

'And you want to get on, do you?'

'Well, of course I do, Mam! I mean, I don't want to end up like . . . well, I can hardly call Os and Mary Jean and Maisie, has beens, can I? They've never been anything yet!' The bright laughter stopped suddenly, as Frances' hand lashed Eve's face. The girl went white, quivering, like a limpet prised out of its shell.

'That's better!' Frances nodded with satisfaction. 'Do you know what sophisticated means?' Eve was about to speak, but thought better of it. 'It means artificial. False. Like you. Just a shell and nothing inside it but a shivering jelly. And you think you'd do well in Hollywood, do you?' Eve sobbed.

'I'm not going to live at Fowler Street, Mam! I'm not!'

'They're your family, Eve!'

'Not to me, they're not!'

'I see.' Frances sighed. 'So, you think I'm going to let my own daughter travel all the way to America, on her own? Am I so bad a mother?'

'Jack said, you and him might take me.' Frances frowned. 'He said he wanted to make a new start with you, and the crossing would be just like a second honeymoon! And it would, Mam! You and him could have a nice holiday, even if you didn't stay!'

'I see. Is your grandma in on this, by any chance?' Eve nodded.

'She's written to the Ridleys in California. They've asked us over on a visit.'

'So that was it. I might've known. And where was the money coming from for the passage?'

'The sale of the shop, I suppose!' Frances bit her lip. 'Mam!' Eve pleaded. 'Don't make's stay here! There's nothing for me in Shields! I don't want to get married and have kids and live in a shop all me life! Please, Mam. Let me try!'

Frances looked at her daughter. She meant it. And if she didn't let her go, what would happen? She would run away, like Frances had done, getting herself into worse trouble than before. Better let the girl go, than lose her. Give her a long rope, but hold on to one end of it, so if she got into any kind of trouble, there'd always be help. And, who knows Eve might even make it!

'I'll think about it.' Eve suddenly gave her mam a hug.

'Thanks! You'll not regret it!' But Frances was crying. 'Come on, Mam! You'll be coming too, won't you?' Frances shook her head.

'No, pet. I'm in no mood for second honeymoons.'

Eve watched her mother walking off down the street. It was as though she was looking at her for the first time. She wasn't a big woman, small by modern standards, middle-aged, her step light but firm. She looked as though she was carrying a heavy burden on her back. What was it? For the first time, Eve found she was anxious for her mother. She had had so much suffering in her life, wasn't it time she was happy? Eve had thought her Mam and Jack . . . What had gone wrong?

Maisie's flat. The old assignation. Frances sighed, as she took off her coat and sat to wait for Jack. Memories of furtive meetings soured the air; Eve discovering them. Had Davey known? How could she have let Jack kid her on it was all right to carry on like that?

'Just like old times!' Jack laughed as he breezed into the room. But his confidence faltered as he saw her face.

'Sit down, Jack,' Frances said quietly. He sat. 'What's all this I hear from Eve, about America?'

'Ah!' He smiled ruefully. 'Cat's out of the bag, is it? Well, sorry we didn't let you in on it sooner, but Eve thought you wouldn't approve.'

'I don't!' Jack was not to be put off.

'We could make a new start over there . . . we deserve it!'

'On my money, I suppose!'

'Well, *I* haven't got any!'

'You're all very keen to spend my money, I must say, but you none of you think of asking me how I might want to spend it! You're making use of me, Jack, just as you always have.'

'I'm thinking of you! You always wanted to get away from Shields. Well, now you can! You can put the past behind you! Shake the dust off! The job's over!'

'It's only just begun!' Jack stared at her. What did she mean? 'It might have been over, Jack, if you hadn't taken the easy way out, as you always do, and killed that Vijay.' Jack went pale. 'Through him, we might have discovered the truth. But you've closed that path, haven't you? We can hardly start making friends with our relations in India now!'

'I did it to protect you.'

'No. That was your excuse, Jack. Really, you did it to protect yourself. Anything for a quiet life! Let the old barsket think Frances is pregnant, then he'll beg you to marry her and come into the business! My, you really landed on your feet there! Avoid the war as long as possible, not because you've got anything against killing people, Jack, but because you couldn't face it! And then when you *did* volunteer, you killed the one man who might have helped my family!'

'He wanted to hurt you!'

'In the short term, maybe. But it would have been worth it!'

'How could I have known that?'

'You weren't willing to find out. Did you ever think of telling Vijay who you were, to see how he'd react?' Jack was silent. 'No. You didn't have the guts for that! And then, how easy it must have been, when you came back, to start up an affair with me; having your cake and eating it. You didn't want to put things on a proper footing again, when Davey died. Don't try to deny it. I know. But, what else could you do? And, as you've discovered, it's actually easier for you, with me around, to do your dirty work for you. Oh yes! You stood and watched me telling our son he couldn't marry his beloved Anna, telling Tom Fairbairn what to do. And then, there's the money; the money you've already planned to spend, gallivanting half way round the world! When are you going to grow up, Jack? There's a depression on, in

360

America as well as here. We'll be lucky to survive!' Jack swallowed hard.

'You said you respected me . . . '

'Perhaps I was trying to persuade myself. I thought you'd changed. You haven't. But I have. And I have to say, you haven't lived up to your part of the bargain, since I agreed to come back to Fowler Street.' There was a long silence.

'What are you going to do?'

'I think I may have sold the shop in Ocean Road. And I've seen a solicitor about Hester's shares in Fowler Street. It seems she has to nominate a trustee. It could be Tom, or my mother, or even me. When I know how things stand, I'll make a decision about the best way to use Davey's money. But, I've told Eve she can go to America, so I'll keep some back for her.'

'You mean to stay on at Fowler Street?'

'Yes. Like I said, Jack. The job's only just begun, and I gave up running away a long time ago.'

'What about me?'

'I ought to throw you out!' Jack sat absolutely still, waiting. But his mind was racing. And Eve?

'Who's going to go to America with Eve? She's my daughter! I can't stand by . . . '

'Your daughter? You don't seem to want to own her! You encourage her in your fly-by-night ideas . . . you don't even want her to call you "Dad"!'

'I thought it would be easier if she called me Jack.'

'Easier!' Frances spat the word at him, and he cringed.

'What'll I do? Where'll I go?' Jack's voice was shaking.

'You can go to hell!'

CHAPTER TWENTY-ONE

Frances went down to Southampton alone to see them off. Maisie was as excited as a girl of nineteen, and Eve was sober as a matron. Who'd be looking after who, Frances thought? Eve certainly had become more responsible since they'd had their row!

'Don't worry, Mam, I'll not be needing any money. I've got a job on the liner. Entertainments. I'll be dancin' me way across the Atlantic!' It was a good sign, but she still needed something by her, not to mention a chaperone. And then, Maisie had volunteered.

'I've made up me mind!' she said. 'I'm goin' to cash in my annuity, and go with our Eve to America!'

'What about your Independence, Auntie?' Frances had asked anxiously.

'Well, you know me, pet,' Maisie answered her. 'Reckless!' Frances smiled, watching the pair of them walk up the gangway onto the great ship. Maisie with her new shingle hair do. At least there was the telegraph, in emergency. Had Eve got enough money with her? Frances chewed her lip, nervously. Ocean Road hadn't produced any money, yet. It was only sold subject to contract. 'Don't worry, Mam. I'll get a lot of tips!' Eve had swanked. The girl had spunk, Frances had to give her that! But she wasn't as tough as she liked to make out. America might make her, but it might also break her. Putting on a brave face, Frances waved, as the ship sailed, and the two small figures on the deck faded from sight. She wiped her eyes, and started out on the journey back home to Shields.

She had a lot of time to think, as the train sped north. Had she been too harsh on Jack? She had to admit he had, at least, made friends with Eve. His easy-going manner had oiled the wheels. And he had been a support, of a kind, to her granda. She was a woman, after all, and her heart ached for affection. She might easily persuade herself to take him back . . . if she wasn't careful. After all, was there a man in England who was not still a child? She sighed, closing her eyes against the dark night, and slept.

It was mid-morning, when Frances arrived back in Fowler Street. The smell of frying bacon made her hungry. But there was no one in the kitchen, when she walked in, and breakfast had been over long ago. She put down her bag, and went through to the shop, where she surprised her son, kissing Mary Jean.

'You might choose a less public place, next time!' Frances rebuked them. Their stifled laughter followed her up the stair to her room, and it made her feel lonely. There was a knock on her door, and Ellen came in with a cup of tea.

'I thought I heard you!' Frances eyed the tea. 'Can I get you anything else, pet?'

'I tell you what, Mam, I'm dyin' for a bacon sandwich!'

'Right you are!' Ellen turned to go but stopped at the door. 'I'll get Jack to make one for you! He's a dab hand!' Frances frowned. What was she going to do about Jack? It wasn't going to be easy with him around. 'I don't know what you've said to him, love,' Ellen grinned, 'but he's been a great help while you were away. He even washed up!'

'Never!' Frances sighed and lay down on her bed. She felt suddenly, very, very tired.

She was asleep when Jack brought up her sandwich. He put it down on the chest of drawers, and waited for a while, watching her. She was a different woman from the one he'd married all those years ago. Her mouth fell open, and her breath came in long, loud

363

gasps, as though she was desperate for air. She was worn out from a life of endless work and sacrifice. And suddenly Jack felt very, very sorry. He sat on the edge of the bed, staring down at her, tears running down his cheeks. She deserved better than him. But he would do his best, if she would let him. After a while, he crept away, to let her sleep. He would make her another sandwich, later.

Ellen was made trustee for Hester's affairs, but it was Frances she turned to, when it came to decisions. The whole house revolved around her. And Jack worked hard, showing her the books, helping her to understand the financial situation. And at last, eight months after putting up for sale, Frances exchanged contracts on Ocean Road. It was the end of a chapter. The sadness surprised her. Memories of her time there with Eve and Davey flooded back to her, and she couldn't sleep for wondering how her daughter was getting on. Was she good enough, tough enough to carve a niche for herself in America? She would almost be there, by now. Giving up on sleep, Frances got out of bed and dressed. She itched to have a look at the sea. A walk might do her good. But Jack heard her, as she crept downstairs to the kitchen, and followed her.

'What's the matter?'

'Nothing. I just fancied a walk, that's all.'

'On your own?'

'Yes.'

'It's still dark.'

'So?'

'You can't go out on your own. I'll go with you.'

'No. Please.'

'Where were you thinking of walking?'

'The sea.' Jack nodded. He could just fancy a breath of fresh air . . .

'Look, I tell you what, I'll run you down there, in the van.' Frances was about to object, but Jack went on, 'Then I'll let you have your walk all on your own, and I'll wait for you, to take you back. Eh? How about it?'

'All right. If it makes you happy.' He dressed quickly, and soon they were careering down Bent House Road.

'I wonder how Eve's getting on,' Jack observed.

364

'*I* was wondering that.' Frances snorted. 'Them pendulum wings of hers are a bit wild to my way of thinking!'

Passengers and crew lined the room, and the cheeks of the band bulged, trumpeting enthusiastically, as Eve's feet flew, tap stepping across the dance floor. From her seat near the front, Maisie watched, proudly. She thought them wings were wonderful! Then Eve splayed out both her hands, grinning, and the music ended, amidst tumultuous applause. Immediately, people were crowding round Eve, offering congratulations.

'That's my niece, you know,' Maisie explained to the neighbouring table.

'Oh yes?' An American voice answered her. 'Are you travelling on business or pleasure?'

'Oh well, a bit of both really!' Maisie opened like a flower. 'Our Eve's goin' into films, you know . . . '

'Really? Well, that's just great!'

'We're going to be staying with family, though, while we're over there.'

'Oh! Where?'

'California. I've got some pictures, somewhere . . . ' And Maisie started digging out the photographs the American cousins had sent over. Their names were written on the back. Maisie put on her glasses to read them. 'That's Uncle Ernie and his wife Ursula. Now this one's somebody called June. I'm not sure what relation she is, oh yes, and this one's Uncle Luis with Auntie Titia. I think that's Alexandra . . . ' She turned it over to check. 'Yes . . . that's right.' The Americans were stifling their yawns, and suddenly, Maisie realised she was tired.

'It's all the fresh air!' her neighbours told her. Waving to Eve, over the heads of the crowd, Maisie made her excuses, and walked out onto deck. The moon was sinking. Its silvery path reached out across the ocean, as the ship sped on, silent, smooth, like a white swan. They would be in America in the morning. Maisie looked over the side at the pale foam. If Will could see her now. Aye, she missed him, especially here, where lovers and honeymooners huddled, each pair pretending to be alone on a deserted deck. Eeh, well. No point in being a gooseberry. She turned away, and the red carnation from her dress fell to the ground. She picked it up and smelt it. Not as nice as they had in the shop, but still, it was nice of them to give it to her. All the ladies had been given one that night. It was a special day. Independence Day. Maisie threw it over the side, and watched the crimson petals fluttering into the dark churning waters beneath.

'Oh, Cabin boy!' she called to a passing waiter. 'Would you show's to me State Room, please!' She always got lost, on this great ship, with its maze of corridors. 'State Room' indeed! Maisie chuckled, as she followed the lad in his white jacket. My this was the life! A bit different from that time she and Frances had stowed away on a coal steamer!

Standing on the beach at Shields, Frances stared into the darkness of the Northern Ocean. Its cold waters rustled to her feet, and moonlight crested its waves with silver. The foaming white horses of the sea. Riderless horses. Like her. No knights in shining armour these days. Aye, Eve did right to take off for America. They were maybe different over there. Not a man in Shields . . . But Frances felt so alone. And it hurt her. Her body shook with the pain, and hot tears scalded her cheeks.

'Fran . . . ' It was Jack. He'd come up behind her, though he'd said he wouldn't. She tried to shut him out, keeping her back to him. Gingerly, he touched her shoulders. 'Fran . . . I'm sorry.' Why wouldn't he shut up? He just made it worse! Hurting her more! 'I . . . don't know if I can change. I don't know how. But, if you'll give me time . . . ' The sobs wrenched out of her, and he took her in his arms, holding her. 'I'll try . . . Show me how, Fran. Please show me how.' Together, they walked up the beach to the van, and Jack started it up, as the moon sank below the horizon.

'Eeh, I'm that tired!' Frances smeared her hands over her face.

'Don't worry about Eve.' Jack tried to reassure her. 'I bet you what you like, within the space of a week, she'll have some bloke falling over himself to look after her!' Frances suddenly laughed.

'If she'll let him!'

Eve was looking wistfully after her Auntie Maisie, as she left, when, suddenly hoisted onto the broad shoulders of an American, she was paraded round the ballroom, trumpets blaring, and streamers flying in an atmosphere of carnival. Then, there was a roll of drums. It was twelve o'clock. Independence Day. Slithering to the floor, Eve joined hands with her American, who joined hands with a Chinese woman on his left, she to a Frenchman, he to an Indonesian, he to a South African, and so on, in a great circle, young and old, men, women and children, of all nationalities, linking arms as the band struck up 'The Stars and Stripes'. And then, the lights were dimmed. Eve craned her neck to see above the crowds. A flickering light flared across the darkness, and there were cheers and applause, as the flaming punch bowl was brought into the hall. Someone handed Eve a cup. She raised it, as the toastmaster held up his glass,

'Ladies and gentlemen, I give you Freedom!'

Silent and unseen, the slippery time spirit moved, as one who works unseen, at night, while people slumber, waking to find everything has changed. The world might be peopled with the same beings we knew the day before, but the impression of familiarity is deceiving. Try as we might, to go on as before, sooner or later, we are brought up against it. Admit it. It's a New World we have entered on and all our ideas on how to live in it will have to change. As Jack and Frances slept, they entered the last darkness, the darkness before the dawn, and the great ship steamed on, taking Eve into the waters of the New World.